About the Author

MICHAEL KNIGHTS has a rich background in research and consulting pertaining to the security affairs of the Gulf Cooperation Council states, along with Iraq, Iran, and Yemen. A London-based associate of The Washington Institute, he has been a visiting lecturer in intelligence and national security policy at Brunel University. Dr. Knights supplies political risk and political violence assessments to a range of business-intelligence and corporate-security services providers dealing with the Gulf. He is also a frequent contributor to Jane's Information Group, the author of *Cradle of Conflict: Iraq and the Birth of Modern U.S. Military Power* (U.S. Naval Institute Press, 2005), and the editor of The Washington Institute compilation *Operation Iraqi Freedom and the New Iraq: Insights and Forecasts* (2004).

• • •

TROUBLED WATERS

Future U.S. Security
Assistance in the Persian Gulf

Michael Knights

THE WASHINGTON INSTITUTE FOR NEAR EAST POLICY

© 2006 by the Washington Institute for Near East Policy

Published in 2006 in the United States of America by the Washington Institute for Near East Policy, 1828 L Street NW, Suite 1050, Washington, D.C. 20036.

Library of Congress Cataloging-in-Publication Data

Knights, Michael.
   Troubled waters: future U.S. security assistance in the Persian Gulf / Michael Knights.
   p. cm.
   ISBN 1-933162-01-5
   1. Military assistance, American—Persian Gulf Region. 2. Persian Gulf Region—Strategic aspects. 3. United States—Military policy. 4. United States—Military relations—Persian Gulf Region. 5. Persian Gulf Region—Military relations—United States. 6. National security—Persian Gulf Region. I. Title.
   UA832.K55 2006
   355'.032530973—dc22

                                                                    2006008639

Design by Daniel Kohan, Sensical Design & Communication
Front cover: Copyright AP Wide World Photos/U.S. Navy, Alta I. Cutler

Table of Contents

Figures

Acknowledgments

THE WRITING of this book would not have been possible without the assistance of The Washington Institute, and particularly of Steve and Nancy Mendelow, whose great generosity provided a seat for me at the Institute. The Washington Institute's unparalleled background in Near Eastern affairs gave me a platform to meet and exchange ideas with Gulf security specialists at the U.S. Department of Defense, Central Command (CENTCOM), the Department of State, and other governmental agencies. Research director Patrick Clawson and head of military studies Michael Eisenstadt stand out as central influences on the book. Both spent considerable time and effort honing the text. Where errors remain, they are entirely my own responsibility, but there are doubtless far fewer errors thanks to the sterling efforts of my two key collaborators.

This study would also not have been possible without the intellectual and logistical support of the U.S. Department of Defense and other governmental agencies. In addition to many serving officers, a range of former military and civilian decisionmakers provided key support and deserve individual recognition, including but not limited to Anthony Lake, Kenneth Pollack, Bruce Riedel, Rear Admiral John Sigler, and General Anthony Zinni (Ret.). I would like to thank my many interviewees for setting aside so much of their valuable time to talk with me. All in all, I was staggered by the hospitality shown to me by the U.S. Department of Defense and other governmental agencies. The individuals I met in these organizations were truly the finest community of Americans I have encountered during my twenty-nine months in the States.

The author of a book always owes a debt of gratitude to the family and friends who supported him or her throughout the writing process. In particular, I would like to thank my wonderful mother-in-law, Mary Bartholomew, for hosting me in her charming home during the most intensive part of the drafting process. I have many warm memories of this home-away-from-home. Last but definitely not least, I would like to thank my beautiful wife, Maria, for putting up with me during the writing process, and the rest of the time, too.

Preface

AT PRESENT, U.S. FORCES remain heavily involved in countering the insurgency in Iraq, requiring a robust U.S. military presence nearby in the friendly, conservative Arab monarchies that make up the Gulf Cooperation Council (GCC)—Kuwait, Saudi Arabia, Bahrain, Qatar, Oman, and the United Arab Emirates (UAE). But a large U.S. presence in Iraq will not be permanent. Whatever the outcome of the Iraq conflict, the day will come when the U.S. military commitment in Iraq is reduced substantially. In preparing for that inevitable reduction, we must now consider the future shape of U.S. security involvement in the Persian Gulf.

U.S. forces have been in the Persian Gulf since World War II and are not likely to leave entirely any time soon. The reason is simple: the stability of the Gulf region will remain vital to America's economic and physical security for the foreseeable future. Even if initiatives on energy security ultimately succeed in reducing U.S. energy imports from the Gulf region, its tremendous oil and gas resources will make the region an important influence on world energy prices. Furthermore, Iran's quest to develop nuclear weapons threatens both regional and global security. And the Gulf has provided the base of support for some of the most threatening radical Islamists.

For at least a decade, the U.S. military has effectively shouldered the burden of ensuring Gulf security, because the members of the GCC were not able to defend themselves against the threats posed by Iraq and Iran. While necessary, this arrangement has been less than ideal: a large U.S. military presence in the Gulf is one pretext used to justify Islamist terrorism, and the large-scale commitment of U.S. forces in the region reduces their overall readiness and flexibility.

To investigate the forces that will shape the U.S. military presence in the Gulf over the next decade, The Washington Institute has turned to Dr. Michael Knights. Knights is uniquely qualified for this project, having spent the last decade reporting on Gulf security developments for respected journals such as *Jane's Intelligence Review* and researching U.S. military involvement in the region, first for his doctoral dissertation at King's College's War Studies Department and then for his excellent book *Cradle of Conflict: Iraq and the Birth of Modern U.S. Military Power* (Naval Institute Press, 2005). We are pleased that after his two years with us in Washington, he remains an associate of The Washington Institute, based in London.

Knights's assessment of security fundamentals in the Gulf suggests the possibility of a better balance of effort and division of labor between the United States and the GCC states. Though the Gulf monarchies were ill suited to deter invasion from Iraq, they are far better able to deter and defend against today's main security threats: internal unrest, transnational terrorism, and the conventional threats posed by Iran. Unless Iran's standoff with the international community escalates into a full-blown conflict, these threats will remain the region's most serious into the next decade.

In today's scene, the GCC states must be pressed to take a more active role as agents of national and collective defense. Knights argues that the United States should seek to build four core competencies in the GCC states' security forces: intelligence sharing to develop a common picture of the operational environment; securing of land borders; patrolling at sea; and the ability to hold the line against low levels of Iranian pressure. To build these competencies, the United States should make greater use of cost-effective U.S.-approved arms sales, U.S.-funded training, and grants of surplus U.S. military equipment.

To meet maritime and aerial threats from Iran, Knights proposes that the United States encourage a reorientation of the GCC collective defense effort. Because Iran will likely view such measures as a threat, the GCC states should simultaneously attempt to launch a program to reduce military tensions in the Gulf, including developing a Gulf security forum.

With Iraq unstable and the Iranian nuclear program progressing unchecked, it may seem optimistic to envision a more peaceful Gulf region. But we can still benefit from thinking about steps to take if the United States achieves its immediate objectives of stabilizing Iraq and freezing the Iranian nuclear program. Knights's study shows how the United States can best build on and extend these possible achievements through its security relations with the Gulf monarchies.

Robert Satloff
Executive Director

Patrick Clawson
Deputy Director for Research

Executive Summary

THOUGH MANY MIGHT wish it otherwise, the stability of the Gulf region will be vital to America's economic and physical security for the foreseeable future. In time, U.S. government initiatives may diversify America's supply of energy enough to reduce its direct exposure to supply instability in the Gulf. Even in the absence of policy changes, the U.S. Energy Information Administration predicts that by 2020, only 20 percent of oil used in the United States will originate in the Gulf. Yet the Gulf remains a vital source of direct physical supply for the United States if and when other sources become unstable. Furthermore, diversifying U.S. energy sources cannot hedge against the broader second-order economic effects of an interruption of Gulf hydrocarbon supplies. If Gulf oil and gas supplies are interrupted—or do not grow fast enough to accommodate increasing energy demand in the fast-developing economies in India and China—then prices for oil and gas will rise in every world market, including the United States. In other words, a shortfall in Gulf energy supply will drive up energy prices in U.S. markets whether or not the United States imports its oil from the Gulf. A sharp increase in energy prices could hurt the U.S. economy directly, and throw the world economy into a recession that harms the U.S. economy even more deeply.

In addition to these economic threats, the Gulf has spawned a range of direct threats to the physical security of America and its citizens. The U.S. National Security Strategy of 2006, in particular, highlights the need to "Prevent Our Enemies from Threatening Us, Our Allies, and Our Friends with Weapons of Mass Destruction." In this context, Iran's quest to develop nuclear weapons threatens both to embroil the United States in a showdown with a rogue state and to encourage other states in the region to develop weapons of mass destruction (WMD). Stopping Iran from acquiring nuclear weapons is an important national security interest of the United States.

A second major physical threat originating from the region is Islamic terrorism. The U.S. National Defense Strategy of 2005 notes two interrelated ways in which the United States must counter this threat: by disrupting terrorist networks and by countering ideological support for terrorism. The Gulf is one of the world's most active arenas for operational counterterrorism, and it also contains the most influential ideological institutions in the Islamic world. All but two of the September 11 hijackers were from GCC countries, showing that threats originating in the Gulf region do not always stay there.

Need for a Sustainable Security Framework

In the four decades since the United States replaced Britain as the key external guarantor of Gulf security, the U.S. government has at different times tried and failed to cultivate Iran and Saudi Arabia as effective security partners. By the mid-1990s, the U.S. military was shouldering the entire burden of directly ensuring Gulf security.

Despite the discomfort and cost of hosting U.S. forces, for GCC decision-makers depending on the United States for security proved far easier than developing as military powers in their own right, or tackling the thorny issues required to reduce interstate threats in the Gulf. The U.S. and regional decision-makers became accustomed to direct U.S. military intervention, even though it evolved from policy failures rather than policy choices.

The arrangement by which the United States ensures Gulf security is by no means ideal. Among other problems, a large U.S. military presence in the Gulf is one pretext used to justify Islamic terrorism. The substantial presence of U.S. forces in the Gulf—a region far removed from U.S. shores—also reduces the readiness and flexibility of U.S. forces for deployment in the event of crises elsewhere. The U.S. National Defense Strategy, meanwhile, envisages a worldwide reduction of the number of forward-deployed U.S. forces. For U.S. planners, the challenge in the Gulf is to maintain stability while finding a way to lighten the U.S. footprint.

The question that inevitably follows is whether the GCC states can shoulder more of their security burdens themselves. Speaking broadly, the National Defense Strategy calls on U.S. planners to "identify areas where our common interests would be served better by partners playing leading roles," and to "encourage partners to increase their capability and willingness to operate in coalition with U.S. forces." An assessment of security fundamentals in the Gulf suggests that the balance of effort and division of labor between the United States and the GCC can and should be changed. The strong U.S. role post-1990 was needed to deter a short-warning overland invasion from Iraq while simultaneously hedging against a threat from Iran—roles for which the small GCC states were ill suited. They are far better suited to deterring and defending against today's main difficulties: the internal and transnational threats posed by substate adversaries (e.g., terrorists and criminals) as well as the aerial and naval threats posed by a conventionally armed Iran. In the next decade, assuming the Iranian nuclear program is refrozen, these will likely remain the principal security threats in the Gulf. Given this scenario, the GCC states will need to stand on their own feet as the primary agents of national and collective defense.

Principles to Guide U.S. Regional Security Strategy

In determining principles for defense of the Gulf, U.S. planners should first recall the mistakes made over the past four decades with Iran and Saudi Arabia. In other words, Washington should avoid the temptation to build its efforts around a new "anchor" state. Instead, the United States should continue to develop a wide range of basing options and military partnerships throughout the GCC states, embracing new allies among the smaller GCC states without neglecting older allies such as Saudi Arabia and Kuwait.

Second, the United States should focus on strengthening formalized multinational cooperation within the GCC, between the GCC and its neighbors, and between the GCC and extraregional partners such as NATO. Though Washington draws advantages from bilateral alliances with individual GCC states, the transnational threats facing the Gulf states require transnational solutions. Such multinational cooperation need not be developed through the sort of collective defense initiatives that failed in the past, but could instead result from multilateral initiatives fostered by the United States.

Third, more cost-effective means for meeting security needs should be sought. This would include keeping to a minimum the long-term deployment of U.S. forces in the region. At the same time, Gulf states should not purchase highly expensive weapons systems except when necessary. The GCC states can work to ensure their security by using their resources to address pressing problems in job creation, education, and social welfare, rather than through any dramatic increases in defense spending.

The final principle underlying U.S. security assistance in the Gulf should be a commitment to threat reduction. If U.S. support to the GCC is not managed carefully, it could exacerbate military tension in the region. The United States needs to use its considerable influence over GCC military-development policies to guide states toward "nonoffensive" defense, creating regional militaries that are responsible as well as capable. This also means supporting regional dialogue and confidence-building measures.

Key Recommendations

In dealing with their internal security problems, GCC states already play the lead role. As a result, the United States should focus its efforts on increasing the regional allies' ability to defend against transnational threats and deter interstate aggression by Iran—with the understanding that if Iran were to acquire even an ambiguous nuclear capability, deterring it would require a substantial U.S. role. These missions are both long term and open-ended. To the extent that regional allies can reliably replicate or even improve upon the performance of U.S. forces in either of these roles, the GCC nations could greatly reduce the burden on the overstretched U.S. military. Many of the steps required to improve GCC capability against transnational threats will also strongly enhance the GCC's ability to respond effectively to lower-scale Iranian actions.

The United States should seek to build four core competencies in the GCC security forces:

- **Common operating picture.** A tiered intelligence-sharing network that can provide an up-to-date picture of land, maritime, and aerial environments. A central element of this network will be a collaborative sensor grid that relies primarily on GCC assets and uses multinational "plug-in" assets as needed.

- **Land-border security.** The establishment of effective points of entry, denial points, and patrolling along land borders.

- **Maritime patrolling.** The ability to carry out effective drug and alien-migrant interdiction, vessel-boarding search-and-seizure operations, interception of unsafe or suspicious vessels at a safe distance from shore, and the enforcement of exclusive economic zones.

- **Hold the line in Iranian scenarios.** GCC forces need to be able to defend against and deter low levels of Iranian pressure without calling on the U.S. military for assistance, though the GCC will continue to rely on the United States in the event of a full-scale Iranian attack and to provide protection against potential Iranian nuclear capability. GCC forces must also be capable of a strong initial defense of the basing infrastructure and regional reception points that the United States relies on to project its power. "Nonoffensive" defense capabilities hinge on the GCC states' air-defense and civil-emergency capabilities.

To build these competencies, the United States should make greater use of cost-effective security-assistance mechanisms, including U.S.-approved arms sales, U.S.-funded training, and equipment grants. One way to ensure more efficient defense spending would be to guide GCC procurement with increased financing credits through the U.S. Foreign Military Financing (FMF) program and the provision of U.S. military surplus. As a result, the GCC states might be encouraged to focus greater resources on manpower development, maintenance, and interoperability both amongst themselves and with the United States. Meanwhile, use of U.S.-funded training opportunities such as the International Military Education and Training (IMET) and Nonproliferation, Antiterrorism, Demining, and Related (NADR) programs should be pushed energetically throughout the GCC. These types of programs are vital for ensuring that future generations of GCC political and military leaders have a positive experience of American social, political, and military culture.

In the field of security cooperation—including exercises, intelligence exchanges, and coalition operations—the United States should develop a formal regional cooperation framework similar to existing frameworks in other areas of strong U.S. interest (e.g., the "Caspian Guard" or "Gulf of Guinea Guard" programs). Such a program could be undertaken by expanding the scope of the U.S.-GCC Cooperative Defense Initiative (CDI), or else it could be pursued as an entirely new initiative. NATO assistance, extended under the Istanbul Cooperation Initiative (ICI) framework, could be a highly useful aspect of this effort. For NATO, one primary contribution could be to aid GCC states with defense reform and budgetary planning. NATO could also provide useful assistance to GCC states in developing a blueprint of military integration, measures to justify costs and avoid duplication of efforts, and better-synchronized procurement. In the fields of counterterrorism, border security, countertrafficking, and civil-emergency planning, NATO countries could assist GCC states directly.

While a more formal regional security framework would focus primarily on transnational threats, the United States should also use its security cooperation framework to increase GCC ability to deter Iranian pressure. Such a program should seek to develop a multinational maritime presence in the Gulf—what might be called a "peninsula shield at sea." As this name implies, the aim would be a reorientation of the GCC collective-defense effort to meet maritime and aerial threats from Iran. To demonstrate U.S. military commitment to the Gulf, the United States should mount an annual exercise similar to the "Reforger" reinforcement exercises it enacted during the Cold War. Such maneuvers would periodically test U.S. ability to deploy forces to the region, maintain strategic airlift capabilities and regional reception capacity, and send a strong deterrent signal to potential aggressors.

Because Iran could perceive the measures noted here as a threat, a counter-balancing program of threat reduction is necessary to reduce military tensions. The United States should therefore support any steps to develop a Gulf security forum. If practical, the United States should seek to guide such a forum to be (1) inclusive of all regional states (including Iran, Iraq, and Yemen); (2) focused on both bilateral and multilateral issues; and (3) insulated from broader regional issues such as the Israeli-Palestinian or Israeli-Syrian conflicts. Such a forum could perform a vital role in developing regional responses to the trans-national threats facing the Gulf, and allow confidence- and security-building measures to reduce interstate tension in the region. The Association of Southeast Asian Nations (ASEAN) Regional Forum—or ARF—provides a useful model for this proposal.

Acronyms

A2AD: antiaccess and area denial threat

AAM: air-to-air missile

ACRS: Middle East Arms Control and Regional Security working group

AEF: Aerospace Expeditionary Force, a concept of the U.S. Air Force

AESA: active electronically scanned array radar

AEW: airborne early warning; *also* Aerospace Expeditionary Wing

AMRAAM: advanced medium-range air-to-air missile

AOR: area of responsibility

AQAP: al-Qaeda Organization in the Arabian Peninsula

ARG: amphibious ready group

ASEAN (or ARF): Association of Southeast Asian Nations

AShM: antishipping missile

ATA: Antiterrorism Assistance, a training program of the U.S. State Department Bureau of Diplomatic Security

ATACMS: army tactical missile system

AWACS: airborne warning and control system

BVR: beyond-visual-range (air-to-air missiles)

C3: command, control, and communications

C^{4}ISR: command, control, communications, computerization, intelligence, surveillance, and reconnaissance

CBW: chemical and biological weapons

CDI: Cooperative Defense Initiative; a collection of U.S.-sponsored measures aimed at deterring Iran's missile capabilities

CENTCOM: U.S. Central Command

CEP: circular error of probability, a means of determining weapons accuracy

CINC: CENTCOM commanders-in-chief

CONUS: continental United States

CSBM: confidence- and security-building measure

CSL: cooperative security location

CVBG: aircraft carrier battle group

DIO: Defense Industries Organization; an umbrella group of Iranian defense industries that comprises 250 sites and employs 50,000 workers

EACTI: East African Counter-Terrorism Initiative

ECCM: electronic counter-countermeasure

EDA: excess defense articles (U.S. military surplus)

EIA: Energy Information Administration

ESG: expeditionary strike group, *also* expeditionary sensor grid

EXBS: Export Control and Related Border Security Assistance, a U.S. program

FIU: Financial Intelligence Unit

FMF: foreign military financing

FMS: foreign military sales

FOS: forward operating site

GAMCO: Gulf Aircraft Maintenance Company

GCC: Gulf Cooperation Council. Formed in 1980, includes Saudi Arabia, Bahrain, Kuwait, Oman, Qatar, and the United Arab Emirates.

GID: Saudi General Intelligence Directorate

GLCM: ground-launched cruise missile

GPS/IN: global positioning system inertial navigation

GSS: General Security Service of Saudi Arabia's Interior Ministry

IACI: Iranian Aircraft Industries

IAFAIO: Iranian Armed Forces Aviation Industry Organization

ICDL: International Computer Driving License training, now being under-taken by all UAE AFAD personnel

ICI: NATO's Istanbul Cooperation Initiative

IFF: Identification, Friend or Foe system

IMET: International Military Education and Training

INCSEA: incident at sea

IRGC: Islamic Revolutionary Guard Corps (of Iran)

IRIAS: Islamic Republic of Iran Armed Services

IRIN: Islamic Republic of Iran Navy

ISR: intelligence, surveillance, and reconnaissance

HAS: hardened aircraft shelter

JLENS: joint land attack cruise missile defense elevated netted sensor system

JSF: joint strike fighter

JSTARS: joint surveillance target attack radar system

LCS: littoral combat ship

MCM: mine countermeasure

MEMAC: Marine Emergency Mutual Aid Center; works to prevent pollution in the Gulf. *See also* ROPME.

MOB: main operating base

MOIS: See VEVAK.

MPA: maritime patrol aircraft

NADR: Nonproliferation, Antiterrorism, Demining, and Related Programs of
   the U.S. State Department

NCW: network-centric warfare

NDS: National Defense Strategy

NEO: noncombatant evacuation operation

NESA: Near East and South Asia

NIC: National Intelligence Council

NPT: Nuclear Non-Proliferation Treaty (also Nuclear Nonproliferation Treaty
   of 1968)

NSS: U.S. National Security Strategy

PAC-3: Patriot Advanced Capability 3 radar systems

PISCES: Personal Identification Secure Comparison and Evaluation System;
   software provided by the United States to facilitate international intelligence
   sharing and "watch list" monitoring

PSI: Proliferation Security Initiative; a U.S. program that provides for the
   interdiction of maritime traffic suspected of carrying WMD or illegal missile technology

QDR: Quadrennial Defense Review

ROPME: Regional Organization for the Protection of the Marine Environment; works to prevent pollution in the Gulf. *See also* MEMAC.

RPG: rocket-propelled grenade

SAG: surface action group

SALW: Small Arms and Light Weapons Program; a U.S. initiative that assists
   in border security and disarmament

SAM: surface-to-air missile

SANG: Saudi Arabian National Guard

SAR: search and rescue

SASO: support and stabilization operation

SSM: surface-to-surface missile

SWAT: special weapons and training

TBM: theater ballistic missile

THAAD: Terminal High-Altitude Area Defense

TIP: Terrorism Interdiction Program; a U.S. program that provides immigration software. *See* PISCES.

TSCTI: Trans-Sahara Counter-Terrorism Initiative

UAE AFAD: UAE Air Force and Air Defenses

UAV: unmanned aerial vehicle

UCAV: unmanned combat aerial vehicle

USMTM: U.S. Military Training Mission

UUV: unmanned underwater vehicle

VBIED: vehicle-borne improvised explosive device

VEVAK: Iranian Ministry of Intelligence and National Security. Also known as MOIS.

WMD: weapons of mass destruction

WTO: World Trade Organization

Introduction

The Enduring Strategic Importance of the Persian Gulf

FOR U.S. FOREIGN policy, the Persian Gulf region has been and will continue to be an area of extraordinary importance. The record of U.S. activism in the area speaks for itself. Since the 1980s, U.S. Central Command (CENTCOM) has undertaken fourteen major contingency operations in the Gulf, including two major wars, numerous smaller military strikes and operations, and parallel maritime and aerial containment operations lasting twelve years. What vital strategic interests and values drew U.S. forces into the region on so many occasions? Though securing access to strategic energy reserves and waterways has never been the sole reason for U.S. military intervention in the Gulf, energy security will remain a major concern as long as the developing economies of the world rely on hydrocarbon resources to power their industries.

Perhaps just as important, the Gulf has emerged as a central front in the open-ended fights against terrorism and nuclear proliferation. The connection between Gulf security and the global war on terror goes deeper than the oft-quoted fact that Osama bin Laden and all but two of the nineteen September 11 hijackers were citizens of Gulf states. The Gulf states rest at the very heart of the Islamic world, and the Gulf remains the theater in which the West, particularly the United States, has most often clashed with Islamic societies. Iran's quest to develop nuclear weapons threatens both to embroil the United States in a showdown with a rogue state and to encourage other states in the region to develop weapons of mass destruction. The threats to Gulf states—whether the internal threats of failed leadership and terrorism, or the external challenges of conventional and unconventional arms races—will likely expand beyond the region, becoming more likely to harm the economic and physical security of the United States. As one observer wrote: "The Gulf has shown a dismaying ability to affect the lives of people throughout the world, not only as their principal supplier of energy, but as one of the major fonts of terrorism."[1]

Future Energy Security and the Gulf

All signs indicate that, for the next two decades at least, Gulf stability will be vital to the economic well-being of the global economy. For the developing nations of the Asia-Pacific rim in particular, these decades will see a strong growth in demand for oil and gas supplies. To meet this demand, while keeping oil prices within a reasonable range, extensive energy reserves will be needed. The Gulf countries, particularly Saudi Arabia, will continue to own the most significant and accessible reserves. As far as existing excess production capacity, proven oil reserves, and low extraction costs are concerned, the Gulf states maintain key advantages over other oil-producing regions (see figure 1). The six Gulf Cooperation Council (GCC) countries (Bahrain, Kuwait, Oman, Qatar, Saudi Arabia, and the United Arab Emirates) plus Iraq, Iran, and Yemen maintain proven reserves of 730 billion barrels of oil—some 61.4 percent of proven global reserves—and one-third of proven global reserves of natural gas.[2]

In meeting global demand for hydrocarbons, individual regional states have different roles to play. Saudi Arabia, through its pivotal control of oil reserves, will maintain the greatest influence on global oil prices (and therefore on the growth of developing countries and the global economy) for the next two decades. Currently Riyadh controls about 25 percent of proven global oil reserves and, even more important, 50 percent of global shut-in excess production capability, a level now at 2.4 to 2.9 million barrels per day (b/d).[3] With their capacity as a "swing producer," the Saudis can lower oil prices and reduce the impact of supplier instability elsewhere in the world. This has prompted oil industry analysts to refer to Saudi Arabia as "the central bank of oil."[4] Respectively, the UAE and Kuwait maintain .59 million b/d and .48 million b/d excess capacity.[5] Though production numbers may vary in the coming decade, the GCC states will likely remain the only oil-producing countries to keep spare capacity as a matter of policy. Iraq currently controls around 10.7 percent of global proven oil reserves and Iran 8.5 percent, but neither of these countries maintains significant shut-in excess production capacity.[6] The result is a precarious concentration of strategic energy reserves along the Gulf littoral, which boasts the world's largest oil processing facility at Abqaiq and the world's largest oil export facilities at Ras Tanura, both in Saudi Arabia. Almost 40 percent of internationally traded oil already flows through the Strait of Hormuz, which is less than forty kilometers wide at its neck.

In the next two decades, developing countries are expected to become more dependent on the Gulf states' ability to maintain a steady and afford-

Figure 1. Hydrocarbon Reserves in the Gulf

	Proved oil reserves (billion barrels)	Percentage of global proved oil reserves	Proved natural gas reserves (trillion cubic feet)	Percentage of global proved natural gas reserves
Bahrain	0.5	<0.1	3.2	0.1
Kuwait	99.0	8.3	55.5	0.9
Oman	5.6	0.5	35.1	0.6
Qatar	15.2	1.3	910.1	14.4
Saudi Arabia	262.7	22.1	238.4	3.8
UAE	97.8	8.2	213.9	3.4
Iran	132.5	11.1	970.8	15.3
Iraq	115.0	9.7	111.9	1.8
Yemen	2.9	0.2	16.9	0.3

Source: Data compiled from BP Statistical Review of World Energy 2005.

able supply of hydrocarbons. Bahrain alone, of the Gulf states, is expected to expend its oil reserves in the next decade (see table above). According to the U.S. Department of Energy, oil produced in the Gulf—three quarters of which will be produced by GCC countries—is projected to make up a greater proportion of global production in 2010 than it does today.[7] Projections by Cambridge Energy Research Associates suggest that by 2010, 31.9 percent of global oil supply will originate in the Gulf, with this figure rising to 33.9 percent by 2020. And reports from the International Energy Agency suggest that Gulf oil supplies will remain the preponderant source in 2030.[8] In the increasingly important field of natural gas supply, regional states will become key suppliers to fast-growing economies in India, Pakistan, and perhaps even farther afield. Iran now controls 14.8 percent of global proven natural gas deposits, and sizeable deposits are also controlled by Qatar, Saudi Arabia, and the UAE. The supply of natural gas, particularly that delivered by pipeline, is often difficult to replace quickly in the event of supplier instability. Because many developing nations are integrating natural gas into their national systems for power generation, such replacement fuel can be critical for their competitiveness and ability to provide basic services.

For the United States, stable supply of Gulf hydrocarbons will continue to matter for the foreseeable future both because of the United States's own thirst for hydrocarbons and because of the increasing interconnectedness of the global economy. In 2003, the United States consumed 19.7 million b/d of crude oil, including 10.6 million b/d of imported oil. Energy Information Administration (EIA) projections suggest that by 2020, two-thirds of U.S. oil consumption—projected at 30 million b/d—will consist of imports. Put simply, where the United States has 5 percent of the world's population, it consumes a full quarter of global oil supplies every year. And while the United States is the world's third largest consumer of oil, it has only the tenth largest proven oil reserves, with the proportion it can provide for its own consumption declining rapidly. Politicians are unlikely to regulate U.S. oil consumption and stimulate the development of alternative energy sources through the unpopular steps of applying vehicle fuel efficiency standards designed in the 1970s or taxing hydrocarbons. As a result, imports will likely continue to increase. U.S. energy-security policy, however, does include efforts to ensure that the U.S. economy maintains access to oil supplies if access to Gulf oil is lost. This policy includes tapping alternative supply sources in Latin America, Eurasia, and Africa. Indeed, by 2020, the EIA predicts, only 20 percent of oil used in the United States will originate in the Gulf.[9] But such an approach provides no panacea, even in terms of ensuring physical supply of oil. In all non–Middle East supply sources, there are risks, as evidenced by the recent earthquake in Alaska, Hurricane Katrina, serious unrest in Columbia and Nigeria, and a major interruption of access to oil supplies from Venezuela.[10]

The focus on diversification in U.S. energy security policy also fails to hedge against the broader second-order economic effects of an interruption of Gulf hydrocarbon supplies. The critical issue here is that of general oil pricing and the sensitivity of global oil markets to instability in the Gulf. Maintaining the stability of Gulf oil producers represents a net gain for oil consumers across the world because, as Anthony Cordesman has noted, "The United States competes on a world market. Any shortage or price rise in a crisis forces us to compete for imports on the same basis as any other nation."[11] As for future global demand for oil, estimates vary widely—from as low as 83 million b/d in 2010 to 115 million b/d by 2020[12]—and Gulf oil supplies continue to represent the most significant resource for meeting high-end estimates. If demand cannot be met—either because of the impact of long-term instability in the Gulf on investment in regional production capacity, or due to specific crises—the Asia–Pacific rim economies would be affected dramatically by a shortfall in supply and higher prices. In addition to causing higher prices at the pumps in the United States, recession in these economies would have other negative effects on both the U.S. and global economies. Such effects would include knock-on recessions (e.g., those caused by prolonged high oil prices) in addition to a loss of markets and interrupted supply of low-cost services and energy-dependent manufacturing. For India, Pakistan, China, and Japan—nations with increasingly vital national interests tied up in the steady provision of Gulf hydrocarbons—it will only make sense to remain uninvolved in Gulf security as long as the United States stays involved. Put simply, other major powers will only stay out of the Gulf as long as the U.S. stays in it.

As this brief analysis suggests, maintaining Gulf security is not a choice for the United States, but instead a strategic necessity. On the issues of economic and energy security, Anthony Cordesman concluded:

> These energy reserves make the Gulf the one region in the Middle East that is a truly vital American strategic interest, although the United States does have strategic interests in friends like Israel and Egypt. The fact remains, nevertheless, that the only vital U.S. strategic interest in the region is the security of energy facilities and exports. Fundamental strategic interests still matter.[13]

State Failure, Terrorism, and WMD in the Gulf

The 2002 United States National Security Strategy introduced the prevention of state failure—defined as areas of weak or lapsed government authority within a nation—as a means of restricting the spread of terrorist havens and ensuring that WMD and other advanced weaponry do not fall into the hands of terrorists. In assessing the possibility of state failure around the globe, the U.S. Nuclear Posture Review of January 2002 identified the Middle East as the fastest growing area of concern for U.S. defense planners as they develop nuclear deterrence plans for the twenty-first century. Similarly, one observer noted:

> While it might be too dramatic to suggest that the Middle East effectively replaces the Soviet Union as the central targeting requirement for sizing and configuring the U.S. strategic deterrent, it seems clear that regional contingencies will assume a more prominent role in the nation's nuclear strategy.[14]

In the Middle East, an increasingly ominous security climate owes itself to mounting challenges to state cohesion, an advanced terrorist threat, and proliferation of conventional and unconventional weapons. When such challenges are placed alongside the immense value of the strategic assets in the region as well as the proven potential for regional threats to harm U.S. interests both inside the Gulf and on U.S. soil, it becomes clear that the United States must make effective management of Gulf instability a security priority.

In the Gulf, Islamic militancy poses two interrelated challenges to vital U.S. strategic interests: that of disrupting terrorist networks and simultaneously countering ideological support for terrorism. These challenges are highlighted in the U.S. National Defense Strategy of 2005. On the first count, strategists point to strong evidence that the Gulf is developing from a support base for the al-Qaeda movement and its affiliates into an operational theater. If the attacks of September 11, 2001, showed the United States one principal lesson, it was that threats originating in the Gulf do not necessarily stay within the Gulf anymore. And Gulf citizens not only made up a plurality of hijackers in that attack, they are also well represented within al-Qaeda and its regional affiliates. Further, Gulf citizens have been the main source of al-Qaeda's leaders, jihadists, and logistical facilitators, and the Gulf represents a transit point for both terrorist actors and terrorist funding. At present, al-Qaeda's affiliate groups based in Saudi Arabia and Iraq are developing offshoots that occasionally reach into Bahrain, Kuwait, Qatar, and that may, in time, infiltrate the other GCC states. These cells threaten the vital strategic interests of the United States and its regional allies in the region, ranging from the safety of U.S. citizens to the stability of energy supplies and friendly governments, as discussed before.

Whereas attacks such as that in October 2002 on the Limburg oil tanker off the coast of Yemen present a limited threat to oil supply, future terrorist attacks such as the February 24, 2006, assault on the vital Abqaiq oil-processing facility in Saudi Arabia could pose a serious threat to energy security. In Saudi Arabia, major attacks since May 2003 indicate a fundamental shift in the relationship between the global body of Islamic militants and the Saudi royal family. Though still viewed as a distant prospect, the radicalization or collapse of the government of a major oil-producing country, such as Saudi Arabia, could have a sustained negative impact on global oil markets. Diversified U.S. energy supply and relatively small Western strategic reserves would not be able to counterbalance the impact of major instability in Saudi Arabia, termed by Hess oil analyst Edward Morse "the ultimate strategic petroleum reserve."[15] As the following chapters will note, social and economic trends in the Gulf could contribute to such a radicalization or collapse in Saudi Arabia within the coming decade if conditions are left unchecked. Meanwhile, the threat posed by terrorism is growing in seriousness, and it will most likely remain at the forefront of U.S. global and regional security policy at the start of the next decade. As one analyst put it:

> We have to think in generational terms, which means we are still going to be dealing with al-Qaeda for the rest of our lives. Most al-Qaeda operatives are in their twenties or thirties, and will continue to fight until they are in the autumn of their lives. Furthermore, aside from their use of terrorism, they are drawing on an ideology and a relatively mainstream intellectual framework that has deep roots, giving further longevity to the threat.[16]

Securing the Gulf

The question "Who should police the Gulf?" is an enduring conundrum that has elicited few enduring solutions. To begin with, the Gulf has always been a truculent and violent neighborhood. In 1903, the British viceroy of India Lord Curzon remarked:

> [A] hundred years ago there was constant trouble and fighting in the Gulf, almost every man was a marauder or a pirate; kidnapping and slave-trading flourished; fighting and bloodshed went on without stint or respite; no ship could put out to sea without fear of attack; the pearl fishery was a scene of annual conflict; and security of trade or peace there was none.[17]

At intervals, this fundamentally unstable region has been shaken by the collapse or retreat of major powers. Lasting formally from 1920 to 1971, the period of Pax Brittanica saw the British assume the role of Gulf policeman in the aftermath of the First World War collapse of the Ottoman Empire, relinquishing this role in the years 1968–1971. In January 1970, the U.S. government issued the Nixon Doctrine, which identified the security of the Gulf as a vital U.S. national interest. At this point, the United States could have stepped into the field along the same lines as the previous "policemen," inserting itself as the region's dominant military power and discouraging the development of a militarily powerful regional proxy.

But the United States did not follow this path. Instead, the role of Gulf policeman fell increasingly to the growing military power of imperial Iran. Between 1970 and 1973, the U.S.-backed Shah represented the willful local ally of the United States. In 1973, when the oil embargo illustrated Saudi Arabia's tight grip on oil prices and its huge economic potential, a second pillar of U.S.

influence began to form. This oil-based partnership developed further, when in the years after King Faisal's assassination in 1975—during the Ford administration—Saudi Arabia ramped up its active financial diplomacy against Soviet-supported radical states in the region such as South Yemen and Iraq. At the same time, U.S. military planners designed for the Saudis a ten-year force design program, which aimed to make the kingdom capable of limited self-defense by the 1980s. This presumably would have allowed it to hold off an attack by any given radical states until the United States intervened directly using its newly constituted Rapid Deployment Force.[18]

As the United States sought to balance the power equation in the Gulf with its "twin pillar" approach, Iran and Saudi Arabia were engaged in their own bilateral machinations. Starting in the late 1950s, Saudi Arabia had been rejecting Iranian proposals concerning a bilateral defense pact. Though the idea of carving up the Gulf between the two largest states was not wholly unattractive to Riyadh, the Saudis saw the move as a risky leap into the unknown for two reasons. First, in keeping with the Shah's focus on expelling foreign military powers, it would require a cutting of ties with Britain, then the external guarantor of security in the Gulf. Second, it represented a move away from inter-Arab cooperation and trust at a time when Arab nationalism wielded powerful influence. In June 1967, following the weakening of radical Arab nationalism after the defeat of Arab armies in the Six Day War, and with Britain expected to leave the Gulf starting in 1968, both of these disincentives lost some potency. Between 1975 and 1978, Saudi-Iranian dialogue began once again on the issue of a collective defense pact that would exclude foreign military forces from the Gulf. This time, stumbling blocks largely involved the pressure exerted on Saudi Arabia by Iraq and the smaller Gulf states, which demanded equal inclusion and guarantees in the developing security dialogue. This entire diplomatic exchange was wrecked by two events: the Islamic revolution in Iran in 1979, and the subsequent outbreak of the Iran-Iraq War in 1980.[19]

With the Islamic revolution in Iran, the stronger of America's two pillars in the Gulf crashed down. Newly hostile relations between the two countries were cemented by the seizure of U.S. hostages, and later the failed hostage rescue bid in April 1980. Though the Saudi pillar remained intact, even with the formation of the Gulf Cooperation Council (GCC) in 1980, the military power it could muster fell far below that required to counterbalance Iran or Iraq. Nor could Baathist Iraq be developed into a lasting security proxy for the United States and the GCC. This was because of its long-standing role as a radical Soviet-supplied Arab nationalist state and its penchant for external aggression and pursuit of weapons of mass destruction. Though the United States removed Iraq from the State Sponsors of Terrorism list in March 1982, officials had little doubt that Baghdad continued to sponsor terrorist acts and shelter international terrorists who threatened U.S. interests and those of its allies. [20] In pursuing weapons-of-mass-destruction capability, Saddam's Iraq was poised to alter the regional military balance in a decisive way.

With a single weak pillar—Saudi Arabia and the GCC—supporting U.S. policy objectives in the region, U.S. officials knew into the late 1980s that they would have to increase direct U.S. military intervention in the region. The visible shift began in 1987, with the escort of reflagged Kuwaiti oil tankers in the Gulf and air and naval strikes on Iranian facilities. Then, on August 2, 1990, U.S. security policy in the Gulf reached its low point when Iraq invaded Kuwait. The Gulf War and the subsequent decade of air and maritime patrolling drew massive and prolonged U.S. military presence into the Gulf, necessitated mainly by the short-warning overland threat posed by Iraq. For the military capabilities of GCC states, CENTCOM developed objectives consisting of three tiers. In Tier I, individual Gulf States (led by Saudi Arabia) would develop the capability to defend their own territories (though the idea of developing the Saudi kingdom as a new pillar of military strength became widely discredited during the 1990s). Tier II sought to integrate the forces of individual Arab Gulf states into a more effective GCC-wide collective defense structure. The 1991 Damascus Declaration, meanwhile, would draw Egyptian, Syrian, and perhaps Pakistani forces into GCC defensive arrangements. As Ambassador Chas Freeman explained, the United States "would provide command and control and support, but basically the bulk of the forces would be provided by regional allies of the Gulf states."[21] With the rapid collapse of the Damascus Declaration due to Egyptian and Syrian unwillingness to engage with Gulf security fully, and due to inertia in GCC military development, the key focus was thrown on Tier III. This entailed the development of GCC allies' ability to host U.S. forces and operate alongside them through access and prepositioning agreements and the construction of military bases.[22]

For the United States, direct military intervention proved to be an effective way of policing the Gulf, but it had distinct drawbacks. Among these, open-ended U.S. military presence and activity in the region instigated radical Islamist tendencies, providing a basis for real discontent from which Salafist terrorists could draw. U.S. strategists quickly learned that the political burden of basing U.S. troops on foreign soil cannot be solved entirely by moving the U.S. presence to remote desert locations. In the Arab world, "out of sight" is not necessarily "out of mind." Though U.S. forces in Saudi Arabia moved to desert basing as long ago as 1996, their residual presence in Saudi society and the widespread knowledge that they were in the country remained a constant political liability for the Saudi government. Even after U.S. forces had largely been removed in 2003, the shock of having hosted and relied upon Western military power did not fade quickly from the Saudi public mind. The effective garrisoning of the Gulf also carried mounting financial costs and had a strong negative impact on the readiness of U.S. military forces elsewhere in the world. Continued U.S. military presence in the Gulf was driven wholly by the threats posed in the region, not by U.S. preferences.

Moreover, the experience of direct U.S. military intervention in the region had disturbing effects on both the United States and its regional allies. Though it tested U.S. military endurance, direct intervention in the Gulf represented a seductively simple solution to the problem of Gulf security. Direct military presence placed the Gulf squarely under military jurisdiction and gave U.S. decisionmakers a relatively high degree of control over security issues in the region. For GCC decisionmakers, despite the discomfort and cost of hosting a U.S. military presence, it proved far easier to depend on the United States for security than to develop as dependable military pillars in their own right, or to tackle the thorny issues required to reduce the interstate threat in the Gulf. In effect, the U.S. and regional decisionmakers could easily become addicted to direct U.S. military intervention in the Gulf.

The Need for a New Approach

The current U.S. approach to Gulf security needs to take into account the character of threats in the future and the competing pressures on the U.S. military. Key future threats include terrorism and a nuclear-armed Iran. As far as the U.S. global defense posture is concerned, officials argue that the military must aim to reduce its presence, visibility, and costs overseas without weakening the security of regional allies or compromising U.S. interests. This balancing act is doubly difficult when it comes to the politically sensitive and strategically vital Gulf region.

For the U.S. military to reduce its presence in an era of increased threats may sound like a tall order. Under conditions short of a major new confrontation in the region (say between Iran and the United States), such a readjustment is both possible and necessary. In the 1970s, the U.S. government pursued a strategy of balanced deterrence in the region by developing the military bulwarks of Iran and Saudi Arabia, on opposite ends of the Gulf. Meanwhile, the same two Gulf states and, later, the smaller states of the region sought to reduce the threat of regional instability by developing a nonaggression pact. This mixture of deterrence and confidence- and security-building might have worked had it not been for the Islamic revolution in Iran and the invasion of Iran by Saddam Hussein's Baathist state. In the current climate, a similar mixture of strengthened deterrent capabilities bolstered by outside powers and confidence- and security-building measures developed by regional powers can work. Indeed, this approach should be central to the future security of the region.

A U.S. security strategy grounded on the provision of assistance to regional security forces rather than exclusive use and deployment of U.S. forces is the key to building sustainable deterrence in the Gulf. Though helping build the defensive capabilities of local allies at Tier I–III levels is hardly a new prescription, several factors suggest that such a strategy can finally work. Central to this study is the premise that the evolution of the Gulf threat away from a short-warning overland invasion from Iraq and toward regional states' internal instability—along with an emphasis on aerial and naval operations, and nuclear deterrence—means that the GCC states will be capable of playing a more prominent role in their own defense than ever before. Where the small, slow-developing armies of the GCC were ill suited to counter the threat from Iraq, they are surprisingly well suited to face the future threats. Though America will continue to be the ultimate counterweight to extremely serious threats such as Iranian military aggression, the Arab Gulf states can function as the primary agents of national and collective defense in the region during a host of more probable threat scenarios. The United States needs to continue its current policy of developing a broader-based set of military allies that does not rely on one or two so-called anchor states. At the same time, it must not neglect its longstanding military allies such as Saudi Arabia and Kuwait.

Because increased security assistance to the GCC states could create heightened tension and arms races in the region, the United States should consider taking a leaf out of the regional dialogues that first occurred in the late 1970s and are beginning to develop once again. Where the United States instinctively looks to bolster local deterrence through building regional states' military capability, the Gulf nations place equal importance on reducing threats through dialogue and economic interconnectedness. Along with helping local allies develop self-defensive capabilities, the United States should play a low-key role in encouraging the development of a Gulf security forum. In the coming years, such a forum might support a fourth tier of a theater security cooperation plan developed by CENTCOM, adding a threat reduction focus to the defensive and deterrent focuses of Tiers I–III. Had regional events turned out differently, this same formula might have brought greater stability in the late 1970s. It stands an even better chance of succeeding today, promising a lighter U.S. military presence, a broad base of strong but balanced local allies, and reduction of threats between potential antagonists.

Notes

1. Joseph McMillan, *U.S. Forces in the Gulf: Options for a Post-Saddam Era* (2003), p. 2.

2. Simon Henderson, *The New Pillar: Conservative Arab Gulf States and U.S. Strategy* (Washington, D.C.: Washington Institute, 2004), p. xiv.

3. Joseph Barnes, Herman Franssen, and Edgard Habib, "The West and Gulf Oil: Stability, Security, and Strategy" (paper presented at the conference "Gulf Oil, Global Politics: The Future of Energy Security in the Middle East," London, December 11, 2002).

4. Ibid.

5. Ibid.

6. Henderson, *The New Pillar*, p. xiv. See also Barnes, "The West and Gulf Oil."

7. Anthony Cordesman, *The U.S. Military and Evolving Challenges in the Middle East* (Washington, D.C.: Center for Strategic and International Studies, 2002); Simon Wardell, "Continued Dependence on Gulf Oil: The Shape of Things to Come" (paper presented at the conference "Gulf Oil, Global Politics: The Future of Energy Security in the Middle East," London, December 11, 2002).

8. Barnes, Franssen, and Habib, "The West and Gulf Oil."

9. Geoffrey Kemp, "The Persian Gulf Remains the Strategic Prize," *Survival* 40, no. 4 (1998), p. 132.

10. *Strategic Survey* 2002/2003 (Washington, D.C.: International Institute for Strategic Studies, 2003).

11. Cordesman, *The U.S. Military*, p. 1.

12. Edward Morse and Manouchehr Takin, "Re-drawing the Energy Map: Supply Diversification—Implications for the Gulf" (paper presented at the conference "Gulf Oil, Global Politics: The Future of Energy Security in the Middle East," December 11, 2002). See also Kemp, "The Persian Gulf," pp. 132–135.

13. Cordesman, *The U.S. Military*, p. 1.

14. James Russell, "Nuclear Strategy and the Modern Middle East," *Middle East Policy* XI, no. 3 (Fall 2004), p. 98.

15. Morse and Takin, "Re-drawing the Energy Map."

16. Michael Eisenstadt, interview by author, Washington, D.C., March 2004.

17. M. H. Ansari, "Security in the Gulf: The Evolution of a Concept," *Strategic Analysis* 23, no. 6 (1999).

18. R. K. Ramazani, "Security in the Gulf," *Foreign Affairs* (1979).

19. Ansari, "Security in the Gulf."

20. Douglas Borer, "Inverse Engagement: Lessons from U.S.-Iraq Relations, 1982–1990," *Parameters: U.S. Army War Quarterly* 33, no. 2 (Summer 2003), pp. 54–55.

21. CENTCOM, "Southwest Asia: Approaching the Millennium—Enduring Problems, Emerging Solutions" (1996), p. 57.

22. Binneford Peay, "The Five Pillars of Peace in the Central Region," *Joint Force Quarterly* (Autumn 1995), p. 34. See also United States Security Strategy for the Middle East (1995), pp. 21–22.

PART I

Threats to Future Gulf Security

1

Local and Transnational Threats to Internal Stability

RISK CAN BE defined as the nexus of a threat and the set of assets that stand to be affected by that threat. As the previous section showed, the Gulf has many strategic assets. This chapter will review the many threats originating from the Gulf that are capable of striking U.S. strategic assets both inside and outside the region. While successful threat assessment is essential to strategic planning, planners too often base tomorrow's force requirements on today's threats. By the year 2000, for instance, U.S. Central Command (CENTCOM) and the Kuwaiti armed forces had developed a posture ideally suited to countering the threat of overland invasion posed by Iraq in August 1990. Strategic planners need to understand future threats so that they can design solutions in advance. To support the development of a reformed program of future U.S. security assistance in the Gulf, planners must first create a baseline threat assessment that imaginatively reaches into the future. Both this and the next chapter will provide an assessment of threats to the status quo in the Gulf over the next ten years. Threats will be presented at three levels: (1) internal threats posed by indigenous political forces; (2) transnational threats involving antagonists moving between nations; and (3) threats between nations themselves.

Socioeconomic Change and Weakening States

Before the post-1950s era of high oil revenues—which, to an unparalleled extent, centralized control of wealth and security capabilities within separate tribal confederations—few observers expected internal peace or stability in the states along the Gulf littoral. But contrary to popular perceptions of Gulf states as unchanging societies led by inflexible autocrats, the Gulf royal families have proved adept at managing periods of radical change, such as the sudden transition to oil-based economies and urban-centered societies. In 1996, reflecting on the internal stability in the Gulf states, CENTCOM long-range planners remarked:

If one looks at the regimes that came to power in the 1960s and 1970s, a kind of region-wide regime stability has resulted unlike any six other contiguous countries anywhere else in the developing world. Their individual and collective resilience in the face of one daunting challenge after another has, therefore, not been lacking.[1]

The phrase "rentier state" describes a government that distributes wealth among its population, by either heavily subsidizing services or providing them for free. In the Arab Gulf states, a rentier approach has helped governments limit discontent among its citizens. Powerful state security services dealt with the remainder of hard-core radicals. Yet, while the patronage-based system of low populations, plentiful oil revenues, and long-serving leaders supported this system until the 1990s, since then, each of its pillars has been slowly eroded. In a number of Gulf states in the coming decade, rapid population growth, unreliable oil revenues, and political successions will test the ability of leaders to redefine the existing social contract between rulers and ruled.

Particularly in Saudi Arabia, Kuwait, and Oman, population growth will place increasing strain on national economies (see figure 2). This is because subsidized government services represent a fixed expense for the GCC states, all of which remain highly reliant on unpredictable oil revenues. As a result, GCC leaders will effect reforms in the welfare state over the next decade, a process that will necessarily reduce the standard of living in some states. For most

Figure 2. Population Growth in the Gulf: Annual Percentage Change

Country	2000	2001	2002	2003	2004
Bahrain	2.11	2.07	2.03	1.99	2.0
Kuwait	3.86	3.81	2.3	2.29	3.2
Oman	2.61	2.78	2.39	2.38	2.4
Qatar	3.48	2.2	1.99	2.27	2.6
Saudi Arabia	2.57	2.68	2.78	2.89	2.7
United Arab Emirates (UAE)	4.48	6.71	6.88	N/A	6.9
GLOBAL AVERAGE	1.26	1.25	1.17	1.17	1.1

Source: World Bank Development Indicators database.

Gulf nations, reforms will require hiring freezes in government jobs, in part to streamline bloated bureaucracies.

Such reforms will exacerbate already high levels of unemployment in the GCC, requiring job creation as a counterbalancing measure. Because of population growth in recent decades, most Gulf states have demographic "bulges" that will soon result in tens of thousands of employment-age job-seekers entering each country's national workplace each year. In the long term, only a transformation in cultural attitudes and outlook will stabilize population growth, including the cessation of pronatalist policies and "changes that strike at the core of Gulf culture, concerning the arranged and young marriage, the sexual division of labor, and the female role as mother and wife."[2] In the near term, Gulf states need to implement meaningful educational and economic reforms to improve vocational training opportunities, change the overall work ethic to encourage natives to undertake a full range of jobs, and reduce incentives to hire nationals from outside the Gulf ("third-country" nationals), or else face growing unemployment in their countries.[3] This localization of the workforce will be difficult to achieve for a number of reasons. First, the potential for job creation is greatest in private sector nonoil industries, which are presently small in size and poorly managed. Second, the duplication of industries across the GCC has made growth harder to sustain. And, third, localization will be complicated by procedures requiring less manpower in traditionally labor-intensive industries, and by existing legal mechanisms that make local workers considerably more expensive to hire than third-country nationals, who currently make up an average of 60 percent of the national workforce of Gulf states (see figure 3, next page).[4]

In each GCC state, economic trends will likely play out slightly differently. In Qatar, for instance, the economic underpinnings of the rentier state—high revenues and a small population—are alive and well. After successfully preparing to make the transition from an oil-based to a gas-based economy in the 1990s, Qatar has begun to export its enormous natural gas resources throughout the Gulf and farther afield, and now ranks as one of the world's best-performing economies. Even while reinvesting up to 42 percent of its revenues in improved export infrastructure in recent years, the government has produced a string of unbroken budget surpluses, forecast conservatively at 20 percent of the gross domestic product (GDP).[5] Qatar's small population will likely continue to enjoy one of the world's highest per-capita incomes through the coming decade. Per-capita incomes in Bahrain, Kuwait, Oman, and the United Arab Emirates (UAE) have also increased steadily since the late 1980s. But—with the possible exceptions of Qatar and the Emirates—these states will be unlikely

Figure 3. Expatriate Populations in the Gulf

	Total Population (millions)	Number of Expatriates (millions)	Proportion of Expatriates
Saudi Arabia	22.757	5.360	24%
Kuwait	2.041	1.159	57%
Bahrain	0.645	0.228	35%
Qatar	0.769	0.576	75%*
UAE	2.407	1.576	65%
Oman	2.622	0.527	20%

* The *CIA World Factbook* does not provide a figure for expatriates living in Qatar. The generally accepted estimate is 75 percent.
Sources: Simon Henderson, *The New Pillar: Conservative Arab Gulf States and U.S. Strategy* (Washington, D.C.: Washington Institute, 2003); *CIA World Factbook 2003*, available online (www.cia.gov/cia/publications/factbook).

to sustain rentier state welfare services or sufficient job creation throughout the coming decade. Despite its great hydrocarbon reserves, of the GCC states Saudi Arabia is least capable of reducing unemployment and maintaining a decent standard of living for its citizens, who have witnessed a precipitous drop in per-capita incomes, from $16,267 in 1980, to a low point of $5,010 in 1988, then back up slightly to $8,530 in 2002.[6]

As GCC governments grapple with the problems associated with raising revenues, reducing welfare-related expenditures, creating private-sector job opportunities, and grooming more capable job-seekers, popular frustration will likely mount. The reality of high unemployment and reduced standards of living will breed resentment throughout the Gulf, as has already occurred in the region's Shiite communities, which were systematically excluded from the benefits of the rentier system.[7] Inequality plays a major role in this discussion. Economic-austerity measures for ordinary citizens, when contrasted with the apparent corruption of elites (particularly in Saudi Arabia and Bahrain), will generate anger within the Gulf's predominantly young and semieducated populations, who are, in the words of National Defense University academic Judith Yaphe, "politicized, articulate, indignant, and obsessed with social and economic justice."[8] For this generation, increasing globalization will likely have two effects: that of fostering unattainable material expectations, and that of encouraging media-fueled pan-Islamic identity politics—calls for militant Arab nationalism that some call the "manufacture of dissent." A number of analysts have commented on the potentially polarizing effects of globalization on Gulf countries, plus the potential for a foreign presence, commercial or military, to serve as a lightning rod for socioeconomic and regional frustrations.[9]

Managing Simultaneous Social Change and Leadership Succession

Royal succession represents a unique feature of Gulf security, with its central import lying in the redistribution of influence that can occur during protracted or inconclusive transitions. As with economic issues, the political challenges posed by succession vary greatly from one GCC state to another. Two variables dictate the likely impact of Gulf successions over the next ten years. The first regards the actual number of leadership changes to be expected. In many Gulf states, both the current rulers and their immediate heirs are already quite old, suggesting that several successions could periodically disrupt government activity and decisionmaking over a relatively short period (see figure 4, next page). A second indicator is whether potential successors have broad support and can wield strong powers of command. Contested or weak succession processes will only magnify the disruption created by each change in leadership.

In terms of risks posed by succession over the next ten years, Gulf states can be divided into three broad categories.[10] Future succession in Bahrain and the two key emirates within the UAE—Abu Dhabi and Dubai—present a relatively low risk for serious disruption, though not without potential complicating factors. In the medium-risk category, Oman remains a concern because Sultan Qaboos, who will be seventy-four in 2015, has no children and is unlikely to sire any in the future. Though a family council system has been established to manage succession by drawing from a select list of relatives, no clear-cut successor has been identified. Qatar has a long history of contested successions and may also see a complicated dispute over leadership if the designated successor Crown Prince Tamim is required to accede to the throne at too young an age. Kuwait recently clarified its cluttered line of succession (see Appendix 6) and moved through two successive elderly and infirm leaders. Nevertheless, deft power-sharing will be required to maintain the balance between competing wings of the royal family and ensure stability in future successions.

Arguably the highest-risk succession case is Saudi Arabia, where successions may be frequent, contested, and potentially inconclusive. Though King Fahd's death gave nominal full authority to King Abdullah, the new monarch is eighty-three years old, and his nearest successors are not much younger. Within the wings of any royal family, each succession creates a significant risk of disagreement. The effect in Saudi Arabia may be slowed decisionmaking at precisely the moment when the kingdom must take bold and decisive steps to avoid state failure. A detailed analysis of succession issues in the GCC can be found in Appendix 6.

Redefining the Social Contract through Power Sharing

As a result of growing social dissatisfaction over the slow collapse of the rentier state, combined with increasingly transient and weakened leaderships, a redefinition of the social contract between the royal families and their subjects in the Gulf will likely take shape. Though Gulf Arabs certainly desire a say in the exciting and unsettling changes now rippling through their nations, their

Figure 4. GCC Succession at a Glance

Country		Current Ruler	Age/Health of Ruler	Current Successor (Age/Health)	Risk of Problematic Succession
Bahrain		King Hamad	56/good	Crown Prince Salman (37/good)	Low
Kuwait		Emir Sheikh Sabah al-Ahmad al-Sabah	77/poor	Crown Prince Sheikh Nawaf al-Ahmad al-Sabah (68/good)	Medium
Oman		Sultan Qaboos	65/good	Not established	Medium
Qatar		Emir Sheikh Hamad	56/poor	Crown Prince Tamim (27/good)	Medium
Saudi Arabia		King Abdullah	83/average	Crown Prince Sultan (82/average)	Medium-High
UAE	Abu Dhabi	Emir Sheikh Khalifa	57/average	Crown Prince Muhammad bin Zayed al-Nahayan (45/average)	Low
	Dubai	Ruler Sheikh Muhammad bin Rashid al-Maktoum	47/average	Not established	Low

greater participation in politics will result not from some universal yearning for democracy, but rather from the collapse of this unsustainable state system.

This is not the first time GCC rulers have had to alter their relations with other sources of influence in their countries. Before the oil boom, the royal families presided over more evenly balanced power-sharing arrangements between themselves, other tribes, the merchant or middle classes, and even foreign labor movements than they did afterward. But the centralization of oil revenues in the hands of the ruling families changed this balance radically, considerably strengthening the position of the Gulf leaderships vis-à-vis the other centers of power, and forming the basis of the rentier state. Even so, the royal families remained, and still remain, sensitive to the opinions of other social groups, particularly in the presence of instability, social dissatisfaction, or succession disputes. As University of Vermont academic Gregory Gause noted: "Ruling family factions would seek alliances, as they have in the past, with whatever groups are powerful. In the 1950s and 1960s, those were the Arab nationalists and labor; today, it would be the Islamists."[11]

Though Gulf states have employed repression systematically and used internal security forces to keep their populations in check, they also have other arrows in their quiver. One alternative to maintaining the standard of living promised under the rentier state is to develop democratic and electoral conventions. And Gulf rulers are increasingly recognizing reform processes as ways of reducing international and internal pressure on their regimes. In the near term, the ruling families within some GCC states may use mainly cosmetic reforms in these areas to placate an increasingly dissatisfied public. But such a limited approach will come at a cost and cannot be maintained forever.[12] Civil society has a knack for breaking down the barriers erected to contain it, and—as demonstrated by a brief survey of the power-sharing processes in individual Gulf states—pluralist ambitions are clearly taking root in the region. (An in-depth analysis of emerging power-sharing structures and democratic institutions appears in Appendix 7.)

In the UAE, one of the Gulf's more stable and economically successful states, the royal families of the six emirates have hardly begun to initiate meaningful reform programs, nor have they engaged in new alliances or power-sharing arrangements with internal partners. Both the UAE federal government and the governments of its constituent emirates appear disinclined to broaden the political franchise.[13] Qatar, which boasts the most successful economy in the Gulf, might have taken a similar approach into the coming decade, relying on the established mechanisms of the rentier state to co-opt internal opposition. Instead, it has moved toward political reform as Emir Hamad initiated a "top-down" campaign of democratization that has gathered pace as Qatar's citizens adapt to the idea of democracy. In Oman and Bahrain, economic and political factors have driven the respective governments to engage in broader power-sharing with local interest and identity groups. Sultan Qaboos is slowly developing a form of constitution and a concept of citizenship through relatively informal mechanisms, building on the Omani government's longstanding efforts to develop a tolerant and pluralistic system. Bahrain's move toward pluralism has involved the creation of more formal power-sharing mechanisms than that of Oman, resulting in regular clashes between the feisty parliament and the royal establishment.

Many of the problems now facing Bahrain have been constant features of Kuwaiti politics since it first developed a limited parliamentary system in 1963,[14] and even more so since the mid-1990s. Kuwait's experience of representative government contains a cautionary note for other Gulf states. Though parliamentary democracy is typically equated with political liberalization, the opposite has been true in Kuwait, with the parliament acting as a brake on economic and political modernization. The overarching trend in parliament has been toward a more powerful Islamist and tribal (or traditionalist) bloc. Further reforms to Kuwait's political system may not necessarily offset these factors. In time, Kuwait's voting rights may be broadened to include women, military personnel, and naturalized citizens, reducing the "elitist democratic" nature of the current system. Yet, at just the time when economic, political, and social liberalization are needed to reduce tension and increase opportunity, it is uncertain whether the Kuwaiti government, which tends to lag behind parliament on most political reform issues, will be able or focused enough to promote liberalization. And there is little chance that the parliament will be able to promote such changes on its own.[15] Thus, while increased democratization has helped address broadly held concerns in Kuwait, such as the difference between economic expectations and realities, and will assuage educated internal petitioners and external opposition groups, it has also given a voice—and a vote—to traditional and Islamist elements that support the imposition of Islamic law, oppose sectarian and gender equality, and reject other forms of modernization—along with interaction with the Western world, particularly the United States.[16]

In Saudi Arabia, meanwhile, the ruling monarchy continues to develop two very different approaches to power-sharing simultaneously. Of these, the first and more familiar is the division of responsibilities between the royal family and the Wahhabi religious establishment. The second track, now emerging, involves political pluralism, through which the government could negotiate a new and radically different social contract with the Saudi Arabian people. Serious consideration of this possibility was first sparked between June and September 2003, after a series of announcements by then–Crown Prince Abdullah, who had commissioned a royal group to develop a gradualist reform plan beginning with municipal elections in March and April 2005. These elections resulted in municipal councils with an equal number of elected and government-appointed candidates. When the government-appointed Majlis al-Shura (consultative council) was appointed in April 2005, the membership was increased to 150, with the system reshuffled to include a greater number of liberal voices. In upcoming years, more and more seats will be added the council, until it reaches 360 members. On the council's next reappointment in 2010, half of its members could be elected.[17]

Prospects for State Failure

In the next ten years, a serious risk facing some Gulf states is that of slowly emerging state failure. A failed or failing state is typically defined as a weak central authority with very limited ability to deliver security, service provision, or economic opportunity throughout most of the country. Examples include Afghanistan, Burundi, the Republic of Congo, Liberia, and Sierra Leone. Between 1994 and 2000, the U.S. Department of State's State Failure Task Force undertook a comprehensive unclassified analysis of the phenomena surrounding failed or failing states.[18]

No GCC states can yet be considered failed or failing. In each, the absolute autocracy retains the ability to make and enforce meaningful national policies. Though serious terrorist activity and crime are on the increase throughout the GCC, local governments continue to guarantee the security of almost all their citizens. And all Gulf states continue to provide basic goods and social services, including advanced health care and social safety net systems and the modernization of physical infrastructure. The weak point in these states is arguably their provision of economic opportunity, characterized by a growing inequality in the distribution of wealth, increasing unemployment, and poor educational preparation for the work market. Though no GCC state shows symptoms or indicators of failed statehood, a few—notably Saudi Arabia and Kuwait—have the characteristics of weak states and could conceivably slip in their classification.

Of the indicators of future state failure identified by the State Department task force, a country's prevailing security situation—interestingly—is identified as a symptom but not a major cause. Perhaps more damaging to these states' stability as well as their oil-exporting ability are long-term factors such as emerging democratization, sectarian strife, and economic collapse. In the section of the task force report focusing on Muslim states, several indicators of impending state failure are identified, including:

- **Partial democratization.** Both globally and regionally, partial democracies are five times more likely to become failed states than to become either total autocracies or full democracies. This prognosis is attributed to the fragility of new or incomplete democracies, and their inability to cope deftly with shifts in public opinion and major security challenges.

- **Islamic sectarianism.** Muslim countries with a predominant Islamic sect are three times as likely to become failed states as Islamic states with more demographically balanced sectarian communities.

- **Closed or nondiversified economy.** Export specialization (e.g., oil revenues), lack of foreign investment, and income instability may make states more likely to fail.

- **Overpopulation.** States with larger and faster-growing populations may be more likely to fail.

- **Civil conflicts in neighboring countries.** States bordering conflict zones may fail more often.

- **Declining quality of life and economic opportunity.** States with higher infant mortality, unemployment, and inflation rates may fail more regularly.

To this list should be added consideration of succession politics, identified in the previous section as a key impediment to government decisionmaking during crisis periods.

The indicators of state failure noted in the previous section are mapped in summary form in figure 5, giving a picture of each individual GCC state's prospects for the coming decade. Taking into account weighting by the State Department task force for each indicator, the states fall into three categories:

- **Low risk:** Qatar and the UAE have the lowest chance of experiencing weakened state authority because they face neither uncertainty as

Figure 5. Indicators of State Failure in GCC Countries

	Bahrain	Kuwait	Oman	Qatar	Saudi Arabia	UAE
Frequent, contested successions	Low	Moderate	Moderate	Low	Strong	Low
Partial democratization	Strong	Strong	Moderate	Moderate	Moderate	Low
Islamic sectarianism	Strong	Moderate	Low	Low	Strong	Low
Closed economy	Moderate	Strong	Strong	Low	Strong	Moderate
Overpopulation	Moderate	Moderate	Moderate	Moderate	Moderate	Moderate
Neighboring instability	Moderate	Strong	Strong		Strong	Moderate
Quality of life	Strong	Moderate	Moderate	Low	Strong	Low
Overall threat of weakening	Medium	Medium	Medium	Low	Serious	Low

Key: ● = Strong   ◉ = Moderate   ○ = Low

to succession nor other chronic destabilizing factors, and their economies should continue to perform well.

- **Medium risk:** Oman is considered to face a medium risk of becoming a weakened state, largely due to general economic stagnation as well as other destabilizing factors. In Kuwait, a combination of succession issues and destabilizing socioeconomic factors heighten the risk that state authority will weaken. In Bahrain, potential causes of instability include the adversarial nature of relations between the royal establishment and the parliament, serious sectarian tensions, and a combination of socioeconomic factors.

- **High risk:** Saudi Arabia faces the most serious threat to its state authority. The Saudis will need simultaneously to manage a range of stubborn sectarian and socioeconomic factors along with multiple contested successions. Considering the overwhelming concentration of economic resources in the kingdom, the prospect of a weakening or failing Saudi Arabia requires further attention.

Internal Weakness in Saudi Arabia

As the previous analysis illustrates, a number of indicators point to weakening central government authority in Saudi Arabia. Though the current Saudi government continues to provide advanced health care and social safety net systems, deliver basic services, and modernize the country's physical infrastructure, demographic expansion in the coming decade will undoubtedly cause the nation's capabilities in these areas to deteriorate. Equally important, the government will be unlikely to offer economic opportunities to citizens both because the private sector has grown too slowly and because the educational system has failed to prepare Saudis for a modern, competitive job market. Over the next ten years, the gap between the rich and poor in Saudi Arabia will likely increase, with unemployment rising above 25 percent.

According to several analysts, unless the Saudis can enact successful economic and political reforms in the coming decade, the kingdom will enter a period in which centralized authority either declines or is forced into alliances with radicalized Sunni elements of the population and the Ulama (Saudi Arabia's Wahhabi religious leaders). Gregory Gause has noted that, in the broader context of the GCC states, mismanaged economic reform and factionalism could draw Islamists and other groups into the state decisionmaking process.[19] This potential for "internal alliances and power-sharing" between Gulf royal families and radical Islamists has also been cited by the U.S. National Intelligence Council (NIC), which identifies the advent of a "new destabilizing regime" in Saudi Arabia as a possible problem for any Middle East nation during the next two decades.[20] The U.S. National Defense University Near East and South Asia (NESA) center, meanwhile, has identified the collapse of state authority and the development of a radicalized regime in Saudi Arabia as the worst of the "wild card" scenarios that the Gulf area might face in the coming decade.[21]

When applied to Saudi Arabia, the indicators of future state failure, as determined by the State Department task force, are deeply worrying. They include:

- **Partial democratization:** King Abdullah's Charter for Arab Reform and the March 2005 municipal elections signal that Saudi Arabia's royal family has consented to initiate a cautious program of reform. Into the coming decade, such a program could slowly push the country into the dangerous territory of partial democratization.[22]

- **Islamic sectarianism:** In particular, the State Failure Task Force cites the government's treatment of Shiite minorities as examples of pervasive Islamic sectarianism in Saudi Arabia.[23] Though the royal family has attempted to quash overt Wahhabi extremism in the clergy, 500 mosques are under construction in the kingdom, the Ulama controls the educational system, and many extremists operate outside the controlled environs of the mosque. Royal counterterrorist policies are only now beginning to focus on the causes of Wahhabi extremism as well as the symptoms. With regard to the Shiites, the Saudi government has sent mixed indicators. On the one hand, it made a gesture of religious tolerance by creating a new, predominantly Shiite council district in Qatif (near Dammam) just before the March 2005 elections, allowing prospective Shiite council leaders to share local governance of both Shiite and Sunni villages with the government-appointed municipal council members. In other districts, however, Shiite candidates were prevented by government efforts from winning seats, pointing to the continuing problems of politically integrating Sunnis and Shiites in Saudi Arabia.[24]

- **Economic drivers:** In the economic sphere, Saudi Arabia will need many years to diversify its oil-dominated economy (presently at 90 percent of export earnings and 75 percent of budget revenues), suggesting that export specialization and income instability will characterize Saudi economics for some time. Openings for foreign investment remain slow. Against this backdrop, the Saudi birthrate increased by 2.9 percent in 2004, compared to a global average of 1.2 percent. Though certain indicators, such as infant mortality, underline the basically satisfactory living conditions in Saudi Arabia, and others such as low inflation are impressive even by standards of the developed world, most forecast a decline in Saudi living conditions if the nation's economy continues on its current course. GDP growth is highly dependent on oil revenues, zigzagging above and below the global average (see figure 6, next page). More important, job creation consistently falls short of meeting demand, with the median age of Saudi Arabia's male population at 20.9 years and unemployment soaring from between 13 and 25 percent.[25]

Ultimately, Saudi Arabia displays to some extent (or will display, if its current policies are continued) every indicator of a state bound for failure. Of the two key indicators of impending state failure, one (sectarianism) is well documented in Saudi Arabia and the other (partial democratization) may begin under Abdullah, ushering Saudi Arabia into a period of very high risk. The remaining four indica-

Figure 6. GDP in the Gulf: Annual Percentage Change

Country	2000	2001	2002	2003	2004
Bahrain	5.3	4.5	5.1	5.7	5.5
Kuwait	1.9	0.6	-0.4	10.1	2.8
Oman	5.5	7.5	1.7	1.4	2.5
Qatar	9.1	4.5	7.3	3.3	9.3
Saudi Arabia	4.9	0.5	0.1	7.2	3.6
UAE	12.3	3.5	1.9	7	3.6
GLOBAL AVERAGE	4.7	2.4	3.0	3.9	5.0

Source: International Monetary Fund, World Economic Outlook database, September 2004.

tors will slowly increase the Saudi state's level of risk. Though common perceptions of state failure in Saudi Arabia have focused on the swift and dramatic rise of a radical regime, this scenario is the unlikeliest form of collapse. More likely would be a slower atrophy of state power. In the nearing period of economic and political crisis, the Saudi government has little margin for error or delay, with the most likely immediate cause of state failure being paralysis of government decisionmaking caused by regular and contested succession of leadership. Whoever accedes to the throne, power will surely remain diffused among King Abdullah's half-brothers, creating a significant risk for disagreement among the wings of the royal family and inertia in the process of creating reform.

In the coming decade, economic policy failures in Saudi Arabia could result in a slowly diminishing standard of living for citizens, a factor that would be exacerbated by slow collapse of the social safety net and the government's decreased ability to deliver basic services. Islamist groups within the country would provide alternative social safety nets for citizens, with the central government becoming less relevant. Crime numbers would continue to increase and personal security would decline. In other nations where this has occurred—e.g., Afghanistan and northern Nigeria—strict interpretations of Islam have gained influence. Growing urban slums (what might be termed "failed cities") and some rural areas, particularly those where independent political views or Wahhabism thrive, could become increasingly violent and "Talibanize" their codes and rules more quickly than others. Shiite areas of the Eastern Saudi province could become semiautonomous to offset the growing breakdown of social norms.

It is possible that future Saudi kings will lack the Islamic credentials and widely perceived piety of King Abdullah, and will thus be more vulnerable to manipulation by respected members of the Ulama and susceptible to dealmaking, particularly during leadership successions, which the Ulama must consecrate. The Ulama's hand would further be strengthened by popular disillusionment with the government's decisionmaking powers in the case of a stalled or unsuccessful economic and political reform effort. To garner popular support, government decisionmakers might stress their Islamist and nationalist credentials, and endorse isolationist or anti-Western policies. National policymaking could become even more inflexible, and implementation of government policy undependable, finishing off any prospect of recovery driven by direct foreign investment. Perhaps most important, without foreign investment and effective government management, the maintenance of oil production capacity would become impossible—let alone the development of excess or new capacity—creating major global production shortfalls and intense price hikes. Even assuming a nonviolent collapse of state power, as described here, the effects would be devastating for both the regional and global economies. Considering Saudi Arabia's central role both in global oil markets and as the birthplace of Islam (Mecca), even the *possibility* of state failure would have a tremendous impact on U.S. strategic interests.

Weak Central Government Authority and Transnational Threats

The 2002 U.S. National Security Strategy states that "America is now threatened less by conquering states than we are by failing ones."[26] According to the 2001 U.S. Quadrennial Defense Review, transnational threats emanating from weak and failing states and the diffusion of power and military capabilities to nonstate actors represent two key features of the twenty-first century strategic environment.[27] Over the last twenty years, the uncontrolled movement of Gulf residents (including terrorists, criminals, and illegal immigrants), funds, and goods (weapons, drugs, and other contraband) has emerged as a serious threat to the region's security, with these transnational threats likely to develop further in sophistication and potential impact in the coming two decades. Economic downturns and unstable leadership will likely exacerbate these threats, which thrive in areas of weak government authority and economic inequality.

Of these transnational threats, the most serious facing the GCC states is Islamic terrorism. For the West and its allies, the Global War on Terror is likely to be a protracted, generational struggle and terrorist threats are likely to persist as features of the GCC threat profile. Critical to determining the threat level facing individual GCC states is the potential for recruitment of homegrown Salafist terrorists. Factors to consider in such a calculation include:

- **Size of population indoctrinated into Wahhabi Islam:** Islamic terrorists represent only a tiny percentage of the broader population of conservative Sunni Islamists, and are typically adherents to the "Salafist" interpretation of the Wahhabi brand of the Hanbali school of Sunni Islam., As a result, the size of a country's Sunni population is an important factor in determining the potential scale of the terrorist threat it faces. In assessing the potential for militancy, analysts must consider the historical breadth and depth of religious intolerance taught or preached in a country's educational and religious establishments. States with strong Wahhabi establishments have already provided jihadist recruits for prior jihads in the 1980s and 1990s, fostering a jihadist tradition that younger generations will seek to follow. Countries with particularly young populations, or with high unemployment or underemployment, make for ideal recruiting grounds.

- **Perception of anti-Islamic activity by the state:** Islamic militancy is more likely to emerge in countries that perceive themselves as playing a special role in Islam (e.g., Saudi Arabia, for its custodianship of the two great mosques at Mecca and Medina). Militancy may also be spurred in countries seen as playing a role in purportedly anti-Islamic activities such as the occupation and political reconstruction of Iraq. States may draw further criticism for allowing globalization to threaten traditional and Islamic ways of life.

Terrorist actors operating in the Gulf fall into three broad categories, with experienced, nonnative terrorists making up the first group. This set of actors is characterized by relatively advanced skills and experience gained in foreign jihads or training camps, but may be disadvantaged and relatively conspicuous due to its nonnative profile. Unlike the experienced native terrorist who returns to his home country for logical reasons, the experienced nonnative must have a compelling reason to choose a particular country over other theaters of jihad. Recent experience has shown that target-rich environments (e.g., soft Western targets) tend to be less of a draw than iconic theaters (such as the purported legitimate defensive jihad in Iraq or the land of the two holy mosques, Saudi

Arabia). A role in supporting U.S. military operations is a key factor drawing such actors to individual Gulf states.

A second category consists of experienced native terrorists. These actors have connected with the broader global Salafist jihad in some way, gaining skills and experience, before returning to their home countries to continue waging jihad. The ability of such operatives to blend back into their native societies depends on the care of their reinsertion, the homeland-security practices of local security services, and the antiterrorism awareness of local populations. It is important to note that such terrorists *may be natives, but not necessarily nationals.* They may be drawn from the massive communities of non-Gulf Arab (Egyptian, Syrian, Sudanese, etc.) or Asian (Pakistani, Indonesian) foreign workers. This kind of terrorist can also spring up in any Gulf state but the incidence of such returnees or migrants is based on the existence of a jihadist tradition that witnesses sons and grandsons follow their relatives into the jihadist experience. In many cases, involvement in such jihad is the only way to "plug in" to networks of experienced terrorist cells.

The third and final type comprises "disconnected" or inexperienced native terrorists. For whatever reason, this set of actors remains disconnected from the broader global Salafist jihad and perhaps from any other native resistance groups. They receive inspiration primarily through broadcast media, and their operational capabilities rely on online research and their given professional skill sets. Typically mimicking known terrorist tactics and targeting schemes, they adapt these strategies to serve their own operational concepts. But without drawing on the resources of former jihadist "brokers," these inexperienced terrorists cannot achieve what terrorism analysts call the "articulation" of terrorist functions. This refers to the development of specialist cells to undertake financing, bombmaking, planning, and attacks, widely recognized as necessary precursors to the development of advanced terrorist capabilities. These scattered and isolated groups therefore have two choices: they can either travel abroad independently to connect with the global Salafist jihad, or they can form their own amateur cells and strike haphazardly at accessible targets in their home countries using the weapons available to them. This kind of terrorist can theoretically spring up in any Gulf State, but the incidence of such homegrowns will ultimately be derived from the local base of radicalized manpower—the raw numbers of Sunni males of military age exposed to radical interpretations of Islam.

Terrorism Threat Assessment

General. Maritime attacks remain a key threat, and deserve further attention, considering the growing terrorist interest in such targets in recent years.

In January 1999, al-Qaeda attempted but failed to launch a suicide attack on the USS *The Sullivans* in Aden Harbor, a feat it had achieved against the USS *Cole* in October 2000. In October 2002, al-Qaeda operatives attacked the French-flagged oil tanker *Limburg* off the coast of Yemen.[28] In June 2002, three suspected Saudi operatives who had been arrested in Morocco informed their captors that al-Qaeda had directed them to monitor the movement of NATO ships through the Straits of Gibraltar. In a further development, al-Qaeda operatives mounted video surveillance of shipping traffic in the Straits of Malacca.[29] Assuming al-Qaeda is surveying maritime choke points, logic suggests that it views the Straits of Hormuz as a potential target. Though the terrorist organization's key maritime specialist, Abdul Rahman al-Nashiri, has been captured, al-Qaeda's interest in littoral targets has a broad base. Translations of captured al-Qaeda manuals on naval targets include sophisticated advice on the economic impact of maritime attacks and selection of targets, such as liquefied natural gas tankers and chains of oil tankers. Indicators also suggest that the April 2004 attack on Iraq's oil terminals included an attempt to detonate collocated oil tankers whose hulls had almost no remaining oil, leaving them filled with explosive oil vapors—an opportunity highlighted in the al-Qaeda manuals.[30] Other manuals advise on the placement of limpet mines and the correct use of rocket-propelled grenades (RPGs) and incendiary devices, urging readers to recall the use of Molotov cocktail–type devices in naval warfare against the Crusader forces during the Siege of Acre in 1190.[31] From amateur to expert, Islamic terrorists are focusing increasingly on a range of maritime targets, which are made ever more vulnerable by growing congestion at maritime choke points and the use of skeleton crews. As terrorist attacks grow more difficult to execute on land, analysts note that maritime targets will become more attractive, particularly in the Gulf, which has a longstanding tradition of unimpeded water navigation.[32]

Saudi Arabia. Saudi Arabia is both the hub of efforts launched by global Salafists in the Gulf region and the base of the al-Qaeda Organization in the Arabian Peninsula (AQAP), al-Qaeda's regional affiliate. The kingdom of Saudi Arabia is also the birthplace and heartland of the Wahhabi sect of Sunni Islam, closely connected to the Salafist creed forwarded by the al-Qaeda movement. Al-Qaeda's leadership has been studded with Saudi citizens, including Osama bin Laden and a range of planners and operators. Saudis are also at the heart of al-Qaeda's funding networks, including a list of twenty Saudi al-Qaeda financiers described by Osama bin Laden as "the golden chain."[33] Saudi Arabia's contiguous borders with Yemen and Iraq—both key theaters of operation for transnational jihadists—make the country a critical transshipment point for weaponry and jihadists engaged in a multidirectional flow of personnel and equipment throughout the GCC. The role of Saudi Arabian citizens in the attacks of September 11, 2001, is notorious, and their role in the al-Qaeda network is reflected in the presence of 127 Saudi Arabian nationals out of the 500 or so inmates at the Camp X-Ray military prison in Guantánamo Bay, Cuba.[34]

Saudi Arabian society remains an ideal recruitment ground for Salafist terrorists. This is because of the country's broad network of radical Wahhabi clerics, a large population (20 million) that has been exposed to such clerics since childhood, and because of its self-perception as the guardian of the twin holy cities of Mecca and Medina. In addition to its native terrorists, Saudi Arabia has been used as a base by militants from many different countries. Some of these militants turned radical in Saudi Arabia itself. In neighboring Yemen, the population of 20 million has provided an ample pool of militant recruits since the 1980s, and the jihad against the Soviet Union in Afghanistan. Also through the 1980s and 1990s, Muslims of all nationalities moved through Saudi Arabia to receive religious education, attend Hajj, and receive funding and support to undertake jihad overseas. Though at the time of this writing Iraq represents the central site of jihad, the struggle in Saudi Arabia will continue to draw Saudi and foreign jihadists for the foreseeable future.

All four types of terrorists described earlier exist in large numbers in Saudi Arabia, and the nation's strong tradition of Islamic militancy will likely continue into future generations. As many as 20,000 Saudi citizens are believed to have gone to Afghanistan to fight the Soviets, from which emerged a hardened cadre of genuine jihadists and a tiny elite of committed intellectual activists such as Osama bin Laden. In the 1990s, hundreds more Saudis fought in Afghanistan, Bosnia, Chechnya, and a host of smaller jihads throughout the Islamic world. In the late 1990s, Osama bin Laden succeeded in boosting the representation of Saudi and Yemeni foot soldiers in al-Qaeda's ranks. As before, most fighters were drawn from tough tribal constituencies among the uneducated Saudi upper-working and lower-middle classes. The most striking example of this phenomenon is the selection of Saudi Arabians (mainly from the southwestern provinces) to fill all but one of the positions as "muscle" hijackers in the September 11 attacks.

At the same time al-Qaeda was planning global operations against the United States, strong evidence suggests that Osama bin Laden was preparing the ground for a parallel campaign in the kingdom. Locally, the effort was coordinated by bin Laden loyalist Yusuf Salih Fahd al-Ayiri, a highly respected first-generation Saudi jihadist and a rare example of a committed intellectual activist and a skilled military insurrectionist. Al-Ayiri had returned to Saudi Arabia in 1991 from Afghanistan and had stayed in the country ever since. The buildup for the internal campaign had two elements. The first entailed logistical stockpiling of weaponry—including antitank and surface-to-air missiles—and explosives brought over from Yemen, as well as the development of recruitment networks and other functions such as media operations, bombmaking, and planning. The second strand of activity centered on escalating intimidation against the Western expatriate community in Saudi Arabia, resulting in more than a dozen antipersonnel bombing plots—some successful, others foiled—in the period between 2000 and 2003. Eventually four operational cells were established, built predominantly around young loyalists who had given their oath of allegiance to bin Laden.

Though al-Ayiri preferred to continue building the logistical and recruitment base of the organization before making the transition to major attack operations, he was overruled by the al-Qaeda "board of governors," in this case Osama bin Laden and Ayman al-Zawahiri. The motivation behind a sudden attack on three compounds housing Westerners in Riyadh on May 12, 2003, is believed to have been a desire to display offensive capability at a time when al-Qaeda had been evicted from Afghanistan and was on the run everywhere else. Though the attack threatened to upset years of careful planning for larger and more coordinated attacks against expatriates and even government targets, al-Ayiri acceded to the order to execute it. The results were catastrophic for the al-Qaeda effort in Saudi Arabia. Within three weeks of the May 12 attacks, al-Ayiri was dead and the bulk of al-Qaeda's local cells were dispersed and being pursued. In response to the backlash in Saudi public opinion at the death of Muslims in the compounds, theologians associated with the Mujaheddin Military Committee in the Arabian Peninsula spent the remainder of 2003 and much of 2004 struggling against the flow of public sentiment to lay out the theological grounds for mass casualty attacks. Saudi Arabia's terrorists quickly came to recognize the difficulty of creating such a model for a campaign within their own homeland.

Since summer of 2003, Saudi terrorist leaders have made no systematic attempt to restore centralized leadership of operations or place them under direct al-Qaeda command. Instead, they have used the Internet to provide a loose form of leadership to the scattered cells of Saudi terrorists, urging them to self-organize in small groups of trusted individuals and encouraging them to undertake actions at will. The expulsion of Westerners has been stressed as the key aim of Saudi militants. To avoid further Muslim casualties, terrorist communiqués have sought to guide terrorist targeting and develop more discriminating attack methods through the fortnightly online digest *al-Battar Training Camp* (*Mu'askar al-Battar*), which ran throughout 2004. In this publication, leaders such as Abdulaziz al-Muqrin proposed a more deliberate approach emphasizing careful selection of targets and close-range assaults using small arms, grenades, and knives. Around this time, a sequence of small-arms attacks was launched on security forces. The May 1, 2004, attack on oil industry offices in Yanbu, hailed by al-Muqrin as an example of local groups acting on their own initiative, was quickly followed by a similar operation directly commissioned by al-Muqrin, on May 29, 2004. The rampage consisted of attacks on three expatriate targets in Khobar. Following these attacks was a sequence of small-arms, knife, and hit-and-run attacks on Western expatriates, culminating in the abduction and decapitation of U.S. contractor Paul Johnson. In all cases, pains were taken to discriminate between Muslims and non-Muslims. And since al-Muqrin's murder on June, 18, 2004, the sporadic attacks have stayed broadly within the parameters adopted during his tenure. Though large vehicle-borne improvised explosive devices (VBIEDs) have been used since summer 2004, they have been used sparingly and never in circumstances that might risk mass casualties among Muslim civilians, such as against residential compounds.

Alongside refinement of its targets, a second and arguably more significant change for terrorists in Saudi Arabia occurred later in 2004, when momentum increased for a diversion of Saudi recruits to Iraq. Saudi jihadists in Iraq have numbered in the low hundreds at the least, with the Saudi General Intelligence Directorate (GID) estimating the number conservatively at 350 and some estimates reaching as high as 1,500. Iraq gave a major boost to terrorist recruitment in Saudi Arabia, representing a legitimate defensive jihad against the U.S. military in a foreign country. The infusion of young Saudi volunteers likely contributed to the acceleration of suicide bombings in Iraq in 2005. Though very few volunteers appear to travel to Iraq with suicide missions in mind, radicalization is a relatively simple matter in the isolated and inward-focused environment of the covert foreign jihad. The intensive use of suicide operations by Saudi terrorists plus the difficulty of surviving normal combat operations in Iraq and reinserting themselves into Gulf societies indicates that Iraq may not generate significant blowback in the GCC.

However, if such militants do return to Saudi Arabia from Iraq, these men will have matured as Salafist militants and come into extended contact with al-Zarqawi's particularly brutal model of Salafist terrorism. Assessment of the motives and intentions of returning jihadists is critical to judging whether these returnees will try to apply al-Zarqawi's style in Saudi Arabia or maintain the more discriminating approach developed by the al-Qaeda Organization in the Arabian Peninsula. The young, impressionable, and tough jihadists in Iraq have learned to ignore public opinion and to isolate themselves from societal pressures.

Jihadists may also return from Iraq with heightened intentions and capability to target the oil infrastructure. Though the hydrocarbon infrastructure remains an extremely difficult target for even the most experienced terrorists, certain vulnerabilities exist. Half of Saudi Arabia's oil reserves are concentrated in eight oil fields, while two-thirds of its export capability relies on the Abqaiq gas-oil separation plant, which Saudi terrorists attacked on February 24, 2006. Since summer 2002, various sabotage plots against Saudi oil processing and export infrastructure have been foiled.[35] Extended oil pipeline infrastructure continues to be vulnerable to attack, a possibility emphasized by the experience in Iraq. And maritime terminals could also be targeted, as they were in Iraq in April 2004 when a group of al-Zarqawi-employed suicide bombers executed three explosive-laden motor launches.[36]

Kuwait. Though Kuwait does not suffer from the same breadth and depth of religious intolerance as Saudi Arabia, the country's deeply conservative tribal and religious base is a fertile breeding ground for Islamic militancy. In the political sphere, a struggle will soon take place between the modernizing elements of the government and the secular portions of society on one side, and the traditionalist elements on the other. As this power struggle unfolds, Salafist political expression is particularly likely to attract government scrutiny and suppression. Though the coming political struggle will resolve itself mainly through political mechanisms, Kuwait's young and underemployed Sunni Arab population of around 1.6 million creates the potential for a serious terrorist threat even if only a very small slice of this Sunni community chooses a militant course.

Since the jihad against the Soviet Union in Afghanistan, Kuwait has been a provider of militants willing to undertake violent acts in the name of Islam. Some of these jihadists, including Khaled Sheikh Muhammad and Suleiman Abu Ghaith, filled senior positions in the al-Qaeda general staff and played key roles in the September 11 attacks. The tradition continued with the involvement of scores of young Kuwaitis in later jihads in the Balkans, Caucasus, post–September 11 Afghanistan, and now Iraq. By October 2005, eleven Kuwaitis remained under U.S. custody in Guantánamo Bay, having been detained in

Afghanistan or Pakistan as alleged "enemy combatants," while many more appear to have been detained while in transit to the UAE after returning via Iran. While the surviving 120 or so veterans of the original Soviet-era jihad in Afghanistan are under tight surveillance, their sons and grandsons may be apt to seek out their own jihadist experiences. Being too young to recall Palestinian support for the Iraqi invasion of Kuwait, younger Kuwaitis have responded to continuous coverage of the Israeli-Palestinian conflict on Arab satellite channels with increasing anger against the United States and the West at large.

Kuwait's role in supporting U.S. policy in Iraq appears to have been a watershed event in the broadening of the Salafist terrorist threat in Kuwait. The scale and intrusiveness of the Western military presence in Kuwait had no post-1991 precedent, and the offensive nature of Operation Iraqi Freedom engendered similarly unprecedented levels of resentment in Kuwait. Meanwhile, Saudi Arabia's and Turkey's unwillingness to host major coalition ground forces threw Kuwait's role in the war into sharp relief. Since the beginning of the military buildup in autumn 2002, Kuwait's involvement with the U.S. military presence in Iraq has been the primary driver of insurgent activity originating within Kuwait. Initial terrorist attacks took the form of uncoordinated local actions against U.S. forces in 2002 and 2003 by novice native terrorists. As Iraq flowered into the central theater of the global Salafist jihad in 2004, the Kuwaiti security establishment began to detect and address the threat posed by the funneling of Kuwaiti youths to Iraq as jihadist volunteers.

When recruitment cells in Kuwait were raided in early 2005, interrogators discovered that the cells were also preparing to undertake attacks on U.S. forces and Western expatriates in Kuwait. The composite picture of the Kuwaiti Mujaheddin and Peninsula Lions groups projected an ambitious and well articulated association that was intimately connected to the broader al-Qaeda network in the Gulf. The Kuwaiti Mujaheddin cell operated mainly as a facilitator for jihadists to travel to Iraq via Syria, while its sister movement, the Peninsula Lions, was destined to be the principal attack cell operating inside Kuwait. This group included individuals with bombmaking experience and most of the group's young members had secure jobs in Kuwait's well-cosseted public sector. They were bored rather than destitute, and members lived mainly in urban settings. With their operational intentions synchronized with those of the Iraqi resistance, they focused on attacks on U.S. convoys, aiming to explode roadside bombs and undertake ambushes that would result in the capture and execution of U.S. personnel. Both types of activity were intended to be videotaped to support recruitment. The violent events of early 2005 were, in many respects,

"Kuwait's September 11." The spate of shootouts caused Kuwaiti families to question whether their own young men, too, would become involved in Islamic militancy.

Other GCC states. None of the four other GCC states (Bahrain, Oman, Qatar, or the UAE) bears the same range of factors that has made Saudi Arabia the linchpin of Salafist operations in the Gulf, or made Kuwait a base for Salafist terrorists. To begin with, these states have a combined population of only 9.4 million, a figure that includes many nonnationals and other groups unlikely to become involved in the global Salafist jihad. This figure highlights the tiny potential recruiting base compared against countries providing the personnel backbone of the global Salafist jihad: Indonesia (241.9 million), Pakistan (162.4 million), Egypt (77.5 million), Algeria (32.5 million), Saudi Arabia (26.4 million), and Yemen (20.7 million). Though the educational systems and mosques of Bahrain and Qatar are suffused with Wahhabi influence, their diminutive size and lack of a jihadist tradition limits sharply the number of militants they are likely to spawn. In the relatively tolerant southern GCC region, militancy and even malcontentedness are rare occurrences.

Nor are the smaller four GCC states a key focus for Salafist terrorist groups. Since 2003, efforts to incorporate these states into the regional struggle have been haphazard, of secondary importance compared to the struggle to reorganize and escalate operations in Saudi Arabia itself or support the jihad in Iraq. And while al-Qaeda might view the GCC as a single area of operations, Saudi Arabia has always been first among equals. Experienced nonnative terrorist actors have focused on Saudi operations. At an ideological level, there are few factors to draw attackers to the smaller GCC states, which lack the central role in Islam of, say, Saudi Arabia. Though states like Qatar and the UAE host huge numbers of Westerners, these countries lack unique "target sets," and Saudi-based terrorists have a far easier time gathering intelligence on and attacking the numerous expatriate targets in their own country.

Vulnerable assets, particularly soft targets like Western expatriates, are not enough to attract terrorist activity. In the smaller GCC states, two explanations dominate consideration of the likelihood of future terrorist attacks. The first suggests some form of shadowy compact between the local government and terrorists. The second predicts that further attacks will inevitably occur, and that it is only a matter of time before they do. Both explanations offer ways of interpreting the lack of terrorist attacks in these states *without* contemplating factors that may have dissuaded terrorists from striking in the first place. In fact, the lack of violent activity in these states indicates a scarcity of Salafist militants on the ground, and a lack of motivation on the part of outside terrorists to travel to the southern GCC to carry out attacks. The size of the recruitment and former jihadist base, "top cover" mentoring and support from senior jihadists, and national involvement in apparently anti-Islamic activity all drive local terrorist activity. Long-term local structural factors such as traditionalist backlash against Westernization, local power shifts, and under- or unemployment may also increase the recruiting pool. But a clear casus belli such as Iraq appears to be the spark that ultimately ignites local sentiment.

In reviewing the causes of local terrorism, we find that none of the four smaller GCC states carries the same combination of features that has prompted the radicalization of homegrown terrorists in Saudi Arabia and Kuwait. With the notable exception of Oman, these nations' economic situations have a stabilizing effect on society. None of the southern GCC states contains high numbers of Sunnis who have been exposed for long periods to intolerant Wahhabi doctrine, though a radical fringe puts Qatar at some risk. Similarly, none of the four smallest GCC states has a well-established jihadist tradition or top cover from senior terrorists who might take an interest in stirring militancy in their home countries. Though Muslim expatriates, particularly Egyptians and Pakistanis, may present an additional risk, the vast majority of such migrants have invested heavily to work in the Gulf, and typically many relatives at home depend on their continuing employment. As a result, cases such as that of the March 19, 2005, suicide bombing in Qatar (in which an Egyptian expatriate was the sole attacker) will likely be rare.

In the smaller Gulf Coast nations, perhaps the most alarming development involves local reaction to the U.S. military's use of local facilities, which can act as a lightning rod for dissent and draw attention to government activities perceived by local radicals to be anti-Islamic, such as supporting Western presence in Iraq. Qatar's al-Udeid air base and Dubai's port facilities are notable examples of such a scenario, and U.S. use of Abu Dhabi's al-Dhafra air base will likely attract similar attention before long. Because these bases are well fortified, dissenters typically attack less protected elements such as personnel in transit or Western civilian targets unrelated to the base, and expatriate gathering places with lax security. Though the Qatar bombing illustrates the high end of capabilities by "disconnected" novices—albeit a former jihadist in this case—most local terrorists will likely use the tools closest at hand, such as firearms and vehicles for ramming into structures and personnel. More advanced capabilities would often require the outside intervention of experienced nonnative terrorists. But this does not imply that such actors will necessarily be drawn to the southern GCC.

In the broader GCC, Saudi Arabia remains the focus of terrorist operations. Furthermore, terrorists within the kingdom are struggling to survive and diverting most of their efforts into supporting the war in Iraq. With rare exceptions, attacks have spread into the GCC nations only when local affiliates—at present, only Kuwaitis—have sought deliberately to open a new cell in their country. This phenomenon could occur in the four smaller GCC states, but the threat level is not particularly high.

Border Security and Transnational Threats

The threat posed by terrorists from Iraq, Saudi Arabia, and Yemen can be further reduced by getting serious about border security. The activities of the al-Qaeda Organization in the Arabian Peninsula suggest that the terrorists consider today's state borders to be illegitimate, viewing the Gulf states instead as a single operating area. For officials of the GCC countries, the expanse of land and maritime border areas combined with the migratory and mercantile nature of people in and around border areas present an acute border security challenge. Terrorists have found the Gulf a convenient thoroughfare, in part, because organized criminal activity supports uncontrolled movements and activities across both land and sea borders, and through the bustling maritime entrepots of the Gulf littoral. A culture of smuggling and sanction-busting also prevails in the Gulf, where UN sanctions on Iraq slowly died in the 1990s, and where Iran does not recognize U.S. sanctions. Oil smuggling networks, established during the containment of Iraq, continue to operate as part of the entrepreneurial "gray economy" of the Gulf, costing Iraq an estimated $200,000 a day in lost petroleum.[37] In the UAE, a range of actors—Gulf smugglers, radical Islamists, and Asian mafiosi—congregate to engage in trans-Gulf shipments.[38] According to the intergovernmental Gulf Contraband Forum, smuggling costs GCC states an estimated $21.9 billion annually in loss of tax revenues and other commercial losses. The illegal importation of tax-free tobacco, textiles, car parts, and electronics hurts local industries and can prevent them from creating vital jobs.[39] Moreover, organized criminal activity may provide avenues for terrorists to travel around the Gulf, move weapons, launder money, and raise funds. The UAE was identified as a key node in Iran's procurement of nuclear materials via the Abdul Qader Khan network.[40]

Arms smuggling is one part of the problem with respect to border security. Terrorist cells using Saudi Arabia as a base rely on cross-border movements to replenish armaments and other logistical support, and they frequent large unregulated arms bazaars such as the one at Sadah, some twenty-five miles inside Yemen. In attempting to stop illegal movements across the Yemeni border, thirty-six Saudi Arabian border guards were killed in the Jizan area alone between March 2002 and February 2003. Other arms shipments arrive from Iraq via the lengthy border with Saudi Arabia, and then are moved across the GCC's internal borders. Cross-border movements are also a useful way to avoid pursuit by Saudi security forces, and a well-established trend in terrorist activity, because borders are commonly areas of weak government control or poorly integrated international cooperation over enforcement.[41] Without adequate coordination between national border security forces, terrorist cells are simply "pushed" across national borders, instead of being penned against them and engaged decisively.

In the Gulf, the connection between organized crime and terrorism is also evident in narcotrafficking. Originating in Afghanistan and Pakistan—including areas under al-Qaeda and Taliban control—shipments of illegal drugs cross Iran on their way to Europe and the Gulf. Though Iran has undertaken a major campaign to stop such trafficking, according to the UN Office on Drugs and Crime, the Islamic Republic will likely remain the most profitable smuggling route for central Asian drugs during the next decade.[42] As recent U.S. captures show, maritime smuggling across the Gulf is a major route of transfer for these drugs. During a two-month period in winter 2003–2004, U.S. and coalition ships in the Straits of Hormuz and the North Arabian Sea intercepted 2.93 tons of hashish and 40 kilograms of heroin.[43] In the northern Gulf, a coalition against oil smuggling continues to turn up shipments of illegal drugs moving from Iran to Kuwait.[44] Though the Islamic Republic of Iran Navy (IRIN) has provided low-profile support to U.S. efforts to prevent both oil and drug smuggling since the late 1990s, the same cannot be said for Islamic Revolutionary Guard Corps (IRGC) naval forces, also under Iran. While IRIN has accounted for almost all of Iran's drugs seizures in the Gulf, the IRGC remains heavily involved in corruption and smuggling of all kinds.[45]

Since the collapse of Baathist rule in Iraq and the subsequent opening of the country's borders to Iranian pilgrims from the east and businessmen from the south, both the Kuwaiti and Saudi Arabian land borders have seen increased transshipments of drugs.[46] In traversing the Gulf region, drug smugglers use many of the same channels as terrorists and weapons smugglers. They pose an exceptionally difficult threat for governments in part because of the enormous profit ratios involved in the trade; traffickers can accept the loss of a certain proportion of shipments without being deterred. Still, Gulf countries cannot afford to continue acting as transshipment hubs for narcotraffickers. Over time, nations on drug routes tend to develop their own indigenous drug problems, such as in southern Iran and increasingly in Kuwait, where in a country of only 750,000 citizens, around 20,000 residents are estimated to use illegal drugs—a low level for Western societies but a matter of concern for a strict Islamic country.[47] Of these users, 600 are in treatment for addiction, with deaths from drug use ranging from 28 to 40 since 1998.[48] The UAE and Saudi Arabia are beginning to acknowledge similar, though smaller, problems with drug use.[49]

Characterizing Future Internal and Transnational Security Challenges

In the coming decade, the Gulf states will no doubt face stern internal security challenges. Factors that cause the disintegration of state systems exist in a number of Gulf states, including closed and nondiversified economies, overpopulation, and declining quality of life and economic opportunities. Though economic reforms have been initiated in many states, these changes will likely develop too slowly in the near- and midterm. Residents will therefore be disappointed at the states' failure to provide adequate economic support and advanced public services. Succession-related issues will likely also play a role in these delays, with progress held up by local democratization initiatives, as officials experience the difficulties of setting up representative government. Though democratization may protect citizens in certain ways, as one analysis noted, "Parliamentary pressure can cut both ways; Majlis members can act as a lobby for transparency and accountability, but they can also exert pressures for public spending and services for their constituencies." As Gulf Research Center academic Muhammad Salem al-Mazroui noted with regard to the young, anxious, and increasingly restless GCC populations, "All GCC states today have a growing class of university graduates who nourish the ambition to have a better future. If doors are kept tightly sealed in the face of this class, it might resort to violence as a means of venting its pent-up frustration."[50]

Emerging from the analysis in this chapter are a number of potential threat scenarios. The most pressing is that of persistent terrorism originating in both urban and rural areas. Alongside an increasingly frustrated citizenry, which may or may not be sufficiently placated by political power-sharing, Gulf leaders will need to contend with the long-term threat of alliances between Islamic militants and dissatisfied or threatened conservative elements throughout the region. Embedded terrorist groups will exploit popular disenchantment and, for the foreseeable future, will continue to present a major challenge to government authority. Terrorists will be able to exploit nearby sanctuaries, such as Iraq and Yemen, and areas of weak central government authority, including restive urban ghettos, border areas, and rugged rural regions. Such attackers threaten the numerous Western expatriates who play key roles within the Gulf states, as well as the continuity of government, economic infrastructure, freedom of maritime navigation, and civilian aviation.

Management of major civil disorder and other internal crises represents the second internal and transnational security challenge in the coming decade. Traditionally the Gulf states' security establishments have envisaged major breakdowns in public order originating in their large communities of foreign workers. While such scenarios are still possible, Gulf security managers must also take into account the need to manage crises stemming from dissatisfaction within the younger segments of their own population, should the effects of increasing political pluralism boil over into periodic instances of civil disorder. During such moments, the GCC governments will need to employ levels of force commensurate with the seriousness of unrest. Otherwise they risk exacerbating the situation and allowing the rise of a major threat to the regime. Gulf countries need to develop more effective integrated capabilities to prevent, manage, and recover from natural and man-made disasters.

The third and final international security challenge facing the Gulf states in the forthcoming decade is border security, including maritime patrolling and interdiction. These missions will be required to mitigate the risks posed by weak government control of both sea lanes and land borders. Because terrorist groups and organized crime thrive in areas of weak central government authority, transnational threat actors can operate freely in the maritime and littoral areas of the Gulf. In view of the known threat posed by al-Qaeda to shipping in the Gulf, plus its expressed interest in attacking key maritime choke points and oil export infrastructure, GCC nations must develop patrol and interdiction capabilities in order to protect themselves and the region.

Notes

1.   CENTCOM, "Southwest Asia: Approaching the Millennium—Enduring Problems, Emerging Solutions" (paper presented at the Southwest Asia Symposium 96, Tampa, FL, May 14–15, 1996), p. 167.

2. "Gulf States: Pressures Mount as Populations Grow," Oxford Analytica, May 28, 2004. Available online (www.oxweb.com).

3. Daniel Byman and Jerrold Green, *Political Violence and Stability in the States of the Northern Persian Gulf* (Santa Monica, CA: RAND, 1999), pp. 35–47; Gregory Gause and Jill Crystal, "The Arab Gulf: Will Autocracy Define the Social Contract in 2015," in Judith Yaphe, ed., *The Middle East in 2015: The Impacts of Regional Trends on U.S. Strategic Planning* (Washington, D.C.: National Defense University, 2002), p. 69; Judith Yaphe, "The Middle East in 2015: An Overview," in Yaphe, ed., *The Middle East in 2015*, p. 5.

4. Jamal Jassem al-Fakhri, "The Demographic Structure of GCC States," in Abdulaziz Sager, ed., *Gulf in a Year, 2003* (Dubai: Gulf Research Center, 2004), pp. 73–75.

5. Jon Marks, "Buoyant GCC Grapples with Dollar Black Spot," *Gulf States Newsletter* 28, no. 726 (2004), p. 13.

6. Ibid., p. 14.

7. Byman and Green, *Political Violence and Stability*, pp. xiv, 8.

8. Yaphe, "The Middle East in 2015," p. 6.

9. Byman and Green, *Political Violence and Stability*, p. 8.

10. Simon Henderson, *The New Pillar: Conservative Arab Gulf States and U.S. Strategy* (Washington, D.C.: Washington Institute, 2004), pp. 34–45; Paul Melly, Nick Carn, and Mark Ford, *Succession in the Gulf: The Commercial Implications* (Hastings: Middle East Newsletters, 2002).

11. Gause and Crystal, "The Arab Gulf," p. 184.

12. Ibid., p. 190.

13. Melly, Carn, and Ford, *Succession in the Gulf*, pp. 32–36; Marks, "Buoyant GCC," p. 14.

14. R. Burrell, "Policies of the Arab Littoral States in the Persian Gulf Region" (1975), in Abbas Amirie, ed., *The Persian Gulf and Indian Ocean in International Politics* (Tehran: Institute for International Political and Economic Studies, 1975), p. 254.

15. "Kuwaiti Reformists Seek Governance Breakthroughs," *Gulf States Newsletter* (April 30, 2004), p. 6.

16. Byman and Green, *Political Violence and Stability*, p. 8; Paul Pillar, "20/20 Vision? The Middle East to 2020," *Middle East Quarterly* XI, no. 1 (2004) p. 63.

17. "Winning the Initiative: A Saudi Timetable for Elections and Reform," *Gulf States Newsletter* (March 19, 2004), p. 3. See also "Saudi Arabia: Modest Reforms

Strengthen Shura," Oxford Analytica, May 28, 2004. Available online (www. oxweb.com).

18. State Failure Task Force Report: Phase III Findings (September 30, 2000), p. 131. Available online (www.cidcm.umd.edu/inscr/stfail/SFTF%20Phase%20III%20 Report%20Final.pdf).

19. Gause and Crystal, "The Arab Gulf," p. 192.

20. Pillar, "20/20 Vision?" pp. 63–66.

21. Rear Admiral John Sigler, *Post-Saddam Framework for CENTCOM: Military Considerations* (Washington, D.C.: National Defense University, 2003).

22. Marks, "Buoyant GCC," p. 13; Henderson, *The New Pillar*, p. 35; Melly, Carn, and Ford, *Succession in the Gulf*, pp. 24–32.

23. Marks, "Buoyant GCC," p. 29.

24. Paul Melly, "Saudi Arabia's New Politics," *Gulf States Newsletter* 29, no. 754 (2005).

25. Ibid.

26. The National Security Strategy of the United States (White House, September 2002). Available online (http://www.whitehouse.gov/nsc/nss.html).

27. Department of Defense, "Quadrennial Defense Review Report," (Washington, D.C.: U.S. Department of Defense, 2001), p. 11.

28. Blanche, "Terror Attacks Threaten Gulf's Oil Routes," pp. 6–9.

29. Eric Watkins, "Facing the Terrorist Threat in the Malacca Strait," *Terrorism Monitor* 2, no. 9 (2004), p. 4.

30. Ibid., p. 4.

31. Stephen Ulph, "Anti-Ship Warfare and Molotov Cocktails at the Siege of Acre, 1190," *Terrorism Monitor* 2, no. 9 (2004).

32. Andrew Holt, "Plugging the Holes in Maritime Security," *Terrorism Monitor* 2, no. 9 (2004).

33. Matthew Levitt, "Drawing a Line in the Saudi Sand," *National Review Online*, April 16, 2003. Available online (www.nationalreview.com/comment/comment-levitt041603.asp).

34. Stephen Ulph, "The War Within," *Terrorism Monitor* 1, no. 6 (2003), p. 5.

35. Ed Blanche, "Terror Attacks Threaten Gulf's Oil Routes," *Jane's Intelligence Review* 14, no. 12 (December 2002), p. 7; Michael Knights, "Western Expatriates Are the Weakest Link," *Gulf States Newsletter* 27, no. 705 (2003), p. 7. See also John Daly,

"Saudi 'Black Gold': Will Terrorism Deny the West Its Fix?" *Terrorism Monitor* 1, no. 6 (2003).

36. Michael Knights, "Maritime Intercept Operations Continue in the Gulf," *Gulf States Newsletter* (April 3, 2004).

37. Tim Ripley, "Securing Iraq's Maritime Flank," *Jane's Intelligence Review* (January 2004), pp. 1–4.

38. Jon Marks, "Dubai, Qatar Confront the Realities of Life as a Global Hub," *Gulf States Newsletter* (February 20, 2004), p. 16.

39. Knights, "Maritime Intercept Operations," p. 1.

40. Marks, "Dubai, Qatar Confront the Realities of Life as a Global Hub," p. 7.

41. David Fulghum, "Frontiers Disappear," *Aviation Week and Space Technology*, March 15, 2004, p. 56.

42. Knights, "Maritime Intercept Operations," p. 3.

43. Ibid.

44. Reuters, "U.S.-Led Naval Forces Hold Exercises," January 17, 2004.

45. IRO, *Illicit Drug Report in the Islamic Republic of Iran* (International Relations Office, Drug Control Headquarters, March 14, 2004). Available online (www.diplomatie.gouv.fr/routesdeladrogue/textes/iran.pdf); Ripley, "Securing Iraq's Maritime Flank," p. 3.

46. IRO, *Illicit Drug Report,* p. 3. See also *Middle East News and Events* 2004 (UN Office on Drugs and Crime, March 14, 2004); available online at www.unodc.org/egypt/en/news_and_events.html.

47. Rasha Owais, "GCC Electronic Link Takes Shape to Fight Drugs," *Gulf News*, March 13, 2004 (available online at www.gulf-news.com/Articles/news.asp?ArticleID=11165); Knights, "Maritime Intercept Operations," p. 1.

48. Tanya Goudsouzian, "Kuwait Declares War on Drug Trafficking," *Gulf News,* March 13, 2004, p. 1.

49. *UN Office on Drugs and Crime*, p. 1.

50. Mohammed Salem al-Mazroui, "Elections and Referendums in the GCC," in Abdulaziz Sager, ed., *Gulf in a Year, 2003* (Dubai: Gulf Research Center, 2004), p. 51.

2

Interstate Conflict and Future Gulf Security

REGARDLESS OF HOW settled the security situation in the Gulf may appear, the GCC states will always feel vulnerable to interstate aggression. Both the ruling elites and nationalistic populations are subject to a range of influences that have no parallel in the contemporary United States or Europe. One factor is that each of the GCC states was formed within the living memory of its national leadership. Despite rapid modernizing trends, Gulf denizens still view impermeable borders and exclusive national identities as relatively new features of the region. And each of the GCC states has faced external depredation and threats to its existence since being formed. Even within the last twenty years, armed clashes between GCC states have taken place. In April 1986, Qatari helicopters fired on Bahraini positions on Fasht al-Dibel, while in June 1991 the Bahraini air force penetrated Qatari airspace to warn against further actions. In both 1978 and 1992, Omani and United Arab Emirates (UAE) forces clashed in disputed border areas, and Saudi and Qatari forces have engaged periodically in tense military exercises in disputed wadis near the coast.

Today only three intra-GCC border disputes persist—concerning areas of Saudi Arabia's borders with Oman, Qatar, and the UAE—and even these may have been essentially settled in closed-door agreements between the states involved.[1] Considering the nationalism that frequently accompanies the development of civil society in young states, this settling of border disputes removes a potential trigger for the militarization of rivalries within the GCC. Such rivalries will likely grow as smaller Gulf states such as Qatar and the UAE undercut Saudi Arabia's traditional leadership in the region by capitalizing on their greater political stability and economic sustainability.

Despite a healthy distrust of each other, the GCC states will continue to view depredation from larger external powers as the central interstate threat facing all of them. In this context, the range of states both capable of and interested in influencing Gulf security is slowly expanding. The updated list is highlighted by increasing missile ranges from China, India, Israel, and Pakistan, placing the Gulf states within the threat radii of a host of new nations. For several assertive Asian nations that depend on regional oil and gas supplies for economic growth, stability in the Gulf is of growing importance. Still, in the near term, the key interstate threats to the GCC nations originate within the Gulf itself, falling into two broad categories: first, Iraq and Yemen, once known as the radical Arab states of the Gulf and Arabian Peninsula, and second, Iran, representing the longstanding threat to dominate the Gulf region. With the notable exception of the UAE, the GCC states have not regularly committed their armed forces to operations beyond the Gulf.

The Declining Threat from Radical Arab States

Of the three non-GCC states in the Gulf, Iraq has undergone the most dramatic transformation over the last decade. In 1990, the now-deposed Baathist leadership threatened the UAE explicitly and leveled harsh criticism against all the GCC states as they supported Iraq's containment in the 1990s. Most keenly affected by the Iraqi threat were the northern GCC states: Saudi Arabia, Bahrain, and, especially, Kuwait—the result of Iraq's invasion in August 1990, its brutal occupation lasting more than five months, and Iraqi missile strikes executed in 2003. For these reasons, Kuwait is unlikely ever again to underestimate the threat from Iraq. Saudi Arabia and Bahrain were meanwhile exposed to Iraqi ballistic missile attacks in 1991, played major roles in both the 1991 and 2003 coalition offensives, and supported Iraq's containment through military and economic measures. Despite a powerful shared interest in Iraq's rehabilitation, the GCC will continue to treat Iraq cautiously. The scars inflicted on Iraq-GCC relations and overall Arab solidarity in the Gulf may take some time to heal, particularly because Iraq has not yet formally renounced its territorial claims in Kuwait. Iraq may once again emerge as an expansionist, or at least muscular, force in the Gulf. As Gulf Research Center academic Issam Salim Shanti noted: "For both ideological and historical reasons, a post-Saddam Iraq, irrespective of ideology and political character, will, in the long term, continue to harbor the same aspirations to become a regional hegemon."[2]

Yet, while the strategic intentions of the reconstituted Iraqi state remain uncertain, the country has a far-downgraded ability to threaten its southern neighbors. Its economic recovery will likely be slow and guided heavily by watchful foreign governments and international organizations. Defense spending will probably remain far below the level needed to build an effective offensive military capability, with any sign of a major military buildup in Iraq triggering international censure that the fragile national recovery effort could ill afford.[3] The New Iraqi Army, currently under development, will be unsuitable for high-intensity offensive warfare and is unlikely to be supported by strong offensive airpower in the foreseeable future. Put in concrete terms, the short-warning overland invasion threat to the northern Gulf states has been eliminated up through 2015. As the Stanley Foundation's Michael Kraig noted in late 2004:

> About Iraq, participants are still thinking in terms of the old Iraqi army: 400,000 men, Scud missiles, and great military power. This military power is not there any more, and it will not be for some time. Whether this military power will rise again or not is a decision that should be made by an Iraqi government that doesn't even exist today. The military power of Iraq is so distant that it doesn't merit consideration [in future dialogues].[4]

Though regional states, particularly Kuwait, will remain watchful, Iraq's potential to collapse poses a greater threat to Gulf security than any chance that it could expand.[5] Gulf states will therefore work to ensure Iraq's territorial integrity, and will seek to fence off the country's borders to prevent it from functioning as a cross-border sanctuary for terrorists.

Though not a Gulf state, Yemen is nonetheless connected to the Arabian Peninsula and has played a role similar to Iraq's with regard to the southern Gulf borders of Oman and Saudi Arabia, though in a less threatening manner. During the era of radical Arab nationalism, a divided Yemen represented an opportunity for both the Soviet Union and Nasser's Egypt to develop military toeholds on the Arabian Peninsula. Before, during, and since the unification of Yemen in 1990, border disputes led to military clashes with Yemen's neighbors. Throughout recent decades, Saudi Arabian and Yemeni border forces have intermittently tangled in skirmishes, and Omani forces repelled a Yemeni incursion as recently as 1987. To Oman and Saudi Arabia, Yemen remains a dangerous and militaristic neighbor. The country is unstable and engaged in the nationalistic task of state-building, with large swaths of its population consisting of tribesmen with a disposition for warfare.

Like Iraq, however, the interstate military threat from Yemen is diminishing due to economic weakness and intensive reliance on international financial assistance. Foreign aid—which reached $2.3 billion in 2005—underpins the Yemeni economy, making the country highly dependent on the approval of international institutions. Unless new oil exploration is successful, Yemen's production will likely decline from approximately 435,000 barrels per day (b/d) in 2001 to less than 143,000 b/d in 2010.[6] Attracting investment in both the oil industry and vital job-producing sectors such as transshipment and berthing or tourism will necessitate continued stability in Yemen's foreign policy, and the development of closer economic ties to the GCC. Though further skirmishes and border spats are always possible, the primary threat to the GCC from Yemen originates not from the government in Sanaa, but from the uncontrolled areas of the country that host terrorist and criminal networks.

Dissecting Iranian Strategic Intentions

Of the three non-GCC states in the region, Iran presents the most serious military and intelligence threat to the GCC states. Despite a sustained period of pragmatism and stability in Iran's relations with the GCC states in the 1990s, including a virtual cessation of attempts to export the Islamic Revolution across the Gulf, GCC leaders today can still consider Iran a threat for several reasons. Basic geography is an important factor: the coastline of every GCC country faces Iran, offering a mode of close if indirect contact. And most of the vital economic and political centers of the Gulf states are arrayed along this exposed coastline. Along with the UAE and Oman, Iran acts as a custodian of the Straits of Hormuz, the vital oil artery relied upon by the regional and global economies. Even before the Islamic Republic of Iran was created in 1979, the predominantly Persian Imperial Iran of the Shah presented an overt threat to the Arab Gulf states.[7] During a period of massive military expansion, backed by Iran's apparent interest in a parallel nuclear weapons program, it welcomed the retreat of British influence in the Gulf by dominating areas of the Shatt al-Arab waterway and annexing the islands of Abu Musa and the Greater and Lesser Tunbs in 1971, an episode during which three Sharjah policemen were killed.

Following the Iranian revolution, a number of GCC states were attacked or otherwise pressured by the new Islamic state. During the Iran-Iraq War of 1980–88, Iran made aerial and maritime incursions into Kuwaiti territory and ten times launched antishipping missiles at Kuwaiti tankers and terminals. In clashes with Saudi fighters during the war, a number of Iranian aircraft were destroyed. In 1980, elements of the Omani and Iranian navies faced off in shows of force, and armed clashes between Iran and the UAE occurred at al-Bakush in 1986 and involving offshore structures on the Sharjah coast in the years since.[8] Along with to overt military actions, Iran has supported internal dissent and acts of terrorism within a number of Gulf states since the 1980s.[9] In addition to the early focus of the Islamic Republic on exporting the revolution, these actions took place against the backdrop of Iran's desperate struggle to survive and win the war against Iraq.

In the aftermath of that war, Iran adopted a more moderate foreign-policy stance. This approach focused on containment of Iraq, improvement of relations with Saudi Arabia and other GCC states, use of Iranian influence to spur higher oil prices, and expulsion of foreign forces from the Gulf, to be replaced by a regional security condominium—objectives not recognizably different from those pursued by Imperial Iran.[10] The 1990s saw a decline in overt Iranian military actions and covert Iranian state sponsorship of dissent and terrorism in the Gulf. Even so, Tehran continued its support for Lebanese Hizballah and Palestinian rejectionist groups, viewed by all wings of the Islamic Republic establishment as acceptable faces of terrorism. Despite constant sanctions imposed by the United States against the Islamic Republic, the decade of peace since the end of the Iran-Iraq War has given Iran breathing space to rebuild its shattered military forces and industries.

Iran's future strategic intentions in the Gulf remain difficult to ascertain. At its heart, Iranian foreign policy will be influenced by stable nationalistic aims—namely Tehran's desire to exclude external security guarantors that threaten its role as "policeman of the Gulf."[11] This sentiment remains pervasive in postrevolutionary Iran, where key political figures from the reformist and conservative factions, plus military leaders, are united by their calls for U.S. military withdrawal from the Gulf.[12] Like the Shah-led government that preceded it, Iran's theocratic leadership assumes Iran to be the natural leader of the Gulf region. In defending its national interests and security, the Iranian government continues to give significant support and funding to the development of strong conventional military forces, an indigenous arms industry, and a range of weapons of mass destruction (WMD).[13] Since the Islamic Revolution, Tehran has continued to insist on retaining Abu Musa and the Tunb Islands, and may continue to compete with Iraq for ownership of parts of the Shatt al-Arab waterway. [14] Most recently, Iran warned Qatar to slow its exploitation of the North Field and South Pars gas reserves, shared by the two countries, or else Iran would "find other ways and means of resolving the issue."[15]

Alongside the perennial features of Iranian policy, we must consider the style of foreign policy that has developed in the fifteen years since the death of Ayatollah Khomeini. This period witnessed what has been called the "economization of foreign policy."[16] Economic pragmatism began under President Ali Akbar Rafsanjani in the early 1990s and accelerated when President Muhammad Khatami took office in 1997. The period was characterized by relative lev-

els of restraint and engagement, compared to the 1980s, and pursuit of normal-
ized international and regional status and increased foreign direct investment.
Under this policy, the Islamic Republic has enjoyed considerable success since
the late 1990s in tapping international capital markets. Remarking on this trend,
Iranian Deputy Minister of Foreign Affairs Hossein Adeli explained that following the postrevolutionary institution-building and national defense (Iran-
Iraq War) stages of the Islamic Republic—known as the "first Republic"—Iran
pursued reconstruction and internationalization. The next stage, Adeli noted,
would see "active interaction with the world economy," including more open-
ness to foreign investment and an attempt to join the World Trade Organization (WTO).[17]

All these advances appear to be in peril due to Iran's determination to
develop nuclear technology, which has resulted in an open-ended confrontation with the international community. The election of President Mahmoud
Ahmadinejad in 2005 may well prove to be a less significant development than
Iran's strategic decision to initiate the nuclear stand-off. In the longer term, the
rising power of Ahmadinejad's backers might threaten to take Iran back to the
foreign policy outlook of the first Republic. Made up of former Islamic Revolution Guard Corps (IRGC) officials and members of the conservative Abadga-
ran (developers) coalition, Ahmadinejad's clique has not rejected the security,
diplomatic, and economic policies of the revolutionary era. The faction also
displays two apparently contradictory traits: overconfidence and paranoia.
Boosting the morale of the Ahmadinejad faction has been the effective defeat
of reform at home, the situation in Iraq—with America bogged down and Iran
gaining influence—and the deliberate pace of international attempts to slow
Iran's nuclear progress.

Eventual nuclear ownership by Iran—at this stage a highly plausible outcome—could lead to more assertive foreign policy in the Gulf, as well as a
strengthened strategic position. Though the roots of Iran's pragmatic foreign
policy run deep, the development of nuclear capability might raise confidence
enormously, as when Iraq developed chemical weapons before attacking Iran
in 1980 and when India played for Kashmir during the Kargil Crisis of May–
July 1999. Iran is well aware that though America did attack Iraq—which U.S.
planners believed to possess chemical weapons in 1991 and 2003—the United
States has never attacked a country with nuclear arms, a fact that could tempt
the Iranian regime to assert itself more brashly.

Yet even ownership of nuclear arms will not immunize Tehran against likely
international isolation should it continue moving away from the economics-

based pragmatism of the last fifteen years. From the vantage point of the Islamic Republic, threats appear everywhere, with the so-called *touts azimuts* doctrine a cornerstone of Iranian security policy since the 1970s.[18] And Iran *is* surrounded by U.S. allies on all sides, including the increasing deployment of U.S. forces. For a number of years at least, large U.S. military contingents will remain in Afghanistan and Iraq, plus smaller contingents and basing options throughout the Caucasus and central Asia, while U.S. naval and air forces will remain present along Iran's Gulf and Indian Ocean coastlines. Peer competitors surround Iran, with Israel's strategic partner Turkey to the northwest; Russia across the Caspian to the north; and a potentially unstable and nuclear-armed Pakistan to the southeast.[19] Specifically, the threat of regime change sponsored by United States—whether through covert or military action—would radicalize Iranian foreign policy. In the face of international isolation, the Ahmadinejad faction appears prepared ideologically to call for a new period of self-reliance, mirroring the approach taken by Iran during the 1980s.

This dynamic sets the stage for a three-way struggle in Iran for control of the country's foreign policy. On the one hand, the old-new school of thought put forward by the Ahmadinejad faction could see Iran adopt a more assertive and less predictable regional foreign policy. This could mean increased meddling in the internal affairs of other Gulf states or political and military showdowns with the United States and the international community. On the other hand, the quiet but influential community of traditional conservative technocrats and businessmen (the "thinking conservatives")[20] will argue for a continuation of the "economization of foreign policy," claiming that this policy is necessary to allow Iran to open up new oil, gas, and nonhydrocarbon sources of revenue and jobs. Somewhere between the two camps lies the Supreme Leader, Ayatollah Ali Khameini, who has worked at the highest levels of government and the state under both camps.

Though the result of this struggle is impossible to predict, Iranian foreign and regional policy will likely zigzag even more than it has in the past. The Ahmadinejad faction does not enjoy absolute or unchecked control of the foreign and security apparatus. Furthermore, there is no reason to assume that the current president's nontraditional conservative faction will have greater political staying power than other Iranian political movements, such as the technocrats and reformists. In Iran, economic imperatives often steer policy. While the country's birthrate is now declining, Iran will still require significant expansion of its nonoil sectors to generate sufficient jobs for the generation of Iranian youth soon to come of age.[21] According to the traditional conservatives and technocrats, economic development will depend largely on the Islamic Republic's willingness to avoid expansion of policies threatening to other Gulf nations, and to rein in extremist elements within the multifaceted ruling elites. Under this model, Iran would develop much as China has done, seeking to offer a stable diplomatic and foreign direct-investment partner to states outside the region,[22] while promising incremental improvement in economic and social conditions to a broadly apathetic electorate.[23] As the very survival of Iran's theocratic regime depends on maintenance of political apathy anchored in economic improvements, such an approach strives to achieve what Peter Jones terms "external calm."[24] Though such an outcome cannot be guaranteed, it is at least as likely as the worst-case scenarios that attended the election of President Ahmadinejad. With neither renewed activism nor continued economic pragmatism assured, Iranian policy will likely fluctuate between the two poles in the coming decade.

Iranian 'Full-Spectrum' Deterrence

However Iranian foreign and regional policy develops on a broad scale, Tehran will want the means to deter or resist foreign interference in its domestic and foreign affairs. In pursuing these ends, Iran may undertake offensive actions (e.g., through terrorism or weapons proliferation), but its overriding focus will be to develop deterrent options that blunt external attempts to spur regime change or impose military or economic sanctions. Deterrence can be achieved through one of two models—punishment or denial. A threatened nation typically employs punishment-based deterrence when it cannot prevent an action from occurring but still retaliates to inflict damage on the attacker that will affect its future strategic calculus. Deterrence by denial, meanwhile, is used to reduce the attacker's chances for success, thereby making the attacker less likely to risk the costs of an attack. Ever since the Iran-Iraq War—when Iranian air and naval forces proved unable to protect Iranian shipping from Iraqi attacks, and when Iranian air defenses lacked the means to intercept Iraqi Scud missiles—Iran has adopted a predominantly punishment-based deterrent model. As Michael Eisenstadt noted, this system has relied on a "strategic triad" of state-sponsored terrorism, antishipping (or "sea-denial") attacks on oil tankers, and air or missile attacks on strategic targets, with or without the use of WMD.[25] Though each element appears to have been developed to deter an opponent from launching an initial attack, or to prevent further attacks or escalation, each leg of the strategic triad could also be used offensively. And while deterrence by punishment will remain Iran's principal and most reliable deterrent mechanism, Iran's growing conventional military capabilities have led to a renewed effort to develop denial-based deterrent capabilities. Through the combination of punishment- and denial-based deterrence, Iran appears to be developing what might be termed "full-spectrum deterrence" against the full range of its external threats.

Though Iranian development of nuclear weapons is not inevitable, the likeliest outcome of the current nuclear standoff will be that Iran retains at least the technological base and reactor infrastructure to develop a closed nuclear fuel cycle and a nuclear arsenal at short notice—the so-called bomb in the basement or virtual nuclear arsenal. Military counterproliferation strikes could seriously retard development of nuclear reactors (thereby removing one of Iran's "shortcuts" to creating fissile material), but such strikes would likely spur increased efforts in the parallel field of uranium enrichment, the sites for which are considerably less vulnerable to military strikes (see Appendix 8). As Iran crawls toward achieving embryonic nuclear weapons capability by the end of the decade, the United States will try to slow the advancement of the nuclear program by isolating the nation internationally and making it pay a diplomatic and economic price for pressing ahead with proliferation. The United States will also try to influence Iran to moderate its behavior within the region.

In its default response to such measures, Tehran will likely assert its refusal to tolerate any limitations on its ability to research and develop nuclear technology (e.g., uranium enrichment and a nuclear fuel cycle). This is seemingly a point of consensus between conservative and reformist politicians and street-level Iranians of all political hues. Hassan Rouhani, the former coordinator of Iran's nuclear portfolio, confirmed that Iran reserved the right as a signatory of the Treaty on the Non-Proliferation of Nuclear Weapons (NPT) to develop nuclear technology under appropriate International Atomic Energy Agency (IAEA) safeguards. Rouhani clarified that "European negotiators had the [mistaken] assumption that Iran would forgo uranium enrichment in case of political, security, and economic concessions."

Even if Tehran is allowed to develop this kind of virtual nuclear capability, the Iranian government may be convinced to maintain strategic ambiguity along the model used by Israel. Traditional conservatives would certainly prefer to couch Iran's foreign policy in the warm and fuzzy language of the "dialogue of civilizations" and to remain within the NPT, preserving Tehran's ability to sound its support for international institutions and agreements. This standing would also allow the Iranian government to conform to previous rulings made by Supreme Leader Khameini, who has denied that Iran is pursuing nuclear weapons. On June 24, 2004, for instance, he stated: "If the Europeans are concerned about Iran's access to nuclear arms...Iran will never go after nuclear arms. But, if they want to prevent Iran from acquiring nuclear technology, Iran will not accept such extortion."

A strong argument exists that Iran's development of immature nuclear weapons capability will not immediately change the strategic or military balance in the Gulf as much as some might think. Though strategists understand very little about how Iran might use nuclear weapons, they can learn important lessons from early nuclear weapons capability in other states, where the key influence on strategy has been nuclear scarcity—that is, the limited amount, reliability, and ease of delivery of their small deterrent arsenal. As for the latter two points, such a scenario would be particularly applicable if Iran does not test its nuclear devices, and even more so if it does not divert nuclear materials required to construct an atomic weapon until shortly before the onset of a crisis. If Iran remains within the Non-Proliferation Treaty and does not develop an extensive covert program in parallel of its declared nuclear activities, it is likely that only a handful of bombs could be created at one time, with crude results. Design of weapons would probably draw heavily on Chinese warhead plans sold by Pakistani nuclear scientist Abdul Qadir Khan's network, suggesting warheads weighing from 1,000 to 2,000 pounds. Uncertain explosive yields would be produced by the near weapons-grade material used, and the weapons would be questionably reliable, especially if delivery placed stress on the devices, or if delivery systems with a low chance of surviving were used, such as aircraft.

Under such conditions, the general taboo on the use of nuclear weapons is reinforced by the need to maintain both the stockpile and the perceived efficacy of the deterrent threat. The exception to these powerful incentives for nonuse is that of a "second strike" retaliatory force in the case of an attack that threatens the existence of the nuclear power. As indicated by U.S. war plans during the late 1940s, nuclear scarcity channels primary responsibility for deterrence back to conventional forces. Specifically, this involves deterrence by denial, in which conventional forces are used to blunt the attacker's efforts, and deterrence by punishment, in which techniques such as aerial bombing and naval blockades are wielded to inflict costs on the attacker after the transgression. In increasing its own nuclear capability, the United States has adopted a nuclear-led deterrent posture, including the development of the "Pentomic military"—which replaced expensive conventional forces with relatively inexpensive nuclear weapons at all levels of the force structure. Ultimately this strategy was only of limited use in conflicts taking place below the nuclear threshold (e.g., Korea and Indochina). As regards Iranian nuclear and conventional defense spending and procurement, a Pentomic era is clearly not imminent—and nuclear scarcity will factor into Iranian defense planning up through 2015. In place of an emphasis on nuclear weapons, Iran has opted to develop "full spectrum deterrence," building nonconventional and conventional forces in tandem to ensure a range of politically and technologically credible deterrent options. Nuclear ownership may influence the way a nation is treated by its peers, but Iran, like other nuclear nations, will find nuclear weapons to be of surprisingly little offensive use in most conflicts and of almost no use as a strategic prod in any situation falling short of an existential crisis, as assessment that recalls Henry Kissinger's commentary:

> Given the power of modern weapons, a nation that relies on all-out war as its chief deterrent imposes a fearful handicap on itself. The most agonizing decision a statesman can face is whether or not to unleash all-out war; all pressures make for hesitation, short of direct attack threatening the national existence. In any other situation he will be inhibited by the incommensurability between the cost of war and the objective in dispute....A deterrent which one is afraid to implement when it is challenged ceases to be a deterrent.[26]

Strengths and Weaknesses of Iran's Future Armed Forces

For the next ten years at least, conventional military forces are likely to play the main role in Iran's deterrent—and possibly its offensive—capabilities, highlighting the need to develop an up-to-date and forward-looking assessment of Iranian military potential. Throughout the 1990s, CENTCOM commanding officers and planners made a distinction between the near-term threat posed by Iraq and the longer-term threat posed by Iran. A number of CENTCOM commanders-in-chief (CINC) recognized that, compared to the crumbling Iraqi military, the Iranian armed forces presented an increasingly capable potential foe.[27] Contemporary Persian military culture bears little relation to the traditional Soviet-influenced outlook of major Arab military powers such as Iraq, Syria, and Libya. Though purges removed many Western-trained officers from the Islamic Republic of Iran Armed Services (IRIAS), the remaining senior military leadership struggled to ensure that Western, rather than Soviet-inspired, military doctrine and equipment remained in service. A vein of Western military thinking is strongly evident in the contemporary Iranian military, despite the contradictions created by the character of the Islamic Republic.

This dichotomy is mirrored in the very uneven development of different aspects of Iran's nonnuclear armed forces. For instance, while Iran remains wedded to maintaining massed armed forces that include an army of 450,000, an equal number of army reserves, plus 500,000 in Basij militia forces, today's IRIAS places strong emphasis on qualitative enhancement of military capabilities.[28] In contrast to many Arab forces, Iran stresses the value of developing competent junior leaders, and undertaking a busy schedule of realistic training exercises. While practice often lags far behind theory, Iran is moving in the right direction in terms of military preparedness. At the operational level, Iran has developed increasingly sophisticated structures for joint command and control, and stresses the value of initiative and maneuver in warfare, avoiding enemy strengths and exploiting observed weaknesses. At the tactical level, however, Iran still suffers from crippling training inferiority compared to that of the United States. Heavy reliance on conscript manpower could negate many of the potential advantages of Iran's military modernization.[29]

Iran has taken advantage of its front-row seat to observe the evolving strengths and weaknesses of Western military forces in regional contingencies. During the Iran-Iraq War, the Islamic Republic came into direct conflict with U.S. forces during Operation Nimble Archer on April 18, 1988 (an element of Operation Praying Mantis). In this painful series of U.S. naval air strikes, Iran deviated from its previous naval tactics by attempting to use major surface combatants to fight the United States. The defeat reiterated lessons that Iran had already begun to internalize: that the Islamic Republic could benefit from maintaining ambiguity with regard to operations such as its mining of the Straits of Hormuz; and that in any future conflict with the United States, Iran must keep U.S. naval forces as far away from Iranian littoral areas as possible and engage them using guerrilla tactics.[30] According to the U.S. Department of Defense, the Iranian military also drew a host of lessons from Operation Desert Storm.[31] At tactical levels, Iran appears to have accepted further the utility of mine warfare against Western warships, and noted the importance of deception and mobility in reducing the impact of Western air superiority.

At the doctrinal level, Desert Storm appears to have strengthened the Iranian military's basic proclivity toward Western practices and technology. At the operational and strategic levels, Desert Storm hinted at what capabilities might be required to deter a U.S. invasion of Iran, particularly in the sphere of WMD development. Following Desert Storm, Indian Brigadier General V. K. Nair, noting that the United States had not been deterred by Iraq's chemical or biological weapons, mused, "If you fight the United States, you'd better have nuclear weapons." Iran also appears to have heeded Iraq's error in allowing the coalition access to local air bases and uninterrupted logistical buildup, increasing Iranian awareness of the need to develop antiaccess and area denial (A2AD) capabilities. In May 2000, Muhammad Hassan Tavalai, general manager of the Iranian Armed Forces Aviation Industry Organization (IAFAIO), noted the need to develop offensive doctrine, when he observed:

> Evidence from recent wars shows that defensive warfare will be replaced by offensive warfare. Offensive wars revolve around offensive arms, and their philosophy is that the first offensive move is the deciding factor, and whoever strikes this first blow will keep the momentum.[34]

In its military planning, Iran has also reportedly incorporated lessons from U.S. operations in the Balkans, Afghanistan, and Iraq since 2003, including further means to counter U.S. air superiority, maneuver warfare, and psychological operations.[35]

Above all, Iran has drawn the lesson that technologically inferior armed forces suffer disastrously in military engagements with Western adversaries, particularly in the aerial and naval arenas, which remain the most likely venues for clashes between Iran and either the United States or the GCC states. U.S. sanctions on Iran, combined with pressure by the U.S. government on Western and Russian arms manufacturers, led the Islamic Republic to institute a major rehaul of its defense industries. Still, a number of Shah-era defense initiatives provided fertile ground for Iran's postrevolutionary drive toward self-sufficiency. Highly ambitious, Iran's early aerospace industry worked intimately in the development of key U.S. aircraft types. The Persian King program was envisaged in the early 1970s, and included substantial orders of U.S. equipment, worth $2 billion, including three hundred YF-16 Fighting Falcon fighters and seventy-nine F-14A Tomcat fighters. Between 20,000 and 30,000 Iranian technicians took part in the program, huge Northrop plants were constructed at Mehrabad Airport, and Imperial Iran provided partial funding for key projects, earning a seat in the development process for the F-14A Tomcat and the AGM-65 Maverick missile.

During the Iran-Iraq War, the Iranian armed forces utilized Persian King and other production deals licensed during the Shah era to provide infrastructure and expertise to rebuild damaged equipment and airframes, as well as to reverse-engineer (or copy) platform and weapon components so that technology did not have to be obtained abroad. Since the Iraq-Iraq War, Iran has applied considerable resources to defense industries, with $5 billion worth of investment reportedly injected into the Defense Industries Organization

(DIO) during a five-year plan that lasted from 2000 to 2005. The DIO is an umbrella group of Iranian defense industries that now sprawls across 250 sites and employs 50,000 workers, a third of whom boast graduate-level education.[36] Because of Iran's relatively low personnel costs and large labor market, it has been able to increase defense expenditures for operations, maintenance, and research and design. At the Northrop plant at Mehrabad, where an enormous plant still rivals the McDonnell Douglas plant in St Louis, Missouri, IAFAIO oversees aerospace projects. The area is now run by Iranian Aircraft Industries (IACI), which carries out upgrades on existing airframes and develops new combat aircraft. To reduce duplication and allow greater focus on the neglected fields of avionics and battle management, IAFAIO is encouraging the merging and centralization of aerospace projects. The Iranian Helicopter Support and Renewal Company (known as Panha) manages helicopter repair and production from its facilities at Isfahan—a site built by American company Bell Textron in 1976–1978. In a major program at Isfahan, older U.S.-supplied airframes will be replaced by high-quality reverse-engineered types.[37]

Since the 1970s, Iran has used laser-guided munitions, guided antishipping missiles, and beyond-visual-range (BVR) air-to-air missiles, while in 1984 the Islamic Republic became perhaps the first user of unmanned combat aerial vehicles (UCAVs).[38] In order to maintain its antitank, antishipping, and antiaircraft missile stocks, Iran first became adept at reverse-engineering decaying fuel packs, later progressing to updating guidance and other electronic features. These advances laid the foundations for Iran's successful reverse-engineering of Western and Chinese surface-to-air missiles and glide and powered standoff guided munitions, and its production of a range of indigenously designed unmanned aerial vehicles (UAVs) and engines suitable for use in cruise missiles.[39] Furthermore, IAFAIO and the Communications Industries Group of DIO maintain strong links with research facilities at a number of Iranian universities and military research institutes, where they sponsor research into advanced flight control systems, long-range radar, night-vision equipment, electronic counter-countermeasures (ECCMs), secure communications, and Identify Friend and Foe (IFF) systems.[40] Iran has also modified its stock of Western and Russian avionics and radars to allow compatibility with both Western and Russian guided munitions, and has installed digital datalinks and global positioning systems (GPSs) on UAVs and standoff weapons.[41] These programs, in combination with deepening defense relations with potential high-technology partners like India,[42] suggest that throughout the coming decade, Iran's defense industries will transition from mechanical and electronic self-sufficiency to more advanced fields of military research and design.

Unless Iran's modernization can move beyond the mechanical and electronic spheres, its military will remain a second-rate force. The extent to which Iran weakens or strengthens in view of the global and regional military balance will be determined by its success in at-home development and external procurement of command, control, communications, computerization, intelligence, surveillance, and reconnaissance (C⁴ISR) technologies. As U.S. Coast Guard Rear Admiral Patrick Stillman has noted, "Seamless C⁴ISR is the sine qua non for success in the [networked] battlefield of the twenty-first century."[43] Though Iran has likely developed strategies to challenge its adversaries' C⁴ISR strategies, both in terms of complicating enemy decisionmaking and reducing ability to perform surveillance on Iranian military forces,[44] Iran's own ability to maintain command, control, and communications while under attack by a modern military adversary appears limited at present. Though Iran is laying fiber-optic land and sea lines, investing in satellite communications, importing and developing encrypted communications, and installing limited computerization within its command centers, once Iran comes under attack, it may quickly lose the ability to maintain high-volume tactical communications among its regional commands.[45]

As both its immobile ground-based surveillance radar network and its slowly expanding airborne early-warning fleet are exposed to enemy attacks, Iran will have to develop a more effective and durable network of intelligence, surveillance, and reconnaissance (ISR) sensors.[46] In maintaining effective situational awareness in Iran's own airspace and territorial waters during such an attack, the Islamic Republic's extensive array of passive sensors—observation positions, listening posts, acoustic naval sensors, and perhaps other electronic intelligence–gathering equipment mounted on oil rigs,[47] dhows, and on shore—would likely complement surviving elements of the radar system to provide the basic intelligence required to give early warning to defenses at key economic and military hubs. For tasks beyond Iran's borders, which will be more demanding, such as "over the horizon" location and tracking of a U.S. aircraft carrier, Iran will have to develop considerably more advanced wide-area surveillance capabilities, possibly including satellite reconnaissance capability and durable long-range UAVs. [48]

Deterrence by Denial: Iranian Defensive Capabilities in 2015

Though Iran will continue to guard against the unlikely prospect of a new overland invasion by Iraq, the United States represents the default opponent in Iranian planning. Following Operation Iraqi Freedom, Iranian planners are well aware that Iran's inefficient land forces would struggle to dislodge or stop a U.S.

invasion and march on Tehran. In planning to defend Iranian territory, they no doubt maintain schemes that aim to limit U.S. mobility while utilizing both conventional and guerrilla tactics. In battle, Iranian forces would likely remain close to their bases, lacking adequate mechanization or air cover to do otherwise, and would likely fail to halt an invasion conclusively. Still, to counter such an approach by the Iranians, the United States would need to commit all available ground forces, representing an immense challenge that the U.S. military will not be ready to undertake for a number of years. Nevertheless, Iranian planners would be remiss in failing to plan for such an eventuality, in which they would work to keep the U.S. military as far away from the Iranian homeland as possible, creating aerial and littoral defensive capabilities that might thicken their defensive wall or deter the U.S. military from launching more than a limited foray into Iranian territory (e.g., a temporary annexation of certain islands or ports). In summary, the most plausible conflict scenarios involving Iranian defensive capabilities revolve around air and littoral defenses.

Influenced by American training and force-development assistance in the 1970s and by the experience of the Iran-Iraq War in the next decade, the successive regimes of Imperial Iran and the Islamic Republic stressed the need for effective air defenses. As Shah-era planners recognized, however, defending Iran's airspace was easier said than done because of the country's size and its mountainous topography. These features would have required hundreds of ground-based radar stations and surface-to-air missile (SAM) units to create an integrated radar picture and fill in the large gaps—or radar "shadows"—created by the terrain. The solution adopted by Imperial Iran—culminating in the 1977 Seek Sentry arms deal—was to procure seven E-3A AWACS aircraft from the United States, as well as seventy-nine F-14A Tomcat fighters, with each of the latter type carrying a powerful long-range AWG-9 radar, to build a large airborne early warning (AEW) network. Though the AWACS aircraft never reached Iran, the F-14A aircraft, ordered earlier, were delivered before the revolution, giving Iran a fleet of "mini-AWACS" aircraft that remains in service to this day.

Iran's air defenses have evolved uniquely, fusing elements of the Shah's grandiose plans with more than twenty-five years of improvisation, cannibalization, and, most recently, modernization. At heart, the military philosophy underpinning the air-defense system remains Western rather than Soviet; that is, both interceptor aircraft and SAMs play an equal and synergistic role in a system that derives most of its radar coverage from airborne rather than ground-based sensors. Since 1979, Iran has added only one ground-based surveillance radar station, on the Afghan border. Iran's air-defense and air forces continue to rely, instead, on the F-14A Tomcats, including thirty aircraft on active duty in carefully managed, phased rotation from a fleet of forty-five to fifty.[49] Extensive maintenance efforts are likely to keep these aircraft, and their vital AWG-9 radars, active until 2015,[50] by which time Iran will be an experienced operator of a new fleet of locally licensed Antonov An-140 AEW aircraft. These small AWACS aircraft are likely to enter service in sufficient numbers to permit full twenty-four-hour radar coverage along Iran's Gulf coast during crisis periods.

Besides this coverage, Iran is unlikely to seek to develop a fully integrated nationwide air-defense system along the Iraqi model of the 1980s. Instead, Iran's experience of air defense in the Iran-Iraq War appears to have inculcated belief in a point-defense BVR, with Iran's strongest defenses located around "neuralgic" points such as Tehran, Isfahan, Kharq Island, Bandar Abbas, and the potential site of Iran's nuclear reactors at Bushehr. Local networks of interceptor aircraft and ground-based SAMs will provide layers of protection for these areas, employing a mobile defense based on regular relocation of SAMs plus a network of low-flying fighters screened by mountain ranges and teamed up with F-14A controllers operating farther inland and at higher altitudes. In such a setup, the aim would be to ambush penetrating attackers and their supporting AWACS or tankers with salvos of long-range SAMs, BVR air-to-air missiles (AAMs) fired by the F-14As, and shorter-range AAMs delivered by other fighters.

In continuing to present a meaningful air-to-air combat threat, Iran is well aware that Western air forces—of the United States, Europe, and Israel—have destroyed regional air forces in every major regional conflict since the 1980s. Yet, the Islamic Republic, and Imperial Iran before it, continues to think of itself as an exception to most rules, including the developing trend toward purely ground-based air defenses for non-Western armed forces, and has trained accordingly. The Islamic Republic of Iran Air Forces (IRIAF) continues to use syllabi adapted from U.S. training modules and requires trainees to have completed at least four hundred flying hours before moving on to advanced missions, and up to an additional three hundred to five hundred on combat aircraft before they qualify as combat pilots.[51] Iran is developing flight simulators locally.[52] Because Iranian pilots are trained to overcome the limitations of their aircraft, avionics, and weapons when faced with more advanced opponents, they stand out as a different breed of non-Western regional air force.[53] Vital teamwork is practiced between F-14A "mini-AWACS" controllers and partnered sets of F-4D/E or MiG-29 interceptors, which will continue to be the main types of combat jets in service in 2015.[54] With sixty-four aircraft deployed and seventy well-maintained aircraft on the side, the F-4D/E has been upgraded extensively with new electronic countermeasures, enhanced radar, as well as aircraft moving-target indicators, in-flight refueling capability, and new flexibility in the range of weapons it can carry. The MiG-29, meanwhile, will operate as a point-defense fighter, its short range extended through drop tanks, in-flight refueling, and engine modifications. Its poor radar will be compensated for by AEW support. Reputedly aggressive, Iranian pilots have learned to make use of advanced radar tactics, terrain masking (hiding in the radar "shadow" of mountains), maneuver, and ECCMs to surprise opponents, minimize their warning time, and limit their shooting opportunities.[55] To improve the survival rates of Iran's aircraft on the ground, the IRIAS maintains several hardened aircraft shelters, a range of aircraft dispersal options, and distributed sets of support packages at a number of potential operating bases.

Alongside its aerial interceptors, Iran will deploy increasingly sophisticated ground-based air defenses. For the foreseeable future, Iran will continue to field sufficient air defense artillery and shoulder-launched SAMs to keep attackers at medium to high altitudes, thereby denying them the ability to exploit Iran's serious vulnerability to low-level, or below-the-radar, intrusions. At critical targets, Iran is developing missile engagement zones built around well-designed Russian SAMs. Iran has reportedly explored the purchase of S-300V (NATO code name: SA-12a Gladiator or SA-12b Giant) wide-area defense systems, plus the highly capable localized S-300PMU (NATO code name: SA-10) and S-400 (NATO code name: SA-20) point-defense systems. The S-300V system could protect key centers at a maximum radius of 109 miles, while the S-400—which is highly mobile—would add modern missile units to roaming SAM defenses now composed of mobile versions of reverse-engineered and substantially upgraded Western SAMs.[56] The S-300 and S-400 series, some versions of which are likely to enter Iranian service in the coming decade, are particularly difficult to target based on their radar emissions, because they are able to continually communicate with radars in other locations.[57]

Iran's Gulf island bases and oil rigs remain among the most vulnerable parts of its territory, and Iran spends considerable effort in simulating protection of these holdings.[58] As well as providing observation outposts and mooring points for missile boats, these islands prevent commercial shipping from moving outside Iranian missile or artillery range, as they sit astride the easterly and westerly shipping lanes. Abu Musa, the most significant and farthest flung of Iran's presumed territories, is its most vulnerable. When revealed by commercial satellite imagery in 1999, the island's fortifications appeared relatively limited, though like other Iranian-controlled islands, such as Sirri, the island is likely stocked with sixty to ninety days of munitions supply, and cocooned with shelters and weapons caches. In both October 1994 and February 1995, Iran fortified Abu Musa, reportedly bringing additional SAMs, chemical artillery shells (probably nonlethal tear gas), and 4,500 troops.[59] Iran's limited amphibious and airmobile units could also reinforce its offshore assets, though only at great cost and with limited success. Though Iran has four brigades of Islamic Republic of Iran Navy (IRIN) and IRGC naval infantry, it lacks sufficient amphibious craft to lift more than twenty-five to thirty tanks and 800 to 1,200 troops in a single wave.[60] Even if Iran's merchant marine were used to support an amphibious operation, only a single brigade of troops could be transported.[61] This weakness in reinforcing the Gulf islands makes it highly unlikely that Iran could launch offensive amphibious operations elsewhere in the Gulf, already considered a remote possibility by military analysts.[62] As an Emirates Center for Strategic Studies and Research study concluded, "Invasion of a GCC state by sea would require enormous amphibious capabilities and air bridges, which Iran lacks."[63]

In addition to air defense of Iran's immediate territory and littoral holdings, the Islamic Republic has learned both directly, through operations against the United States in 1988, and indirectly, through Iraq's experiences in the 1990s, that in the case of hostile U.S. intervention in the Gulf, Iran must keep U.S. forces as far away from the Iranian coast as possible. In using its A2AD strategies, Iran could target either local air bases available to the United States, or else U.S. aircraft carriers or surface warfare vessels sailing in or near the Gulf. Antiaccess and area denial are related strategies, because while area denial typically concentrates on physically destroying or degrading the infrastructure supporting a nation's military access to the Gulf, the threat alone of such attacks may represent an antiaccess threat, reducing the political willingness of host nations to provide access to the United States.[64] As a number of studies have shown, advances in cruise and ballistic missile technology will give Iran the capability, well before 2015, to launch heavy area-denial attacks on most of the unfortified military facilities in the GCC states.[65] This will be particularly relevant if Iran utilizes chemical or biological warheads as well as conventional munitions in attacking these fixed targets.[66] As a result, the United States may not be able to count on the access points and reception facilities required to connect troops with prepositioned equipment or station land-based expeditionary units. This would undermine critical elements of a deterrent posture in the Gulf based on projection of power.

Because of weaknesses in Iran's wide-area naval surveillance, the Islamic Republic is far less capable of locating and attacking moving A2AD targets such as a carrier battle group or other naval surface warfare groups than it is of hitting a stationary target. As defense writer William O'Neill has noted, finding a U.S. carrier remains a very difficult task for developing nations, even in the confines of the Gulf. In the Gulf of Oman, such a task becomes more difficult by an order of magnitude. Even if targeting information can be gathered, it only stays relevant temporarily; and if, for instance, a weapon is launched at a range of 270 miles, the carrier will have moved 3 miles by the time the weapon hits, necessitating the use of smart weapons that can search a twenty-five-square-kilometer area. Iranian naval doctrine stresses the need to maintain secure communications between deployed forces and home command, suggesting that Iran will seek to overcome weaknesses in this field over the next ten years.[67] Even if Iran were to improve its striking ability, a U.S. carrier could sustain multiple hits from all but the largest specialized antishipping missiles (AShMs) or nuclear-armed missiles.[68]

For its three Russian-built 877EKM Kilo submarines, Iran clearly has offensive plans. These plans exist despite doubts over whether Iran can maintain communications with these vessels or use them to carry out "over-the-horizon" targeting of enemy naval forces. The very existence of the Kilos may compel U.S. naval forces to advance at a slower rate and operate at longer ranges from Iran, and indications suggest that Iran may be considering aggressive tactics, such as the use of "wake-homing" torpedoes (which follow ships) to attack adversaries' escort warships.[69] In pressuring the United States to deploy its naval forces away from the Iranian coast, the Islamic Republic's most potent capability remains operation of its three Kilos in the Indian Ocean.

According to Iranian naval doctrine, "The Navy must consider the Sea of Oman as its specific operational field for deployment of submarines in both offensive and defensive postures." To support these operations, Iranian doctrine calls for the development of port facilities and "special logistics craft to support the seabound naval units."[70] One port being developed to serve this role is Chah Bahar, where Iran's Kilos will likely have been transferred from Bandar Abbas well before 2015. Such a transfer would reduce U.S. ability to track and trap the craft in the Straits of Hormuz.[71] By increasing the length of submarine cruises—currently at around ten days per month—improving their reliability in the warm waters of the region, and utilizing technical assistance from both

Russia and India, Iran is extending the forty-five-day limit on the missions undertaken by these submarines.[72] Iran is also developing the ability to carry out covert replenishment of supplies at sea, using logistics and replenishment vessels produced at home. [73]

Deterrence by Punishment: Iran's 'Strategic Triad' in 2015

No matter how much Iran increases its defensive capabilities by 2015, Tehran will not rely entirely on conventional military force-on-force engagements to deter external aggression. The strategic triad described by Michael Eisenstadt will continue to allow for additional dimensions of deterrent capability, but could also be made to serve offensive ends.

Interdiction of oil exports through sea denial. In the Straits of Hormuz, Iranian interference against tanker traffic will not likely occur, except as a deterrent measure against an existing blockade on Iranian exports. As Iran learned during the Iran-Iraq War, interdiction of Gulf shipping is a double-edged sword. Even before the Islamic Revolution, the Iranian military had long recognized the strategic significance of the Gulf shipping lanes, particularly the Straits of Hormuz. When Oman—one custodian of the Straits—faced internal unrest during the 1970s, Imperial Iran sent a contingent of 18,000 troops to stabilize the country.[74] And the vital role of maritime export routes was driven home to the Islamic Republic in 1983 when Iraq initiated unrestricted attacks on Iranian shipping and oil platforms.[75] In response, Iranian president Ali Rafsanjani asserted, "We will block the Straits of Hormuz when we cannot export oil....Even if [the Iraqis] hit half of our oil, it will not be in our interest to block the Straits of Hormuz." A year later he reinforced this point: "We would close the Straits of Hormuz if the Gulf became unusable for us. And if the Persian Gulf became unusable for us, we would make the Persian Gulf unusable for others." Then, as now, Iran considered attacks on shipping—or "sea denial"—to be a weapon of last resort, only to be employed if its own oil exports were under attack. Against the background of rising tension between Iran and the international community, Iranian leaders have continued to threaten the closure of the straits.[76]

The experience of antishipping attacks in the Iran-Iraq War suggests that no combination of attacks by aircraft, missiles, mines, submarines, and naval special-warfare forces could close the Gulf to all shipping for a sustained period. As Michael Eisenstadt noted, only four of three hundred ships struck by enemy fire were sunk during that war, and traffic through the Straits did not thin appreciably.[77] Iran could, however, impose serious direct financial costs and loss of market share on GCC states, with important side consequences on global oil markets, as uncertainty and increased insurance premiums drive up the cost of crude oil deliveries. Over the next two decades, the Straits of Hormuz will contain even more targets than it does today, as daily maritime passages increase from 1,400 to 4,200 and the daily transit of oil rises from 15 million b/d to an estimated 30 to 45 million b/d.[78] GCC states have invested heavily in Gulf littoral processing plants and export terminals for oil and liquefied natural gas, and pipelines such as the East-West Crude Oil Pipeline boast neither the capacity nor the cost-effectiveness to serve as long-term alternatives to the Hormuz export route. If oil markets are tight to begin with, Iranian harassment of shipping could have a direct impact on oil prices for some months and induce a "fear factor" in prices for much longer.

In the Gulf, the IRIN and IRGC naval forces are diverging increasingly in their operational roles. IRIN is moving toward the long-term development of "blue water" capabilities that could give Iran "sea control" rather than just "sea denial" capabilities—that is, allow Iran to use regional waterways while denying access to its enemies. IRIN doctrine notes that "it is vitally important for the Iranian navy to maintain its supremacy in the Persian Gulf, and to extend its supremacy to the enemy shores and islands in the region." To support these aims, IRIN doctrine calls for improved escort capabilities, including naval air defenses and instruments for antisubmarine warfare,[79] and Iran has started to procure modern surface combatants to carry out these roles. In March 2003, Iran launched the Sina-1 frigate, followed by the Mowj—a 289-foot, 1,000-ton displacement destroyer—in September 2003. Two more destroyers of this class are being planned, each armed with sonar and other antisubmarine equipment, plus four air-defense missile launchers and close-in antimissile weapons.[80] These developments follow the pattern of Shah-era plans to create a blue-water navy that could escort vessels throughout the Indian Ocean and Red Sea, equipped with six U.S. Spruance-class destroyers and up to six attack submarines.

Meanwhile, IRGC naval forces, backed by IRIAF aircraft, are developing Iran's near-term sea-denial capabilities. In the face of modern AShM and other precision-guided munitions, IRIN's new major surface fighters are unlikely to remain combat-effective for long on a major military engagement over the next two decades. Iran's ability to interfere with maritime shipping will instead be drawn from more durable IRGC vessels, including classes that specialize in mine warfare, small fast-attack craft, and AShM operations. Iran has certain advantages in developing highly effective sea-denial capabilities. The Zagros

Mountains and the country's uneven coastline provide numerous sites for hiding AShM and coastal artillery, plus inlets from which to operate fast-attack craft. As Iranian naval doctrine notes, the geography of the Gulf—long, narrow, and shallow—forces targeted vessels into known areas and denies them much room to maneuver or hide.[81]

Also noted by the Iranian navy—and connected with the channeling of maritime traffic—is that the "capability to lay mines and also to sweep mines must occupy a special place in...operational doctrine."[82] A cost-effective way to obstruct maritime lanes, mine warfare causes major disruption and delay to military forces, and imposes untold costs and uncertainties on commercial traffic.[83] Not to mention that minesweeping is slow business. During Operation Desert Storm, when coalition military operations off the Kuwaiti coast were delayed by Iraqi mine warfare, sixteen minesweepers were required to clear just four mines per day, and sweepers located only a quarter of the mines laid.[84] U.S. military documents suggest that Iran would need to deploy 2,000 to 3,000 mines to constrain movement severely in the shipping channels of the Straits of Hormuz. At present, Iran can manufacture advanced (i.e., nonmetallic and remote-controlled) mines—both moored and bottom-influence—in very large numbers, meaning that it can block the shallow waters of the Straits and other areas of the Gulf.[85] To increase its control in the deepwater channels and parts of the Indian Ocean, Iran would need to develop an arsenal of rising mines, perhaps including rocket-propelled mines. But this should not present the Islamic Republic with an insurmountable technical challenge as its defense industries mature in the coming decade. The task could be made even easier if specimens could be procured from Russia or China and thereafter reverse-engineered.[86] Because Iran can deliver mines through a variety of means, such activities will be difficult to prevent completely. As well as delivery via helicopter, Iran has a small number of dedicated minelayers and can convert many different surface vessels, including innocuous-looking dhows, into minelayers. Iran can also deploy mines from miniature submarines, and mines or torpedoes from its Kilo-class submarines. When running silent and remaining stationary on a shallow bottom just outside the Straits of Hormuz, these battery-powered or diesel submarines would be "effectively immune to detection," representing a major threat to shipping as long as they can avoid detection and maintain operations while submerged.[87]

Iran could also interfere with Gulf shipping with its large fleet of small fast-attack craft—referred to as "swarm boats" in U.S. naval planning. Using its extensive experience in operating these craft—as well as its air-launched

AShMs—Iran can add flexibility to its AShM inventory.[88] Iran's arsenal already includes around two hundred fast-attack craft, including types that are produced locally. In using these craft to harass shipping, Iran would arm them "lightly"—with heavy machine guns and rocket-launchers—and position them on Iranian-controlled islands and maritime platforms, or from an extensive range of inlets along the Iranian coast. According to Iranian naval doctrine, such craft would "carry out hit-and-run operations and exploit the protective umbrella of the inlets."[89] IRGC naval special-warfare troops have experimented with many different types of light craft, including the military use of jet skis. Since the late 1990s, such craft have been used operationally against oil smugglers, leaving a number of oil tankers damaged from rocket-propelled grenade attacks.[90] IRGC naval forces also employ about fifty heavier fast-attack missile craft, which present a far more serious threat to commercial shipping than do light craft. Along with ten highly capable Chinese-supplied Houdong craft—the delivered portion of an order for forty suspended by the Chinese government[91]—plus a motley assortment of other missile craft, Iran received an unspecified number of Chinese-built C-14 high-speed catamarans in May 2002, each armed with eight C-701 AShMs, and then another unspecified number of North Korean missile craft in December 2002.[92] By 2015, Iran will likely be building and equipping locally produced fast-attack missile craft, allowing the Islamic Republic to interdict naval vessels using a potent and durable mix of smaller harassing craft and heavier vessels armed with AShMs.

The key to Iran's ability to seriously damage large commercial and military vessels in the Gulf lies in its sea-, air-, and land-launched AShM arsenal. This responsibility remains almost entirely under IRGC control,[93] and its capability in this area should increase in the coming decade. In AShM operations in the Gulf, Iran has certain advantages. A wide network of mobile hilltop radars, coast watchers, island and offshore platform observers, and so-called spy dhows would complement traditional intelligence-gathering capabilities to allow Iran to identify maritime targets inside the Gulf or near the Iranian coastline with relative ease.[94] If Iran were desperate enough to launch strikes on shipping in the Gulf, this would probably take place under blockade conditions and would include unrestricted attacks on all shipping. In such a scene, Iran would not require highly refined information for identifying targets or avoiding friendly fire.

Since their origins in the 1980s "tanker war" in the Gulf, Iran's AShM capabilities have already advanced considerably. Older land-based Chinese AShMs (HY-1 Seersuckers and HY-2 Silkworms) are being phased out of operation, as more modern Chinese missiles are incorporated into service, reverse engineered, and provided with upgraded guidance and extended ranges. Iran's C-801K and C-802 AShMs have allowed the Islamic Republic to field an advanced sea-skimming missile, with the latter of these types now in production in Iran and coined the Noor missile. In upgrading the Noor missile, Iran's defense industries are improving its guidance, along with its ability to be fired "over the horizon" and to identify targets once it reaches a predetermined point. Requiring relatively few support vehicles and capable of quickly issuing twelve salvos, these three missile types provide durable close-range AShM cover along the Iranian coastline and island chain. Iran is also producing a larger and more modern Silkworm, the 150-kilometer land-based Raad AShM, to give it long-range reach across the Gulf from the Iranian mainland. The more varied acquisition path and lower-profile testing required to develop cruise missile technology means that Iran could produce substantially upgraded Noor and Raad variants in short order. These dedicated antishipping weapons will be complemented by a range of aircraft-delivered laser-guided bombs and missiles, both of which Iran has used since the late 1970s and produces locally.[95] Both the Sattar 1 and 2 laser-guided munitions and the Zoobin and Qadr television-guided bombs are either rocket assisted or equipped with glide attachments, allowing them to be released at up to thirty kilometers from their targets, thereby improving the ability of Iranian aircraft to avoid air defenses and deliver their attacks against maneuvering targets, including ships.

Thanks to Iran's growing number of potential launch platforms for antishipping weapons, the country will be increasingly able to initiate attacks, with potential targets no longer able to skirt known AShM positions or assume that attacks are coming from a given direction. As in Operation Iraqi Freedom, when Iraqi AShMs fired throughout the war from positions on the small and heavily monitored al-Faw Peninsula, missiles based both on islands and the mainland remain difficult to locate. In addition, it is likely that not all of Iran's fixed HY-1, HY-2, and future Raad sites have been identified or distinguished from dummy sites. Because the C-801, C-802, and Noor land- and island-based batteries are mobile, they do not need to employ associated radars, making them very difficult to locate. With the same tactics used successfully by the Argentine forces in the Falkland Islands, Iran will likely move these missiles throughout island and coastal areas by helicopter. Presurveyed launch points connected to Iranian targeting radar by fiber-optic cable are likely to allow Iran's mobile AShM units to plug in to the targeting network, much as U.S. ground-launched cruise missiles (GLCMs) did during the Cold War or Iraqi air defenses did in the 1990s.

Already, Iranian AShMs have the ability to veer on launch, allowing them to be fired from behind escarpments. Future guidance systems will offer even more precise firing options, allowing for increased concealment of the platform. In addition to these land-based missiles, conventional Iranian tube and rocket artillery have ranges spanning across much of the Straits of Hormuz. More and more, Iran will mount AShMs on its growing fleet of fast-attack missile craft, which also can be difficult to track, and may locate others on coastal barges, large dhows, or other offshore platforms and islands. In developing air-launched versions of the C-801K and C-802/Noor, Iran poses a future multidirectional threat, boosting the range of its AShMs to up to 120 kilometers, and increasing the number of missiles it can launch at a given moment.

In developing its ability to interfere with enemy shipping, Iran will also focus on vessels in port. Iranian naval doctrine notes that the "numerous ports, oil terminals, industrial installations, and rich resources in the Persian Gulf area" make the Gulf "a specifically vulnerable target for special commando operations."[96] A particularly serious threat to ships is posed by combat swimmers and demolition teams of the IRGC naval commandos, deployed from small boats and minisubmarines. In addition to a number of older minisubs,[97] Iran received seven new Taedong-B/C from North Korea in 2002—capable of firing thirty-two-centimeter torpedoes—and began fielding Alsabeh-15 minisubs in September 2003, produced at home.[98] The combination of naval special operations and land-, air-, and sea-launched AShM capabilities threatens to multiply the number of "choke points" for shipping, placing Gulf harbors as well as the Straits of Hormuz under threat.[99] For Silkworm or Raad batteries, missile emplacements on Abu Musa face the GCC, putting Abu Dhabi, Dubai, and Doha within range.

Countervalue military capabilities. Alongside its sea-denial operations, Iran has developed capabilities that provide it with a flexible range of options to deter, or indeed compel, actions by foreign states. In the Iran-Iraq War, considerable military countervalue attacks were waged against strategic targets such as oil production and export facilities, and other industrial or military infrastructure. The so-called war of the cities saw months of surface-to-surface missile (SSM) attacks against Tehran, causing a major disruption of Iranian morale and prompting the Islamic Republic to assemble quickly a missile force capable of striking back at Baghdad. In the 1980s, Iran also developed the capability to foment subversion within other regional states and to sponsor terrorist acts on a global scale. Though Iran slowly reduced its attempts to export the revolution in the 1990s, the Islamic Republic still manipulates local communities in regional states, particularly Shiite populations, and employs terrorist proxies to threaten or wreak instability for any number of reasons.

In the coming decade, Iran is likely to augment its military countervalue strike capabilities in two ways. Using conventional explosive warheads, it will increase the reach and accuracy of its air and missile forces, allowing more effective targeting of critical military and civilian infrastructures throughout the Gulf. For use in more serious situations, Iran will continue to develop WMD munitions to provide new countervalue deterrent options. The parallel development of conventional and nonconventional strike options reflects Iran's increasingly sophisticated defense industries and the Islamic Republic's drive to develop full-spectrum deterrence against threats of differing levels.

For its long-range strike capabilities, Iran relies first on its missile delivery systems and second on a range of air-delivery systems. Though in 2015 Iran will still be flying Su-24 and F-4E strike aircraft, neither will necessarily be able to survive in the Gulf's hostile air-defense environment. As a result, Iran's range of missile systems will likely play the main role in future Iranian offensive strike operations, offering the Islamic Republic a relatively inexpensive capability that relies less on fixed-base infrastructure and is harder to intercept than other weapons delivered by air. In operational wartime use of surface-to-surface missiles (SSMs), Iran has a wealth of experience, including up to nine hundred launches during the Iran-Iraq War and action as recently as April 2001, when it fired sixty-six SSMs during an attack on bases of the Mujaheddin-e Khalq Organization in Iraq.[100] Iran also maintains an active test program, and can drill its missile forces in its expansive eastern exercise areas.

To date, analysis of Iran's missile programs has focused on the Shahab-3 missile, which was first tested in July 1998, when it successfully traveled 850 kilometers. Since then, Iran has tested the Shahab-3 on four more occasions, resulting in three successful flights, including one of about 1,000 kilometers. Though typically accorded a maximum range of 1,300 kilometers, the Shahab-3 is likely to provide the basis for longer-range versions, potentially including a true intercontinental missile that could strike the United States. Indeed, variants that can travel 2,000 kilometers have begun to emerge in Iran. As the expensive Shahab-3 will be deployed in small numbers and is believed to carry a warhead of up to 1,000 kilograms, which it can deliver within a circular error of probability (CEP) of 3 kilometers—meaning 50 percent of missiles launched will land within that radius—the missile is seen as a long-range delivery system. If the Shahab-3 can reliably reach targets within a range of

1,300 kilometers, Iran will be able to strike the capital cities of Israel, Turkey, and Pakistan, as well as each of the Arab Gulf states, complicating these nations' threat profiles. By 2015, Iran is likely to have a small and well-tested strategic arsenal of Shahab-3 weapons, and a number of longer-range variants under development.

For the Arab Gulf states, however, Iran's theater ballistic missiles (TBMs) and tactical rocket artillery—both of which Iran possesses in greater number than the long-range options—also pose a major threat. As its domestic defense industries have grown, Iran has demonstrated increasing ability in the fields of guidance, propulsion, aerodynamic reentry, and command/engine synchronization.[101] These advances have allowed Iran to begin producing several mobile ballistic missiles with ranges of 200 to 600 kilometers. The Mushak 200/Zelzal series, with a range of 200 kilometers, is already in production, and Iran can manufacture most of the components required to produce Scud-B variants (Shahab-1) and extended range Scud-C variants (Shahab-2), reaching 320 and 600 kilometers, respectively.[102] At most points, the Gulf measures 200 to 250 kilometers in width—nowhere exceeding the range of the Scud-B—and all the GCC states' key economic, military, and population targets are arranged along the coast, with the exception of Riyadh, located 600 kilometers away from the Iranian mainland. So, while more distant states could have to contend with limited Shahab-3 missile attacks, the Gulf states must now recognize the large arsenal of TBMs capable of striking their shores. In the coming decade, Iran will likely continue to increase the accuracy and range of its TBMs through global positioning system inertial navigation (GPS/IN) guidance and more efficient engine design, presenting a missile threat to the Gulf states that balances quantity with quality.[103] Having made extensive use of TBMs to target Iraqi cities and other sites both during and after the war, Iran could now use longer-range TBMs against the GCC states.[104]

In the coming decade, Iran is highly likely to add a new dimension to its missile threat by developing a cruise missile arsenal. During Operation Iraqi Freedom, Iraqi cruise missile attacks on Kuwait showed that these low- and slow-flying projectiles remain difficult to defend against. In a short matter of years, Iran will possess all the technical requirements to build cruise missiles, if it does not possess these requirements already. In using this technology, Iran could build on its existing UAV and reverse-engineered AShM projects, which have produced GPS-assisted flight management systems, data-linked in-flight targeting updates, and turbojet engines.[105] First, however, Iran might follow Iraq's example by converting old AShMs into crude land-attack cruise missiles. (A number of Iraqi HY-2 Seersucker missiles were converted into land-attack variants with a range of 150 to 180 kilometers.)[106] One strong possibility for a land-attack variant is the Raad program. According to many Western analysts, large salvos of sophisticated Iranian GPS-assisted cruise missiles armed with unitary explosive warheads or cluster-bomb-type submunitions represent Iran's most potent future threat to regional radar, airfields, and other fixed-location military installations.[107] Also pointing to the Islamic Republic's longer-term plans are the six KH-55 cruise missiles it purchased from Ukraine. With an optimal range of 2,975 kilometers, the KH-55—or, more likely, a reverse-engineered and upgraded domestic version—would give Iran a heavy cruise missile capable of delivering nuclear weapons weighing two hundred kilotons, or large biological, chemical, or conventional payloads with great accuracy over long ranges. Even accounting for some inefficiencies in payload design, KH-55 technology gives Iran a strong option for reaching into Israel, Pakistan, and throughout the Gulf. The missile is smaller than the Shahab series and simpler to launch. Most likely, Iran will develop the weapon type as a mobile ground-launched cruise missile—though such missiles are typically launched from the air—using solid-fuel booster stages.

In time, GPS-assisted cruise missiles will give Iran a true long-range precision-strike capability, but for most of the next decade, Iran's countervalue strike force will consist of TBMs and larger Shahab-3-type rockets. These weapons will likely continue to lack great precision; and even with GPS-assisted launches and other likely advances such as steering jets on warheads, they will have a CEP of 150 to 200 meters at best. Armed with conventional warheads, they will need to be fired in salvos and targeted at large installations or populated areas, as they were during the Iran-Iraq War. As in that war and subsequent Gulf wars, physical destructiveness may take a backseat to the strikes' political and terror-inducing effects, giving Iran a powerful countervalue capability against each of the Gulf states. The large number of TBMs likely to be available to Iran by 2015 will need to be countered with an extensive missile defense strategy. Even then, a considerable number of strikes, known as "leakers," would penetrate the various antimissile defenses.

To this threat must be added Iran's potential to produce and field WMD warheads on TBMs and cruise missiles. Aside from Jordan, Iran is unique in the region in having signed every major nonproliferation treaty. But having seen Iraq's initiation of WMD go virtually unpunished in the Iran-Iraq War, notes writer Peter Jones, the Islamic Republic, too, uses treaties for its own needs.[108] In 1987, Iranian president Ali Rafsanjani explained:

Chemical and biological weapons are a poor man's atomic bombs and can easily be produced. We should at least consider them for our defense. Although the use of such weapons is inhuman, the war taught us that international laws are only scraps of paper. With regard to chemical, bacteriological, and radiological weapons training, it was made very clear during the [Iran-Iraq] war that these weapons are very decisive. It was also made clear that the moral teachings of the world are not very effective when war reaches a serious stage and the world does not respect its own resolutions and closes its eyes to the violations and all the aggressions which are committed on the battlefield. We should fully equip ourselves both in the offensive and defensive use of chemical, bacteriological, and radiological weapons. From now on you should make use of the opportunity and perform this task.[109]

In November 2003, Iran was estimated by the U.S. Central Intelligence Agency (CIA) to be producing and stockpiling chemical weapons, including "blister, blood, choking, and probably nerve agents." Using equipment procured in the late 1990s, Iran was seen as capable of producing about 1,000 tons of agents per year. Though estimates concerning biological weapons are less confident, the U.S. government believes that, considering Iran's advanced laboratory and medical science capabilities—and factoring in an apparent effort at procurement of biological weaponry uncovered throughout the 1990s—Iran is probably already creating small supplies of biological agents for research and possibly to develop immunization stocks. Over the coming decade, these stocks could also be expanded, manufactured into dry-storable or aerosol forms, and converted to weapons with relative ease.[110]

By 2015, Iran will deploy a range of delivery options such as TBMs; UAVs and cruise missiles; helicopters and aircraft; and artillery and rocket systems. In the Iran-Iraq War, Iran used battlefield chemical weapons, and has since used them in land and naval simulations,[111] and reportedly deployed them to Abu Musa during a period of tension in 1994–1995. Though Iran's use of WMD in the naval environment could affect Gulf states, nonbattlefield uses of WMD—aimed at the Arabian Peninsula—represent the most serious threat faced by the GCC and its military allies. U.S. planners are broadly confident that, unless Iran's future were imperiled, the regime in Tehran would not use chemical and biological weapons (CBW).[112] And indicators suggest that even in this instance, the Iranian government would not gain national approval to use such weapons against civilian population centers.[113] Instead, in future A2AD operations, Iran could use or threaten to use CBW against regional military installations, causing potential damage to key military hubs.[114] Yet, even this scenario may be far-fetched, considering Iran does not appear to have used CBW during the Iran-Iraq War.[115] Furthermore, WMD use could be counterproductive for Iran. As Anthony Cordesman noted, "Iran's possession of these weapons provides only a marginal enhancement to Iran's conventional war-fighting capabilities, and any offensive use of chemical weapons would almost certainly do more to provoke retaliation than enhance Iran's war-fighting capabilities."[116]

As noted previously, Iran is also likely to develop a small nuclear arsenal by 2015, though for the sake of comparison, it may be smaller and less reliable than the stockpile held by the U.S. Army and Air Force in the late 1940s. It is uncertain whether Iran will have created devices small enough to use with longer-range ballistic or cruise missiles, or whether Iran will remain limited to delivering bulky nuclear devices through unconventional means—truck or ship—or via aerial platforms with lower resilience, such as strike aircraft. Iran will thus possess a relatively immature nuclear capability that—though still presenting the ultimate countervalue threat to Gulf states and the ultimate A2AD threat to the United States—will still be an uncertain instrument, potentially vulnerable to interception or technical malfunction. Under such circumstances, delivery of valuable and crude nuclear devices may be carried out by Iran's intelligence and security apparatus by ship or container.

Other countervalue capabilities. Alongside some of Iran's more large-scale conventional and unconventional military options, it could also threaten the Gulf states using its ability to manipulate regional proxies and sponsor terrorist activities. According to the U.S. State Department's Patterns of Global Terrorism report of 2005, Iran remains "the most active state sponsor of terrorism in the world." While this judgment mainly reflects Iran's very active involvement in sponsorship of terrorist groups that reject the Arab-Israeli peace process, the Islamic Republic maintains dormant but highly effective unorthodox capabilities in the Gulf. Such capabilities were first demonstrated during the Iran-Iraq War, when Iran manipulated Shiite communities in Bahrain, Kuwait, and Saudi Arabia in seeking to undermine or overthrow the northern GCC states. The networks and operating practices forged during this period came to some use in the 1990s, culminating in the development of Iranian-trained cells in the Bahraini Shiite community—cells eventually implicated in an attempted coup against the Bahraini monarch in 1996—plus the disruption of several Hajj festivals at Mecca.[117] Iranian agents appear to have been involved directly in the 1996 bombing of the Khobar Towers, in which nineteen U.S. military personnel died.[118] And Iran's intelligence and unconventional warfare institutions have established a presence in Iraq, where the pattern of financial and social-welfare provisions and agent recruitment appears to have begun alongside more aggressive transfer of improvised explosive device–making knowledge and materiel. Such developments have resulted in the death of a number of British troops and other international personnel.

Though Iran maintains all the resources necessary to undertake terrorist actions in the GCC states, such activities might not meet the approval of all national-level decisionmakers. With Israel alone representing a "consensus issue" when it comes to justifying terrorist strikes, similar actions in the Gulf states could result in a major escalation of regional tensions and increased international isolation for Iran. Such attacks would likely only be initiated if the Islamic Republic perceived a serious near-term threat to its interests. For masterminding terrorist activity, the key executive bodies are the Gulf Affairs section of the Intelligence Directorate of the IRGC and the Qods paramilitary wing, each of which maintains an active presence in Iranian embassies and front companies throughout the Gulf.[119] Less significant but still potent, the Ministry of Intelligence and National Security (known as VEVAK or MOIS) maintains a foreign intelligence directorate of two thousand personnel and is active in intelligence collecting and network building in Iraq, Saudi Arabia, and the remaining Gulf states. Both VEVAK and IRGC have considerable freedom of movement in the GCC—utilizing unregulated dhow and speedboat traffic or other means to enter the Gulf States, then either seeking cover among the 100,000 Iranians living in the GCC or operating under diplomatic cover[120]—and both are capable of cultivating individuals and communities to act as long-term local proxies.

This scenario is particularly true in the Shiite communities of the Gulf. While it would be disingenuous to suggest that Shiites in the GCC are disloyal to their countries, regional Shiites maintain transnational ties that make them amenable to cooperation with other groups. In particular, the Gulf's Shiite communities are often characterized by secretiveness and a level of self-organization that reduces the ability of domestic intelligence services to monitor their Iran-related activities. Through the establishment of informal community funding schemes, these communities can provide an easy conduit for funding from Iran, which VEVAK and IRGC are aggressive in providing.[121] Finally, clerics in the Shiite communities in the Gulf states have often studied in Iranian seminaries and may retain links to clerics now serving in the IRGC Gulf Affairs section, or else be subject to influence in some other form.[122]

None of this suggests, however, that Iran's covert agencies limit their work to sponsoring terrorism by Shiite proxies. IRGC intelligence and the Qods forces

Figure 7. Potential Conflict Scenarios with Iran

Scenario: Conflict between Iran and the United States or between Iran and the U.S.-backed GCC states	
Subscenario	**Iranian courses of action**
U.S. threat of invasion toward regime change	Use of all military means at its disposal to defend homeland, perhaps seeking to block the deployment of U.S. forces with either threatened or actual A2AD attacks, potentially striking any nation that supports the U.S. campaign.
Iranian response to a U.S. strike on Iran (punitive or counterproliferation)	Beginning of a persistent campaign of military and terrorist actions in the Gulf and beyond, striking any nation that supported the U.S. action.
Iranian response to imposition of U.S.-policed maritime sanctions	In retaliation, threats to blockade the Straits of Hormuz, or carry out more selective attacks on shipping from nations that support the U.S. policy.
Iranian response to U.S. searches of selected Iranian shipping	Attempts to escort its shipping within the Gulf and engage in tense naval skirmishes with U.S. forces.
Iranian response to a third-party action (e.g., reclamation of Abu Musa by UAE)	Threats to retaliate against a U.S. ally for a specified act. In the case of a UAE reclamation of Abu Musa, threats to attack UAE shipping and reinvade the island.

are both highly active in financing and training Sunni Arab Palestinian rejectionists, and have shown a strong capability to woo initially resistant allies in Fatah and other Sunni organizations. Such an approach to proxy warfare renders outdated an exclusive focus on subversion of the Shiite communities in the Gulf.[123] It also means that future Iranian tactical cooperation with al-Qaeda, its local affiliates, and other Sunni Salafist groups cannot be dismissed. Though senior al-Qaeda members have passed through Iran and communicated attack orders from within Iran, it remains to be seen whether their presence was sanctioned officially or even detected by Iran's security services.

Characterizing the Security Challenge Posed by Iran in the Coming Decade

After a decade broadly defined by economic pragmatism, Iran no longer has a default policy in the Gulf. Apparently it remains committed to a range of provocative positions on the pursuit of WMD, the use of shared economic zones, and the continued occupation of disputed islands in the Gulf. Though highly sensitive to its threat environment, Tehran has taken steps that will lead to growing international isolation and periodic international attempts to compel changes in its policy. Management of potential conflicts, therefore, represents the central challenge facing the United States and its Gulf allies in the tense period now emerging. With Iran's set of capabilities allowing it to engage adversaries at all levels, the Islamic Republic could potentially test U.S. willingness to deploy and sustain forces in the Gulf. The United States and its allies must now be ready, as CENTCOM theater strategy dictates, to deter Iran at all levels of conflict. This suggests a range of subscenarios that must be considered, the scope of which are represented in figure 7.

Across the range of potential conflict scenarios, Iran represents a formidable foe—perhaps more sophisticated than the Iraqi military at its peak. Among the commendable traits of the Iranian military are its adaptability and an instinct for the unorthodox aspects of warfare. In organizing around a revamped set of equipment and doctrines, this military will have strong capabilities in areas that affect the United States, such as antiaccess and area-denial forces, sea-denial capabilities, and the ability to take regional allies hostage using its strategic strike capabilities and sponsorship of terrorism.

Notes

1. Simon Henderson, *The New Pillar: Conservative Arab Gulf States and U.S. Strategy* (Washington, D.C.: Washington Institute, 2004).

2. Issam Salim Shanti, "Defense and Security Issues in the Gulf Region," in Abdulaziz Sager, ed., *Gulf in a Year, 2003* (Dubai: Gulf Research Center, 2004), p. 174.

3. Jon Marks, "Buoyant GCC Grapples with Dollar Black Spot," *Gulf States Newsletter* 28, no. 726 (2004), p. 15.

4. Michael Kraig, "Conference Report," *Middle East Policy* 11, no. 3 (2004).

5. Pillar, "20/20 Vision? The Middle East to 2020," *Middle East Quarterly* XI, no. 1 (2004).

6. Marks, "Buoyant GCC," p. 11.

7. Burrell, "Policies of the Arab Littoral States in the Persian Gulf Region," Abbas Amirie, ed., *The Persian Gulf and Indian Ocean in International Politics* (Tehran: Institute for International Political and Economic Studies, 1975).

8. For the definitive account of Iranian clashes with GCC forces, see Tom Cooper, *Iran-Iraq War in the Air, 1980–1988* (2003).

9. NWC, "Global 94: Volume III—Southwest Asia/Middle East Regional Estimate and Regional Action Plan" (Newport, RI: Naval War College, 1994), p. 25; CENTCOM, "Southwest Asia: Approaching the Millennium—Enduring Problems, Emerging Solutions" (paper presented at the Southwest Asia Symposium 96, Tampa, FL, May 14–15, 1996), p. 180.

10. M. H. Ansari, "Security in the Persian Gulf: The Evolution of a Concept," *Strategic Analysis* 23, no. 6 (1999).

11. Larry Velte and U.S. Navy Commander Jonathan Christian, interview by author, Washington, D.C., 2003.

12. Saideh Loftian, "A Regional Security System in the Persian Gulf," in Lawrence Potter and Gary Sick, eds., *Security in the Persian Gulf: Origins, Obstacles, and the Search for Consensus* (New York: Palgrave, 2002), p. 123.

13. Kori Schake and Judith Yaphe, *The Strategic Implications of a Nuclear-Armed Iran* (McNair Paper 64) (Washington, D.C.: Institute for National Security Studies, National Defense University, 2001), pp. 14, 18. Available online (www.isn.ethz.ch/pubs/ph/details.cfm?id=10548).

14. Hassan al-Alkim, "On the Persian Gulf Islands: An Arabian Perspective," in Lawrence Potter and Gary Sick, eds., *Security in the Persian Gulf: Origins, Obstacles, and the Search for Consensus* (New York: Palgrave, 2002).

15. Paul Melly, "Iran Delivers Warning to Qatar over North Gas Field," *Gulf States Newsletter* 28, *no. 727* (2004), p. 5.

16. This phrase was coined by Professor Anoush Ehteshami of Tehran University. See Mohammed Hossein Adeli, "Iran's Foreign Policy Future" (paper presented at the World Economic Forum, Davos, 2004), p. 1.

17. Adeli, "Iran's Foreign Policy Future," p. 1.

18. Amir Taheri, "Policies of Iran in the Persian Gulf Region," in Abbas Amirie, ed., *The Persian Gulf and Indian Ocean in International Politics* (Tehran: Institute for International Political and Economic Studies, 1975), p. 273.

19. Anthony Cordesman and Ahmed Hashim, *Iran: Dilemmas of Dual Containment* (Boulder, CO: Westview Press, 1997). See also Loftian, "A Regional Security System," p. 129; Peter Jones, "Iranian Security Policies at the Crossroads?" in Jamal al-Suwaidi, ed., *Emirates Occasional Papers* (Abu Dhabi: Emirates Center for Strategic Studies and Research, 2003), pp. 13–15.

20. Johannes Reissner, "Political Stability in Iran: Internal and External Threats to the Status Quo," in Johannes Reissner and Eugene Whitlock, eds., *Iran and Its Neigh-*

bors: Diverging Views on a Strategic Region, vol. 2 (Berlin, Deutsches Institut fur Internationale Politik and Sicherheit, 2004), p. 56.

21. Marc Gasiorowski, "Iran: Can the Islamic Republic Survive?" in Judith Yaphe, ed., *The Middle East in 2015: The Impacts of Regional Trends on U.S. Strategic Planning* (Washington, D.C.: National Defense University, 2002), p. 120.

22. Marks, "Buoyant GCC," p. 17.

23. Jones, "Iranian Security Policies," pp. 27–30.

24. Jones, "Iranian Security Policies," p. 27.

25. Michael Eisenstadt, "The Challenge of U.S. Preventative Military Action," in Henry Sokolski and Patrick Clawson, eds., *Checking Iran's Nuclear Ambitions* (Carlisle, PA: Strategic Studies Institute, 2004).

26. Henry Kissinger, *Nuclear Weapons and Foreign Policy* (New York: Harper and Brothers, 1957), p. 133.

27. See comments by General Binneford Peay in CENTCOM, "Southwest Asia" and NWC, "Global 94: Volume III—Southwest Asia/Middle East." In conversations with the author, Peay's successor, General Anthony Zinni, also expressed the view that Iran presents the most advanced military threat in the Gulf.

28. Riad Kahwaji, "Iran Is Ready for U.S. War, Says Defense Minister," *DefenseNews,* March 1, 2004, p. 16.

29. Anthony Cordesman, *Iran and the Future of Gulf Security* (Washington, D.C.: Center for Strategic and International Studies, 2004), p. 17; *Iran: Country Handbook* (Washington, D.C.: Department of Defense, 2004), pp. 125–127.

30. Iran suffered fifty-seven killed and one hundred injured, plus the loss of one frigate and a number of speedboats and static oil-rig outposts. Two Americans were killed when an AH-1J helicopter crashed while in action. See Cooper, *Iran-Iraq War,* pp. 267–273.

31. *Iran: Country Handbook,* p. 125.

32. Quoted in CENTCOM, "Southwest Asia," p. 54.

33. See Bruce Hardcastle's analysis of Iranian lessons from Desert Storm in CENT-COM, "Southwest Asia," p. 94. See also Andrew Krepinevich, Barry Watts, and Robert Work, *Meeting the Anti-Access and Area-Denial Challenge* (Washington, D.C.: Center for Strategic and Budgetary Assessments, 2003), pp. 7–8.

34. No Author, "Interview with General Manager of Iranian Aviation Industry," Foreign Broadcast Information Service, IAP20000501000095, 1997.

35. Kahwaji, "Iran Is Ready," p. 16.

36. Cordesman and Hashim, *Iran*. Tom Cooper, of the Air Combat Information Group, gave invaluable assistance in the development of this section.

37. Michael Knights, "Iran's Military Aerospace Industry" *Aerospace International* (November 2002).

38. See Cooper, *Iran-Iraq War,* for an account of Iran's use of armed UAVs in the Iraq-Iraq War.

39. Cordesman and Hashim, *Iran*, pp. 16–18.

40. Knights, "Iran's Military Aerospace Industry."

41. Tom Cooper, "IRIAF," Air Combat Information Group, March 16, 2004; available online (www.acig.org). See also Cooper, "Islamic Republic of Iran Armed Forces," Air Combat Information Group, December 6, 2003.

42. Schake and Yaphe, *The Strategic Implications of a Nuclear-Armed Iran*.

43. Rear Admiral Patrick M. Stillman, "Small Navies Do Have a Place in Network-Centric Warfare," Naval War College Review, March 2004. Available online (www.nwc.navy.mil/press/Review/2004/Winter/dr1-w04.htm).

44. *Iran: Country Handbook*, pp. 126–127.

45. Michael Knights, "Faced by Strategic Encirclement, Iran Develops Full Spectrum Deterrence," *Gulf States Newsletter,* April 16, 2004. Tom Cooper, of the Air Combat Information Group, gave invaluable assistance in the development of this section.

46. Ibid.

47. Iranian platforms are festooned with directional antennae.

48. Knights, "Faced by Strategic Encirclement, Iran Develops Full Spectrum Deterrence."

49. This is true even though 53 percent of Iran's operational aircraft and 60 percent of its stored aircraft have already flown for 25,000 hours; according to IAFAIO, many airframes will now fly for up to 40,000 hours.

50. As noted above, this possibility is quite feasible. Iranian F-14As were not exposed to the strains of carrier-based employment and have been upgraded extensively in midlife, including the installation of digital avionics. Also, large numbers of them (15 percent at any given time) are held in storage.

51. As Anthony Cordesman noted correctly, however, Iran will need to engage in more active squadron-level training exercises. See Cordesman, *Iran and the Future of Gulf Security*, p. 21.

52. Michael Knights, *Unfriendly Skies: The Development of GCC Air Forces* (Hastings: Cross-Border Information, 2002), p. 62.

53. Shmuel Gordon, *Dimensions of Quality: A New Approach to Net Assessment of Airpower* (Tel Aviv: Jaffee Center for Strategic Studies, 2003), p. 103. Gordon notes the strength of Iran's pilot and ground crew training, operational culture, and the ability of the IRIAF to maintain its sortie rates and preserve combat power in the face of enemy action.

54. It is quite conceivable that in 2015, Iran will continue to deploy a force centered on F-14As, F-4D/Es, and, to a lesser extent, MiG-29s. Upgrades to the durable U.S. fighters preferred by the IRIAF will ensure their continued service, while the newer—but less favored and less durable—MiG-29s will reach the end of their life span early in the next decade. Iran's indigenous fighter aircraft project—a twin-tailed, twin-engine fighter of Western extraction called the Sa'eqeh-80—is unlikely to have entered serial production by 2015.

55. Cooper, *Iran-Iraq War*, p. 287.

56. Tony Cullen and Christopher F. Foss, *Jane's Land-Based Air Defense 2000–2001*, 13th ed. (Old Coulsdon: Jane's Information Group, 2000), p. 133. Iran has reverse-engineered a range of Western, Chinese, and Russian SAMs, increasing their ranges and modernizing both guidance and ECCM.

57. Krepinevich, Watts, and Work, *Meeting the Anti-Access*, p. 22. See AW&ST, March 2001.

58. CENTCOM, *2001 Desert Promise Storybook*, pp. 6–15. Available online (www. globalsecurity.org/military/library/report/2001/DP_storybook.htm).

59. Cordesman and Hashim, *Iran*, pp. 127–134.

60. Michael Eisenstadt, *Iranian Military Power: Capabilities and Intentions* (Washington, D.C.: Washington Institute, 1996), p. 51.

61. Edward Atkeson, *A Military Assessment of the Middle East, 1991–1996* (Carlisle, PA: Strategic Studies Institute, U.S. Army War College, 1992), p. 70.

62. Ibid. See also Darius Bazargan, "Iran, Politics, the Military, and Gulf Security," *Middle East Review of International Affairs,* March 19, 2004. Available online (http://meria.idc.ac.il/journal/1997/issue3/jv1n3a4.html). As pointed out in Cordesman and Hashim—*Iran*, p. 128—Iran could perhaps gain a toehold in the rugged Musandam Peninsula on Oman's Gulf coastline.

63. Sean Foley, "What Wealth Cannot Buy: UAE Security at the Turn of the Twenty-first Century," In Barry Rubin, ed., *Crises in the Contemporary Persian Gulf* (London: Frank Cass, 2002), pp. 33, 42–43.

64. Chris Bowie, Robert Haffa, and Robert Mullins, *Future War: What Trends in America's Post–Cold War Military Conflicts Tell Us about Early Twenty-first Cen-*

tury Warfare (Washington, D.C.: Northrop Grumman Analysis Center, 2003), p. 2.

65. Chris Bowie, *The Anti-Access Threat and Theater Air Bases* (Washington, D.C.: Center for Strategic and Budgetary Assessments, 2002); Krepinevich, Watts, and Work, *Meeting the Anti-Access*; John Stillion and David T. Orletsky, *Airbase Vulnerability to Conventional Cruise Missile and Ballistic Missile Attacks: Technology, Scenarios and U.S. Air Force Responses* (Santa Monica, CA: RAND, 1999).

66. Brian Chow et al., *Air Force Operations in a Chemical or Biological Environment* (Santa Monica, CA: RAND, 1998); Gregory Giles, "The Islamic Republic of Iran and Nuclear, Biological, and Chemical Weapons," in Peter Lavoy, Scott Sagan, and James Wirtz, eds., *Planning the Unthinkable: How New Powers Will Use Nuclear, Biological, and Chemical Weapons* (Ithaca, NY: Cornell University Press, 2000).

67. Rear Admiral Ashkbus Daneh-Kar, "Operational Doctrine of the Navy of the Islamic Republic of Iran," *Saff*, no. 235 (1999), p. 3.

68. William O'Neil, "The Naval Services: Network-Centric Warfare," in Has Binnendijk, ed., *Transforming America's Military* (Washington, D.C.: National Defense University, 2002), pp. 136–138.

69. Norman Friedman, "New Technology and Medium Navies," RAN Maritime Studies Program, March 16, 2004. Available online (www.fas.org/man/dod-101/sys/ship/docs/working1.htm).

70. Daneh-Kar, "Operational Doctrine of the Navy of the Islamic Republic of Iran," p. 3.

71. *Iran: Country Handbook*, p. 157.

72. Russia is contracted to provide support until 2008 but still has not delivered $1.2 million worth of support services related to these vessels, or $1.5 million in construction services on six bases for the Kilos. By 2015, India will likely have replaced Russia as Iran's main naval partner. Iran has already authorized Indian use of ports such as Chah Bahar in the case of a major Indo-Pakistani war.

73. Cooper, *IRIAF*; Eisenstadt, *Iranian Military Power*.

74. Burrell, "Policies of the Arab Littoral States," p. 248.

75. Cooper, *Iran-Iraq War*; Anthony Cordesman and Abraham Wagner, *The Lessons of Modern War*, vol. 1, *The Iran-Iraq War* (Boulder, CO: Westview Press, 1990).

76. Jalil Roshandel, "On the Persian Gulf Islands: An Iranian Perspective," in Lawrence Potter and Gary Sick, eds., *Security in the Persian Gulf: Origins, Obstacles, and the Search for Consensus* (New York: Palgrave, 2002). For a description of the negative consequences of an oil blockade on Iran, see Hisham Nazer, "Energy Security in the Gulf," in Jamal al-Suwaidi, ed., *The Gulf: Future Security and British Policy* (Abu Dhabi: Emirates Center for Strategic Studies and Research, 2000), p. 47.

77. Eisenstadt, *Iranian Military Power*, pp. 49, 59. See also Geoffrey Kemp, "The Persian Gulf Remains the Strategic Prize," *Survival* 40, no. 4 (1998), p. 47.

78. Claire Rak, *The Future of the U.S. Navy in a Post-Saddam Persian Gulf* (Monterey, CA: Center for Contemporary Conflict, 2003), p. 1. See also Cordesman, *The U.S. Military and Evolving Challenges in the Middle East* (Washington, D.C.: Center for Strategic and International Studies, 2004, pp. 64–66).

79. Daneh-Kar, "Operational Doctrine of the Navy of the Islamic Republic of Iran," pp. 2, 5.

80. "Iranian Navy," Global Security, March 19, 2004 (available online at www.globalsecurity.org/military/world/iran/navy.htm); "Persian Gulf and the Middle East," March 16, 2004 (available online at www.hazegray.org/worldnav/).

81. Daneh-Kar, "Operational Doctrine of the Navy of the Islamic Republic of Iran," p. 2.

82. Ibid., p. 3.

83. Michael Eisenstadt noted that during the Iran-Iraq War, mining operations costing Iran an estimated $200,000 caused about $100 million in setbacks to international commerce.

84. *Iran: Country Handbook*, p. 161.

85 Ibid., p. 161. See also Eisenstadt, *Iranian Military Power*, p. 55. Iran's mine stocks included an estimated 4,200 floating contact mines, plus 200 bottom-influence mines.

86. "Iranian Navy." See also Friedman, "New Technology."

87. Friedman, "New Technology." U.S. naval officers involved with Gulf operations stress the serious threat of submarine warfare in the areas east of the Straits of Hormuz, near the Iranian towns of Larak and Jask. See the following interviews by the author: Velte and Christian; and Rear Admiral John Sigler, August 2003.

88. Cooper, *Islamic Republic of Iran*.

89. Daneh-Kar, "Operational Doctrine of the Navy of the Islamic Republic of Iran," p. 3.

90. Knights, interview with Source A75. See also "Iranian Navy."

91. Known locally as the Thondar fast-attack missile craft.

92. See Global Security's review on the Iranian Navy. Available online (www.globalsecurity.org/military/world/iran/navy.htm).

93. *Iran: Country Handbook*, p. 174.

94. Friedman, "New Technology."

95. Cooper, *Iran-Iraq War*.

96. Daneh-Kar, "Operational Doctrine of the Navy of the Islamic Republic of Iran," p. 3.

97. *Iran: Country Handbook*, p. 161.

98. Michael Knights, "Iranian Navies Mix Sea Control and Sea Denial Capabilities," *Gulf States Newsletter,* February 25, 2005.

99. Cordesman, *The U.S. Military*.

100. Cordesman and Wagner, *Lessons: The Iran-Iraq War*, p. 495.

101. Stillion and Orletsky, *Airbase Vulnerability*, p. 8.

102. Bowie, *The Anti-Access Threat*, p. 38.

103. Krepinevich, Watts, and Work, *Meeting the Anti-Access*, p. 28.

104. Cordesman and Wagner, *Lessons: The Iran-Iraq War*, p. 498.

105. Dennis Gormley, "Missile Defense Myopia: Lessons from the Iraq War," *Survival* 45, no. 4 (2003), p. 73.

106. Ibid., p. 62.

107. Bowie, *The Anti-Access Threat*; Stillion and Orletsky, *Airbase Vulnerability*.

108. Jones, "Iranian Security Policies at the Crossroads?" p. 25.

109. Schake and Yaphe, *The Strategic Implications of a Nuclear-Armed Iran*, p. 15.

110. Cordesman, *Iran and the Future of Gulf Security*, pp. 24–26.

111. Michael Knights, "Iranian Forces Focused on Deterrent Role, Exercises Provide Practice and Boost Morale," *Gulf States Newsletter,* November 14, 2001.

112. Each of the U.S. officers interviewed by the author believed that Iran would use CBW only if facing a serious or existential security threat.

113. Giles, "The Islamic Republic of Iran," p. 98.

114. CENTCOM briefings stress that even the existence of Iranian CBW requires certain precautions that degrade U.S. military effectiveness. See CENTCOM, "Southwest Asia," p. 117. A RAND study on the issue concluded that Iran would need to launch one CBW warhead per day onto a military airfield or similar target to force the United States to either abandon the facility or suffer degraded performance as a result of measures to protect or decontaminate the site. See Chow et al., *Air Force Operations*, p. 3.

115. See the article by Joost R. Hiltermann of ICG in MERIP; available online (www.merip.org/mero/mero011805.html). Also of interest is the work of Jean Pascal Zanders of SIPRI; available online (www.cns.miis.edu/pubs/programs/dc/briefs/030701.htm and http://projects.sipri.se/cbw/research/monterey2_iran_cw.pdf).

116. Cordesman, *Iran and the Future of Gulf Security*, p. 32.

117. Byman and Green, *Political Violence and Stability*, pp. 59–71. See also Cordesman, *Iran and the Future of Gulf Security*, pp. 31–32.

118. For an overview of the issue, see Matthew Levitt's testimony to the House Committee on International Relations. Available online (www.house.gov/international_relations/109/Lev021605.pdf).

119. Mahan Abedin, "The Iranian Intelligence Services and the War on Terror," *Terrorism Monitor* 2, no. 10 (2004), pp. 2–3.

120. Cordesman and Hashim, *Iran*, p. 138.

121 Recently Iran has shown an aggressive instinct by funding Palestinian terrorist groups previously funded by the Saudis. Iran is also reported to be providing major funding to gain influence inside Iraq. A good summary of these activities is given in Matthew Levitt, "Iranian State Sponsorship of Terror: Threatening U.S. Security, Global Stability, and Regional Peace," *PolicyWatch* no. 964 (Washington Institute for Near East Policy, February 16, 2005). Available online (www.washingtoninstitute.org/templateC05.php?CID=2263).

122. Byman and Green, *Political Violence and Stability*, p. 29.

123. Levitt, "Iranian State Sponsorship of Terror." I am indebted to Colonel Zohar Palti of the Israel Defense Forces for his insights on this issue.

PART II

Sharing the Burden of Gulf Security

3

The United States' Planned Contribution to Regional Stability

THE PREVIOUS SECTION developed a comprehensive threat assessment for the Gulf states in the coming decade. But U.S. theater strategy in the Gulf is not driven wholly by the nature of the threats facing U.S. and allied interests in the region. Rather, the development of U.S. theater strategy responds to global factors and decisions made by the U.S. Department of Defense. At the level of grand strategy, one of the factors driving reform by 2015 will be a drawdown in the military assets the United States is willing and able to deploy overseas. While U.S. Central Command (CENTCOM) will remain the main security guarantor in the region throughout the coming decade, the Gulf is not the only theater in which the U.S. military needs to be ready to intervene.

The 2002 and 2006 U.S. National Security Strategies (NSSs) provided top-level strategic guidance for U.S. planners, stressing the need to preempt, deter, and defeat threats to the U.S. homeland and interests on a global scale. The National Defense Strategy (NDS) terms of reference issued in January 2005 provided a strategic guide for military implementation of NSS requirements. The NDS terms of reference will in turn guide the development of the Pentagon's roadmap for the next four years, known as the 2005 Quadrennial Defense Review (QDR), as well as subsequent defense posture reviews. The NDS calls on the U.S. military to pursue four overarching objectives:

1. secure the United States from direct attack;

2. secure strategic access to resources and markets and retain global freedom of action;

3. strengthen alliances and partnerships; and

4. establish favorable security conditions.

Changing Force Design and Training

A constant theme in both previous and emerging QDR documents is the need to refocus U.S. military basing away from traditional "cantonment" areas in Europe and northeastern Asia and closer to the perceived "arc of instability" running from the Middle East to Central and Southeast Asia.[1] This change will end the so-called garrison era of the Cold War,[2] when massive U.S. bases in Europe and Asia developed into miniature American cities, and mark the beginning of the expeditionary era of "frontier forts rather than mini Americas."[3]

This does not mean that all large bases will disappear. Some large, permanently manned main operating bases (MOBs) will remain outside the United States, including permanently manned facilities in Manama, Bahrain, and Qatar (the al-Udeid air base), though the last of these will not accommodate "accompanied tours" in which U.S. servicemen are joined by their families. What will change is the number of smaller, less permanent bases. A large portfolio of forward operating sites (FOSs) will provide "warm bases." These well-maintained but lightly staffed facilities will serve as training hubs and equipment prepositioning sites through which forward deployed troops will rotate, reducing stress on local hosts. Finally, a wide range of cooperative security locations (CSLs) will be identified and surveyed as contingency access sites that may serve as "lily pads" (chains of bases) for deploying U.S. troops.[4] To reinforce the lighter overseas presence, the forward-deployed troops will have a greater ability to call on intelligence and strike assets based in the continental United States (CONUS). Afloat and ashore prepositioning will make it easier and faster to assemble air and ground forces in distant theaters.

This lighter model of permanent forward presence will see increasing numbers of personnel based in CONUS, driving force design toward larger numbers of deployable expeditionary units. To ensure greater availability of U.S. Navy and Marine Corps units, under their new Global Concept of Operations the maritime services will reorganize naval task forces to create more units, making it easier to deal with multiple problems at once with forces tailored to each. Though U.S. Navy shipbuilding will slow between 2006 and 2009, by the end of the current decade the navy aims to field eleven or twelve carrier strike groups, twelve expeditionary strike groups, nine strike/theater ballistic missile defense surface groups, and four naval special warfare groups (composed of submarine-deployed missiles and special forces).[5] This reorganization will increase the number of naval task forces from twenty-one to as many as thirty-seven. A new fleet-readiness plan will increase the availability of these task forces. [6]

The U.S. Air Force will continue to develop its Aerospace Expeditionary Force (AEF) concept, maintaining ten AEF divisions (each with 175 aircraft). Two will be deployed or alerted in CONUS during each 120-day period. During crisis periods, one AEF can be deployed within forty-eight hours and a total of five AEFs can be sent to a theater within fifteen days.

The U.S. Army, meanwhile, is also reorganizing and reequipping itself to create a larger number of medium-weight, air-portable, brigade-size units. Under the U.S. Army modularity initiative, the number of combat brigades in the active Army may increase from thirty-three to either forty-three or forty-eight. Figure 8 outlines the anticipated numbers of light, medium, and heavy brigades and battalions that would be available for global employment. Heavy units are based on mechanized infantry and armor units and are equipped with tanks and other armored vehicles. Medium units are equipped with the Army's new Stryker light-

Figure 8. Potential U.S. Army Reorganization

	Active Component	Reserve Component	Total Army
Brigades			
Current force	33	36	69
43-brigade force	43	34	77
48-brigade force	48	34	82
Battalions			
Current force	98	108	206
43-brigade force	92	70	162
48-brigade force	102	70	172
Companies			
Current force	297	327	624
43-brigade force	353	265	618
48-brigade force	393	265	658
Personnel			
Current force	170,000	170,000	340,000
43-brigade force	195,000	150,000	345,000
48-brigade force	215,000	150,000	365,000

Source: Congressional Budget Office.

armored vehicle. These are more easily deployed than heavy forces but more lethal than light forces, which are based on light-infantry, airborne, or air-assault units.

Special operations forces are likely to increase during this time frame, reflecting strong funding increases set to be phased in between 2004 and 2009. All U.S. ground forces are likely to receive increased training in "full-spectrum operations," ranging from high-intensity warfare to humanitarian support. Marine Corps Lieutenant General Martin Steele outlined the future concept:

We are convinced that the notion of a "three-block war"—that is, Marines feeding and nurturing hungry children one morning in a humanitarian assistance role, separating tribal factions at noon in peacekeeping operations, and fighting a mid-intensity conflict that same night, all within a three-block radius—requires us to think anew about the problem of operations other than war and to recognize that the old paradigms have indeed broken down.[7]

New Technologies

Alongside changes in force design and training, the U.S. military is integrating a range of new technologies associated with defense "transformation."[8] These include:

- advanced remote sensing;

- long-range precision strikes; and

- faster and longer-range maneuver, including the defeat of antiaccess and area denial (A2AD) threats and the deployment of expeditionary forces.[9]

According to Kent Carson of the Institute for Defense Analyses, U.S. forces are already employing next-generation concepts of operations alongside current-generation military technology, and by 2012 they will have shifted to next-generation technology as well.[10] In other words, we have begun to fight in a different and more advanced way, but will be fully enabled by advanced or "transformational" technologies only by 2012. Though the importance of individual weapons platforms and technologies can be overrated, it is important to note some of the advances that will occur between now and the next decade.

U.S. Army and Marine Corps ground forces are likely to fight smarter and lighter thanks to many small advances in land combat systems, particularly the more capable sixteen- to twenty-ton vehicles of the Future Combat Systems family, due to enter service from 2010 to 2032. The key advances, however, are likely to take place in air and naval warfare. U.S. land- and sea-based aviation will continue to improve its capability to establish air superiority and undertake precision-strike missions in three ways:

- the incremental improvement of munitions and sensors;

- the procurement of more unmanned aerial vehicles; and

- two important new combat platforms.

Beginning in 2006, the U.S. Air Force will deploy small numbers of the stealthy F/A-22 fighter, bolstering the aircraft's precision-strike capabilities during the 2008–2014 time frame. The F/A-22 is the centerpiece of a concept of operations called the Global Strike Task Force, and will allow the United States to seize air superiority and degrade enemy air defenses at a greater pace and at lower risk than ever before—a capability that U.S. planners colloquially refer to as "kicking down the door."[11]

Complementing the F/A-22, in 2008 the U.S. Navy and Marine Corps will field the F-35 joint strike fighter (JSF). The advanced air-to-air and air-to-ground capabilities of this aircraft will increase the ability of all U.S. carrier battle groups and marine amphibious ready groups (ARGs) to establish local air superiority and undertake precision-strike missions using only their own assets. Like increasing numbers of other U.S. aircraft, the F/A-22 and JSF will carry advanced electronically scanned array (AESA) radar, which will give them (and any other units they are networked with) a greatly improved ability to monitor and engage ground targets.[12]

Due to payload fractionation (the reduction in the weight and size of modern munitions), U.S. aircraft will pack increasing punch throughout the next decade. The precision-guided 250-pound Small Diameter Bomb will enter U.S. service between 2006 and 2009, vastly increasing the number of targets each aircraft can engage. Further reductions in munitions size (to 150-pound weapons) will occur early in the next decade.[13] In theory, existing payload fractionation already permits each U.S. carrier battle group to hit hundreds of targets per day (compared to dozens per day in 1991).[14]

Alongside the existing range of aircraft carriers, surface combatants, and submarines that will still represent the majority of U.S. naval forces in the coming decade, the U.S. Navy is introducing two important new platforms. The first and more significant is the littoral combat ship (LCS), a shallow-draft vessel designed to operate in the challenging littoral (coastal) combat environment. It will be charged with patrolling and intelligence-gathering in peacetime, and clearing the littoral zone of antiaccess threats (mines, enemy "swarm boats," and others) during conflicts. The first LCS will enter service in 2007, with eight or nine vessels expected to launch by 2009. A key feature of the LCS will be its ability to carry out mine countermeasures (MCMs) using unmanned underwater vehicles (UUVs) and to cooperate with advanced MH-60 helicopters made optimal for the littoral environment.[15]

Existing naval combatants and the very small numbers of new DDX-class Land Attack Destroyer will be ever more suited for a land-attack mission, adding greater precision-strike capabilities to future U.S. amphibious and littoral operations.[16] The Tactical Tomahawk missiles already fielded in 2004 will also strongly boost land-attack capabilities; these can loiter over the battlefield until directed to strike time-sensitive targets. Among other platforms, these missiles will be loaded on four Ohio-class cruise missile submarines, each of which theoretically will be able to launch its full load of 154 Tomahawks in just a few minutes. [17]

Network-Centric Warfare

The military value of these new technologies will be multiplied by a suite of new software packages being incorporated into U.S. forces under the rubric of network-centric warfare (NCW). Put simply, NCW fuses together data produced by sensors and human reporting to give forces a fuller picture of the situation around them. NCW could have profound effects in certain types of military operations, many of which are pertinent to Gulf scenarios.

For example, littoral environments such as the Gulf present a challenge because the movement of civilian and military vehicles, vessels, and aircraft creates clutter, and also because topographical and maritime features can confuse electronic sensors or interrupt their line of sight. The best way to counteract these effects is to link together many different types of sensors, looking from different angles at the same time, and thereby eliminate false signals and see around obstacles. NCW will also increase U.S. ability to monitor and target missile launchers, locate and strike small groups of enemy combatants (such as terrorists crossing borders), and track ships that may contain weapons of mass destruction (WMD) or terrorists.

The most high-profile use of NCW in the following decade will probably concern its contribution to missile defense, particularly in the relatively neglected field of theater anti–cruise missile defense. Though existing U.S. upward-looking radar systems and launch warning satellites have a good ability to detect ballistic missiles, the inability of low-level air defenses to detect or intercept Iraqi cruise missiles and unmanned aerial vehicles (UAVs) during Operation Iraqi Freedom has underlined a current weakness in U.S. defensive capabilities.[18] To rectify this shortfall, the U.S. military is developing increasing numbers of specialized "look-down" aerial sensors capable of observing low-and slow-flying inbound cruise missiles.[19] For most of the next ten years, this coverage will be provided by existing airborne platforms such as enhanced E-2C Hawkeye and E-8 joint surveillance and target attack radar system (JSTARS) aircraft, supplemented by look-down radars carried by joint land-attack cruise missile defense elevated netted sensor system (JLENS) aerostats and U.S. tactical aircraft. Other cover will be provided by ship-based Aegis and land-based Patriot Advanced Capability 3 (PAC-3) radar systems. U.S. Navy Cooperative Engagement Capacity systems provide a network through which to share a common operating picture. Around 2013, the first four E-10A Multi-Sensor Command and Control Aircraft will supplement these platforms and systems.

After one of these systems identifies a missile, a range of weapons could be deployed to shoot it down. During the ascent phase of ballistic missiles, U.S. Navy ships armed with enhanced Standard surface-to-air missiles would take the first shot. By 2010, U.S. Air Force airborne laser aircraft (if deployed to the theater and on-station near the launch) could attempt a second shot during the missile's vulnerable boost phase. Thereafter, the U.S. Army Terminal High-Altitude Area Defense (THAAD) missiles would attempt to intercept the missile during high-altitude descent, and the U.S. Army Patriot PAC-3 systems would make final attempts to intercept any "leakers" during low-altitude descent.[20] Cruise missiles would face the new U.S. Navy RIM-116 Rolling Airframe Missile and Rearchitectured NATO Sea Sparrow missile, or land-based PAC-3 and other air-defense systems.

CENTCOM Theater Strategy

Within this relatively firmly established global framework of basing concepts and force development, CENTCOM theater strategy can still be modified in a number of ways. After well over a decade of intensive deployment to the Gulf, the specifics of U.S. basing in the region (where to locate MOBs, FOSs, and CSLs) are largely set. More important is the division of labor between the United States and its regional allies, for which U.S. planners need to identify an ideal sustainable balance of effort. To what extent should various parties have specialized roles? How can the U.S.–Gulf Cooperation Council (GCC)

Figure 9. CENTCOM Gulf Theater Strategy

War-fighting	Protect, promote, and preserve U.S. interests in the Central Region, to include the free flow of energy resources, access to regional states, freedom of navigation, and maintenance of regional stability.
	Develop and maintain the forces and infrastructure needed to respond to the full spectrum of military operations.
	Deter conflict through demonstrated resolve in such efforts as forward presence, prepositioning, exercises, and confidence-building measures.
	Maintain command readiness to fight and win decisively at all levels of conflict.
	Protect the force by providing an appropriate level of security and safety.
Engagement	Maintain support and contribute to coalitions and other collective security efforts that support U.S. and mutual interests in the region.
	Promote and support responsible and capable regional militaries.
	Promote efforts in the region to counter threats from weapons of mass destruction (WMD), terrorism, information warfare, and drug trafficking.
	Establish and maintain close relationships with regional political and military leaders.
	Develop integrated regional engagement approaches through cooperation with counterparts in the interagency, other unified commands, and key nongovernmental and private volunteer organizations.
Development	Promote and support environmental and humanitarian efforts and provide prompt response to humanitarian and environmental crises.
	Educate key leaders and the American public on the mission of CENTCOM, the importance of the Central Region, and the contributions made by our friends in the region in supporting vital U.S. interests.
	Develop a positive command climate that encourages innovation, develops tomorrow's leaders, provides a high quality of life, promotes respect for others, and increases appreciation of regional cultures.
	Participate in concept and doctrine development, assessment of desired operational capabilities, and integration of validated capabilities.
	Maintain regional awareness of security, political, social, and economic trends.

Source: CENTCOM, *Shaping the Central Region for the 21st Century*, March 13, 2004.

security partnership serve U.S. strategic objectives in the Gulf? To serve these objectives, CENTCOM has designed a theater strategy that breaks down into three key areas: war-fighting, engagement, and development. A full summary of the strategy is given in figure 9.

Initially established as the Rapid Deployment Force in 1977, CENTCOM was formed to protect the Gulf, and though the Gulf region is now only one of the areas within CENTCOM's area of responsibility (AOR), representing nine of the twenty-seven countries it covers, the Gulf remains the chief focus of the command. Further, though other areas such as south Asia and the Horn of Africa demand increasing attention, key passages of the January 2005 NDS suggest that CENTCOM is likely to remain focused on Gulf security for the foreseeable future.

Ever since the Carter Doctrine came into effect in January 1980, the United States has been committed to a presence in the region.[21] The NDS envisions that, following an adjustment of global defense posture, the CENTCOM AOR will be one of four areas in which the United States maintains a permanent presence. In addition, the three central tasks the NDS sets for the U.S. military could have been written with Gulf security in mind:

1. countering Islamic extremism by reducing ideological support for terrorists and disrupting terrorist networks;

2. dealing with an emergent failed state armed with nuclear weapons; and

3. managing the conventional military power and disruptive capabilities of potential adversary states.

The key question facing U.S. force planners is not whether the U.S. will retain a presence in the Gulf, but what will be the precise mix of forward-deployed (or "in-place") forces stationed in the Gulf and deployable reinforcements (or "augmentation forces") stationed outside the region.

Benefits and Risks Associated with In-Place Forces

On the one hand, stationing U.S. military forces in the Gulf carries key benefits. At the most general level, some U.S. military presence in the Gulf states and the Gulf waterways has become standard, becoming a symbol of U.S. commitment to the region through its willingness to share the operational risks of maintaining a regional presence. Between crises, forward presence allows forces to train in local conditions with allies, which cements relations and builds interoperability and local defensive capabilities. Forward presence is necessary to undertake longstanding U.S. initiatives such as the Freedom of Navigation program as well as newer ones like the Proliferation Security Initiative (PSI), which provides for the interdiction of maritime traffic suspected of carrying WMD or illegal missile technology.[22] Forward basing supports the ability to develop early warning and to respond to contingencies on short notice, allowing the U.S. to undertake early shows of force and security assistance actions to deter or defend against local aggression or instability—what CENTCOM terms "flexible deterrent options."[23] As the NDS notes, "Prevention is a critical component of an active layered defense."

Offsetting these benefits, current models of forward presence also carry a range of risks. In general, the NDS suggests that three interrelated types of risk be considered when making any basing decision.

1. **Risks to current operational success:** those that threaten the successful execution of the current strategy at an acceptable cost.

2. **Risks to future operational freedom:** those that threaten U.S. capability to undertake similar missions in the future.

3. **Force-management risks:** those that threaten the recruitment, retention, training, and equipping of U.S. forces.

Risks to current operational success and future operational freedom. To begin with, U.S. military presence in the Gulf exposes U.S. forces to an increased risk of attack by terrorist groups. But the main risks to current operational success and future operational freedom in the Gulf region revolve around the effect of U.S. military presence on the stability and political climate of local states.

A 1996 CENTCOM report described the delicate issue of "balancing the requirements of deterrence against the dangers of intrusive presence,"[24] an issue that lies at the heart of a number of recent critical studies of forward presence in the Gulf.[25] In 2003, Deputy Secretary of Defense Paul Wolfowitz recognized the role that continued U.S. presence in the Gulf, and specifically in Saudi Arabia, played in the narratives of Islamist terrorists, stating, "I can't imagine anyone wanting to be there for another twelve years to continue recruiting terrorists."[26] Joe McMillan, meanwhile, observed that "a large and visible U.S. military presence has the effect of discouraging evolutionary change. Any perceived association with the United States weakens domestic support for existing governments and makes them less, not more, capable of creating openings for change."[27] Though it can be argued that even a small and remote military presence in the Gulf states may draw a reaction from Islamist groups, logic suggests that steps to reduce the overall size and visibility of U.S. forces in the region will reduce their political impact.[28] "Commitment without presence," as CENTCOM argues, is the ideal.[29] On this theme, Gregory Gause also noted: "What GCC leaders will likely want in 2015 is what they want today, contradictory though it is: an American presence that is virtually invisible but offers protection from serious external and internal threats."[30]

Force-management risks. A separate but equally serious range of force-management risks is posed by continued high levels of U.S. presence in the Gulf, which place extreme strain on the U.S. armed forces, contribute to personnel retention problems, and eat up spare parts and equipment.[31] After Operation Iraqi Freedom, the U.S. Air Force and Navy were quick to scale back their respective in-place forces from the Gulf at the end of the eleven-year Operation Southern Watch no-fly zone and the twelve-year Maritime Intercept Operation. The U.S. Army meanwhile suspended the Operation Desert Spring training of Kuwaiti forces as the occupation of Iraq began, entering into a period when 27 percent of the active component of U.S. military personnel and an unprecedented proportion of the deployable reserves have been stationed overseas. Even maintaining a force of 100,000 troops in Iraq will require roughly two-thirds of both the active and reserve components during this period. After the occupation of Iraq ends, U.S. ground forces will require the same type of strategic reset period that U.S. air and naval forces have undertaken since the end of the militarized containment of Iraq.[32]

In addition to imposing heavy strains on personnel morale, recruitment, and retention, sustained high levels of forward presence in the Gulf also generate acute financial strain due to the incremental operations and maintenance costs accrued by deployed forces. GCC states have provided important burden-sharing contributions over the past two decades, providing more than $36 billion of the $61 billion cost of Operation Desert Storm and absorbing an average of just more than 50 percent of the incremental costs of U.S. forward presence in the Gulf during the subsequent militarized containment of Iraq. Alongside direct financial contributions, in-kind contributions have typically included the provision of fuel, water, billeting, land use, and increased air-traffic costs.[33] Yet, even with these offsets, the added wear and tear of forward presence imposes costs that are typically paid for by slackened modernization (procurement plus research and design). Though defense spending currently remains on an upward trajectory, increasing federal deficits suggest that this will be difficult to sustain.

Risks Associated with Augmentation Forces

At the same time, a force posture that depends on regular and heavy reinforcement by augmentation forces from outside the region has different but still significant risks.

Force-management risk. In terms of force-management risk, military buildups in the Gulf from 1992 to 1998 are estimated to have cost $7 billion, ranging from $100 million in 1992 to $1.4 billion in 1998.[34] Saddam Hussein's repeated "cheat and retreat" tactics in the 1990s demonstrated the ease with which an adversary could draw the United States into expensive deployments to the region at very little cost to itself.

Risks to future operational freedom. A parallel set of risks concern the possibility that reinforcement—and, therefore, the ability to project power—may be disrupted by the withdrawal of host-nation support or the physical interdiction of waterways, ports, and airfields with antiaccess attacks. U.S. planners have recognized that there is no such thing as "assured access" in any of the Gulf states, a situation that is unlikely to change in the coming decade.

Withdrawal of host-nation support. RAND Corporation studies have highlighted the loss of host-nation support as a high-probability threat.[35] If the United States is involved in a conflict between states, for example, the aggressor state could coerce this veto by threatening to widen its attack to the territory of the hosting nation. Regional states might be particularly hesitant to offer crisis basing if Iran were armed with nuclear capability.

More frequently, however, host nations have denied or limited access because they believed U.S. military activity would not serve their national interests. The history of U.S. military operations in the Gulf since 1991 supports this assertion, though it is worth noting that a full "lockout" of regional basing only occurred once in the 1990s, when the United States was forced to use naval and air-launched cruise missile strikes to punish Saddam's incursion into Kurdistan in Operation Desert Strike in September 1996.[36] Other host-nation interventions have shaped and inconvenienced U.S. military operations only marginally. In Operation Desert Fox in December 1998, for instance, the United States was compelled to deploy extra forces because a large proportion of its forward-deployed forces in Saudi Arabia were neutralized by a Saudi veto on the use of combat aircraft from its soil.[37] Most recently, Turkey recast the operational plan of Operation Iraqi Freedom by voting against U.S. military access shortly before the war, while Saudi Arabia again placed some constraints on the profile and operations of U.S. forces in the kingdom.

Whether deployed to counter interstate aggression or to help stabilize an internal security situation, the deployment of U.S. forces to a Gulf state has the potential to bring domestic political pressure to bear on local rulers, and could trigger terrorist attacks against U.S. or local government institutions.[38] Political pressure is likely to be most acute when GCC states feel no immediate threat and receive no other inducement to provide basing access (as occurred in Operation Desert Strike).

Antiaccess attacks. This type of threat involves military strikes on facilities used to receive and host U.S. forces. Issued in 1999, a U.S. Defense Science Board study on military antiaccess threats concluded that most regional states could develop a respectable capability in this field by 2010, even given severe resource constraints.[39]

If Iran is the military opponent, the antiaccess threat in the Gulf is particularly acute. At the lowest and most focused end of the spectrum, the United States could face special forces attacks on air bases and other facilities. Iranian intelligence and security services have a demonstrated capability to attack specific targets using local proxies to deliver large-scale explosive devices.[40]

Other deep-strike assets (ballistic and cruise missiles) pose an additional threat to any facility that cannot be completely hardened against conventional explosives.[41] In February 1991, for instance, Iraq's relatively inaccurate Scud arsenal missed a major munitions storage area at the Saudi port of al-Jubayl by less than a thousand meters, narrowly failing to set off explosions that would have destroyed a large part of the port.[42]

The United States also needs to prepare for the threat of WMD. Aside from the development of deterrence and active antimissile defenses, the threat of WMD dictates that forces be dispersed and rotated through a larger number of bases, including, to a greater extent, bases at sea. It also puts a premium on passive defenses such as hardening and consequence management.[43]

There is a limit, however, to the viability of bases at sea. Though sea-basing concepts might appear to offer an alternative to vulnerable, fixed, land basing, access agreements with regional bases—referred to in one CENTCOM publication as "the coin of the realm"—are unlikely to lose their value.[44] Despite planned improvements to both afloat prepositioning and staging bases, U.S. Navy planners note that sea basing "relies on the basing support of overseas friends and allies."[45] Other analyses have highlighted the continued importance of the Fifth Fleet headquarters and facilities in Bahrain and a range of other primary, forward-based facilities and naval logistical hubs in each of the GCC states.[46]

Similarly, land-based airpower launched from Gulf airfields will remain a key component of U.S. military operations in the region. Despite the powerful showing of long-range bombers in recent conflicts, RAND's analysts calculate that a mix of short-range fighter and long-range bomber operations will remain the optimal profile for U.S. airpower, meaning that the United States must retain access to a range of air bases on the Arabian Peninsula.[47] In fact, authoritative studies have concluded that the United States will need air bases in the Gulf until 2012, preferably within 1,000 to 1,500 nautical miles (nm) of their targets, or even 500 to 1,000 nm if high-tempo operations are required.[48]

CENTCOM will need to develop carefully its portfolio of air bases in the smaller Gulf states in order to reduce its reliance on Saudi bases. But it will be quite difficult to replace Saudi air bases entirely, due to their numbers, dispersal across the large area of the kingdom, top-notch facilities, and ubiquitous hardened aircraft shelters (HASs). As low-profile U.S. operations from Saudi Arabian airfields showed in Operation Iraqi Freedom, the remoteness of many Saudi bases allows Riyadh to deny that they have been used by foreign forces. Bases in the smaller GCC states, with the possible exception of Oman, are neither as strategically dispersed nor as deniable. Iraq *could* offer sizable and remote basing opportunities, but a host of political and security issues may make it unwise to make U.S. strategy dependent on Iraqi basing options.[49]

In addition to the maintenance of agreements on access, prepositioning, military construction, and legal issues, this careful development must include better physical protection. All bases are under the threat of terrorist attack, and by 2015 every GCC base on the Gulf coast (including U.S. bases at al-Udeid in Qatar and Dhafra in the United Arab Emirates) will be well within the range of Iran's ballistic and cruise missiles. The United States should support the hardening of these air bases, including the creation of HASs for larger U.S. aircraft, hardened personnel shelters, and increased aircraft parking or "ramp" space to allow for greater dispersal. Though expensive (each HAS costs around $4 million), these measures will maintain the usability of U.S. hubs in the face of developing antiaccess threats.[50] To reduce adversary incentives for using chemical or biological weapons (CBW), CENTCOM should also focus efforts on developing a "CBW-protected posture" for its portfolio of bases, including additional "collective protection" (sealed facilities) and the ability to decontaminate key parts of U.S. facilities. As the U.S. Civil Reserve Airlift Fleet probably would not fly into CBW-contaminated air bases, the U.S. needs to develop a set of transfer bases where cargo can be delivered in-theater and moved to contaminated fields by military airlift.[51]

CENTCOM Capabilities under the New Force Posture

The above analysis suggests that during the coming decade, global and regional factors will drive the United States toward reducing the number of forward-deployed forces in the Gulf, putting a premium on the ability of in-place forces to offer a "better initial defense."[52] In fact, according to U.S. National Defense University analyses, forward-deployed CENTCOM forces in the Gulf are likely to be reduced by at least 50 to 60 percent. Between 7,500 and 10,000 personnel would be routinely deployed under the command of a permanent forward regional Joint Task Force headquarters at al-Udeid,[53] one of two MOBs in the theater (the other being the Fifth Fleet headquarters in Bahrain).

A reduced peacetime U.S. military presence in the Gulf is likely to be characterized by the phrase "enduring access, episodic employment."[54] This strategy relies heavily on the uncertain prospect of intercontinental reinforcement during major crises.[55]

The left-hand column of figure 10 (next page) gives an approximation of the likely U.S. force posture in the Gulf toward the end of the current decade, assuming a usual level of tension but no specific strategic warnings. The right-hand column gives an approximation of the alert forces that might be dispatched to bolster the forward-deployed forces, short of a major U.S. projection of military power.

Following the reduction of the overland invasion threat from Iraq, the presence of U.S. ground forces is likely to consist of battalion-size groups touring the region to undertake bilateral and multilateral exercise programs. Like ground-based U.S. Air Force units, these U.S. Army units "will move in and out of a variety of locations, even during a single rotation," with the intention of making "the U.S. presence ashore appear less permanent and complicat[ing] terrorist targeting."[56]

One or more Aerospace Expeditionary Wings will rotate through the Gulf states during each year, filling the gaps in airpower when an aircraft carrier battle group (CVBG) or an ARG or other naval surface action group (SAG) cannot be deployed to the region.[57] According to National Defense University stud-

Figure 10. Projected U.S. Force Posture in the Gulf

	Notional in-place combat forces	Notional augmentation forces if access is available
Ground forces	• One battalion of U.S. Army or Marine troops on rotational exercises, potentially with access to heavy U.S. prepositioned armored vehicles in Kuwait and Qatar • Elements of a U.S. Special Forces Group training or exercising with local forces across the Gulf • One or more batteries of PAC-3 Patriot missile air-defense systems	• Special or light forces capable of seizing key infrastructure or access points within 72 hours • One brigade of infantry in 96 hours, either falling in on prepositioned heavy armored vehicles or mounted in air-deployed light armored vehicles • Two further brigades of infantry, plus divisional artillery and engineers, within 120 hours, mounted in air-deployed light-armored vehicles • Additional PAC-3 batteries, which could be added via air bridge
Naval forces	• A squadron of one to three LCSs • Up to 75 percent of the time, one other U.S. naval unit will be present; either a carrier battle group, an expeditionary strike group (ESG), or a U.S. Marine Corps ARG • One or more land-based Maritime Patrol Aircraft based in-theater or at Diego Garcia	• One further carrier battle group, ESG, or ARG, which could probably deploy to the theater within a week
Air forces	• At least 25 percent of the time ("gapping" the period when no naval aviation is in-theater), there will be a deployed Aerospace Expeditionary Wing (AEW) of around sixty aircraft • Small number of specialized "high-value, low-density" assets such as tankers, intelligence-gathering aircraft, or unmanned aerial vehicles (UAVs)	• One AEW capable of deploying within 48 hours • A number of AEW and specialized "high-value, low-density" or airlift assets, which could notionally fall in on regional air bases within 96 hours
C⁴ISR assets	• MOB headquarters in Qatar and Bahrain, maintaining local common operating picture • Strong "reach-back" capability to CONUS-based intelligence architecture	• Latent prepositioned C⁴ISR capability at MOB, fully manned

ies, compared to the past decade, when the United States kept a carrier permanently stationed in the Gulf (known as 1.0 carrier coverage), future carrier coverage may be reduced to 0.75 or even 0.5.[58] The U.S. Navy will probably deploy eleven or twelve carriers at the end of this decade, with six or seven earmarked for operations in other parts of the world. Historically, keeping a carrier in the Gulf at all times has required the United States to dedicate eight carriers to the task each year; the future shortfall of a carrier is likely to be made up with both visiting U.S. Air Force wings and combinations of other naval forces.[59] For typical maritime patrolling, the U.S. Navy will keep a group of LCSs in the Gulf, backed up by periodic cruises by CVBGs or expeditionary strike groups (ESGs).[60] The Navy's Global Concept of Operations should ensure that reinforcements can reach the Gulf faster than in the past.

In the case of an interstate aggressor, it is fairly clear that given sufficient warning and access to local bases, a bolstered U.S. force in the Gulf would prevail over its adversary. But what about other scenarios? Couldn't Iran mimic Saddam's successful use of repeated, low-level provocations? These "cheat and retreat" tactics were simple but effective: the United States would be drawn into expending political capital at the UN Security Council and carrying out costly military deployments to the Gulf, and each time Saddam would back down shortly before the United States resorted to the use of force. Or might Iran be able to engineer an effective antiaccess "shutout," drawing on Gulf states' reluctance to confront Iran, and trading on their fear of Tehran's conventional (and nuclear) capabilities?

First, one might ask, what would reducing local forces do the U.S. military's ability to "deter forward" without recourse to heavy reinforcement? Could the likely mix of forces rotating through the Gulf maintain basic deterrence against the Iranian interstate threat, particularly if those forces faced an Islamic Republic maneuvering beneath the umbrella of a nascent nuclear capability? Second, putting aside the interstate threat, at the end of this decade, how able will military forces in the Gulf be to assist GCC stabilization and interdiction efforts against internal and transnational threats? Third, what effect will changing the U.S. force presence have on the provision of security assistance (training programs, for instance) to local allies?

Testing the Planned U.S. Force Posture against Regional Scenarios

In the preceding chapters on threat assessment, a family of four main Gulf security scenarios were developed:

1. Urban and rural counterterrorist operations

2. Stabilization and key-point defense to prevent major disorder or state failure

3. Maritime patrol and interdiction

4. Interstate deterrence against Iran during a period increased military tension

This section examines how the CENTCOM force posture to be in place at the end of this decade would handle each of the scenarios. Each subsection will evaluate the ability of the future U.S. force structure to provide flexible engagement options to the CENTCOM commander.

Support to urban and rural counterterrorism operations. Historically, counterterrorism operations have not been a strong focus of CENTCOM military flexible-engagement options. But such missions have been given greater precedence in the U.S. National Defense Strategy of 2005, which outlines the disruption of terrorist networks as a key operational task.

As will be highlighted in chapter 4, the GCC states are particularly sensitive about the use of foreign combat forces for their internal security. Any U.S. military involvement in counterterrorism operations in the GCC states would therefore represent a highly sensitive and risky proposition for those states' leaders, placing a premium on covert or low-profile modes of assistance that occur principally in remote rural or border locations. Even then, GCC governments are unlikely to allow U.S. Special Forces to operate as discrete units (as they have in contingencies in Afghanistan, on the Afghan-Pakistani border, in the Philippines, and in the trans-Sahara), despite their undoubted utility in attacking rural terrorist redoubts. Operations in these remote areas could perhaps be undertaken in partnership with local security forces, with the U.S. providing capabilities such as imagery- and signals-intelligence collection. (An appropriate model for this form of highly sensitive and covert operation is the role of U.S. signals intelligence and special operations forces in the killing of Columbian drug baron Pablo Escobar.[61])

In rare instances, the United States could also provide airborne precision-strike capabilities. The November 2001 operation that led to the death of four al-Qaeda operatives in Yemen presents a plausible scenario for U.S. military involvement in the Gulf in the coming decade, although future operations would need to be handled far more discreetly than that in Yemen.

The basing posture outlined above would leave CENTCOM adequately manned to provide these kinds of niche support to GCC allies. Even so, due to the potentially long duration and constant availability required in counterterrorism missions—as well as the impossibility of using U.S. assets in high-visibility urban operations—it would be preferable if local forces developed highly responsive intervention forces of their own and the strongest possible capabilities in the field of wide-area surveillance (satellite geodesy, unmanned and manned airborne reconnaissance, plus attended or unattended ground sensors).

Stabilization and key-point defense to prevent major disorder or state failure. Stabilization operations are another area in which GCC states are extremely sensitive, meaning that local forces must undertake such missions in normal circumstances. Nevertheless, the U.S. National Defense Strategy does anticipate that the United States may have to undertake the manpower-intensive stabilization of an important failing state.

As discussed in chapter 1, Saudi Arabia risks failing in the coming decade if it does not reverse current negative trends in its domestic situation. Considering the kingdom's influence on world oil markets, the United States could not allow an extended period of instability to occur there. To a lesser extent, this is also true of Kuwait and Bahrain, which risk becoming weaker states and could face serious internal instability in the next ten years as a result of internal factionalism and the rise of political Islam. The United States might also be required to prop up an Iraqi government once again in the future. (Though beyond the purview of this study, the United States could be called upon to intervene to support President Ali Abdullah Saleh's government in Yemen were a sufficiently strong coalition of tribal interests to launch a coup against him.) Finally, as the NDS suggests, at some point, the U.S. military may be required to perform stability operations in a failed state that possesses WMD.

As postwar military operations in Iraq have shown, securing key facilities and stabilizing a failing state is a major undertaking made doubly difficult if prompt and prescient action is not taken at its earliest stages. This means that U.S. planners need to be thinking about how to detect and prevent, or—if prevention is impossible—mitigate and reverse the onset of serious disorder or state failure in Gulf states.

Before a crisis occurs, the United States can greatly reduce the potential challenge of stabilization operations by maintaining strong links with local military officers through International Military Education and Training (IMET) and other security cooperation programs, such as the U.S. State Department's

Antiterrorism Assistance (ATA) training program. Among other benefits, such programs help local militaries develop crisis management capabilities and plan courses of action that stress nonviolent or nonlethal force.

If a crisis does occur, a history of cooperative programs may help U.S. officers gain the cooperation of local allies and establish appropriate roles for U.S. and local forces in stabilizing the affected country. Military-to-military cooperation will also help establish compatibility in equipment, training, and language, enabling emergency security assistance to flow more smoothly in a crisis. Without such connections, a host nation may be less likely to help U.S. forces gain access to a failing state at an early stage. This would be a critical impediment, because in the event of serious state failure in the Gulf, the United States might need to make covert use of remote air bases to provide logistical, intelligence, and combat support to government forces, or to undertake humanitarian and noncombatant evacuation operations (NEOs).

CENTCOM currently ranks Iran, Iraq, and Yemen as the Gulf nations in which support and stabilization operations (SASOs) and NEOs are most likely to be required. Qatar and Saudi Arabia are considered the GCC states most likely to require intervention; Bahrain, Kuwait, Oman, and the United Arab Emirates (UAE) are ranked less likely.[62] Under certain extreme circumstances, the United States might be required to secure key oil and military infrastructure support on behalf of an ailing sovereign government. This would require advanced planning and intelligence preparation, but although a sensitive task, it would be fully justified by the U.S. national security interests at stake, particularly in the case of a loss of central government control in Saudi Arabia.

Maritime patrolling and interdiction in the Gulf. Throughout the coming decade, the United States is likely to lead regional and international partners in maintaining maritime patrols and interdiction activities in the Gulf. Regular naval patrolling reassures allies and maintains freedom of navigation in international waters.

It also has an increasingly important role to play in the Global War on Terror. Since September 11, the United States has taken part in naval monitoring and interdiction missions in the Horn of Africa, the Indian Ocean, and the North Arabian Sea and the Gulf. While focused on the potential movement of terrorist personnel, weapons, and funds, such patrols also uncover local criminal activities that may be related to terrorism, including illegal immigration and the smuggling of weapons, drugs, and other contraband for profit. Maritime monitoring and interdiction also improves port and littoral security, a matter of prime concern for the United States, its allies in the Gulf, and the broader international community following suicide boat attacks in Yemen in October 2000, against the French-flagged tanker *Limburg* in October 2002, and the three-boat attack against the Mina al-Bakr oil terminal in Iraq in April 2004.

The United States is also likely to undertake interdiction operations under the Proliferation Security Initiative (PSI), targeting ships believed to be carrying material related to WMD, and to assist in the development of cargo-monitoring initiatives at ports exploited by proliferators.

By the end of the present decade, the U.S. Navy will deploy thirty-three surface warfare groups, including twelve carrier strike groups, twelve expeditionary strike groups, and nine strike/theater ballistic missile defense surface groups. Patrolling and interdiction activities in the Gulf will require the annual assignment of up to eight of these. While these forces are capable of long-term, persistent maritime patrolling, the U.S. Navy would lose some flexibility by undertaking a new and long-term commitment of this kind. A more workable solution is the continued maintenance of a U.S.-led multinational flotilla in the Gulf built around a smaller number of rotating U.S. assets. At present, this flotilla (Task Force 150) includes international rather than GCC force contributions, but an obvious case can be made for the close integration of regional navies into the Gulf interdiction flotilla, not least because of the ancillary benefits to national security and law enforcement in the states of the Gulf coast. The involvement of regional force contributors could also relieve strain on certain overworked elements of the U.S. military: rare, high-value assets such as naval special operations troops and maritime patrol and other ISR aircraft.

Managing conflict following an increase in tensions with Iran. The United States needs to maintain a full spectrum of policy choices—political, economic, and military—if it is to guide or even react effectively to events in Iran. As chapter 2 indicated, Iran, particularly a nuclear Iran, will develop a range of measures aimed at deterring the United States from applying pressure through military or economic sanctions. At the same time, the U.S. will perhaps seek to attain the opposite effect: that of ratcheting up pressure on the Tehran government to prevent it from acquiring or declaring its nuclear arsenal, or from acting more assertively if it develops more advanced conventional and unconventional military capabilities. Building on figure 7 in chapter 2, figure 11 (next page) recalls the range of subscenarios in which the U.S. military could be called upon to deter or defend against Iranian military action in the Gulf.

Figure 11. Potential U.S. Response to Iranian Conflict Scenarios

Scenario: Conflict between Iran and the United States or between Iran and the U.S.-backed GCC states		
Subscenario	Iranian courses of action	U.S. counterresponse
U.S. threat of invasion toward regime change	Use of all military means at its disposal to defend homeland, perhaps seeking to block the deployment of U.S. forces with either threatened or actual A2AD attacks, potentially striking any nation that supports the U.S. campaign.	Develop the credible threat that U.S. forces could defeat the Iranian armed forces and occupy part or all of the country while shielding local allies
Iranian response to a U.S. strike on Iran (punitive or counter-proliferation)	Beginning of a persistent campaign of military and terrorist actions in the Gulf and beyond, striking any nation that supported the U.S. action.	Deter Iranian retaliation on U.S. or allied assets following a U.S. military strike on Iran
Iranian response to imposition of U.S.-policed maritime sanctions	In retaliation, threats to blockade the Straits of Hormuz, or carry out more selective attacks on shipping from nations that support the U.S. policy.	Maintain sea control (i.e., uphold sanctions while demonstrating the ability to defeat Iranian capability to close the Straits)
Iranian response to U.S. searches of selected Iranian shipping	Attempts to escort its shipping within the Gulf and engage in tense naval skirmishes with U.S. forces.	Maintain policy of selective naval interdiction while deterring further Iranian escalation
Iranian response to a third-party action (e.g., reclamation of Abu Musa by UAE)	Threats to retaliate against a U.S. ally for a specified act. In the case of a UAE reclamation of Abu Musa, threats to attack UAE shipping and reinvade the island.	Deter and be prepared to defend against Iranian actions versus U.S. ally

Though the U.S. military could clearly overpower its Iranian counterpart, (particularly in the right-hand four predominantly aerial and naval scenarios), this range of subscenarios suggests that a period of increased tension with Iran would be a distinctly uncomfortable experience for the U.S. military. First, it would not necessarily be a short or discrete crisis, but could instead be drawn out by Iran into a sprawling, long-term confrontation. This would carry costs as great for the U.S. military or even greater than the long military containment of Iraq, in terms of the strain on both U.S. armed forces (particularly on rare assets) and local host nations. Second, Iran would likely broaden the conflict so that local allies of the United States would find their security and prosperity at risk over this prolonged period. As a military clash with Iran means a serious and potentially drawn-out conflict, the risk of accidental clashes with Iran needs to be reduced where possible. The United States must develop improved confidence- and security-building arrangements with its allies.

If a conflict develops, the United States and its regional allies must be able to display the same "full-spectrum deterrence" that Iran is seeking to develop. This means the United States must maintain both a credible extended nuclear deterrence and a commitment to forward-deployed conventional military forces (to challenge Iranian actions that do not cross the nuclear threshold). In the latter sphere, the United States needs regional allies with reliable combat forces and rare assets such as ISR collection facilities and platforms, tankers, and vessels to conduct maritime patrols and mine countermeasures. The emerging U.S. military posture is too reliant on power projection, which could prove an uncertain prospect in the face of future shortages of long-range heavy transport aircraft or enemy A2AD activities. Equally important, the United States and GCC need deterrent power to prevent Iran from employing the "cheat-and-retreat" tactics used by Saddam. Instead, GCC forces need to provide the first line of defense, and function as a forward-deployed "trip wire" that can hold the line until U.S. reinforcements arrive.

The United States also has a strong interest in helping regional allies prepare for future conflict and invest in homeland security capabilities including civil-defense plans, hardened facilities, secure ports, escorted shipping, and meaningful air and missile defenses. These capabilities would force Iran to modify its strategic intentions by making attacks on GCC states more costly and less likely to succeed. That, in turn, would make it easier for the United States to shield allies from Iranian coercion or retaliation. Such steps could also influence the conditions under which Iran might conceive of using WMD (e.g., as a deterrent of last resort rather than a coercive tool).

In particular, the U.S. military will continue to focus on the development of shared early-warning and missile-defense systems, the hardening and dispersal of U.S. and allied military assets, and the development of GCC crisis-management and consequence-management capabilities. This raft of measures, gathered under the existing Cooperative Defense Initiative (CDI), could reduce Iran's ability to threaten its neighbors with nuclear weapons, particularly since in the early stages of its WMD program Iran is likely to have few weapons and immature delivery capabilities. Deterrence, layered defense, and the diffusion of targets together can make the threat or actual use of WMD less attractive to Iran and less credible to its neighbors.

Notes

1. Kurt Campbell and Celeste Johnston Ward, "New Battle Stations?" *Foreign Affairs* 82, no. 5 (September/October 2003), pp. 96–100.

2. Andrew Krepinevich, Barry Watts, and Robert Work, *Meeting the Anti-Access and Area-Denial Challenge* (Washington, D.C.: Center for Strategic and Budgetary Assessments), p. 7.

3. Thomas Donnelly and Vance Serchuk, *Toward a Global Cavalry: Overseas Rebasing and Defense Transformation* (Washington, D.C.: American Enterprise Institute, 2003). Available online (www.aei.org/include/pub_print.asp?pubID=17783).

4. Ibid.

5. Admiral Vern Clark, "Sea Power 21 Series, Part I—Projecting Decisive Joint Capabilities" (presented as part of the *Naval Institute Proceedings,* 2002), p. 2.

6. Vice Admiral Mike Mullen, "Sea Power 21 Series, Part VI—Global Concept of Operations" (presented as part of the *Naval Institute Proceedings,* 2003), p. 1.

7. Lieutenant General Martin R. Steele, *Deep Coalitions and Interagency Task Forces* (Newport, RI: Naval War College, 1999), p. 1.

8. U.S. Congressional Research Service analyst Ron O'Rourke described transformation as "large-scale, discontinuous, and possibly disruptive changes in military weapons, organization, and concepts of operations that are prompted by significant changes in technology or the emergence of new and different international security challenges."

9. Department of Defense, *Quadrennial Defense Review 2001* (Washington, D.C.: U.S. Government, 2001), p. 22.

10. Kent Carson, interview by author, Washington, D.C., July 2003.

11. Krepinevich, Watts, and Work, *Meeting the Anti-Access*, p. 22.

12. Vice Admiral Cutler Dawson and Vice Admiral John Nathman, "Sea Power 21 Series, Part III—Sea Strike: Projecting Persistent, Responsive, and Precise Power" (presented as part of the *Naval Institute Proceedings,* 2002), p. 1.

13. William Schneider, interview by author, 2003.

14. Dawson and Nathman, "Sea Power 21 Series, Part III," p. 1.

15. Ronald O'Rourke, "Navy Littoral Combat Ship (LCS): Background and Issues for Congress" (Washington, D.C.: Congressional Research Service, 2004), p. 5.

16. Ronald O'Rourke, "Navy DD(X) Destroyer Program: Background and Issues for Congress" (Washington, D.C.: Congressional Research Service, 2004), pp. 1, 5.

17. Dawson and Nathman, "Sea Power 21 Series, Part III," p. 1.

18. Gormley, "Missile Defense Myopia: Lessons from the Iraq War," *Survival* 45, no. 4 (2003), pp. 61–85.

19. John Stillion and David T. Orletsky, *Airbase Vulnerability to Conventional Cruise Missile and Ballistic Missile Attacks: Technology, Scenarios and U.S. Air Force Responses* (Santa Monica, CA: RAND, 1999), p. xiii.

20. IISS, *Strategic Survey 2002/2003* (London: International Institute for Strategic Studies, 2003), pp. 27–36.

21. Until a decade before the Carter Doctrine, Britain maintained a small forward presence that would call for the dispatch of nearby reinforcements from the Indian Ocean under the PENSUM contingency plan. See Richard Mobley, *Deterring Iran, 1968–1971: The Royal Navy, Iran, and the Disputed Persian Gulf Islands* (Newport, RI: Naval War College, 2003). During the 1970s, prior to the Carter Doctrine, the U.S. Navy's MIDEASTFOR stationed at least twelve mine countermeasure and special warfare ships in the Gulf. See Rak, *The Future of the U.S. Navy in a Post-Saddam Persian Gulf* (Monterey, CA: Center for Contemporary Conflict, 2003), p. 1.

22. Ron O'Rourke, interview by author, 2004.

23. NWC, "Global 94: Volume III—Southwest Asia/Middle East Regional Estimate and Regional Action Plan" (Newport, RI: Naval War College, 1994), pp. 75–77.

24. CENTCOM, "Southwest Asia: Approaching the Millennium—Enduring Problems, Emerging Solutions" (paper presented at the Southwest Asia Symposium 96, Tampa, FL, May 14–15, 1996), p. 198.

25. Daniel Gouré, *The Tyranny of Forward Presence* (Newport, RI: Naval War College, March 16, 2004); available online (www.nwc.navy.mil/press/Review/2001/Summer/art1-su1.htm). See also James Miskel, "Being 'There' Matters. But Where?" Naval War College, March 16, 2004; available online (www.nwc.navy.mil/press/Review/2001/Summer/art2-su1.htm).

26. Quoted in Christopher Preble, "After Victory: Toward a New Military Posture in the Persian Gulf," *Policy Analysis,* no. 477 (2003), p. 8.

27. Joseph McMillan, *U.S. Forces in the Gulf: Options for a Post-Saddam Era* (2003), pp. 1–2.

28. In separate studies, Daniel Byman and Anthony Cordesman make this case. See Byman and Green, *Political Violence and Stability in the States of the Northern Persian Gulf* (Santa Monica, CA: RAND, 1999), pp. 102–103. See Cordesman, *The U.S. Military and Evolving Challenges in the Middle East* (Washington, D.C.: Center for Strategic and International Studies, March 16, 2004); available online (www.csis.org/burke/mb/me_usmil_evolvingchange.pdf).

29. CENTCOM, "Southwest Asia," p. 172.

30. Gregory Gause and Jill Crystal, "The Arab Gulf: Will Autocracy Define the Social Contract in 2015?" in Judith Yaphe, ed., *The Middle East in 2015: The Impacts of Regional Trends on U.S. Strategic Planning* (Washington, D.C.: National Defense University, 2002), p. 193.

31. McMillan, *U.S. Forces*, pp. 1–2. See also Richard L. Kugler, "U.S. Defense Strategy and Force Planning," in Richard Sokolsky, ed., *The United States and the Persian Gulf: Reshaping Security Strategy for the Post-Containment Era* (Washington, D.C.: Institute for National Strategic Studies, National Defense University 2003), p. 109; and Chris Bowie, Robert Haffa, and Robert Mullins, *Future War: What Trends in America's Post–Cold War Military Conflicts Tell Us about Early Twenty-first Century Warfare* (Washington, D.C.: Northrop Grumman Analysis Center, 2003).

32. Carl Conetta, Charles Knight, and Melissa Murphy, *Is the Iraq War Sapping America's Military Power? Cautionary Data and Perspectives* (Cambridge, MA: Project for Defense Alternatives, 2004); Charles Knight and Marcus Corbin, *The New Occupation: How Preventative War is Wrecking the Military* (Cambridge, MA: Project for Defense Alternatives, 2004).

33. Department of Defense, "Allied Contributions to the Common Defense" (Washington, D.C.: Office of the Secretary of Defense, International Security Affairs, 2003).

34. Michael Knights, *Cradle of Conflict: Iraq and the Birth of the Modern U.S. Military* (Annapolis, MD: U.S. Naval Institute Press, 2005), p. 265.

35. David Ockmanek, "The Air Force: The Next Round," in Has Binnendijk, ed., *Transforming America's Military* (Washington, D.C.: National Defense University, 2002), p. 171.

36. Michael Knights, "Bombing Iraq: Influence and Decision-Making in the Targeting, Phasing, and Weaponeering of Modern Air Campaigns," Ph.D. thesis, King's College, January 2003.

37. Ibid.

38. Byman and Green, *Political Violence and Stability*, p. 101.

39. DSB, "Final Report of the Defense Science Board Task Force on Globalization and Security" (Washington, D.C.: Defense Science Board, 1999), p. vi.

40. Matthew Levitt, "Iranian State Sponsorship of Terror: Threatening U.S. Security, Global Stability, and Regional Peace," *PolicyWatch* no. 964 (Washington Institute for Near East Policy, February 16, 2005). Available online (www.washingtoninstitute.org/templateC05.php?CID=2263).

41. Krepinevich, Watts, and Work, *Meeting the Anti-Access*; Stillion and Orletsky, *Airbase Vulnerability*.

42. Adam Siegel, "Scuds against al-Jubayl" (presented as part of the *Naval Institute Proceedings,* 2002), p. 2.

43. Kori Schake and Judith Yaphe, "The Strategic Implications of a Nuclear-Armed Iran," McNair Paper (Washington, D.C.: Institute for National Security Studies, National Defense University, 2003), p. 79.

44. CENTCOM, "Southwest Asia," p. 186.

45. Vice Admiral Charles Moore and Lieutenant General Edward Hanlon, "Sea Power 21 Series, Part IV—Sea Basing: Operational Independence for a New Century" (presented as part of the *Naval Institute Proceedings,* 2003), p. 1.

46. Rak, *The Future of the U.S. Navy*, p. 1.

47. Ockmanek, "The Air Force," p. 177.

48. See Bowie, *The Anti-Access Threat*, pp. 1–2. See also Krepinevich, Watts, and Work, *Meeting the Anti-Access*, p. 25.

49. Steven Seroka, "Access and Air Bases in Iraq," Air University, 2004. Unpublished manuscript, Washington Institute for Near East Policy, 2004.

50. Stillion and Orletsky, *Airbase Vulnerability*, pp. xv–xvii.

51. Chow et al., *Air Force Operations in a Chemical or Biological Environment* (Santa Monica, CA: RAND, 1998), pp. 5, 7, 36.

52. Kugler, "U.S. Defense Strategy," p. 96.

53. Rear Admiral John Sigler, interview by author, Washington, D.C., 2003; McMillan, *U.S. Forces*. See also James Russell, "Occupation of Iraq: Geostrategic and Institutional Challenges," *Strategic Insights* 2, no. 8 (August 2003); available online (www.ccc.nps.navy.mil/si/aug03/middleEast2.asp).

54. William Schneider, interview by author, Washington, D.C., 2003.

55. Rear Admiral John Sigler, *Post-Saddam Framework for CENTCOM: Military Considerations* (Washington, D.C.: National Defense University, 2003), p. 3.

56. McMillan, *U.S. Forces*, p. 2.

57. Ibid., p. 2.

58. Ibid.; Sigler, *Post-Saddam Framework*.

59. Mullen, "Sea Power 21 Series, Part VI," p. 2. See also Ron O'Rourke, interview by author.

60. An ESG is essentially a CVBG without the aircraft carrier.

61. Mark Bowden, *Killing Pablo: The Hunt for the World's Greatest Outlaw* (Boston, MA: Atlantic Monthly Press, 2001).

62. Interviews with government personnel granted to author on condition of anonymity between June 2002 and October 2004.

4

Reassessing Self-Defense Capabilities in the GCC States

THE PRECEDING CHAPTER showed that due to changes in global defense posture, U.S. forces in the Gulf will not be ideally configured to deal with all the types of threats that are likely to develop in the region during the coming decade. At the internal and transnational levels, U.S. Central Command (CENTCOM) will have only limited ability to undertake sensitive security operations in the sovereign states of the Gulf directly. Nor is the United States in the ideal posture to commit to open-ended operations of long duration, whether they are intended to monitor borders or sea lanes, or to deter persistent low-level aggression. Finally, adversaries may be able to deny the United States access to local bases and vital territory during future contingencies.

All this adds up to the need for dependable local allies committed to their own defenses and willing to develop their security institutions to complement U.S. military posture. At first glance, this seems glaringly obvious. States should contribute to their own defense. In the Gulf, however, both the United States and its partners have fallen into the dangerous habit of considering the United States the first and foremost guarantor of security, particularly with regard to the threats posed by Iran and Iraq. This chapter will review the current condition of Gulf Cooperation Council (GCC) states' military and security capabilities, outlining some of the challenges that U.S. planners will face in the coming decade in designing security assistance. In essence, the United States should seek to bolster local capabilities in four key areas:

- First, Gulf states need to develop stronger capabilities to deter and defend against Iran's potential use of persistent low-level "cheat-and-retreat" tactics, or interdiction of their oil-export infrastructure, shipping, and population centers.

- Second, in the case of major Iranian aggression, Gulf states need to bolster their ability to "hold the line" until U.S. reinforcements arrive—protecting the access points those reinforcements will use.

121

- Third, considering the increasing internal and transnational threats facing them, Gulf states need to develop more effective interagency, joint, and multinational cooperation in order to tackle domestic and cross-border adversaries.

- Fourth, U.S. allies in the Gulf need to increase their compatibility with U.S. forces so that CENTCOM and its local allies can provide interchangeable, rare, high-value assets to supplement one another's operations.

Demonstrated Proficiency in Internal Policing

It is clear from previous chapters that the U.S. military can and should only play a marginal role in GCC states' internal security. Security cooperation within the GCC, and between GCC states and the United States, has focused traditionally on interstate threats—even though some of the fastest growing threats facing Gulf states are internal and transnational. Such threats have rarely been in the purview of the GCC military forces with which CENTCOM works. They have instead fallen to the many police, paramilitary, and intelligence organizations operating in parallel throughout the GCC. Nor have the Gulf states typically involved CENTCOM directly in their internal security affairs.

Fortunately, the longstanding perception that local security establishments can handle internal threats is correct in broad terms. Each of the GCC states invests heavily in internal security, typically maintaining paramilitary forces that benefit from strong funding and the direct oversight of influential royal personages. GCC governments have also enthusiastically welcomed foreign assistance and training in the field, as later chapters will discuss. This has resulted in internal security forces of appropriate sizes for the states and populations they protect, redirecting increasing amounts of GCC spending away from interstate threats and toward homeland defense and border security. In Saudi Arabia, for instance, the continuous development since 1926 of a security and intelligence bureaucracy has culminated in sustained annual internal security spending estimated at around $7 billion by the 1990s, and rising to $9 billion in 2005. This long-term development has transformed Saudi Arabia from an anarchic tribal society into a sophisticated security state.

Reducing ideological support for terrorists and disrupting their networks. GCC internal security forces are well suited to undertake some of the tasks that the U.S. National Defense Strategy (NDS) identifies as future priorities but that U.S. forces are not well positioned to execute. For instance,

GCC states have demonstrated a growing willingness and capability to counter Islamic extremism by reducing ideological support for terrorists and disrupting their networks.

On the first count, GCC security bureaucrats have a far more advanced vision than CENTCOM of how to win the ideological war against Islamic extremism, and are putting wise strategies into effect, particularly in Saudi Arabia. A longstanding focus on messages from mosques and the media (now broadened to include strong consideration of the Internet) gives the GCC states good insight into the ideological battleground. The strong security apparatuses of the Arab Gulf countries have the ability to control both mosques and the media, ranging from the periodic licensing of religious scholars and media outlets to legislative prohibitions on incitement.

GCC states are also highly capable of physically disrupting terrorist networks. Ongoing security actions against terrorist hideouts in Saudi Arabia and Kuwait demonstrated those two nations' strengthened intelligence-gathering and paramilitary capabilities. During such battles, GCC security forces have not flinched at prolonged and intense combat, nor have GCC leaders sought to hide the struggle against terrorism from their people. On June 1, 2005, for instance, Prince Bandar bin Sultan, the Saudi ambassador to the United States, called on his country to begin "general mobilization for war, as individuals and as a whole, in the media and in the culture...a war that does not mean delicacy, but brutality." Significantly, Prince Bandar called on Saudis to deal with the crisis in much the same way that Saudi Arabia's founding father, King Abdulaziz Ibn Saud, did when he forged Saudi Arabia in wars lasting between 1906 and 1932. Such warlike rhetoric is not confined to Saudi Arabia, reflecting recognition in each GCC state of the paramount threat posed by terrorism.

Stabilization and key-point defense to prevent state failure. Internal security forces are also well suited to another NDS task: state stabilization and key-point defense. A detailed look at Saudi Arabia will illustrate this assessment.

Like other GCC states, Saudi Arabia inherited a strong eye for key-point defense (of strategic locations) and control of public gatherings from the colonial policemen who guided the formation of its security establishments. The kingdom's vigilance has been boosted by periodic challenges such as the 1979 seizure of the Grand Mosque by elements associated with the Muslim Brotherhood, the annual Hajj pilgrimage, and occasional breakdowns in public order involving Shiite or expatriate workers, or the Ismailis of Najran province. To reduce the chance of popular dissent during the Hajj and at other times, the Interior Ministry and Ministry of Islamic Affairs rein in the clergy through qualifications boards, which license clerics according to their religious credentials, and funding bodies. Surveillance by the Interior Ministry's General Security Service (GSS) feeds into the National Information Center's records on all Saudi citizens and residents of the country.

Capable of dealing with small-scale or politically sensitive contingencies on its own, the Interior Ministry has called on 35,000 public security police to secure essential infrastructure, and the Muhabith (GSS secret police) and Special Security Force (GSS special forces) for direct-action missions. For larger or more threatening scenarios, the Saudi Arabian National Guard (SANG) is available, handling all serious security issues within the kingdom's cities and oil fields, which the Royal Saudi Land Forces are not permitted to enter. SANG has 57,000 personnel, including 25,000 combat troops and 1,117 heavily armed Piranha wheeled armored vehicles. Already a highly capable combat force (battle-tested at Khafji in 1991), as King Abdullah's personal army SANG may be expanded to 80,000 to 100,000 personnel through a $990 million expansion tendered in November 2003. SANG is also developing forces capable of intervening in less serious cases of public disorder (e.g., with horse-mounted police).[1]

Though the Saudi security apparatus is particularly expansive, smaller versions appropriate to national requirements exist in all GCC states.

Help from the United States. Of course GCC internal security capabilities can always be improved, and the United States can support those improvements without wearing out its welcome. Measures to prevent terrorism and ensure security require constant upgrading, as do civil emergency incident–management capabilities. As the State Department's State Failure Task Force suggested, partial democratization imposes strains on internal security, not least by introducing new limitations on the powers of arrest and detention and requiring greater focus on investigation and crime-scene forensics. During the turbulent years ahead, the Gulf states will need to continue developing their internal security capabilities, and at the same time proceed as consistently as possible with the development of civil society and the rule of law. Finally, it is worth noting that while GCC states have proven highly effective at policing their internal affairs, *regional states are notably less comfortable dealing with transnational threats relating to land and maritime border security.*

Views of GCC Military Capabilities
Shaped by Recent History

Historically, therefore, CENTCOM has had only minor reservations about the policing capabilities of GCC states. But its confidence in those states' ability to undertake the final key category of military tasks set by the NDS—to counter the conventional military power and disruptive capabilities of a potential state adversary—has been far lower. This lack of confidence is based on assumptions that may no longer be valid.

It is a commonly held view in U.S. military and diplomatic circles that the states of the Gulf are unlikely to produce effective armed forces and will be forever dependent on the United States for their security. This impression derives from CENTCOM's experience in close partnership with Gulf militaries since 1990, during which time high numbers of U.S. military and diplomatic personnel have had the chance to observe GCC militaries. Though their often snapshot views may have done a disservice to some elements of GCC capabilities, those views have left a lasting, negative impression that the GCC states are able to contribute little to their own defense.

A rather selective interpretation of GCC military performance in the 1990–1991 Gulf crisis contributed to the initial development of this dismissive attitude. In relation to the destruction of Kuwait's armed forces, a Project on Defense Alternatives Research paper from 1991 asked:

> How can we understand a defense scheme that places the better part of a nation's air force within artillery range of a likely opponent and then fails to put the air force on high alert when the opponent masses his army on the border?[2]

Though correct in essence, such an interpretation of the options open to Kuwaiti decisionmakers is uncharitable to say the least. At a practical level, it does not take into account the extremely small size of the country, and at the political level it fails to recognize that Kuwait's best defense prior to 1990 was always diplomatic rather than military. Nor have U.S. analyses generally noted the positive aspects of GCC military performance in the 1991 Gulf War. The Kuwaiti armed forces engaged in a number of determined tactical actions at the al-Jahra road junction and in defense of the country's airspace on August 2, 1990, and Kuwaiti military officers played a role in the extensive guerrilla operations mounted against the Iraqi occupation over the following six months.[3] Kuwaiti air forces were joined by Saudi Arabian, Qatari, Bahraini, and United Arab Emirates (UAE) air forces in combat and support missions during Operation Desert Storm, and a number of GCC Peninsula Shield ground forces engaged Iraqi ground forces with some success in the battle of Khafji and subsequent coalition offensive operations in Kuwait.[4] In other words, the GCC states have more direct experience of conflict than many partners fighting alongside the United States in "coalitions of the willing."

But American misgivings about the military potential of Gulf states were reinforced in the 1990s.

At the beginning of the decade, there were a number of positive indications of a revolution in GCC military capabilities, with Saudi Arabia emerging as the new pro-U.S. "anchor state" and regional military leader. The inconclusive end of Desert Storm and the U.S. desire to avoid a long-term deployment in the Gulf made it incumbent on the northernmost GCC states—with which the United States has the longest and closest historical associations—to develop the means to blunt or at least delay an Iraqi overland invasion. In response, the militaries of Saudi Arabia, Bahrain, and Kuwait looked to the U.S. defense establishment to design their force planning and doctrinal development. U.S. doctrine was copied into Arabic, and strategic force planning was undertaken by a U.S.-Saudi

Figure 12. Average Annual Military Expenditures by Gulf States, 1986–2000

	1986–1990	1991–1995	1996–2000
Bahrain	$154 million	$246 million	$351 million
Kuwait	$1.342 billion	$6.101 billion	$3.904 billion
Oman	$1.442 billion	$1.703 billion	$2.114 billion
Qatar	$842 million	$580 million	$1.280 billion
Saudi Arabia	$17.371 billion	$23.817 billion	$20.553 billion
UAE	$1.498 billion	$2.549 billion	$2.711 billion
GCC total	$22.832 billion	$34.999 billion	$30.052 billion
Iran	$4.054 billion	$3.171 billion	$4.560 billion
Iraq	$8.869 billion	$3.522 billion	$1.334 billion
Yemen	$683 million	$569 million	$439 million

Source: Data compiled from various annual editions of the International Institute for Strategic Studies compendium *The Military Balance*, 1987–2002.

joint committee. In turn, intimate day-to-day contact with U.S. personnel and procedures appeared to make Saudi Arabian military leaders much more interested in increased professionalism. Kuwait developed a 100-kilometer security barrier on its northern border, and both Kuwait and Bahrain equipped their forces with large amounts of excess defense articles (surplus military equipment) donated by the U.S. Department of Defense. Across the northern GCC, states signaled their commitment to security with large increases in defense spending (see figure 12). The prospect of a solid wall of U.S.-trained militaries armed with the latest land and air armaments raised hopes that the United States could largely withdraw from the Gulf and hand off a measure of deterrence responsibilities to local forces. Local states were equally eager to see this happen due to the political costs of hosting U.S. forces.[5]

By the mid-1990s, however, it was increasingly apparent that the effort to build a Tier II (collective) defense around Saudi Arabia had failed, leaving the United States once again the first and foremost guarantor of Gulf security. As Ambassador Chas Freeman noted at a 1996 CENTCOM conference, the only real progress had occurred in the Tier III category (Gulf States' ability to function as partners and hosts of multinational forces), with the development of unparalleled military infrastructure capable of hosting U.S. reinforcements. Tier I (individual national defense) and Tier II, Freeman noted, were "empty."

The causes of underperformance were different for the various northern Gulf States. For Kuwait and Bahrain, time was the central issue. The armed forces of the former were destroyed completely in 1990, and it took time to rebuild and retrain them. In many ways Kuwait was ideally cooperative, undertaking a determined $12 billion program of military rehabilitation, backed by the extensive Desert Spring training series, which matured in the later 1990s. Bahrain's small armed forces also developed at a steady pace due to close cooperation with the United States and slowly increasing military expenditure, supported by generous U.S. military aid.

The real problem was that Saudi Arabia's military development never became what U.S. force planners had hoped. As early as 1993, RAND Corporation analyst Joseph Kechichian observed that the intended "Saudi awakening"—the development of Riyadh as a military anchor state and a "Gulf power broker"—had already derailed.[6] The Saudi military never fully accepted the guidance offered by CENTCOM, leading to massive overemphasis on procurement of high technology and serious underemphasis on manpower issues, personnel selection, training, and maintenance. The Saudis' focus on expensive procurement left them with unsustainable military spending requirements. In Riyadh's first post–Desert Storm five-year plan, it made immediate and heavy commit-ments, then scaled back through the middle of the 1990s, but still remained saddled with a steady rise in defense spending due to the massive and poorly managed forces it had created. This pattern has continued from 2001 to 2005, with Saudi funding falling increasingly short of what is needed to sustain exist-ing forces, let alone modernize them. As a result, Saudi Arabia may defer a num-ber of major procurements until at least 2006–2010 or even thereafter—and as long as it puts off modernizing procurements, the capabilities of its forces can be expected to further decline, unless corrective steps are taken.

Meanwhile, the southern GCC states largely opted out of immediate post–Gulf War defense modernization, perceiving less of a threat from the geograph-ically distant and militarily contained Iraq. The UAE and Qatar both delayed their major rearmament drives until the second half of the 1990s. After 1993, Oman steadily increased spending, but without a definite commitment to a postwar rearmament plan during the remainder of the 1990s; spending was instead opportunist, closely linked to the price of oil and other economic fac-tors. Its spending hike at the end of the 1990s appears to have been the start of a sustained increase, as the Omani government engaged in a major rearmament drive from 2001–2005, with expenditures of more than $2 billion per year.[7]

As a collective defense organization, therefore, the GCC could not play the role anticipated in Tier II of CENTCOM's theater engagement strategy, the command's plan to manage U.S. military relations with regional allies. Ambas-sador Chas Freeman said in 1996 that "the GCC is, in many respects, a very big shell inhabited by a very small snail. It has fallen far short of what it ought to be in terms of the common expectations we had in 1991."[8] As Jerrold Green noted, the lack of a common, GCC-wide threat perception was one cause for the fail-ure of Tier II: "It is unclear whether U.S. notions of a regional defense con-sensus and the potential for strategic cooperation in the region are shared by the nations themselves."[9] In general, since the first Gulf War the southern Gulf states have invested heavily in air and naval forces focused on the Iranian and Yemeni threats pertinent to them, rather than the overland invasion threat per-tinent to the northern Gulf states. Kuwait has pushed for joint military com-mand and strong land forces, Oman has focused on joint naval and air forces to secure the Straits of Hormuz, and Saudi Arabia has sought to accommodate all views.[10]

From the formation of the small Peninsula Shield force in 1983 to the announcement of a common defense agreement in 2000, the GCC made little progress. The GCC still has no blueprint for military integration equivalent to the principles and aims outlined by the European Union at the Helsinki summit of December 1999. Nor has the GCC developed methods similar to those used by NATO to rationalize costs and avoid duplication of effort in key areas such as airborne early warning systems, intratheater airlift command, and aircraft refueling. This has limited joint procurement to a single combat search-and-rescue unit that became active in January 1999. It appears as if similar capabilities involving expensive equipment and training (e.g., unmanned aerial vehicle operation and satellite imagery) will continue to be procured nationally rather than as interoperable GCC assets. Procurement in land and naval forces remains idiosyncratic and uncoordinated. Though states' air forces are becoming more homogenous in their use of U.S. equipment, this is more a result of market dynamics than of any deliberate plan. More compatible ground troops and an effective Peninsula Shield force remain distant goals.

In other words, joint GCC military assets do not really exist. If a Tier II collective defense arrangement is to be resurrected in the Gulf, little investment would be lost in abandoning the GCC as the central locus for military integration and instead focusing on small "coalitions of the willing" involving one or more GCC states.

From CENTCOM's perspective, therefore, the last fifteen years of developing Tier I and II military capabilities in the Gulf did not contribute significantly to the U.S. mission of deterring an Iraqi overland invasion of Kuwait or Saudi Arabia. When Saddam deftly moved a number of Republic Guard divisions to the Kuwaiti border in October 1994, the United States was forced to make a major deployment to the area. Nor, as Simon Henderson noted, did Saudi Arabia develop as a new strategic pillar in the Gulf to offset Iraq and Iran.[11] Instead, a near-permanent U.S. military presence became the de facto third strategic pillar in the Gulf, while cooperation with the GCC states increasingly focused on Tier III activities: the use of GCC military facilities and consumable supplies to support the U.S. presence. The very idea that GCC states can develop meaningful Tier I and II capabilities or develop as militarily useful Tier III allies became distinctly unfashionable.

Challenging Outdated Conventional Wisdom

With the exception of Anthony Cordesman's numerous works, there are few high-quality, open-source analyses of GCC militaries' current capabilities. Most analyses written by generalists lack detail or military insight, or reflect outdated impressions formed by the historical experience outlined above.

Some writing is skewed by unrealistic views of the security threats facing GCC states. For example, American University of Paris policy analyst Steven Ekovich wrote in late 2003 that "the GCC remains fragmented and vulnerable, able to defend itself only until Western help arrives."[12] But defend itself against what? An Iraqi overland invasion? This is no longer likely. An Iranian amphibious invasion? As the analysis in chapter 3 demonstrated—and as Ekovich later noted himself—this is both unlikely and would not present an insurmountable challenge to the forces of any of the GCC states. Internal revolts? The GCC states have internal security forces designed specifically to quell them, and can be expected to provide for their own internal security.

Arguably, the high-intensity threat Gulf states are most likely to face is that of Iranian naval and aerial/missile attacks. And strong indicators suggest that GCC states are far better equipped and configured to handle exactly this kind of external threat than the old threat of an Iraqi overland invasion.

As Saddam demonstrated in October 1994, and again when he overran the Kurdish autonomous zone in September 1996, an Iraqi overland invasion was prone to develop with little strategic warning. Kuwait's small size and the short distances from Iraq's border to Saudi border towns and oil fields made it imperative that the threat be defeated at the earliest stage possible—a demanding task that even the U.S. Air Force balked at.[13] In contrast, a threat from Iran will mainly involve naval and air forces, taking place in the maritime and littoral arenas, and will probably have limited aims and offer extensive strategic warning. U.S. Joint Staff planners have commented that due to Iran's deterrent posture and the nature of the Iranian state, Tehran's military activity would probably follow "a period of political posturing and military indicators—lots of marching and countermarching."[14]

Together, these factors make the Iranian threat far more manageable for the developing military forces of GCC states than was the Iraqi threat. In air and naval operations, raw manpower is less important than technological sophistication, and the numbers of "warriors" engaged is relatively small.[15] These factors work strongly in the favor of the Gulf states, whose armed forces are small and undermanned and whose cultures do not have the same breadth of military tradition as Iran or Iraq. Effective use of airpower in particular has shaped most modern military campaigns, and GCC militaries have been relatively successful in aerial warfare.[16] Saudi Arabian aircraft supported by U.S. airborne warning and control system (AWACS) aircraft policed the "Fahd" air-defense line during the 1980–1988 Gulf War, destroying at least one Iranian aircraft. In the 1991 Gulf War, Saudi Arabian aircraft scored a further two air-to-air kills and

Figure 13. Quantitative Ranking of Iranian and GCC Air Forces

	Iran	GCC
Offensive airpower	36.3	50.6
Defensive airpower	36.1	54.1
Weapons systems	22	55.3
Manpower	51.1	52.7
Infrastructure	29.7	52.6
Integration*	40.3	37

* Refers to rate of operations and operational culture.
Source: Data obtained from Shmuel Gordon, *Dimensions of Quality: A New Approach to Net Assessment of Airpower* (Memorandum no. 64) (Tel Aviv: Jaffee Center for Strategic Studies, Tel Aviv University, 2003), pp. 94–103.

undertook 1,656 offensive sorties into Kuwait and Iraq, including 1,133 strike missions, 523 close air-support missions, and 118 reconnaissance missions. Bahraini aircraft flew 294 combat sorties in Desert Storm, and Qatari Mirage F-1 and armed helicopter sorties were flown during the battle of Khafji and the liberation of Kuwait. UAE aircraft also flew offensive missions into Kuwait and Iraq.[17] During Operation Iraqi Freedom, Kuwaiti Patriot missile crews intercepted two Iraqi surface-to-surface missiles.[18]

An Israeli military analysis of GCC and Iranian air forces hints at the extent of GCC aerial capabilities. The analysis notes that GCC air forces fly the most advanced combat and support aircraft in the region, and in terms of manpower and infrastructure, compare favorably with nearby air forces such as Turkey and Egypt.[19] A quantitative ranking produced by a complex set of capability indicators can be found in figure 13.

Finally, many analysts have formed a static, negative opinion of GCC capabilities because they have assumed that Saudi Arabia's failed military reform is a model for the military development of the five other GCC states. In fact, despite consistently outspending the rest of the GCC combined, Saudi Arabia's attempt at military modernization is in no way representative. Of the remaining northern Gulf states, Bahrain and Kuwait have both implemented measured and successful modernization programs, becoming Major Non-NATO allies of the United States in 2002 and 2004 respectively.

Similarly, the southern Gulf states have initiated steady, successful defense modernization programs through the late 1990s and early years of the twenty-first century, and moved into closer relationships with the United States than they enjoyed previously. As noted before, the UAE and Qatar waited until the second half of the 1990s to undertake defense modernization, while Oman waited until after 2001 to begin in earnest. These delays have greatly aided all three nations' procurement efforts. To begin with, their procurement drives took place in a post–Cold War buyer's market, and—as illustrated in the following section—they have successfully manipulated this market to gain cutting-edge Western military technology at more affordable prices. Their procurement programs also took shape some years after the 1991 Gulf War, benefiting from the operational lessons of the first post–Cold War operations.

By contrast, Saudi Arabia largely decided on its arms purchases within the first year after Desert Storm, before post–Cold War market and operational trends had changed the arms industries. As a result, Saudi Arabia now fields an unwieldy and financially unsustainable Cold War military, while the other GCC states are building trimmer, post–Cold War forces more relevant to their future threats.

Trends Underpinning Growing Military Effectiveness in the Smaller GCC States

During the 1990s, GCC states changed the way they developed their armed forces. (This is particularly true of the way the southern Gulf states developed during the second half of the decade.) In the 1980s, the Gulf states focused on building fleets, such as tanks and fighter aircraft, rather than on developing capabilities. Geopolitical motives underpinned these purchases, as Kori Schake and Judith Yaphe noted:

> All bought what they wanted in bidding wars from whomever they wanted without a serious thought to how the equipment could be used in a combat situation. Arms purchases were not intended to bolster defense; rather, they were an extension of foreign policy, intended to give as many arms-merchant states as possible a stake in their survival. Kuwait, for example, often bought inferior if not obsolete equipment from the Soviet Union, Eastern Europe, and China as well as other European suppliers in order to help ensure political alliances.[20]

In the 1990s, GCC armed forces instead learned to procure, sustain, and employ real military capabilities, including air defense, offensive long-range strike, amphibious operations, and naval power projection. The following sections will explore key advances in each of these fields, using the UAE as a case study.

GCC procurement trends. The procurement practices of the six GCC states are following five key trends.

Cautious buyers: First, buyers are more cautious, with the Gulf states having slowed their rate of modernization and fleet replacement. In the words of one U.S. officer, they now engage in "a lot of shopping, but not a lot of buying."[21] They are prepared to delay major purchases, push back out-of-service dates, and mothball large numbers of aircraft, despite the risk that their capabilities might fall short as a result. States often prefer to break major commitments and delay delivery rather than order cheaper, less functional equipment. Despite the price difference, newer models with longer operational lives are preferred to second-hand equipment.

Cost-saving measures: At the same time, however, GCC states have become far more willing to upgrade their current equipment rather than replace it entirely. New purchases by some of the GCC states rely increasingly on the resale of types being retired from GCC inventories (for instance Kuwaiti and Qatari Mirage F-1s, Kuwaiti A-4KUs, Saudi F-5E/Fs) to buyers outside the region and reinvesting the funds in new procurement.

Professional procurement: Third, buyers have grown more professional and assertive. GCC procurement practices improved greatly during the late 1990s, led by the UAE, Kuwait, and Bahrain, all of which instituted strong governmental or parliamentary oversight of arms deals.[22] Commissions payments continue at reduced levels, but have been largely pushed underground.[23] Tendering and selection processes in arms purchasing are becoming more effective and more rigorous. Even buyers with comparatively little financial clout are growing intolerant of overpriced and downgraded equipment. Competitive, achievable, and profitable offset agreements are becoming more important, requiring larger sums to be invested by arms vendors in the local industries of GCC states. Features such as pre-offset, cash offset, offset of 100 to 115 percent, deals exclusive of U.S. government commission, and performance bonds are examples of the favorable terms GCC states are securing.[24]

Collaborative design: Fourth, GCC states increasingly collaborate in the design and production of arms. The UAE's $2 billion investment in developing U.S. technologies such as the integrated avionics and Agile Beam Radar on the F-16 Block 60 indicates a change in the status of GCC states (see box below).

Case Study: The UAE's Procurement of Lockheed Martin Block 60 F-16 Aircraft

Even before its major rearmament drive of 1995–2005, the UAE was moving toward increased professionalism in its procurement. The Khalifa Directive of December 1986 stated that no commissions agents or mediators were to be used in the sale of lethal equipment, though this ban has slowly been extended to most military equipment. A professional tendering system operates through UAE armed forces General Headquarters, and over the course of a long evaluation, competing tenders are judged strictly on their technical merits. In selecting the F-16, for example, the UAE carried out ninety-six evaluation flights, including thirty-six in UAE conditions.[*] The UAE Offsets Group strictly requires that offsets worth at least 60 percent of the value of deals be reinvested within the local economy within seven years (ten at the maximum), with milestones at three and five years, and with a strong focus on the profitability of investments, not simply in meeting the letter of the law.

Though the UAE has been outspent by both Saudi Arabia and Iran, its procurement drive has been much better timed and executed. The UAE effectively started from scratch and did not have to service large fleets of outdated aircraft, ships, or land units, as do both Saudi Arabia and Iran. Its 1995–2005 rearmament has taken place in a buyer's market, and the UAE has shown itself a tough negotiator, maintaining competition between French and U.S. vendors and obtaining top-grade technologies rather than the downgraded export versions that Saudi Arabia accepted during the 1980s and 1990s.

The UAE forced Lockheed Martin and the U.S. government to provide a $2 billion performance bond to guarantee F-16 deliveries, and

---

[*] Eric Hehs, "UAE Air Force," *Code One* 18, no. 1 (2003), p. 1.

Increasing U.S. market share: Finally, U.S. arms vendors are increasing their market shares in both traditional U.S. markets (such as Bahrain, Saudi Arabia, and Kuwait) and markets formerly dominated by European vendors (such as the UAE and Oman). The United States continues to open markets and protect its market share in U.S. client states by granting GCC states relatively large amounts of funding credit (U.S. government cash offsets against purchases from U.S. companies) and surplus military equipment. This practice captures future sales in the profit-

extracted a no-questions-asked $160 million advance cash offset on top of the standard 60 percent offset arrangement. The UAE was also allowed to make a direct commercial purchase of the aircraft, saving it the 2.5 percent fee levied by the U.S. Department of Defense on foreign military sales (FMS) deals. Finally, the UAE received the object codes required to update its aircraft mission computers without U.S. assistance, allowing the UAE Air Force to keep track of Israeli aircraft. In other words, in making this deal the UAE forged a military relationship with the United States such as no Arab nation has had before.

The UAE's involvement in collaborative development also makes it unique among GCC states. Though that involvement became highly advanced in the late 1990s, it has been under way in a number of low-profile projects for twenty years. In the 1980s the UAE embarked on a secret relationship with G.E.C.-Marconi-Dynamics (now Alenia Marconi Systems) to design and build the al-Hakim series of powered standoff precision-guided munitions, more than a decade before such weapons showed their value in the 1991 Gulf War. More recently, the UAE made a major and unprecedented investment in the U.S. defense electronics industry, becoming the core partner in systems that will provide the backbone of the United States Air Force (USAF) of tomorrow. The F-16 deal included a $2.5 billion advance payment by the UAE to assist in the development of a new internal avionics suite and $500 million toward the development of the Northrop Grumman APG-68 Agile Beam Radar. For a period of years after the Desert Falcons enter service, the UAE will deploy aircraft more advanced than the F-16s of either the USAF or Israeli Air Force. If either the USAF or any foreign customer buys these systems, the UAE will receive royalties. The UAE has also signaled its interest in becoming involved in the field of advanced, next-generation jet trainers and light-combat aircraft.

able fields of aerospace parts and technologies, military aircraft engines, avionics, and communications technologies. In the past, a lack of restrictions on technology transfer gave European and Eastern bloc countries an important competitive advantage, but this advantage looks likely to diminish as U.S. export restrictions loosen. Once one GCC state is cleared to receive a system, the others soon follow. For example, the number of GCC states ordering the advanced medium-range air-to-air missile (AMRAAM) jumped from zero to four in two years.

Sustainment: manpower, training, maintenance, and infrastructure.
Along with improving the quality and assertiveness of their procurement procedures, GCC states have taken concrete steps to improve their indigenous training, maintenance, and infrastructure, reducing their dependence on foreign
contractors at least to some extent. These factors are vital to the sustainment of
effective military capabilities, and serve as indicators of military maturity in the
Gulf states.

As GCC armed forces do remain undermanned and dependent on foreign
maintenance crews, they have begun to focus greater resources in the fields of
manpower management and training. As noted above, future threats to GCC
states probably will not evolve in the manpower-intensive arena of land combat,
but in the air and on the sea. GCC aircrews are slowly increasing in number,
though only Bahrain has exceeded the comfortable minimum 1.5:1 pilot-to-aircraft ratio. In other Gulf states the retirement of outdated or unneeded aircraft
is improving those ratios, and Kuwait and the UAE continue to train aircrews
in the United States to generate a steady flow of pilots. GCC pilots fly upwards
of 130 hours per year, as compared to around 190 in the United States. The
sophistication of training is increasing, with the integration of "train-as-you-
fight" technologies such as linked simulators that allow units to train together
at lower costs. The BAE Hawk trainer series is the regional standard, operating
or on order in all GCC states. The GCC states collaborate effectively to facilitate training, using Saudi airfields, ranges, and even training aircraft. Increasing
numbers of Western exercises provide additional training opportunities, and
more frequent regional exercises are a sign that GCC states are determined to
improve standards. Though training in the United Kingdom and United States
remain an indispensable part of air-defense training, both Kuwait and the UAE
have established their own air-defense schools.

At long last, maintenance and operations support are also receiving greater
recognition. Bahrain, Kuwait and the UAE have best capitalized on U.S. and
French assistance to increase the number of indigenous maintenance personnel, while Saudi Arabia remains the most reliant on foreign contractors. But
the danger of maintaining insufficient spare parts has been recognized even
in Saudi Arabia, where in 2001 the air force came to a halt through a lack of
technical support. Though expensive foreign contractor–support packages
and overseas overhaul facilities remain the preferred options for GCC states,
signs indicate that the Gulf's largest aerospace spenders—Saudi Arabia and
the UAE—are changing their practices, in particular providing more support
services at home to reduce costs and disruption to fleet readiness. Further-

Case Study: UAE Air Force and Air Defenses Manpower, Training, Maintenance, and Infrastructure Development

The UAE Air Force and Air Defenses (UAE AFAD) were badly under-manned in both aircrew and ground personnel at the start of the twenty-first century. Fortunately, military decisionmakers in the Emirates recognized that their force level was entirely insufficient for an air force that by the end of the decade would boast at least 143 advanced-combat aircraft plus a sizable helicopter fleet and surface-to-air missile force. As early as 1995, the UAE Air Force chief of operations, Colonel Khalid Abdullah, admitted that "we may buy 100 to 200 platforms, but we don't currently have the maintenance personnel to support them."* The UAE determined it would need around 400 trained pilots by 2007 to provide the 2:1 pilot-to-aircraft ratio it has set as a goal. Currently the UAE has between 150 and 190 pilots in service.

To make up for this shortfall, the UAE has embarked on a raft of training programs. The Air Force High School and Khalifa bin Zayed Air College (established in 1984) are important sources of recruits, a number of whom enter upper education in the Air Force and Air Defense Institute (established in 1991). All current UAE AFAD personnel are now going through Computer Driving License (ICDL) training and examinations to bring them up to a minimum standard of computer literacy. This same standard will be an entry requirement for all new recruits. (This is an achievable aim, since the UAE Ministry of Education has committed to giving all students ICDL tuition.) The UAE's commitment to bridging the "digital divide" will have major implications for UAE defense capabilities, allowing future generations of UAE military personnel to coordinate far better with the U.S. military.

Several specialist technical training facilities have also been established in the UAE. In 1995, defense firm Ferranti set up a $45.5 million

---

* Michael Knights, *Unfriendly Skies: The Development of GCC Air Forces* (Hastings: Cross-Border Information, 2002), p. 72.

more, these states have begun to build significant joint-venture, locally based aerospace industry support facilities: the Ali Salam Aircraft Company and the Advanced Electronics Company in Saudi Arabia, and the Gulf Aircraft Maintenance Company in the UAE, with Dassault due to set up a depot-level main-

Air Combat Training Range, which employs target drones produced in the UAE by the National Target Establishment. Air-defense simulations are performed with Hughes Simulation International equipment, which allows multiple, simultaneous simulations over areas of 2,400 km^2. The UAE has also begun purchasing Boeing Distributed Mission Training Systems, which allow pilots to exercise together in joint simulations. One UAE Air Force Squadron leader recently commented:

> I have flown the Block 60 simulator. The technology, the cockpit, and the overall capability are tremendous. The pilot will be the only limiting factor to the Block 60. We will need to invest more in training to get the most out of this aircraft. I think we will have to think, fly, and fight differently with these more capable fighters.[†]

While these advances provide the infrastructure for future skill retention, in the near term the UAE will continue to rely on overseas training programs in its personnel expansion. Up to six hundred UAE personnel are trained in the United States each year, including Apache helicopter crews at the U.S. Army Aviation Centre at Fort Rucker, Alabama, and F-16 crews in training centers in Tucson, Arizona. The latter training regimen, part of more than $1 billion worth of training and maintenance contracts attached to the UAE's $6.5 billion purchase of eighty Lockheed Martin Block 60 F-16s, will include six- to twenty-four-month pilot training and twelve-month ground crew training. UAE pilots and ground crews also train with F-16 operators in the Gulf region, including the Turkish Air Force and Turkish Aerospace Industry, and the Jordanian and Egyptian air forces. The UAE is also likely to train with the Royal Omani Air Force, which it encouraged to select the F-16. Further F-16 familiarization will be carried out with the Dutch Air Force. France's Dassault trains Mirage 2000 aircrews, and its Airco trains ground crews.[†]

† Eric Hehs, "UAE Air Force," *Code One* 18, no. 1 (2003) p. 1.

tenance facility in the UAE. In the future, when Gulf states' fleets are expected to include higher numbers of modern, newly built aircraft and weapons, their maintenance burdens will decrease at the same time as their maintenance capabilities have increased.

The UAE Air Force takes part in CENTCOM Blue Flag command-and-control exercises and hosts the Middle East Air Symposium series, which brings together U.S. and allied air forces to discuss high-level issues such as the command and control of air operations. Furthermore, the UAE hosts annual and biannual summits among the United States and regional air force leaders, which provide a regional focus for advanced military thinking. So do the simulations of regional scenarios conducted at the UAE Air Force Strategic Analysis Center. The Fiscal Year 2004 Department of Defense security assistance report noted: "We support the UAE's recent decision to construct a joint air warfare center for regional cooperative training."§

The UAE is also taking steps to increase its in-country maintenance capabilities, the first step to self-sufficiency. It was announced in 1999 that Daussault will build a $50 million depot-level maintenance plant to service the UAE's Mirage 2000 aircraft. Offset arrangements negotiated as part of the F-16 deal include joint ventures with General Electric (engine overhaul facilities) and the Gulf Aircraft Maintenance Company (GAMCO). These developments represent the beginning of an indigenous aerospace industry that could save the UAE considerable funds while increasing reliability and local workforce skills.

The UAE will also undertake the $1.2 billion construction of a new air base at Liwa along with the expansion of the Dhafra air base. These sites will incorporate advanced features present at other new GCC airfields such as Prince Sultan Air Base in Saudi Arabia and al-Udeid in Qatar, including improved, low-profile HASs, hardened command posts, underground fuel storage, separate ammunition storage areas, and redundant taxiways.**

‡ Michael Knights, "UAE Moves to Stay on Top of Future Military Challenges," *Gulf States Newsletter*, February 20, 2004.
§ Hehs, "UAE Air Force," p. 4.
** Neil Barnett, "UAE Will Upgrade Airbases for Desert Falcons," *Jane's Defense Weekly*, April 24, 2002, p. 1.

In the 1980s and early 1990s, Gulf states developed too many airfields, but of late this area has seen a marked slowing of activity. When new airfields are built, it is for one of three reasons: the need to absorb new fighter fleets, the need to relocate military aircraft from civilian airfields (to facilitate development of the civil air transport and tourist industries), and the U.S. need to diversify its airfield options. GCC nations have ceased building networks of fields to allow them to disperse aircraft, and have instead focused on installing hardened aircraft shelters (HASs) and expansive dispersal hardstands (where aircraft can be spread out if the HASs are attacked). In worst-case scenarios, the littoral GCC states know that they could withdraw their fleets to the expanses of Saudi Arabia or Oman, though this would be undertaken at some cost to national pride and freedom of action.

Airfield development does continue to be oriented toward U.S. requirements, not least because the United States defrays the cost of construction considerably and may provide U.S. Army Corps of Engineers support. The United States commonly requires such modifications as additional hardening, lengthening of runways to as long as 15,000 feet, installation of double security fences, development of living quarters and quality-of-life enhancements, and installation of facilities capable of mixing jet fuel to U.S. military standards. After current construction is completed at one UAE and two Omani sites, the only remaining prospects for new airfield development in the GCC states will be a further airfield each in Kuwait, the UAE, and Saudi Arabia—all of which have been shelved in the recent past. Strong development of Iraqi airfields may follow the stabilization of Iraq.[25]

Network-centric warfare and GCC states. The GCC states have long been committed to developing integrated early-warning networks and improved command, control, and communications (C3) systems, principally in their air-defense systems. In addition to these electronic systems, the Gulf states have embraced the computerization of command, control, and communications, and have increasingly sought to integrate radar networks with other intelligence-gathering platforms—in beginning to develop what have been termed C4ISR capabilities: command, control, communications, computerization, intelligence, surveillance, and reconnaissance. U.S. allies in the Gulf have spent more than $4.17 billion on C4ISR since 1991, including more than $2.8 billion by Saudi Arabia alone. (Though Saudi Arabia has spent the most money, Kuwait's air-defense modernization program is the best developed. Unsurprisingly, the GCC-wide Hizam al Taawun [Belt of Cooperation] air-defense system was initiated under the direction of a Kuwait air-defense officer.)

Gulf States' C^4ISR networks began with ground-based radar systems designed to spot incoming aircraft and missiles at medium or high altitudes. They are now beginning to include a range of radars that provide over-the-hori-

Case Study: UAE Adoption of a Network-Centric Warfare Approach

Though Saudi Arabia operates a massive early-warning network of ground-based radars and AEW aircraft, and also makes military use of commercial satellite imagery and ground-based sensors, the UAE is emerging as the Gulf's most advanced advocate of NCW. The UAE plans to go far beyond the radar networks that previously made up the GCC states' early warning screen, creating a layered network of sensors covering the most likely littoral approaches for interstate and nonstate threats, such as smuggling or terrorism. It is developing an extensive airborne surveillance capability consisting of four EADS/CASA C-295M Persuader maritime patrol aircraft, advanced helicopters, and up to five Northrop Grumman E-2C Hawkeye 2000 AEW aircraft.* In the near term, the UAE company GAMCO is developing a range of unmanned aerial vehicles for reconnaissance,† and later this decade the UAE plans to purchase more advanced unmanned aerial vehicles such as the Northrop Grumman Global Hawk.† The Global Hawk's long endurance will allow it to

---

* Riad Kahwaji, "UAE Rebuffs Amended Proposal for E-2c Buy," *Defense News*, March 8, 2004, p. 40. See also Martin Streetly, *Jane's Radar and Electronic Warfare Systems 2000–2001*, 12th ed. (Old Coulsdon: Jane's Information Group, 2000).
† Brian Walters, "GAMCO Special Projects Makes Debut," *Jane's Defence Weekly*, March 19, 2003, p. 4.

---

zon coverage looking down from airborne sensors. This type of radar is more useful for detecting low-flying or surface threats. Most GCC states are starting to use tethered, aerostat-mounted surveillance radar, airborne early warning (AEW) platforms (aircraft, helicopters, and unmanned aerial vehicles), or maritime patrol aircraft (MPA) for this purpose.

The next planned phase of the GCC radar network—a dense network of short-range, ground-based radars that allow integrated tracking of incoming threats—may only be practicable in very small states like Bahrain, Kuwait, and Qatar. But tighter coordination of existing GCC and U.S. radars could make additional ground-based radars less important. A great deal of work has focused on establishing fiber-optic and wireless links among member states and with the United States, under initiatives launched by the United States, the GCC, and its individual members. The United States also shares airborne surveillance aircraft, satellite, and shipborne early-warning data with the GCC, and each of

survey the UAE coastline almost constantly, providing real-time imagery of maritime and aerial movements, with the ability to zoom in and image an area with high-resolution synthetic aperture radar. The UAE also makes extensive use of commercial satellite imagery through the UAE Space Reconnaissance Center in Abu Dhabi. As one Joint Staff planner noted, "For a regional power, the UAE will have remarkable capabilities in remote sensing and advanced unmanned aerial vehicles by 2010."§

The UAE plans to network these assets and civilian sensors (such as littoral vessel traffic management systems) to create a common operating picture that it and its allies can use during security crises. The air and naval platforms the UAE is now procuring will have tactical data link architectures that allow them to share intelligence and targeting data with each other and with compatible allied forces. The UAE will mount Link 11 data links on its naval vessels, Link 16 data links on its F-16s and E-2Cs AEW aircraft, and compatible European data link systems on its Mirage 2000-9s. These links will give the UAE what the U.S. Navy terms "cooperative engagement capacity": one ship or aircraft will be able to detect a target and cue others to engage it.

‡ Robert Mullins (of Northrop Integrated Systems), interview by author, Washington, D.C., April 2004.

§ Larry Velte and U.S. Navy Commander Jonathan Christian, interview by author, Washington, D.C., 2003.

the GCC states has access to U.S. early warnings of missile launches in the Gulf through the Cooperative Defense Initiative (CDI).

Beyond this, the GCC is beginning to show strong interest in creating networks that encompass all military systems, to provide better information to all member states in real time. To some extent this enthusiasm reflects the U.S. military engagement with GCC states. In the 1990s many members of GCC militaries studied in the U.S. professional military education system and emerged as committed advocates of the information-driven "Western way of war."[26]

As discussed in chapter 4, network-centric warfare (NCW) is profoundly relevant to the Gulf states. This approach makes it easier to operate in the littoral environment by fusing information from many different sources, and its emphasis on improved technology represents a cost-effective way to multiply the capabilities of the small GCC armed forces.[27] Just as important, an NCW approach that incorporates a set of sensors broader than just radar could have important effects on GCC abilities to tackle internal and transnational threats. Obvious examples include undersea monitoring, maritime traffic management, and urban and land-border surveillance. Networks could process information from such sources as Kuwait's "electronic fence" of unattended ground sensors on its border with Iraq, similar sensors that Saudi Arabia may deploy along its border with Yemen, or signals intelligence from terrorist cells in rural areas of Saudi Arabia.[28]

As *Jane's Defense Weekly* noted in 2003, the GCC militaries are increasingly focused on threat detection and tracking within their borders.[29] Considering the relatively slow pace of decisionmaking in many Gulf states, governments are likely to welcome the additional time early and accurate intelligence from C⁴ISR networks gives them to make decisions in a crisis.

Gauging the Appropriateness of Developing GCC Security Capabilities

It is clear that the GCC states do have a sophisticated approach to military development, and are far more capable of contributing to their own defenses than many suppose. Yet developing military capabilities will only make the GCC states safer if they develop the ones they need to meet the coming decades' threats. This section will explore whether GCC military capabilities are in fact emerging in the right directions to defend against the full range of internal, transnational, and interstate threat scenarios identified in preceding chapters.

Urban and rural counterterrorism. As observed in chapter 2, the GCC states face increasing internal threats from terrorist opponents that operate in small mobile groups, moving between major cities and using remote rural and border areas as sanctuaries and logistical routes. Appropriately sized and adequately financed GCC security forces are adapting to this threat and have taken the offensive throughout the region, launching multifaceted drives to disrupt active terrorist networks and combat the ideology underpinning Islamic extremism.

Intelligence is the key to rooting out such elusive groups. At the national level, the extensive intelligence forces of GCC states have begun to reorient themselves from a traditional focus on tribal or sectarian activity toward the risk posed by radicalized members of the prevailing Sunni communities, the religious establishment, and even the security forces themselves.

Public recognition of the terrorist threats in the worst-hit GCC states has strengthened intelligence-gathering capabilities considerably. Alongside existing informer networks and public surveillance systems, GCC security forces are beginning to use the general public as a source of intelligence by establishing confidential hotlines.[30] Saudi Arabia already requests public assistance in locating specific suspects, and has issued a public appeal for all families to report any missing male relatives who might have been recruited by terrorist groups.[31]

At the level of technical intelligence-gathering, GCC security forces need to improve their existing capabilities to gather cues from signals intelligence, email traffic, and financial data. Using their broad surveillance powers, GCC governments are increasing closed-circuit television coverage throughout urban centers.

Prevention of attacks requires improved protection for the sorts of facilities targeted by terrorists, such as expatriate gathering places, and increased detection of terrorist reconnaissance or explosives. To prepare for the immediate aftermath of attacks, GCC states need to develop advanced command-and-control and management skills in scenarios involving explosives, mass casualties, WMD, and hostages. Finally, investigation capabilities (e.g., blast, forensic, and general investigation) require constant development to allow states to track down those responsible after attacks occur.

GCC states must also improve their responses to the transnational aspects of terrorism. They are already taking initial steps to codify border regulations and export licensing, making explicit the circumstances under which border crossing and importation of goods are illegal. The next step is enforcement. To counter rural and cross-border movement by terrorist groups, each GCC state must have a sizable, well-trained, and vetted border security force (including, in particular, a capable coast guard) with modern communications and sensor equipment. Such forces also need closer cooperation and "hot pursuit" agreements with neighboring GCC states. Some borders need electronic fence systems such as the one deployed in Kuwait, including unattended ground sensors, surface radars, and processing systems. Saudi Arabia has been deliberating for ten years over the proposed multibillion-dollar Miska deal that includes such an electronic fence, illustrating exactly how long major programs can take to develop. In fact, the economic and in some cases political costs associated with electronic fences dictate that they should be deployed only in key areas as part of carefully tailored interdiction and monitoring campaigns. An ideal system needs to be able to switch its focus from one area to another as terrorist activity adapts.[32]

Improved intelligence-sharing within the GCC and with foreign partners would improve Gulf states' abilities to counter both internal and transnational terrorist threats exponentially. Yet this remains a major area of weakness in the region. Though the GCC has launched antiterrorism information-sharing initiatives, most recently in May 2004, these have generally fallen short of expectations, providing few tangible results to local governments, the United States, or other external partners. Sometimes access to sensitive information is restricted not only because of national sensitivities but also because the information is fragmented among the bureaucratic fiefdoms of several parallel directorates, each the power base of some government official or royal family member.[33] In particular, GCC states sometimes aim to protect the identities of junior members of important families or other dignitaries, resulting in lengthy delays, while raw intelligence goes through a drawn-out and value-reducing process of sanitization.[34] Gulf states also have an uneven record concerning the extradition of terrorist suspects to the United States, meaning that interrogations—and the information derived from them—are kept under local government control. This trend is likely to worsen as a result of the Abu Ghraib prison scandal and attendant reluctance in the Arab world to surrender prisoners to the United States.

When intelligence provides cues for paramilitary or law-enforcement action, GCC paramilitary special weapons and tactics (SWAT) forces need to reach the relevant area quickly and act with precision. As noted, terrorist groups vary greatly in experience, determination, and armament; intervention forces need to be ready to tackle even the most dangerous cells. Professional urban counterterrorism operations generate public confidence, and in urban settings GCC special forces increasingly succeed in "getting their man" (though there is always room for increased professionalism and responsiveness to reduce the risk of friendly and civilian casualties, and to ensure that as many suspects as possible are captured alive). GCC security forces appear less capable in the rugged rural areas used by terrorists as operational havens and trafficking routes. They generally still lack adequate off-road vehicles, and they are not trained or equipped to operate at night or in rural environments against heavily armed terrorists or traffickers. In the future, GCC states will likely require airmobile or motorized special forces capable of operating in rugged terrain or the littoral environment. All-weather, day/night airborne precision-strike capabilities may also be valuable, as long as targeting data are precise enough to minimize the chance of collateral damage. To trap terrorist cells, the forces in each GCC state will have to cooperate across borders and operate in combination with the forces of neighboring states. To prepare themselves for such operations, GCC forces will need to conduct interagency and joint exercises.

Stabilization and key-point defense. At the moment, key-point and road security in the Gulf states is effective, thanks to the large size and long experience of paramilitary forces. There is still room for improvement, however, particularly in the fields of crisis management and major incident command and control. GCC internal security forces are still largely designed to handle large-scale contingencies involving sectarian groups such as the Shiite or Ismaili communities or expatriate labor. Kuwait, for instance, maintains the ability to isolate and displace large numbers of people despite a decade of relative calm. It showed as much in October 1999 when, following rioting in Egyptian ghettos, 3,000 workers were rounded up and relocated to desert internment camps.[35] In the future, however, large-scale threats may come from a broader rage of adversaries, including some in the prevailing Sunni establishment.

In the case of a failing state, regime security forces may not function with the same reliability as they do now, increasing the potential coercive risk posed by military and paramilitary forces. Though key-point security of government and oil industry infrastructure is very tight, more could be done to protect vulnerable expatriate housing compounds and gathering places through better procedures for processing visitors and the establishment of wider perimeters.[36]

At the same time, the Gulf states need to increase the numbers and training of riot police, including mounted police forces. Such units help governments employ minimum force against internal protestors, who will likely provide an increasingly significant challenge in the coming decade. Saudi Arabian policing of the Hajj provides a dramatic illustration of how difficult it is for GCC governments to use minimum force: in 1987 some 400 deaths occurred at the Hajj in clashes between rioters and police. At the Hajj in 2004, a further 251 Muslims were killed by accidents and police action.[37]

To prevent such high death tolls in the future, SANG is training forces capable of intervening in less serious cases of public disorder, and has turned to Britain—where mountain police are seen as the last option before the use of tear gas and rubber bullets—for help. The British Military Mission in Saudi Arabia has cooperated with the London Metropolitan Police's Public Order Training Centre in Hounslow ("Riot City") to train a SANG mounted riot-control unit with two hundred personnel.[38] Against a background of increasing public dissatisfaction, more pluralist political systems, and more assertive media outlets, GCC governments will need to be careful to use levels of force that contain rather than exacerbate manifestations of civil disobedience. Legal, civil-military, and human rights training programs will be critical in developing the more flexible forces that are needed.

Maritime patrolling and interdiction. Terrorists in particular have shown increasing interest in targeting oil terminals and shipping lanes, and in exploiting unregulated maritime traffic and organized criminal networks to move personnel, weapons, drugs, funding, and potentially materials related to WMD. The relatively large but underdeveloped coast guard and naval forces in the Gulf provide a set of capabilities that could provide the basis for the kind of harbor, littoral, and sea-lane security needed to counter this threat.

As naval and littoral missions have grown more frequent, each Gulf state has developed a fleet of either maritime patrol aircraft or helicopters adapted for naval use to patrol their territorial waters. The former are able to carry a far greater sensor payload and stay aloft longer than the latter. Most Gulf navies have also invested in new or upgraded fast patrol boats, which in combination with helicopters will serve to guard littoral zones and harbors against sabotage and illegal boundary crossings.[39] GCC states are also laying the foundations for highly capable, small, deepwater navies, increasing their abilities to carry out persistent constabulary and benign missions (search and rescue, terrorist and drug interdiction, disaster relief, environmental protection, and migration control) or enforce economic exclusion zones.

Yet to counter both the low-intensity threat of seagoing smugglers and terrorists and the high-intensity threat represented by Iran's sea-denial capabilities, GCC states must do a better job of collecting and sharing intelligence in the littoral and maritime environments.

To extend the duration of sensor coverage and support nocturnal underwater surveillance, GCC states will need unmanned aerial vehicles, unmanned underwater vehicles, and unattended floating sensors. Night-vision equipment and periscope detection radar or laser equipment would boost forces' effectiveness, as would ongoing training, exercising, and vetting. To build on these capabilities, the GCC must focus on transnational intelligence sharing, including real-time, common operational pictures of the surface and undersea, supporting multinational, combined border patrolling and maritime interdiction. The GCC states must establish formal early-warning networks that international military and commercial shipping can use to report suspicious activity, issue alerts, or request assistance in the event of a terrorist incident. The extension of shared automated practices among maritime users of the Gulf—the automatic tagging of ships— will aid the process and reduce civilian and military accidents.

Conflict management during an increase in military tension with Iran.
As noted in previous chapters, GCC militaries need to develop more effec-

tive deterrence against a range of military threats posed by Iran. Though at the moment the Islamic Republic continues to display a reactive and deterrence-focused posture toward the GCC, the perceived military strengths or weaknesses of Gulf states could affect Iran's thinking, especially if Tehran develops a nuclear capability that it believes could deter the United States from activating its security guarantee. Though extended deterrence provided by the United States will remain an essential feature of GCC defensive strength, it would be preferable for GCC states to have sufficient internal strength to deter Iran from low-level or persistent harassment. The ideal outcome would be deterrent capabilities in the GCC that dissuade Iran from adopting a more activist foreign policy but do not add to its sense of military encirclement and give it further reason to build up its conventional and nonconventional arsenals.

As suggested in chapter 3, the GCC states could employ one of two models to deter military coercion by Iran: deterrence by punishment or deterrence by denial. To summarize, punishment-based deterrence is typically employed when an opponent threatens an action that a state cannot prevent, and retaliation inflicts a cost on the attacker that may affect its strategic calculus in future cases. Meanwhile, deterrence by denial aims to blunt an attack and thus reduce the likelihood that the attacker will achieve its goals.

Deterrence by punishment is naturally the easier option, relieving the deterring party of the burdens of eternal vigilance and expensive defensive preparations. This is not lost on the Gulf states, where a number of countries are quickly developing formidable long-range and precision-strike capabilities that could inflict great damage on the infrastructure most vital to Iran's economy. Advances in technology have altered the speed at which nations can develop military capabilities and leveled the playing field to a certain extent, giving a boost to small, technologically advanced countries like the GCC states. Affordable, advanced, long-range strike aircraft and standoff precision-guided munitions that can be launched from well outside the range of enemy air defenses have given GCC states the chance to punch well above their weight in any future conflict with Iran.

Each of the six GCC states has developed a small but powerful air and naval fleet armed with advanced antishipping missiles, arguably making each of the GCC states better prepared to block Iranian tanker and commercial shipping than was either Iran or Iraq during their long war. All GCC states boast modern ship- or land-based antishipping missiles (AShMs). Bahrain and Kuwait have focused on developing short-range, air-delivered strike capabilities, while the other GCC states have increasingly sought out long-range strike capabili-

Figure 14. GCC Long-Range Strike Capabilities

	Platform/munitions combination	Capability
Oman	Block 52 F-16/ Harpoon II	Land-attack cruise missile capability against Iranian coastal oil infrastructure, ports, or ships from outside Iranian air defenses
	Block 52 F-16/Joint Direct Attack Munitions	Precision-strike, satellite-guided bombing on coastal targets under cover of darkness
Qatar	Mirage 2000-5/Matra Black Pearl (APACHE)	Land-attack cruise missile capability against Iranian coastal oil infrastructure and ports from outside Iranian air defenses
Saudi Arabia	F-15S/laser-guided bombs	Precision-strike bombing on coastal targets under cover of darkness
UAE	Mirage 2000-9/Storm Shadow	• Land-attack cruise missile capability against Iranian coastal oil infrastructure and ports launched from within UAE airspace • Credible, limited strategic strike capability against fixed targets as far away as Tehran when supported by Block 60 F-16 escorts
	Block 60 F-16/Joint Direct Attack Munitions	Precision-strike, satellite-guided bombing of coastal targets in daylight or under cover of darkness

ties in addition. Figure 14 gives an indication of the long-range, precision-strike capabilities that either exist already or will be fielded by 2008.

Offense is thus most certainly ascendant in the Gulf, with both Iran and the individual Gulf states capable of causing tremendous economic and social damage with a relatively small number of munitions, perhaps in the course of a very short conflict. Most GCC militaries now have the capability to destroy tens of strategic targets on Iran's coast, with pinpoint accuracy and without exposing themselves to Iranian air defenses, and to block Iranian shipping with some effectiveness. Faced with such a prospect, the United States might wish to ask itself whether mutually assured destruction of vital oil-export capacity is the best way to ensure Gulf security.

The one positive aspect to the precision-strike capabilities proliferating in the Gulf is that GCC states do not appear likely to choose unconventional arsenals to counterbalance Iranian WMD. Indeed, no indications suggest that any GCC state has developed chemical weapons to offset Iran's perceived capability. Though possession of WMD confers certain undeniable advantages on developing states—national prestige and a cost-effective deterrent weapon of last resort—such arsenals also invite a level of international censure and isolation that no GCC state will risk under normal circumstances. Furthermore, despite the apparent success of Iraq's use of terror tactics against Iran in the February–April 1988 "war of the cities," when a quarter of Tehran's population fled the city and Iranian morale was seriously hurt,[40] it is uncertain whether GCC states would embrace weapons that implicitly threaten the lives of thousands of civilians. If any GCC state is likely to develop unconventional weapons, it is likely to be Saudi Arabia: its conventional forces are in decline, and it has been linked in the past to Pakistan's nuclear program and other unconventional weapons procurements (e.g., Chinese CSS-2 East Wind intermediate-range ballistic missiles).

Yet the low likelihood that GCC states will develop WMD is the silver lining of a very dark cloud. The proliferation of offensive capabilities in the Gulf is not necessarily a positive step, or one that the United States should allow to become the basis of deterrence in the region. Though economically efficient, deterrence by punishment has been proven to fail in environments where an aggressor can operate just below the deterring state's threshold for punitive action. Iran has a strong record in such so-called gray area deterrence, particularly through its deniable use of proxies and low-profile military action (e.g., naval mines). GCC states must develop a range of capabilities to provide deterrence by denial against the persistent threat of low-level attacks. To be successful, Gulf states need effective air and missile defenses and the ability to prevent, and thus deter, attacks on their maritime and littoral assets. These capabilities would also take some of the military burden off CENTCOM in more serious contingencies.

Even though U.S. and international naval forces have always been present to secure sea lanes, GCC states, in part because of their dependency on maritime export routes and offshore hydrocarbon recovery, have modernized their navies over the last decade. Their navies now offer a set of capabilities that could be developed into a regional deterrent against Iranian maritime expansionism (see figure 15). Most naval helicopters operated by GCC militaries have been upgraded since 2001, incorporating new sensors, communications equipment, and guided weapons. These aircraft can be quite useful in sea-control operations by monitoring naval movements, relaying over-the-horizon targeting data for antishipping missile strikes, or engaging enemy fast-attack craft with their own weapons. GCC navies' small but growing number

Figure 15. Current GCC Contribution to Maritime Patrolling Capabilities

	Maritime patrol aircraft (MPA)	Mine-countermeasure capabilities
Bahrain	• SA-365F Dauphin and Bo-105 CBS-4 Super-Five maritime surveillance helicopters • Considering purchase of additional MPA	None
Kuwait	• SA-332 and AS-532AF maritime surveillance helicopters • Considering purchase of additional MPA	None
Oman	• Shorts Skyvans and Dornier DO-228-100 police aircraft functioning as MPA • Advanced, new Super Lynx maritime surveillance helicopters • Considering purchase of E-2C Hawkeye or Hawkeye 2000 MPA	None
Qatar	• No naval helicopters	None
Saudi Arabia	• SA 365F maritime surveillance helicopters • Considering purchase of additional MPA	• Three al-Jawf (UK Sandown) • Four Addriyah (U.S. MSC-322) (retired)
UAE	• AS-332/ 532SC Super Puma/Cougar and AS-565SB Panther maritime surveillance helicopters • EADS/CASA CN-295 MPA • Purchasing E-2C Hawkeye 2000 MPA • In the long term, considering purchase of advanced unmanned aerial vehicle such as Global Hawk	• Considering MCM vessel purchases

of new and upgraded air-defense frigates and well armed corvettes could also provide credible escort support for civilian shipping and a first line of defense in the GCC missile- and air-defense screen. The small size of the Gulf means that the GCC should be able to provide air cover using land-based missiles, if states can achieve sufficient coordination. The GCC can also play a useful role by providing mine countermeasure vessels, which are likely to remain a rare U.S. asset until a large number of littoral combat ships (LCSs) have entered U.S. service.

Figure 16. Current GCC Contribution to Regional Missile Defense

	"Look-up" air-defense radar (ballistic missile defense)	"Look-down" air-defense radar (cruise missile defense)	Missile defense systems
Bahrain	• Single AN/TPS-59(v) 3-D ground-based radar	• Considering purchase of MPA	• Eight to ten I-HAWK launchers • Sixty SM-1 Standard missiles aboard the ex-U.S. Perry-class frigate Sabha • Limited low-level air defenses
Kuwait	• Small inventory of ground-based radars (AN/FPS-117L, Thales TR2100 Tiger S-band, Thales TRS 22XX S-band 3D) • Considering short-range radar purchases	• Small inventory of tethered aerostat-mounted radars (AN/TPS-63, L-88) • Considering purchase of MPA	• Four HAWK Phase III launchers (limited operability) • Twenty-five Patriot PAC-2 launchers (considering upgrading to PAC-3) • Strengthening low-level air defenses
Oman	• Small inventory of ground-based radars (G.E.C. Marconi Artello S713 surveillance radars, Alenia Marconi Systems S743D Martello 3D radars) • Considering new radar systems	• Considering purchase of E-2C Hawkeye or Hawkeye 2000 MPA	• No high-level air-defense missile systems • Limited low-level air defenses

(continued on next page)

This vision of an appropriately scaled GCC naval and aerial response force is not new. It was the basis for Oman's launch of the GCC military effort in 1981, and Anthony Cordesman proposed the idea in fuller form as early as 1988. But it may only now be coming to fruition.[41] In fact, a naval/air version of the GCC Peninsula Shield force may ultimately be more successful than its land counterpart. When U.S. interests coincide with those of one or more GCC states, such

Figure 16. Current GCC Contribution
to Regional Missile Defense (*continued*)

	"Look-up" air-defense radar (ballistic missile defense)	"Look-down" air-defense radar (cruise missile defense)	Missile defense systems
Qatar	• Small inventory of ground-based radars (Thales TRS-2100 and 2201)	• None	• No high-level air defense missile systems • Limited low-level air defenses
Saudi Arabia	• Extensive inventory of seventeen ground-based long-range surveillance radar and twenty-eight short-range radar	• Five E-3A AWACS aircraft • Some tethered aerostat-mounted radars • Considering purchase of MPA	• 128 I-HAWK launchers • 160 PAC-2 launchers (considering upgrading to PAC-3)
UAE	• Small inventory of ground-based radars (AN/TPS-70)	• Single tethered aero-stat-mounted AN/TPS-67 radar • EADS/CASA CN-295 MPA • Purchasing E-2C Hawk-eye 2000 MPA • In the long term, considering purchase of advanced unmanned aerial vehicle such as Global Hawk	• Considering purchasing high-level air-defense missiles • Thirty I-HAWK missile launchers

a force could cooperate closely with U.S. naval forces, reducing strain on the U.S. Navy by taking over some of the functions outlined in its new Sea Shield concept of operations (designed to "sustain access for friendly forces and maritime trade" in times of rising tension): "organic mine-countermeasures," maintaining an "expeditionary sensor grid," or providing a "theater missile defense" system.[42]

To be avoided, however, is the development of undeniably offensive capabilities by GCC navies—submarine forces, for example. As defense writer Ed Blanche noted, "Submarines don't lend themselves to confidence-building."[43] Yet the UAE may invest in German Type 206 diesel submarines in the future, and the Abu Dhabi–based Emirates Marine Technologies has already begun production of two-man combat swimmer delivery vehicles.

The UAE has also developed a range of sea-control and amphibious assault assets that, from an Iranian perspective, must seem like they are designed to recapture Abu Musa or the Tunb Islands. By 2015 the UAE will boast the strongest navy in the Gulf, with ten very modern and heavily armed frigates or corvettes, a range of amphibious assault craft and amphibious armored vehicles, and sufficient air forces to extend air superiority over the central Gulf for a prolonged period and create a surface and subsurface exclusion zone around the islands.[44] To Iran, this must look very much like an invasion fleet.

It has been observed that the withdrawal of Soviet naval power from northeast Asia resulted in the strong development of regional naval forces, as states vied for maritime presence. A similar trend may develop in the Gulf if U.S. naval presence becomes more episodic, and that trend would need to be managed.[45] To avoid such a trend, the United States should encourage states to follow the principle of "nonoffensive defense." Mine countermeasures (MCMs) are one example of this principle. Even a better example is air and missile defense. Joe McMillan of the U.S. National Defense University noted that missile defense would reduce the Iranian threat and at the same time "deter an unconventional arms race in the Gulf." This touches on the important point that any security assistance CENTCOM gives to the GCC states should seek to deter the Iranian threat while at the same time reducing the underlying tensions that drive Gulf states to arm themselves.[46]

In fact, the Gulf states broadly support the development of GCC-wide air defenses, not least because the majority of them have experienced air attacks in the last twenty years. In the Iran–Iraq war, Kuwait and the UAE suffered air and missile strikes on their ports and offshore facilities. Saudi Arabia and Bahrain were struck by Iraqi ballistic missiles in 1991. Iraq launched ballistic and cruise missile attacks once again in 2003. [47] But again, only the more compact Gulf states have been able to take decisive steps toward better air defense, particularly the UAE, Kuwait, and Bahrain.[48]

As noted, GCC armed forces could play an important role in supporting the theater missile defense role described in the U.S. Navy Sea Shield concept. GCC air and missile defense sensors could reduce the need for the United States to maintain forces in the Gulf by becoming part of a U.S. early warning and defensive system. Against the ballistic missile threat, GCC forces could provide an integrated upward-looking, ground-based radar network, using surveillance radar sites in northern Saudi Arabia, the UAE, and the southern Omani coast.[49] This capability will develop out of a range of national initiatives being drawn into a network as part of the Hizam al-Taawun air-defense system.[50] Some GCC nations can also make a meaningful contribution at the low-altitude descent stage of ballistic missile defense. Kuwait operates five batteries of Patriot PAC-2 missiles, including twenty-five launchers (Kuwaiti batteries have five rather than the usual eight launchers) and 125 to 210 missiles in total. These forces intercepted two Iraqi missiles during Operation Iraqi Freedom. Saudi Arabia appears to have purchased only two or three of the twenty-one PAC-2 batteries it originally intended to buy, but it may field as many as eight in the coming decade if it can overcome persistent funding shortfalls.[51] According to *Defense News* reporting in 2003, Qatar and the UAE were both considering the purchase of small numbers of Patriot units.[52] Both Kuwait and Saudi Arabia are likely to upgrade their PAC-2 systems to PAC-3 standard in the coming decade.[53]

Gulf states can also make a major contribution to the difficult task of detecting and intercepting low and slow cruise-missile attacks, which some of them (particularly Kuwait) suffered during the Iran-Iraq War. If AEW, maritime patrol, and other multimission surveillance aircraft were equipped with data links compatible with GCC-wide and U.S. C[4]ISR networks, their "look-down" sensors could help track inbound missiles. Networking with the U.S. Navy Cooperative Engagement Capacity system would require the procurement of Link 16 data links and relatively advanced sensors such as those on the E-2C Hawkeye 2000 system being considered for deployment in the UAE and Oman.[54] Other advanced "look-down" sensors could be maintained on aerostats and maritime patrol aircraft already fielded by the GCC states. Meanwhile, the Gulf states are far more capable of providing the dense low-level air defenses needed to intercept a cruise missile than the United States, as they can permanently station a raft of modern antimissile weapons on their naval vessels and land bases. And while they defend their own soil, GCC states should at the same time develop an integrated low-altitude air-defense plan for the Gulf littoral, protecting the air and sea points of disembarkation required for the entry of U.S. forces during more serious contingencies.

Notes

1. Michael Knights, "GCC Raises the Drawbridge and Calls out the Guard," *Gulf States Newsletter,* January 24, 2003.

2. Carl Conetta, Charles Knight, and Lutz Unterseher, *Toward Defensive Restructuring in the Middle East*, Project on Defense Alternatives, monograph 1 (March 16, 2003), p. 3.

3. John Levins, "The Kuwaiti Resistance," *Middle East Quarterly* 2, no. 1 (1995). See also Department of Defense, "Final Report to Congress: Conduct of the Persian Gulf War," (Washington, D.C.: Department of Defense, 1992), p. 42.

4. Anthony Cordesman, *Kuwait: Recovery and Security after the Gulf War* (Boulder, CO: Westview Press, 1997).

5. Andrew Rathmell, "The Changing Military Balance in the Gulf," Adelphi Paper 296 (London: International Institute for Strategic Studies, 1992).

6. Joseph Kechichian, *Political Dynamics and Security in the Arabian Peninsula through the 1990s* (Santa Monica, CA: RAND, 1993), p. 58.

7. Michael Knights, "Omani Defense Feels Growing U.S., UAE Influence," *Gulf States Newsletter,* January 9, 2004.

8. CENTCOM, "Southwest Asia: Approaching the Millennium—Enduring Problems, Emerging Solutions" (paper presented at the Southwest Asia Symposium 96, Tampa, FL, May 14–15, 1996), p. 57.

9. Ibid., p. 189.

10. M. H. Ansari, "Security in the Persian Gulf: The Evolution of a Concept," *Strategic Analysis* 23, no. 6 (1999).

11. Simon Henderson, *The New Pillar: Conservative Arab Gulf States and U.S. Strategy* (Washington, D.C.: Washington Institute, 2004), p. ix.

12. Steven Ekovich, "Iran and New Threats in the Gulf and Middle East," *Orbis* 48, no. 1 (2004), p. 77.

13. Earl H. Tilford, *Halt Phase Strategy: New Wine in Old Skins. With PowerPoint* (Carlisle, PA: Strategic Studies Institute, 1998).

14. Larry Velte and U.S. Navy Commander Jonathan Christian, interview by author, Washington, D.C., 2003.

15. Chris Bowie, Robert Haffa, and Robert Mullins, *Future War: What Trends in America's Post–Cold War Military Conflicts Tell Us about Early Twenty-first Century Warfare* (Washington, D.C.: Northrop Grumman Analysis Center), p. 15.

16. Ockmanek, "The Air Force: The Next Round," in Has Binnendijk, *Transforming America's Military* (Washington, D.C.: National Defense University), p. 159.

17. Michael Knights, *Unfriendly Skies: The Development of GCC Air Forces* (Hastings: Cross-Border Information, 2002), p. 44.

18. Dennis Gormley, "Missile Defense Myopia: Lessons from the Iraq War," *Survival* 45, no. 4 (2003), p. 61.

19. Shmuel Gordon, *Dimensions of Quality: A New Approach to Net Assessment of Airpower* (Tel Aviv: Jaffee Center for Strategic Studies), pp. 94–103.

20. Kori Schake and Judith Yaphe, *The Strategic Implications of a Nuclear-Armed Iran*, McNair Paper (Washington, D.C.: Institute for National Security Studies, National Defense University, 2003), p. 40.

21. Velte and Christian, interview by author.

22. Riad Kahwaji, "Bahrain to Scrutinize Future Defense Buys," *DefenseNews*, February 2, 2004, p. 3.

23. Michael Knights, "Commissions to Diminish as Political Liberalization Impacts on Gulf Arms Markets," *Gulf States Newsletter*, May 1, 2002.

24. Ibid.

25. Steven Seroka, "Access and Air Bases in Iraq" (Air University, 2004).

26. Lawrence Freedman, *The Revolution in Strategic Affairs* (London: International Institute for Strategic Studies, 1998).

27. Rear Admiral Patrick M. Stillman, "Small Navies Do Have a Place in Network-Centric Warfare," Naval War College Review, February 16, 2004. Available online (www.nwc.navy.mil/press/Review/2004/Winter/dr1-w04.htm).

28. Michael Knights, "From Appeasement to Open Warfare: Changing Gulf Attitudes to Jihadist Groups," *Gulf States Newsletter*, June 25, 2004.

29. No Author, "Gaining an Edge: Future Challenges and Requirements for the Armed Forces of the GCC," *Jane's Defence Weekly*, March 17, 2003, p. 12.

30. Knights, "From Appeasement to Open Warfare."

31. Paul Melly, "Al-Sauds Defend against Terrorism Charges with Strong Counter-Terrorism Offense, "*Gulf States Newsletter*, September 19, 2003.

32. No Author, "Saudi Victim of Terror, Internal Splits, and Geopolitical Ambiguities," *Gulf States Newsletter*, May 14, 2004, p. 5.

33. Michael Knights, "Prince Nayef Looks Beyond His Fief," *Gulf States Newsletter*, January 24, 2003.

34. Melly, "Al-Sauds Defend against Terrorism Charges," p. 4.

35. Knights, "GCC Raises the Drawbridge and Calls out the Guard."

36. Michael Knights, "Jihadists Bypass Saudi Security Drive to Hit High-Value Targets," *Gulf States Newsletter*, June 11, 2004.

37. Paul Melly, "Hajj Pressures Add to Pressures of Saudi Leadership," *Gulf States Newsletter* 28, no. 727 (2004), p. 4.

38. Knights, "GCC Raises the Drawbridge and Calls out the Guard."

39. Norman Friedman, "New Technology and Medium Navies" (RAN Maritime Studies Program, March 16, 2004). Available online (www.fas.org/man/dod-101/sys/ship/docs/working1.htm).

40. Michael Eisenstadt, *Iranian Military Power: Capabilities and Intentions* (Washington, D.C.: Washington Institute, 1996), p. 44.

41. Anthony Cordesman, *The Gulf and the West: Strategic Relations and Military Realities* (Boulder, CO: Westview Press, 1988).

42. Admiral Vern Clark, "Sea Power 21 Series, Part 1—Projecting Decisive Joint Capabilities" (presented as part of the *Naval Institute Proceedings,* 2002), p. 2.

43. Ed Blanche, "Terror Attacks Threaten Gulf's Oil Routes," *Jane's Intelligence Review* (December, 2002), p. 7.

44. Walters, "GAMCO Special Projects," p. 1.

45. Lieutenant Commander Duk-Ki Kim, "Cooperative Maritime Security in Northeast Asia" (Naval War College, March 16, 2004). Available online (www.nwc.navy.mil/press/Review/1999/winter/art3-w99.htm).

46. Joseph McMillan, *U.S. Forces in the Gulf: Options for a Post-Saddam Era* (London: International Institute for Strategic Studies), p. 2.

47. Gregory Giles, "The Islamic Republic of Iran and Nuclear, Biological, and Chemical Weapons," in Peter Lavoy, Scott Sagan, and James Wirtz, eds., *Planning the Unthinkable: How New Powers Will Use Nuclear, Biological, and Chemical Weapons* (Ithaca, NY: Cornell University Press, 2000), p. 86. See also William Rugh, *Diplomacy and Defense Policy of the United Arab Emirates* (Abu Dhabi: Emirates Center for Strategic Studies and Research, 2002), p. 73; and Tom Cooper, *Iran-Iraq War in the Air, 1980–1988* (Atglen, PA: Schiffer Publishing, 2003).

48. Velte and Christian, interview by author.

49. American Foreign Policy Council, "Gulf States Rethink Missile Defense Shield," Missile Briefing Defense Report no. 54 (May 21, 2002). Available online (www.afpc.org).

50. Riad Kahwaji, "GCC States Seek Missile Defense System," *DefenseNews,* May 26, 2003, p. 16. See also Kahwaji, "Bahraini Minister Underscores Region's Missile Defense Needs," *DefenseNews,* January 19, 2004.

51. C. A. Woodson, "Saudi Arabian Force Structure Development in a Post–Gulf War World" (Fort Leavenworth, KS: Foreign Military Studies Office, 1998), p. 7.

52. Kahwaji, "GCC States," p. 22.

53. Kahwaji, "Bahraini Minister."

54. Vice Admiral Mike Bucchi and Vice Admiral Mike Mullen, "Sea Power 21 Series, Part II—Sea Shield: Projecting Global Defensive Assurance" (presented as part of the *Naval Institute Proceedings*, 2002). See also Clark, "Sea Power 21."

PART III

Future Security Cooperation: Challenges and Opportunities

5

Deterrence and Defense
in the Coming Decade

THE CENTRAL MISSION of U.S. Central Command (CENTCOM) is to "Protect, promote, and preserve U.S. interests in the Central Region, to include the free flow of energy resources, access to regional states, freedom of navigation, and maintenance of regional stability." How can CENTCOM best achieve this mission under the constraints of the new global defense posture and the resultant reduction in U.S. force levels in the Gulf? As U.S. strategy statements stress time and again, partnership is the key. The National Defense Strategy discusses the need to "expand allied roles and build new security partnerships," and specifically to "support models of moderation in the Muslim world by building stronger security ties with Muslim countries." It goes on to identify security cooperation as the "principal vehicle" used to:

- Identify areas where our common interests would be served better by partners playing leading roles.

- Encourage partners to increase their capability and willingness to operate in coalition with U.S. forces.[1]

Similarly, the peacetime engagement pillar of CENTCOM activity calls on the command to "Maintain support and contribute to coalitions and other collective security efforts that support U.S. and mutual interests in the region." Confidence-building measures are to include the promotion of regional militaries, the development of regional and bilateral relationships, and closer cultural understanding between the United States and its Gulf allies.[2]

In the coming decade, the United States needs reliable security partners among the states of the Gulf Cooperation Council (GCC), and it needs to establish a clear and flexible balance of responsibility for deterring and defending against different types of threats. Increasingly, the threats proliferating in the region cannot be deterred or reduced through U.S. military security guarantees alone. CENTCOM's three-tier system of organizing security assistance provides a useful framework for analysis.

Tier I: Each state's ability to defend itself. In the past, assistance at this level has typically meant providing states with the basic tools and political-military support to maintain their territorial integrity against depredation by larger neighbors. Arguably, with intra-GCC disputes on the wane, Tier I self-defensive capacity now refers chiefly to states' efforts to assure internal stability. Consequently, GCC states are unlikely to welcome the direct involvement of other GCC nations or the United States in Tier I activities.

Tier II: The ability to mount a collective defense of any GCC state threatened by an external aggressor. Theoretically, GCC nations can achieve defensive quasi-independence through common defense policies and armed forces that can collectively defend one or more of the six states. Though it is unlikely that GCC states can mount such a quasi-independent defense against a major external threat such as Iran, *Tier II defense is appropriate for addressing shared transnational threats such as terrorism and trafficking.* It is not only much more realistic for the GCC to mount a collective defense in these cases, it is essential to forge transnational responses to transnational threats.

Tier III: The ability to function as partners and hosts to coalition operations involving multinational forces. In the past, the presumed adversary has naturally been interstate enemies such as Iran and Iraq. Such threats would require U.S. intervention, and would justify U.S. military deployment to the region. In the current scene, *multinational forces may also wish to defend against and deter transnational threats*; indeed, we already see a multinational flotilla in the Gulf to block narcotics and terrorists and intercept proliferation-related shipments.

It is clear that GCC states have taken the lead in Tier I (internal) self-defense and can continue to do so. It is equally clear that the distinction between Tiers II and III is slowly eroding, as a multinational partnership is required to tackle transnational and interstate threats to the GCC. Containing and deterring Iran and monitoring transnational threats are both long-term missions that demand the open-ended vigilance of all security forces deployed in the Gulf. To the extent that regional allies can reliably replicate or even improve upon the performance of U.S. forces in either of these missions, they will greatly reduce the burden on the overstretched U.S. military, freeing up rare, valuable assets and allowing service personnel to spend less time on deployment and more time with their families. Finally, more capable regional allies will to some extent take the United States off the front line of deterring Iran, allowing the region to find a more natural and less confrontational balance of power. Though the United States will remain the ultimate guarantor of security in the Gulf states, it should not be drawn into repeated deployments to the region, or exposed to the "cheat-and-retreat" tactics Saddam Hussein used so effectively in the 1990s.

The following sections will enlarge upon the ideas introduced above.

Defense against Internal Threats

Internal security threats in the GCC take place entirely within the territories of sovereign and fully functioning states (not in "failed states" or "ungoverned spaces" such as Somalia). As a result, stabilization efforts and urban and rural counterterrorism operations will be almost exclusively the responsibility of the Gulf states themselves. For reasons explained previously, the United States has only limited ability to provide direct military or security aid to GCC states' internal policing capabilities. Instead, it must aim to ameliorate the structural causes of instability in the Gulf through democratization, economic integration, foreign direct investment, and public diplomacy.

As these slow mechanisms take effect, however, the United States can improve the security of citizens in the Gulf and the near-term internal stability of Gulf states by continuing to provide training in crisis management, civil-military and human rights, and counterterrorism, along with counterterrorism materiel and technical specialists (e.g., in the fields of forensics and technical intelligence collection). In fact, in the field of counterterrorism training, the U.S. was the only show in town throughout the 1990s, providing hundreds of millions of dollars of support each year as opposed to tens of millions of dollars from Europe.

Today such training occurs principally in programs gathered under the Non-Proliferation, Anti-Terrorism, De-mining, and Related Programs (NADR) family of State Department–administered initiatives, including the Antiterrorism Assistance (ATA) program run by the U.S. State Department Bureau of Diplomatic Security. ATA provides training courses that stress the practical elements of protecting personnel, facilities, and infrastructure from terrorist attack, offering courses in prevention, response, and postincident investigation. The Gulf states perfectly meet ATA's criteria for funding: they face a "critical and high threat from terrorism," and need increased capability to "adequately protect U.S. facilities and personnel."[3] Reassuringly, the scale of combined ATA counterterrorism assistance to GCC states has increased massively since the mid-1990s, rising from less than 1 percent of global ATA funding to an average of 15.3 percent in 1996–2001. According to U.S. government officials interviewed for this study, GCC states have consistently provided some of ATA's best students, and each of the GCC countries now runs "cutting-edge" academies at which local instructors teach the basics learned under ATA to junior members of the security services. ATA training now focuses largely on teaching advanced skills to senior GCC officers who are themselves ATA alumni—and proves that U.S. security assistance can foster local self-defense capabilities at minimal cost to the United States. The program clearly deserves continued support and funding from the U.S. government, yet like many smaller initiatives, its success is largely unheralded. (Full details of U.S. delivery of ATA training assistance can be found in Appendix 4.)

Another key State Department initiative is the Counter-Terrorism Financing program, set up with up to $7.5 million funding in FY2005 to establish Financial Intelligence Units (FIUs) in key terrorist financing hubs, including those in the Gulf (such as Bahrain and Saudi Arabia). In the future, the Gulf might be an excellent setting for a counterterrorism conference organized under NADR's Counter-Terrorism Engagement program.

Demand for NADR programs remains high. Competing ATA projects in Iraq and Afghanistan should not be allowed to detract from aid to the GCC states; the programs offered to GCC states under the NADR initiative should even be expanded in certain directions. In FY2004, of a global total of $96.4 million, only $1.7 million of NADR assistance (or 1.7 percent) went to the Gulf states. The GCC share of ATA assistance also dropped precipitously after September 11, registering less than a 1 percent rise on average each year since 2001, while the global ATA budget increased by an annual average of 344 percent. Though the proportional drops resulted largely from the global expansion of the program, it is important that the Gulf continues to receive strong funding under NADR, as it engages in aggressive counterterrorism policing.

Multinational Defense against Transnational and Interstate Threats

Shared transnational problems are easier to solve with shared transnational responses. Transnational terrorists and criminals who use borders to throw off pursuit can only be fought by countries who share intelligence across borders as well. Land, sea, and air borders are easier to police if authorities on both sides communicate regularly and act in a coordinated manner. And shared international waterways and choke points such as the Straits of Hormuz can be made safer and more secure likewise.

Furthermore, though in the past the northern and southern GCC nations have been menaced by different threats, this is no longer the case. Today all GCC states have similar needs: to reduce the risk of conflict with Iran on the one hand, and on the other to handle transnational problems like narcotics and human trafficking, terrorism, and weapons proliferation. All GCC states can contribute to fights against transnational threats, and future GCC action against them does not rest on the capabilities of any one state (as, for example, in the 1980s and 1990s interstate collective defense hinged on Saudi military development).

For all of these reasons, the United States and its Gulf allies should seek to resurrect the idea of Tier II collective defense in the GCC and continue to integrate multinational actors (principally the United States and other NATO countries) into this framework.

Not only should all GCC states be comfortable in developing Tier II capabilities against transnational threats, those same capabilities (C⁴ISR and border and maritime security) would greatly increase GCC states' ability to deter the Iranian threat. Closer defense ties thus could be formed without unduly or unnecessarily provoking Iran. In particular, the United States needs to develop GCC's confidence to become the first line of defense for its nations, capable of resisting any explicit or implicit intimidation from a nuclear or nonnuclear Iran. Ultimately, the United States' aim is to provide what might be termed "full-spectrum reassurance." As the previous chapters have noted, the U.S. global defense posture does not envision maintaining sufficient forces in the Gulf to deter an expansion of Iranian influence or undertake an initial defense against Iran. It therefore stresses intercontinental power projection, despite the potential for shortfalls of strategic lift, or for political or military restrictions on host-nation access. Previous chapters have also noted that a power projection–based strategy can be weakened by use of "cheat-and-retreat" tactics.

To overcome these weaknesses, the United States needs local allies who (in combination with light U.S. forces) can deter Iranian aggression during protracted periods of tension that fall short of major crisis. At the outset of a crisis, and perhaps during an extended period of tension, GCC armed forces need to be able to provide "always there" assets (including rare, valuable assets such as maritime patrol aircraft and mine countermeasures [MCM] craft). Ideally, the GCC should provide both prompt presence and, later, persistence that U.S. forces may struggle to match. Therefore, just as the GCC attempted to develop the Peninsula Shield joint GCC land forces, the increasingly maritime nature of future transnational and interstate threats argues for the development of a "Peninsula

Shield at sea," an idea that will be explored later in this chapter. To support this concept of operations, GCC states should slowly develop systems compatible with the U.S. Navy Sea Shield concept, at first so that niche GCC assets can fit into United States operations, and later, perhaps, equalizing and reversing the balance of effort. In MCM, and in particular in the use of unmanned underwater vehicles (UUVs) for remote mine hunting, the U.S. Navy has sought to make up for funding shortfalls through innovation, including cost and technology sharing with trusted allies. That shared interest could be further served by joint U.S.-GCC efforts in research, design, and coproduction.[4]

In more serious scenarios, GCC forces need to demonstrate "hold-the-line" capabilities, meaning that GCC forces must be capable of a strong initial defense of the basing infrastructure and regional reception points that the United States relies on to project its power. The United States should also continue helping the smaller GCC states harden their land bases, moving them to a "protected posture" against chemical and biological weapons. Nonoffensive defense capabilities would hinge on the air-defense and civil-emergency capabilities of regional allies. The "Peninsula Shield at sea" would be joined by the activation of a "Peninsula Shield in the air."

When push comes to shove, of course, the United States will remain the only state able to defend the Gulf in a major-theater war. Both the United States and the GCC nations would therefore benefit from the regular exercise of America's ability to reinforce the Gulf states.

U.S. Tools for Building Allies' Capabilities

Broadly speaking, the United States uses two categories of mechanism to build military and security capabilities in allied states. The first, security cooperation, includes combined military operations, combined military exercises, and other ad hoc combined operational and intelligence-sharing initiatives. One key initiative of this type is the International Military Education and Training (IMET) program, which brings foreign officers to the United States to undertake professional military education, particularly English-language training and other courses that increase compatibility and closer fraternal ties. Other programs bring specialists to allied nations as part of Technical Assistance Field Teams or Military Training Missions. The second category, security assistance, entails the approval of arms sales and any offsets made against the cost of procuring military equipment and training. In this category, foreign military financing (FMF) allows the United States to guide procurement in allied states and oversee the selection process by providing credits to buy U.S.-produced military equipment. Security assistance also includes the low-cost lease or no-cost grant of U.S. military surplus (known as excess defense articles or EDA) to U.S. allies. Both FMF and EDA allow the United States to help standardize regional armed forces and improve technical compatibility with the U.S. military.

GCC states' defensive capabilities will only continue to grow with continued and even expanded NATO and U.S. security assistance. All the Gulf states are eligible for all the various forms of U.S. security assistance. This will continue to be the case as they are increasingly recognized as "models of moderation in the Muslim world," identified as especially valuable security partners by the 2005 National Defense Strategy. The United States has granted Bahrain and Kuwait the status of Major Non-NATO Ally, further improving their ability to purchase advanced U.S. armaments. Four of the GCC states (Bahrain, Kuwait, Qatar, and the UAE) have joined NATO's Istanbul Cooperation Initiative (ICI), and Saudi Arabia has entered into direct talks with NATO.

Closer U.S.-GCC ties have also meant fewer restrictions on arms sales to the Gulf states. Restrictions on the release of major technology and transfer started to loosen as long ago as the 1970s, with the precedent-setting sale of airborne warning and control system (AWACS) and F-15 aircraft. Export restrictions were relaxed further in the 1980s and 1990s, giving the Gulf states access to nondowngraded U.S. hardware such as the RC-135 Rivet Joint intelligence-gathering platform, army tactical missile system (ATACMS) long-range strike systems, advanced medium-range air-to-air missile (AMRAAM) beyond-visual-range missiles, and a host of other cutting-edge technologies. As the twenty-first century dawns, GCC states like the UAE are now centrally involved in the collaborative research and design of key U.S. radar and avionics systems. One of the reasons such sales are increasingly approved is that GCC states have not used their growing military capabilities to threaten Israel's qualitative edge. The closest any Gulf state has come was when Saudi Arabia stationed its F-15S aircraft at Tabuk air base, near Israel, in contravention of clauses in the original export license. Indeed, relations between Israel and the Gulf states have improved markedly over the last decade.

This is particularly true in relation to the southern Gulf states. The Israeli Foreign Ministry maintains an Interests Section in Qatar, where Israeli Foreign Minister Silvan Shalom met openly with his Qatari counterpart, Sheikh Hamad bin Jassim al-Thani, on May 14, 2004. Oman has long represented a moderate voice on Israel—it was the only Arab country not to boycott Egypt following President Anwar al-Sadat's peace negotiations. When Israel's former prime minister Yitzhak Rabin seemed close to reaching agreement with the Palestinians, he was invited to visit Oman and an Interests Section was opened in Muscat, though it has been dormant since the beginning of the October 2000 intifada. Israeli-UAE ties have shown signs of rapid improvement since September 2004, when an Israeli delegation of forty (including Minister-without-Portfolio Meir Sheetrit, an official in Finance Minister Benjamin Netanyahu's office, and Bank of Israel Governor David Klein) attended International Monetary Fund and World Bank meetings in Dubai. Dubai ruler Sheikh Muhammad bin Rashid al-Maktoum invited Israelis to visit the emirate, and Israel and the UAE have since cooperated closely on UAE sponsorship of rehabilitation projects in Jerusalem's Old City, reflecting the Emirates' appetite to displace Saudi Arabia in many high-profile pan-Islamic projects.

Security cooperation. CENTCOM has long undertaken a busy program of bilateral and multilateral exercises with the GCC, taking advantage of the almost constant presence of U.S. military forces in the region over the last two decades. Recurring naval, amphibious, and special-forces exercises were commonplace, and the U.S. Army undertook the extended Desert Spring training exercise series with the Kuwaiti military over a period spanning two decades. The increased tempo of operations in Iraq and across the Global War on Terror has changed this picture, and future reduction of the U.S. presence in the Gulf may change it further still. CENTCOM has staged far fewer security cooperation exercises with the GCC since 2001, and the Desert Spring series has come to an end. In addition to a basic shortage of forces available to engage in exercises, the United States also has concerns about protecting its troops following 2002 and 2003 terrorist attacks on forces undertaking exercises in Kuwait.

Military-to-military relations between the United States and regional allies could suffer unless new exercises are scheduled so as to exploit U.S. presence in the Gulf when CENTCOM does rotate its forces there. Though expedient planning, shorter exercises, and increased use of simulation can make a smaller pool of forces stretch farther, policymakers should recognize that a regular commitment of rotational exercise forces will still cost far less than the heavy burden of maintaining a significant forward presence. Similarly, instead of allowing U.S. power-projection capabilities to atrophy—as will probably be the temptation—CENTCOM needs an annual exercise similar to the "Reforger" deployment exercises held by the United States during the Cold War. Such maneuvers would periodically test the U.S. ability to deploy forces to the region, maintain strategic airlift capabilities and regional reception capacity, and send a strong deterrent signal to potential aggressors.

Between visits of U.S. or NATO forces to the Gulf region, GCC forces must maintain their own realistic training programs. The GCC will gain most from exercises with Western armed forces, however, so Western and GCC militaries should seek opportunities to undertake such combined, preferably multinational operations. In other parts of the world, the United States has established such training regimes formally: coastal and aerial border-security training and combined operations are undertaken with key hydrocarbon suppliers through the Gulf of Guinea Guard program and the Caspian Guard program. Counterterrorism training and combined land border security operations are undertaken in some of the world's "ungoverned spaces" through the East African Counter-Terrorism Initiative (EACTI) and the Trans Sahara Counter Terrorism Initiative (TSCTI), formerly the Pan-Sahel Initiative. Though politically sensitive, these counterterrorist initiatives might provide a good model for the Gulf.

Currently the closest analogue is the Cooperative Defense Initiative (CDI), a product of United States counterproliferation policy that brings together GCC states under a U.S.-chaired framework. The CDI has a number of facets, including theater missile defense; passive defense and consequence management in the case of chemical, biological, radiological, or nuclear attacks; environmental security initiatives; and C^4ISR and shared early warning. The group's focus on C^4ISR could give it a broad mandate to guide GCC military policy through its senior-level military-to-military discussions and doctrine-development sessions.[5] Perhaps most important, the defensive character of the CDI provides a climate in which GCC military officers feel comfortable engaging in close collaboration with the United States. One obvious step CDI could take is to link together states' C^4ISR systems to provide a common operating picture of shared transnational threats and, thereby, a better basis for combined decision-making. CDI could also be a venue in which to share information supporting counterterrorism, border control, and countertrafficking operations.

Such efforts toward greater integration of Gulf Arab security capabilities and responses need not suffer the same fate as Saudi-led effort of the 1990s to develop a collective defense against Iraqi overland invasion. The slow-developing GCC proved not to be a good venue for managing defense integration, and Saudi Arabia proved to be a poor locus of military reform. But a less formal approach more evenly distributed across the GCC may stand a better chance of success. Furthermore, Iraqi overland invasion was only ever a threat to the northern Gulf states, while new Tier II coordination could develop in response to transnational threats that affect all GCC states (e.g., terrorism, organized crime, WMD, and Iranian domination of the Gulf).

GCC integration could also benefit from NATO's new willingness to involve itself in Gulf security. Formal NATO involvement in the Gulf began with the launch of ICI in 2004, and, as mentioned, Bahrain, Kuwait, Qatar, and the UAE have thus far joined the initiative. One of the primary contributions NATO could make would be to aid GCC states with defense reform and budgetary planning. From the 1983 formation of the small Peninsula Shield force to the 2000 announcement of a common defense agreement, the GCC has never developed a blueprint of military integration. Nor has it developed methods such as those NATO uses to rationalize costs and avoid duplication of effort in key areas, such as airborne early-warning systems, intratheater airlift command, and aircraft refueling. Instead, joint GCC military procurement has been limited to a single combat search-and-rescue unit that became active in January 1999. Similar capabilities that involve expensive equipment and training (such as unmanned aerial vehicle operation and satellite imagery) are currently procured nationally rather than as interoperable GCC assets. Procurement of land and naval forces remains idiosyncratic and uncoordinated.

In fact, at the time of writing shared GCC military assets do not really exist. As a result, states have little invested in the formal organization of the GCC, and little reason, therefore, to remain focused on it as a node of military integration. The time is right for another try at military integration among the six Gulf states, using a different model of development. GCC states have grown increasingly sophisticated in force planning and procurement, developed cutting-edge Western-style military educational facilities, and taken the first steps toward standardizing their platforms and systems. The UAE military is emerging as a locus of new thinking in the Gulf, and the Saudi military is keen to regain some of its status. U.S. defense equipment and doctrine are far more deeply embedded in the GCC military establishment now than they were in the early 1990s, and GCC states are beginning to display mature plans for military development. These trends need to be reinforced.

Security assistance. Arguably, security assistance mechanisms are underutilized in the Gulf. While GCC states have increasing access to as much U.S. military hardware as they desire, far less effort seems to focus on ensuring that arms sales do not overstrain the purchasing countries or overshadow equally important military-to-military ties. On the first count, it is surprising

Figure 17. U.S. Foreign Military Assistance, 2000–2006

	Global FMF (thousands of dollars)	GCC FMF (thousands of dollars)	Near East share of FMF (percent)	GCC share of FMF (percent)
FY2000	4,788,297	0	97	0
FY2001	3,568,373	0	93	0
FY2002	4,007,256	54,000	85	1.3
FY2003	5,991,632	27,850	93	0.4
FY2004	4,544,810	49,532	87	1
FY2005	4,745,232	38,688	77	0.8
FY2006	4,588,600	39,000	78	0.8

Source: Defense Security Cooperation Agency. Figures for 2005 are estimates; figures for 2006 are requests.

that while FMF has steadily increased over the last decade (and particularly since September 11), the GCC share of this funding assistance is miniscule compared to that of nearby states like Israel, Egypt, Jordan, and Turkey. As figure 17 shows, the Near East as a whole received an average of 87 percent of global FMF in 2000–2006 while the GCC states combined for an average of only 0.6 percent.

The only two GCC countries to have received sustained FMF assistance are Bahrain and Oman. Bahrain is the smallest spender on defense in the GCC, unique in spending under $1 billion per year. Thanks to generous U.S. aid and careful procurement, Bahrain has reversed a trend that saw it consistently over-spending its defense budgets using off-budget cash infusions from Saudi Arabia. Saudi money played a large role in kick-starting the Bahrain Amiri Air Force's F-16 program and underpinned the 1987 Peace Crown I agreement. As Riyadh has backed out of aid commitments to Bahrain, Washington has stepped in, helping Bahrain develop its F-16 fleet and air-defense system through increasing amounts of EDA along with FMF aid totaling $91.8 million since 2002.

Meanwhile, Oman's military role in GCC and Western regional planning has long outstripped its financial capacity. It can typically only sustain its spending through external funding assistance. GCC pledges in 1983 to provide $1.8 billion worth of military aid to Oman were never realized, and Oman spent most of the 1980s and 1990s receiving slender amounts of U.S. military aid compared to Washington's other allies, including Egypt, Jordan, and Bahrain.

The U.S. Defense Security Cooperation Agency reported that foreign military sales credits and training assistance totaled a mere $4.5 million from 1990 to 2001, compared with more than $1.3 billion worth of aid to Egypt and $43 million to Jordan over the same period. But Oman's share of U.S. foreign military financing aid has increased dramatically since September 11. A total of $109 million since 2002 has supported its F-16 procurement and development of border and maritime security.

Bahrain and Oman received FMF funding from the State Department because they are perceived to be under military demands for which they are economically unsuited. Bahrain's defense expenditure remained stagnant throughout the 1990s, as it prepared for the exhaustion of its oil reserves in first quarter of the twenty-first century. Oman's transition from an oil-driven economy dominated economic thinking throughout the 1990s and led the World Bank in 1994 to recommend that Muscat reduce its defense spending, initiating a decade of cutbacks to training, operations, and maintenance. With per-capita GDP hovering just over the global average, Oman nonetheless maintains per-capita defense spending and spending as a percentage of GDP at three times the global average. Modernization efforts initiated between 2001 and 2005 period will see up to $8.57 billion worth of additional defense spending, beginning with a dramatic 38 percent hike in 2001 and the announcement of over $1.7 billion worth of new procurement. This modernization will benefit the United States security posture in the Gulf, but it can only be undertaken with strong sustained provision of FMF and EDA.

Similarly, one could argue that the United States should provide FMF support to other GCC states. It is increasingly difficult for them to maintain high levels of per-capita defense spending while their per-capita incomes are stagnant or dropping. Though GCC nations are considered "rich" by casual observers, in fact this is yet another outdated perception. Of the GCC states, only Qatar has high enough per-capita GDP to meet the United Nations (UN) definition of a high-income nation (one with an average per-capita GDP of at least $26,490). The UAE falls just short.[6] All the other GCC states classify as middle income, with Bahrain, Saudi Arabia, and Oman close to the lower end of the scale and hovering just above the global average (see figure 18).

Yet despite economic limitations, the Gulf states are amongst the highest per-capita defense spenders in the world. Kuwait and Qatar were the world's top per-capita spenders in 2001, investing $2,414 and $2,072 per citizen respectively. That year the global average was $226 per capita. The United Arab Emirates had an official per-capita defense expenditure of $1,137, but large amounts

Figure 18. GCC Per-Capita Income, 1998–2002

	1998	1999	2000	2001	2002
Bahrain	$9,627	$10,032	$11,773	$12,012	$10,500
Kuwait	$12,759	$13,791	$15,947	$13,935	$16,340
Oman	$5,726	$6,202	$7,615	$7,421	$7,830
Qatar	$18,373	$21,739	$30,558	$28,959	unknown
Saudi Arabia	$7,019	$7,507	$8,520	$8,169	$8,530
United Arab Emirates	$16,991	$18,029	$18,906	$19,816	$19,550
United States	$31,261	$32,672	$34,253	$34,788	$35,400
Global average	$5,028	$5,126	$5,172	$5,052	$5,120

Source: United Nations Statistics Division, National Accounts Main Aggregates (http://unstats.un.org/unsd/snaama).

of off-budget procurement make it likely that the Emirates spent as much as Israel on defense per citizen or more. (Israel spent $1,673 per capita in 2001.) Saudi Arabia ($1,156) and Oman ($1,089) officially spent roughly the same per capita as the United States ($1,128), but again, these figures do not reflect Saudi off-budget purchases, the more than $7 billion Saudi Arabia invested in internal security,[7] or Oman's off-budget financial assistance from the UAE.[8] In Bahrain, which spends twice the global average of defense per capita, defense spending continues at the same per-capita rate as the more economically sustainable and less challenged nations of France and the United Kingdom.[9]

The U.S. Department of Defense uses defense expenditure as a percentage of GDP to assess whether a state contributes to the burden of its own defense. Of America's top twenty-seven military allies, it has consistently rated the GCC states highest in this category. In fact, the GCC states are remarkable amongst U.S. allies in consistently spending above the average as a percentage of their GDPs while registering midlevel per-capita GDP. Despite this commitment out of proportion to their economic breadth, however, military inefficiencies and overdependence on the Tier III capabilities of U.S. forces left the GCC countries as net importers of security throughout the 1990s.

Nonetheless, the Department of Defense's other burden-sharing measurements make clear that the GCC states have contributed strongly, both directly and indirectly, to their own defenses. The Defense Department's interim goal is for key allies to pay 50 percent of the incremental costs of U.S. contribution to their defense, a goal already reached by Oman (79 percent), Saudi Arabia (54 percent), and Kuwait (51 percent). Qatar has reached 41 percent and Bahrain 33 percent. The UAE provides $74 million per year, but the overall total of U.S. incremental costs linked to that country have not been calculated and thus a percentage cannot be fixed. The raw dollar total is second in the entire GCC after Kuwait, suggesting a strong contribution. In total, the GCC pays an annual $465 million in cash and indirect in-kind payments of fuel, billeting, land use, electricity, and water.

At a time when pressing demographic and economic trends will require states to reorient their expenditures into job creation, education, and social welfare, the majority of GCC states need to slow or even reduce their defense spending. The United States should encourage this. One means of making sure that reduced defense spending is undertaken efficiently would be to guide GCC procurement with financing credits through the FMF program and the provision of EDA. Strong U.S. support is no doubt planned for traditional recipients like Bahrain and Oman, but consideration should be given to extending U.S. support to other GCC states.

For instance, Kuwait received a strong provision of EDA in the early 1990s as equipment used for its liberation was left in that country, but has never received FMF. It spent heavily on defense throughout the 1990s; since it began rearming in 1992, budgeted defense expenditure has averaged $3.28 billion per year, an average of 12.5 percent of the nation's GDP. Kuwait spends considerably more per capita on defense than its GCC neighbors, at around $1,555 (compared to a NATO country average of $399). Despite its consistently strong defense and security budgets, the royal family recognized that the complete reequipment of Kuwaiti armed forces could not be supported by current GDP alone, and an Emiri decree issued in August 1992 authorized the release of up to $12 billion from Kuwait's strategic reserve to supplement procurement budgets over a ten-year period. Between FY1992 and FY2000, $3.72 billion worth of arms transfers were paid from the defense budget, while at least a further $5.34 billion was drawn from the strategic reserve.

To these costs must be added Kuwait's extensive burden-sharing contributions to U.S. force deployments and the recurring Desert Spring exercise series. Together, these had grown to an annual figure that hovered between $200 and $400 million by FY2000, not including an additional $2.28 billion allocated from the strategic reserve for exceptional U.S. deployments. FY2001 figures showed a steep 35 percent increase in defense expenditure, but, following the diminishment of the Iraqi threat, it is likely that the National Assembly's Public

Accounts Committee will become stricter in its scrutiny of defense procurement. This will make it difficult for Kuwait to commit the remaining $4 billion of supplemental, off-budget funding available from its strategic reserve, slowing planned investment in air and air-defense forces, including antiaircraft systems, advanced air-to-air and air-to-ground munitions, long-awaited upgrades to Kuwait's European helicopters, and transport aircraft.

Saudi Arabia remains the highest spender on defense in the Gulf: despite a crash course of cutbacks initiated in the mid-1990s its extremely large military forces are expensive to maintain, even when much of its planned procurement has been delayed indefinitely. Saudi Arabia has recognized the need to maintain equipment inventories and develop a sufficient manpower base to use them, placing a limit on exactly how low its defense expenditure can fall. At the same time, defense spending is unlikely to rise sharply due to the collapse of the Iraqi threat and the demonstrated terrorist threat to the kingdom. Riyadh has pushed back major fleet replacement decisions, embarked on cautious procurement planning, and shuffled capital from single-nation funds like the al-Yamamah fund (covering British arms sales) to cover general procurement. Saudi Arabia is likely to spend the remainder of this decade reducing its conventional forces to a more appropriate level, training them, and properly maintaining its equipment. During this period, an expansion of the U.S. Military Training Mission (USMTM) and provision of carefully targeted FMF and other forms of U.S. security assistance are needed to guide the rationalization of the Saudi armed forces. As the Defense Security Cooperation Agency noted in its FY2004 report, diminished Saudi defense spending meant that Saudi Arabia's military:

> Sought less expensive—and less effective—training from other countries. These steps have led to a diminished experience with U.S. equipment and techniques, which in turn risks a decrease in the interoperability of Saudi armed forces with those of the United States and a similar loss of influence and defense sales to U.S. contractors.[10]

The need for guidance is particularly acute in the naval and air forces, though the Royal Saudi Land Forces look set to begin receiving increased U.S. military training, providing them with similar levels of support to the U.S.-trained SANG. An officer in the U.S. Army commented:

> We are now looking at expanding that relationship to include for the first time the Saudi army, as well as a deeper relationship extending down to the brigade level so that younger more junior officers are trained by our more junior officers.

I think in the long term that is to everyone's advantage because you can develop relationships with these guys as they progress up the ranks.[11]

Alongside FMF and EDA, the IMET program can be particularly useful in building relationships in this way, but as with FMF, the use of IMET in the Gulf represents a tiny fraction of global IMET—around 9 percent in the decade before 2001 and an average of 1.6 percent since then. To put this in perspective, the GCC states receive a fraction of the IMET aid provided to Balkan states. The number of officers undertaking IMET training in the United States during 2004 from all GCC states combined equaled the number from Lebanon and half that sent by Morocco. Within the Gulf, only Bahrain and Oman are major users of IMET, each sending just less than a hundred senior and midlevel officers for professional military education in the United States each year. Receiving a sliver of IMET funding to allow it to qualify for a cheaper training rate, Saudi Arabia put only twelve senior or midlevel officers through IMET training in FY2004. Despite its status as a Major Non-NATO Ally and the effective end of the Desert Spring exercise series since the occupation of Iraq began, Kuwait receives no IMET assistance. Emerging U.S. allies like Qatar and UAE also receive no IMET. The result is that GCC countries send decreasing numbers of senior and midlevel officers through training in America.

Though the GCC can be congratulated for the increasing levels of technical training it carries out at local training centers to reduce costs and personnel relocation, the failure to fully capitalize on the relationship-building potential of IMET represents a major missed opportunity. IMET is most valuable to CENTCOM because it develops interpersonal ties between Gulf military decisionmakers and Americans, giving future decisionmakers positive formative experiences of the United States. It allows a transfer of American values and ideas, providing influence in episodes of diplomatic crisis, aiding trade development, and building a basis for long-term access to the Gulf. IMET is a key tool for identifying future Gulf leaders, strengthening their crisis management skills, and building influence with them. English-language training and time spent in a Western culture builds compatibility. Any security assistance effort will be hampered unless far greater emphasis is placed on these benefits.

The negative view of GCC militaries that has developed among U.S. planners—which this study aims to address—developed in part because of a slow breakdown in military-to-military contacts between U.S. and GCC militaries. This is particularly true of relations between the Saudi Arabian and U.S. militaries in the middle and late 1990s, partly due to the increasing terrorist threat in the Gulf. If in the future fewer forces are deployed in the Gulf, and if those forces that are deployed are under tighter security lockdown, this trend of decreasing contact between the U.S. and GCC militaries could worsen, with important negative effects for coalition operations. Reduced contact results in a decline in mutual trust between militaries. On this subject Thomas Donnelly and Vance Serchuk noted the particularly negative effects this could have on counterterrorism operations:

> In a war predicated on gathering intelligence and making friends, there is no substitute for having boots on the ground. Specifically, this mission requires joint training exercises between U.S. forces and local militaries, day-to-day interaction on the command and operational levels, and—put simply—a degree of mutual trust. It also requires the sense that the United States has a long-term commitment to the region.[12]

This potential for reduced contact and exercises needs to be countered with a carefully targeted series of rotational exercises and the increased use of low-cost but highly valued training programs supported by U.S. grant funding. The highest ever recorded annual level of IMET in the Gulf was one-third the cost of a single M1A2 main battle tank. Such nominal sums can bear disproportionate fruits.

Of course, making FMF and IMET grants available is not the end of the story. GCC states often underutilize these tools themselves, limiting the requests for support that they forward to the Pentagon through U.S. embassies. In part, this underutilization of U.S. aid is an expression of sovereign independence: acceptance of U.S. aid increases reliance on a single security guarantor and a single vendor nation. When petrodollars are flowing freely, U.S. security assistance loses it appeal. Nevertheless, since security assistance represents such a cost-effective means of strengthening and guiding defense reform in the GCC, the United States should energetically push for its utilization by GCC states. If future U.S. security cooperation and security assistance programs aim to develop the core competencies outlined below, regional states may be more enthusiastic about them. Such a nonprovocative focus on shared threats may not only attract GCC participation, but also the assistance of multinational organizations such as NATO that can enhance GCC defense integration and ability to tackle transnational issues.

Building Core Competencies in the GCC

U.S. security cooperation and security assistance in the Gulf should thus focus on creating a defined set of core competencies in the GCC states. Figure 19 summarizes these focus areas.

The following sections will review several of these areas.

Common operating picture. The United States and GCC forces need to develop multilevel systems to share portions of their intelligence pictures with some or all coalition partners.[13] This kind of tiered intelligence sharing could support ad hoc "coalitions of the willing" that would complement the portfolio-basing model adopted by CENTCOM, strongly benefiting the United States. The GCC could play a very significant role in coalition intelligence-gathering as long as it continues to procure advanced sensors and other C⁴ISR assets of the kind the U.S. Navy uses. The U.S. Navy currently plans to maintain what it terms expeditionary sensor grids (ESGs) in each area where it is present. With stronger C⁴ISR capabilities, the GCC could contribute the bulk of the assets required to maintain an ESG in the Gulf, which the United States could administer using its advanced processing capabilities, feeding information back to the GCC contributors, minus that from a minimal number of U.S.-only intelligence sources. During periods of heavy U.S. presence in the Gulf, the ESG would be bulked up with added CENTCOM collections systems. At other times, the GCC would provide the majority of assets, effectively monitoring maritime traffic in the Gulf and extending air and missile defense and providing persistent coverage to the U.S. C⁴ISR system even when the United States cannot keep rare, valuable assets in the area.

The E-2C Hawkeye 2000 aircraft likely to be deployed by the UAE and Oman will be able to feed data into such a system, as could other locally owned sensors if they are purchased as planned. Extensive, modern lookup radar networks already exist throughout the GCC. In the coming decade, certain Gulf states (most notably the UAE) will make widespread use of commercial satellite coverage, unmanned aerial vehicles, unattended surface sensors, and other advanced sensors mounted on helicopters, multimission surveillance aircraft, and patrol craft.[14]

If guided by the United States, the Gulf states could thus contribute greatly to U.S. global defense posture by providing key elements of the Gulf ESG, freeing up rare, valuable U.S. intelligence collection personnel and equipment for use elsewhere or for valuable downtime between deployments. Along with

Figure 19. Focus Areas for U.S. Security Cooperation and Assistance

GCC core competencies	Explanation
Common operating picture	• Contribute to U.S.-led expeditionary sensor grid (ESG) in the Gulf • Shared traffic-management and tracking capabilities • Shared aerial, surface, and subsurface intelligence picture • Networked radar, sonar, and maritime patrolling reports
Land-border security	• Integrated regional customs and border controls • Collaborative border patrolling and intelligence exchange • Electronic and physical fence systems
Maritime patrolling and surveillance	• Robust maritime patrol aircraft and surveillance helicopter fleets • Computerized near-real-time maritime traffic tracking systems • Experience in drugs and alien migrant interdiction, vessel boarding search-and-seizure operations, and interception of unsafe or suspicious vessels at a safe distance from shore • Harbor security • Mine countermeasures (MCMs) • "Blue water" (e.g., beyond coastal waters) shipping escort capabilities
"Holding the line" against Iran	• Early warning air- and missile-defense network (detection) • Multitier active air and missile defenses (interception) • "Protected posture" against conventional and CBRN (chemical, biological, radiological, nuclear) weapons • Crisis- and consequence-management capabilities

these sensors, the GCC should be encouraged to invest in a range of processing systems, including broadband military communications networks, tactical data links, high-speed processors, and recognition tools capable of characterizing and tracking certain kinds of targets automatically. The United States should start a training effort of the scale of Desert Spring to help GCC states develop a flexible set of options for maritime and missile-defense response. At first, modern GCC naval and missile-defense assets would be integrated into a Western, probably U.S.-controlled C^{4}ISR system, but the ultimate aim would be for the exercises to devolve to local control. The same approach might work to generate a common undersea picture from U.S. and GCC sound-surveillance systems attached to the Gulf seabed, floating free, and towed by air- and watercraft.[15] Both kinds of project could be carried out under the low-profile auspices of CDI.

Transfer of skills and systems rather than platforms would mark a key change in the security assistance the United States provides to the GCC states. As William Schneider of the U.S. Defense Science Board noted, the United States can derive great advantages by plugging other nations into its intelligence architectures: "We don't need to share advanced weapons platforms anymore, we need to share data link technology."[16]

Land-border security. The United States and NATO should help GCC states develop the capabilities they need to effectively patrol their own borders and block threats in their sovereign territory (and the adjoining areas of international waters, where appropriate). Under ICI, a number of NATO countries could assist GCC states in the fields of counterterrorism, border security, countertrafficking, and civil emergency planning. The United States already runs programs around the world to train coast guards and border-patrol forces, but these useful, low-cost tools are not yet sufficiently utilized in the Gulf. They include:

- The Export Control and Related Border Security (EXBS) program, which takes practical steps to assist border regulations and enforcement.

- The Small Arms and Light Weapons (SALW) program, which assists border security and disarmament.

- The Terrorism Interdiction Program (TIP), which provides regional states with immigration software called the Personal Identification Secure Comparison and Evaluation System (PISCES). PISCES facilitates international intelligence-sharing and "watch list" monitoring.

Unfortunately, Saudi Arabia, for example, guardian of the beating heart of the global economy, receives the same level of support as Ethiopia. Though Saudi Arabia received $80,000 worth of EXBS assistance in FY2003, no new funding was requested in FY2004 or 2005. Yemen will receive $525,000 worth of EXBS support, making it doubly surprising that Saudi Arabia did not also qualify. (Saudi Arabia might also qualify for the same SALW assistance Yemen receives.) Kuwait and Bahrain, both trading centers that function as smuggling hubs, have received no EXBS support. No GCC states have yet received TIP support, blinding the United States to Gulf immigration records. Finally, only one GCC state, Oman, qualified for the U.S.-funded Counter-Terrorism Fellowship Program, meaning that only $200,000 (1.6 percent) of $12,350,000 worth of this aid reached the Gulf states.

Until the United States can increase its NADR support to GCC states, it may be able to support their border-security programs with assistance in kind. For instance, the United States can contribute to Gulf security by supporting border-security operations in Iraq and Yemen. In the latter case, this might mean continuing to operate Special Forces advisors on the Yemeni side of the border. Future U.S. military and antiterrorism assistance training to Yemeni and GCC forces should include rural border-patrol and mountain-warfare training and specialized training for attack-helicopter crews in night operations and strike missions. Where possible, trainees should be accompanied on training and operations by United States instructors, and be supported with a baseline of equipment that includes GPS navigation, night-vision equipment, and body armor.[17] This form of training has resulted in excellent results in both the Caucasus and Yemen. One Yemeni national security official commented following a successful operation:

> Previously we kept cameras away from the military in case of disasters, but this time we were very confident. We had helicopter backup and received U.S. satellite pictures of the site. Our Special Forces troops were masked and wore body armor. It was one beautiful success story.[18]

What works in Yemen could work in Iraq too. Bilateral exercises involving the United States and the GCC states should regularly focus on border security scenarios. As the NDS noted: "One of our military's most effective tools in prosecuting the Global War on Terrorism is to help train indigenous forces."[19]

Maritime patrolling. The unregulated flow of maritime traffic in the territorial and international waters of the Gulf poses a range of threats to the GCC, Iraq, and indeed Iran (plus all those who depend on the Gulf for energy supplies and stable oil prices). At the most basic level, the existing heavy traffic is due to increase as higher volumes of oil are transported from Gulf terminals and as increasing nonoil imports and exports cross the Gulf. Public health, safety, and environmental concerns demand closer monitoring and tracking of this increased number of ships. Ships and crews passing through the Gulf need to be held to baseline standards to ensure that they do not pose a risk to the economic and ecological systems in the area. The GCC states, Iraq, and Iran have all indicated their desire to prevent pollution in the Gulf through their memberships in the Marine Emergency Mutual Aid Centre (MEMAC) and the Regional Organization for the Protection of the Marine Environment (ROPME).

The GCC states and potential NATO allies also have strong incentives to block organized criminal activities. In the past, European and GCC states have worked with Iran to cut down the trade in drugs, justly praising the Islamic Republic's internationally recognized counternarcotics program (which has also received plaudits from the U.S. State Department). All the GCC states have bilateral agreements with Iran that seek to bolster cooperation on narcotrafficking. Alongside the antitrafficking measures agreed within the GCC, Iran has also signed bilateral drug-control agreements with Kuwait and Qatar, and is completing others with Saudi Arabia and the UAE.[20] Recent multinational interdictions in the international waters of the Gulf have derived their authorization from the 1988 UN Convention Against Illicit Traffic in Narcotics, Drugs, and Psychotropic Substances.[21] This convention has been ratified by Iran and all other regional states, in addition to the United States and the NATO and European states currently involved in maritime patrolling in the Gulf.

Similar support for maritime interdiction can be found in UN conventions dealing with the trafficking of human beings, slavery in all but name. Reasonable suspicion that a vessel is facilitating slavery removes that vessel's rights of "innocent passage" through international waters and makes it liable to be boarded and searched under the UN law of the sea. All the states of the GCC (save Qatar), NATO, and European Union are also in the process of ratifying the December 2000 UN Convention Against Organized Crime, plus the related Protocol to Prevent, Suppress, and Punish Trafficking in Persons, Especially Woman and Children.[22] This protocol in particular justifies interdiction of traffic under a light burden of proof. Like the UN narcotrafficking convention, the protocol's articles encourage states to develop cooperative, interdiction-related rules and practices, including information sharing, interdiction training, and tighter legislative authority to enforce documentary requirements. Following the bad grades they received in the June 2005 U.S. State Department Trafficking in Humans Report,[23] GCC states are eager to improve their records and therefore are likely to give strong backing to multinational interdiction efforts. In particular, Oman, Qatar, Saudi Arabia, and the UAE were placed in the Tier

3 category alongside such notorious centers of the slave trade as Burma, Cambodia, North Korea, and Sudan. The report shed light on the role of Iran as the key supplier state to the GCC.

GCC navies are thus likely to want to get involved in joint exercises that focus on the range of trafficking threats they face. Those navies will benefit from closer interaction with multinational navies that already boast high levels of proficiency in carrying out drug and alien migrant interdiction, vessel-boarding search-and-seizure operations, interception of unsafe or suspicious vessels at a safe distance from shore, and the enforcement of exclusive economic zones. For NATO countries, such interface would advance ICI objectives. Aid in maritime patrolling and interdiction might offer CENTCOM a good way to promote combined GCC and multinational operations and the eventual formation of a multinational naval task force based in the Gulf. Multinational exercises are also an excellent way to draw the GCC states into international waters, preparing them for a broadened role in policing the high seas as well as their territorial waters. Integrating their navies into multinational command and control networks will engender greater sharing of information, providing collateral benefits for U.S.-GCC monitoring and interdiction of shared transnational threats.

"Peninsula shield at sea." The creation of combined GCC-NATO maritime patrols in the Gulf would be one important step toward the creation of a peninsula shield "at sea," in effect reorienting the GCC collective defense force to meet the threats of the twenty-first century rather than the diminished threats of the late twentieth. This new maritime force would be composed partly of a rotating set of GCC naval vessels, an idea similar to early Omani plans for a multinational force to preserve freedom of navigation in the Straits of Hormuz.

Developments that could speed the establishment of such a multinational force are already under way. In response to the attacks of September 11, a multinational flotilla called Task Force 151 was formed in October 2001 to patrol and escort shipping in the Arabian Gulf, the Straits of Hormuz, and the North Arabian Sea/Gulf of Oman. It comprised ships and aircraft from the United States, United Kingdom, Canada, France, Italy, Greece, and New Zealand. The flotilla has now been folded into a U.S. naval force, Expeditionary Strike Group 1 (ESG-1). In an average month, the group reports boarding 27 vessels, querying 1,027, and escorting 9 through the Straits of Hormuz. A similar NATO naval group, Task Force 150, comprised the United Kingdom, France, Germany, Italy, and Spain. This force carried out counterterrorist patrolling in the

Bab el Mandab straits off the Horn of Africa and Indian Ocean, boarding 18 vessels and querying a further 109 during its first two years of operations.

The development of a "Peninsula Shield at sea," would offer the GCC considerable benefits, including the opportunities to feed into the U.S. C⁴ISR network and join with other navies to receive hands-on experience of drug and alien-migrant interdiction, vessel-boarding-and-seizure operations, interception of unsafe or suspicious vessels at a safe distance from shore, and the enforcement of exclusive economic zones.[24]

Multinational naval forces could make a major contribution to combating narcotrafficking in the Gulf. As an example, the UAE Interior Ministry Anti-Drug Department undertook interdiction within its own territorial seas and seized 6.1 tons of hashish and 100 kilograms of heroin in the whole of 2003. In comparison, in just two operations during December 2003, U.S. and coalition ships in the international waters of the Straits of Hormuz and the North Arabian Sea seized 2.93 tons of hashish and 40 kilograms of heroin. In another spate of raids in February 2004, the U.S.-led ESG-1 captured 3 tons of drugs and detained 48 suspected terrorists aboard four dhows.[25] Three terrorist suspects were captured along with the drugs during one capture in the Straits of Hormuz.

Increased multinational naval patrolling could also help block WMD shipments.

Building Partnerships

Contrary to the prevailing view, the GCC states are good security allies, willing and able to do business with the United States. This text, it is hoped, has shown that there is nothing intrinsically foolish about the idea that GCC states can produce effective military forces and play a range of useful roles in Gulf security. Naturally gaps exist in GCC military and security capabilities, but they can and should be filled by reinvigorated U.S. security assistance and security cooperation programs. In cases where CENTCOM is incapable of providing direct assistance (e.g., in counterterrorism operations in Gulf cities or in controlling widespread, internal civil disobedience), the U.S. military should make special efforts to find ways to prepare or indirectly assist the GCC states. In every case, however, the more GCC countries can do for themselves, the less the United States will need to do for them.

Adopting a strategy based on security assistance will allow the United States to manage risks to its abilities to sustain future operations and continue to recruit, retain, train, and equip its forces. Some U.S. allies among the smaller

Gulf states will never seek greater responsibility for their own external security while the United States is willing to pour out its own blood and treasure on their behalf. They need to be helped to stand on their own two feet: as well as being good for the United States, a security assistance–based approach is good for the Arab Gulf states, offering them a way to reduce the visibility of Western security support without losing its protective value.

Yet security assistance and security cooperation have been important but strictly secondary parts of CENTCOM operations in the Gulf since 1990. Recent history has instead seen CENTCOM provide most of its protection in the form of deployed forces and power projection. In the future, this pattern needs to change. Now that this chapter has shown that GCC states do show increasing willingness and capability to become robust security partners, the remaining paragraphs will address how U.S. security assistance could facilitate greater adoption of security roles heretofore played by the United States.

Certain principles should guide the effort. First, the United States should recall the lesson of the last twenty-five years of alliance politics and avoid the temptation to build its efforts around a new "anchor" state. First Iran and then Saudi Arabia have failed to provide the United States with a stable regional proxy or strategic pillar. Simon Henderson has written that the five smaller Gulf states represent a "new pillar," a reflection of CENTCOM's shift toward the so-called portfolio approach, using a wider range of basing options.[26] The key lesson is that one can never have too many allies or too many options; the United States should neither give up on its security relationship with Saudi Arabia nor fall in love with some new and enticing miniature "anchor state" such as the UAE. There is no denying that the UAE looks set to emerge as a locus of military develop-ment. It is establishing training centers that will teach Western military doctrine and technological skills to Arab militaries, and providing low-profile funding of Omani military purchases, guiding the sultanate to buy latest-generation Block 52 F-16 aircraft that will be highly interoperable between UAE and United States forces.[27] But while the United States may recognize particularly close military-to-military ties with nations like the UAE, the portfolio approach must not suffer. No matter how attractive the al-Dhafra or al-Udeid air bases may appear today, it is worth recalling the billions of dollars worth of U.S.-constructed air bases that sat idle during Operation Iraqi Freedom just across the border in Saudi Arabia. The portfolio approach is certainly high maintenance, as U.S. government official Bob Pelletreau noted in 1996 when he cited "the frustrating costs in inefficiency and capability of this still-too-ad-hoc security structure," but it offers the best guarantee of access to the Gulf in an emergency.[28]

The second principle underlying U.S. security assistance should be a commitment to threat reduction. CENTCOM theater strategy calls for maintaining regional stability, supporting regional dialogue, and building confidence. The United States needs to use its considerable influence over GCC military development policies to guide states toward nonoffensive defense, where practical.[29] It is not in the interests of the United States or the GCC states individually or collectively for the UAE to operate attack submarines, for Saudi Arabia to buy modern replacements for its CSS-2 intermediate-range ballistic missiles, or for any GCC state to develop weapons of mass destruction. Nor is it in America's interests to encourage, actively or passively, the proliferation of advanced land-attack missiles that breach the Missile Technology Control Regime. Offensive capabilities are in danger of overheating in the Gulf, leading to instability. States could increasingly face a "use-it-or-lose-it" dynamic in future crises and as each side amasses weaponry of greater precision and effectiveness and the potential pace of those crises accordingly accelerates. As CENTCOM theater strategy noted, the U.S. military should promote the development of regional militaries that are responsible as well as capable. The United States surely should not encourage the continued development of devastating "push-button" strike capabilities in such young and aspiring countries.

Notes

1. Department of Defense, "The National Defense Strategy of the United States of America" (Washington, D.C.: Department of Defense, 2005).

2. CENTCOM, *Strategy* (U.S. Central Command, May 28, 2004). Available online (www.centcom.mil/aboutus/strategy.htm).

3. A summary of NADR assistance is available online (www.state.gov/documnents/organization/28971.pdf).

4. Mark Haskins, "Iran and the Arabian Gulf: Threat Assessment and Response," thesis, Air University (Maxwell Air Force Base, Alabama, 1998).

5. No Author, "The Role of the Armed Forces in Environmental Security" (Muscat: Sultan's Armed Forces, 2000), p. 1.

6. See http://unstats.un.org/unsd/snaama

7. Paul Melly, "Al-Sauds Defend against Terrorism Charges with Strong Counter-Terrorism Offense," *Gulf States Newsletter,* September 19, 2003, p. 4.

8. Michael Knights, "Omani Defense Feels Growing U.S., UAE Influence," *Gulf States Newsletter,* January 9, 2004.

9. See http://unstats.un.org/unsd/snaama

10. Department of State, "Congressional Budget Justification for Foreign Operations Fiscal Year 2006" (Washington, D.C.: Department of State, 2005), p. 459.

11. Colonel Richard Lechowich, interview by author, 2003.

12. Thomas Donnelly and Vance Serchuk, "Toward a Global Cavalry: Overseas Rebasing and Defense Transformation" (Washington, D.C.: American Enterprise Institute, 2003), p. 1. Available online (www.aei.org/include/pub_print.asp?pubID=17783).

13. Daniel Byman and Jerrold Green, *Political Violence and Stability in the States of the Northern Persian Gulf* (Santa Monica, CA: RAND, 1999); CENTCOM, "Southwest Asia: Approaching the Millennium—Enduring Problems, Emerging Solutions" (paper presented at the Southwest Asia Symposium 96, Tampa, FL, May 14–15, 1996).

14. Vice Admiral Cutler Dawson and Vice Admiral John Nathman, "Sea Power 21 Series, Part III—Sea Strike: Projecting Persistent, Responsive, and Precise Power (presented as part of the *Naval Institute Proceedings*). See also Norman Friedman, "New Technology and Medium Navies" (RAN Maritime Studies Program, March 16, 2004), available online at www.fas.org/man/dod-101/sys/ship/docs/working1.htm; Stanley Carvalho, "UAE: Plans Satellite for Space Imagery 2003," *Gulf News,* March 17, 2004 (available online at http://gulfnews.com/Articles/news.asp?ArticleID=105211).

15. Mark Hewish, "No Hiding Place: Undersea Networks Help Flush out Littoral Targets," *Jane's International Defense Review* (June 2004), p. 46.

16 William Schneider, interview by author, Washington, D.C., 2003.

17. Roger McDermott, "Countering Global Terrorism: Developing the Anti-Terrorist Capabilities of the Central Asian Militaries" (Carlisle, PA: U.S. Army War College Strategic Studies Institute, 2004), p. vi.

18. Michael Knights, "Yemen Security Steps Up the Pace," *Gulf States Newsletter,* October 3, 2003, p. 2.

19. Department of Defense, "The National Defense Strategy of the United States of America" (Washington, D.C.: Department of Defense, 2005).

20. International Relations Office, *Illicit Drug Report in the Islamic Republic of Iran* (International Relations Office, Drug Control Headquarters, March 14, 2004). Available online (www.diplomatie.gouv.fr/routesdeladrogue/textes/iran.pdf).

21. Access to the convention is available online (www.unodc.org/pdf/convention_1988_en.pdf).

22. Access to the protocol is available online (http://untreaty.un.org/English/notpubl/18-12-a.E.doc).

23. Access to the report is available online (www.state.gov/g/tip/rls/tiprpt/2005/).

24. U.S. Coast Guard, *Coast Guard 2020: Ready for Today, Preparing for Tomorrow* (U.S. Coast Guard, March 14, 2004), p. 1. Available online (www.dtic.mil/jointvision/cgsmcolor.pdf).

25. Knights, "Maritime Intercept Operations Continue in the Gulf," *Gulf States Newsletter*, April 3, 2004.

26. Simon Henderson, *The New Pillar*: Conservative Arab Gulf States and U.S. Strategy (Washington, D.C.: Washington Institute, 2004).

27. Knights, "Omani Defense Feels Growing U.S., UAE Influence," *Gulf States Newsletter*, January 9, 2004.

28. CENTCOM, "Southwest Asia," p. 216.

29. All of the U.S. officers interviewed for this book agreed that the GCC states have not developed sophisticated force-planning capabilities and that these states remain guided heavily by assessments issued by U.S. military personnel at annual or ad hoc security reviews. As Kori Schake and Judith Yaphe note: "Since their independence, the six [GCC states] have preferred to have—or rather, allowed—outsiders to define their security policies and needs." See Kori Schake and Judith Yaphe, "The Strategic Implications of a Nuclear-Armed Iran," McNair Paper (Washington, D.C.: Institute for National Security Studies), p. 39.

6

Threat Reduction in the Gulf in the Coming Decade

FOR THE GULF states, Tiers I to III security assistance and cooperation aim to improve both internal and transnational security capabilities. In this arrangement, U.S. military forces will be better integrated as contributors of niche capability with regard to internal threat scenarios facing the GCC, and the role of Gulf states themselves will ultimately expand to that of primary force provider in both transnational and interstate relations. As a net result, a significant boost will occur in the national and coalition capabilities of the United States and its Gulf allies, a development that Tehran will likely perceive as a threat. A counterbalancing program of activity, therefore, is necessary to reduce military tensions in the Gulf.

Whereas U.S. Central Command (CENTCOM) traditionally has focused on military-to-military ties with its allies, the growing transnational threats in the Gulf and the dangers associated with isolating a nuclear Iran suggest that CENTCOM must develop a fourth level of regional capability—what might be termed Tier IV. The ultimate objective of Tier IV security assistance would be the reduction of military tension in the Gulf region.

U.S. planners have approached threat reduction from a number of angles in recent years. The U.S. National Security Strategy of 2002 called for the strengthening of alliances and for multilateral initiatives to defuse regional conflicts, while the *Quadrennial Defense Review* (QDR) of 2001 called for the development and sustainment of regional security arrangements.[1] The U.S. National Security Strategy of 2005 identified prevention as the outermost ring of an "active, layered defense" of the U.S. homeland. CENTCOM theater strategy calls for the promotion of "stability" and "confidence-building measures" in the Gulf, and the development of closer ties with "regional political and military leaders." U.S. regional strategy also calls for the "maintenance of regional awareness of security trends," the "development of integrated regional approaches" to these threats, and the "promotion of efforts in the region" to crack down on transnational threats such as terrorism and drug trafficking.

In the context of Gulf security, threat reduction is a two-sided coin. The first entails transnational threats shared by the region's GCC and non-GCC countries. These threats do not affect individual states alone, and they cannot be solved at the national level. Environmental security represents one example: while an oil spill might take place within the territorial waters of one state, the impact will be felt all along the coastline. Another example is the uncontrolled cross-border movement of drugs, contraband, or terrorists. Borders cannot be policed effectively from one side only. As states become more effective at counterterrorism efforts, terrorist actors will cross unguarded borders on their way to easier operating locations. To close down illicit cross-border trafficking, the GCC needs partnerships with Iraq and Yemen, as well as with Iran, which is a major transshipment route for drugs and terrorists bound for the Gulf.

The flip side of the coin involves the need to reduce interstate tensions in the Gulf, particularly between Iran on one side and U.S. allies in the GCC (and the United States itself) on the other. As the preceding chapter argued, improved collective security in the GCC needs to be counterbalanced with confidence-building measures. A stronger U.S.-GCC partnership could cause increased tension with Iran, making closer security relationships with the GCC counterproductive unless a balancing mechanism is established. If Iran develops as a nuclear-armed power, the emergence of dialogue among the region's states will become particularly important. Nuclear crisis management relies not just on the involvement of rational actors, but also on good peacetime and wartime communications channels. In works such as *The Strategy of Conflict* and *Arms and Influence,* nuclear strategist Thomas Schelling argued that successful nuclear crisis management relies on means of communication in which intent can be accurately conveyed and received.[2] As National Defense University scholar James Russell noted:

> In the Middle East, however, there exists no institutionalized process for adversaries to ensure structured communications on a routine basis outside of formal political channels—and even these do not exist in the cases of Iran and the United States and Iran and Israel. Interstate communications tend to occur through other means: the media and more traditional forms of political or diplomatic communications. These forms of communication leave a lot to be desired.[3]

As Michael Kraig has said, the United States will only destabilize Iranian foreign policy and security strategy in the Gulf by refusing to grant the Islamic Republic a "minimal level of existential security" (e.g., by threatening regime change) or by carrying out preemptive military strikes on nuclear facilities, which may delay but could ultimately spur Iranian WMD development. Alternative options exist, Kraig argued, citing the patient U.S. strategy vis-à-vis a nuclear-armed China—entailing bilateral contact and the encirclement of China with stable neighbors protected by U.S. security guarantees—and successful U.S. management of a nuclear-armed India, which used diplomacy to keep the Indian nuclear program in latency between tests in 1974 and 1998.[4]

Moreover, isolating Iran is not a policy that U.S. allies either inside or outside the GCC support collectively. As Patrick Clawson noted concerning this international context, "The United States' containment of the Communist bloc had the consistent support of America's allies; its dual containment of Iran and Iraq did not." With Iran as the sole surviving "rogue state" in the Gulf, this policy is not looking any more popular with allies in Europe or the Middle East. As long as Iran respects certain U.S. interests in the region, reduced military tension will benefit everyone. Moving toward such an end would have few if any political costs, and there is a pressing need for dialogue on key interstate security issues. As ambassador Chas Freeman noted in a speech given to CENTCOM:

> Think boldly about some of the possible implications [of shared security interests of Gulf states]. Do these common interests mean that there should be some kind of naval forum in the Gulf? If we have an interest in freedom of navigation, isn't there a need for understanding on that among the littoral states? Isn't there a need for discussion among all the states in the region about mines? Is there room for an understanding about missiles in a region which saw the "war of the cities" between Iraq and Iran? Is there a need for a regional security forum—if so, how should it be constructed?[5]

The time is right for the United States to guide the development of a Gulf security forum. One result of Washington's preferential treatment of the more assertive set of smaller GCC states has been the slow erosion of Saudi Arabian leadership of the GCC, which in turn has led Riyadh to seek to bolster the six-country pact and develop a new Gulf-wide security forum that maximizes Riyadh's traditional political and economic clout. As Saudi Arabia and Iran weather socioeconomic challenges and external criticism more severe than that of the smaller GCC states, they are likely to draw closer together. Furthermore, if the United States maintains an increasingly exclusive focus on developing bilateral security and economic relationships with the smaller GCC states, Saudi Arabia will also turn toward its fastest growing client states—China, India, and Japan—as well as its long-term ally Pakistan. Closer strategic alignment with these powers presents a long-term proliferation threat, with Riyadh likely to consider the replacement of its aging Chinese CSS-2 intermediate-range ballistic missiles in the coming decade. Already, as an increasingly marginalized Saudi Arabia has reengaged with Iran, the Saudis have restarted the process of codesigning a regional security architecture after a hiatus of twenty-six years. On a call that took place on December 5, 2004, Saudi Arabian foreign minister Prince Saud al-Faisal expressed support for an inclusive Gulf-wide security arrangement (involving the GCC, Iran, Iraq, and Yemen). In calling for a radical reordering of Gulf security, the minister invited an Iranian-GCC security agreement recognized by the UN Security Council and invited the increased involvement of India and China in Gulf security, reflecting the direct and growing interest that both states have in the stable supply of Gulf hydrocarbons.

The Saudi proposal is a reflection of the declining condition of the U.S.-Saudi strategic partnership and an indicator that Riyadh is increasingly concerned at the way its traditional hegemony is being undercut by bilateral security and free-trade deals between the smaller GCC states and the United States. These currents are drawing the smaller GCC states and Washington's former strategic pillars, Iran and Saudi Arabia, in different directions. U.S. security policy in the region should draw the GCC states closer to each other and to Washington, not create internal fissures between them that can be exploited by Iran or extra-regional states.

Designing a Gulf Security Forum

In the same way that CENTCOM took the initiative in creating the Cooperative Defense Initiative (CDI), the United States now needs to play an important, if less visible, role in the establishment of a Gulf security forum. Indeed, as long ago as 1994, CENTCOM identified the need to "foster regional forums to address transnational issues, such as environmental pollution, mass migration, terrorism, and drug trafficking" and to "develop multilateral organizations to investigate and resolve regional disputes."[6] Though GCC states have participated in a number of multinational security forums or organizations—including the Middle East Arms Control and Regional Security (ACRS) working group, and meetings of GCC and Arab League interior or defense ministers—these processes have not yielded significant results. In 1995, the ACRS process collapsed as a result of disagreements between Israel and Egypt over an issue related to weapons of mass destruction (WMD), while Arab League and GCC meetings have produced few substantive initiatives pertinent to Gulf security. In contrast, local appetite for substantive security agreements has grown markedly in recent years, with increasing numbers of informal security agreements taking root between the GCC states and Iran or Yemen.[7] In May 2004, GCC interior ministers signed an antiterrorism agreement, but they had no formal mechanism for extending its provisions for intelligence-sharing to states with a vital stake in the issue, such as Iraq and Yemen. Such a mechanism could be provided by a Gulf security forum.

Like U.S. security assistance, a Gulf security forum should be developed with certain principles in mind. These principles have been encapsulated neatly by security studies analyst Craig Dunkerley as "cooperative, comprehensive, and compartmentalized." In plain terms, "cooperative" means that the forum would be inclusive and not aligned against any state in the region; "comprehensive" refers to the need to discuss both "hard security" (interstate military threats) and "soft security" (intrastate and shared transnational threats); and "compartmentalized" means that any diplomatic, economic, and security processes would be specific to the Gulf itself and not tied to the success or failure of the Israeli-Palestinian or Israeli-Syrian negotiations.[8] Further, the forum should be local in character, focusing on the issues that local states care about. Some form of U.S. support or facilitation must underpin the development of a Gulf security forum, giving the project initial impetus, structure, and funding. To attract genuinely enthusiastic regional participation, particularly from Iran and Iraq, however, it must be seen to be homegrown.

This necessity would mean that the United States, along with any other interested extraregional states, would attend the forum with observer status only. As suggested by National Defense University scholar Michael Yaffe, this arrangement could perhaps entail a special envoy for the Gulf, who would be invited to attend certain working groups but not others.[9] Also reducing Washington's overt involvement in the forum would be a means to channel its sponsorship through a multilateral security organization such as NATO, whose membership includes a number of Iran's major European trading partners. A basic model is provided by NATO's Mediterranean Dialogue, which facilitates regional workshops and meetings, though NATO-member involvement in a Gulf security forum would need to be commensurately subtler than its assertive, even stultifying, role in the Mediterranean Dialogue. Any project launched under NATO's Istanbul Cooperation Initiative (launched in 2004 to increase NATO involvement in the Gulf) would have to take such lessons into account. NATO would also have to overcome an image problem in the GCC, where it is seen as a U.S. proxy and a military organization that would seek to solve the region's problems with military solutions. In reality, a strong case can be made that NATO is evolving into a predominantly political organization with a strong interest in fostering inclusionary confidence-building measures and systematic security dialogue in the region.

Though the European Union (EU) might seem a more natural organization to work with the GCC—because of its long history of economic ties to the GCC and greater "distance" from U.S. policies—the EU has a far shallower record on security cooperation and would lack the thrust that can be generated by U.S. involvement in regional initiatives.

Inclusive Membership

As indicated earlier, the forum should be inclusive, meaning that all regional countries—the GCC states, Iran, Iraq, and Yemen—should be offered membership, alongside international and regional nongovernmental organizations (NGOs) dealing with security issues. The glaring, potential hitch would seem to be Iranian involvement. Could the United States support inclusion of Iran, even at the moment when the international community is withholding full rehabilitation for the Islamic Republic in a last-ditch effort to halt its nuclear development? And how would grassroots Iranian reformists view this low-key cooperation on the part of the international community with the Iranian government? Arguably, the balance of cost and benefits to United States strategic interests favors inclusion of Iran in a progressive security forum of limited scope. The United States and Iran already cooperate on many issues that a Gulf security forum would address, ranging from search and rescue (SAR) and the avoidance of incidents at sea (INCSEA),[10] to agreements to repatriate U.S. pilots who might be forced to eject or crash-land in Iran,[11] to support for coalition reconstruction efforts in Iraq, including electricity and oil swaps.[12] In effect, the United States is already engaging in "cooperative security" arrangements with Iran, defined by academics Stan Windass and Eric Grove as "a relationship between antagonists, not between allies. Although they are antagonists, both sides nevertheless share significant areas of common interest: (1) in avoiding war, and especially nuclear war; and (2) in reducing the level of their military expenditure to their minimum necessary for security."[13] Reducing tensions with Iran might, in fact, support rather than undercut the U.S. objective of minimizing Iran's nuclear threat, offering a course of action that can function in parallel with the no less problematic or uncertain multilateral diplomatic effort now under way.

Just as tense relations between the United States and Iran should not block Iran's participation in a security forum, neither should potential objections on the part of GCC states prevent a forum from going forward with Iran. This is true even considering Tehran's continued occupation of Abu Musa and the Tunb Islands. After all, GCC-Iranian security cooperation already exists and is growing on the ground. The aforementioned "security pacts" between a number of GCC governments and Iran are, in part, motivated by the appreciation held by Arab Gulf states for the progressive role being played by Iran in interdicting drug trafficking in the Gulf. The need for cooperative security between all Gulf states has been stressed by the Kuwait Center for Strategic Studies, the Emirates Center for Strategic Studies and Research, as well as Dubai's Gulf Research Center.[14] And GCC states strongly support increased security through the development of interdependent infrastructural networks and economic systems, as shown by a $1 billion water-export deal between Iran and Kuwait, a Saudi role in developing important Iranian industries, and the creation of shared economic zones.[15] Despite the United Arab Emirates' (UAE's) continued bitterness over the occupation of the islands, it has welcomed Iranian involvement in its Environmental Research and Wildlife Development Agency working groups.[16] Such forms of cooperation are mirrored in other regions, where, for instance, China and Taiwan maintain a tense strategic standoff yet manage simultaneously to keep up vibrant trade and investment links.[17] As Iranian academic Saideh Loftian noted, it is possible to discern "an undercurrent of belief among the Arabs and non-Arab elite in the region that the time is right to look for areas of possible cooperation, to unmask common interests suppressed by competing ideologies."[18]

Yet even assuming that the United States and the Arab Gulf states supported Iranian membership, Tehran itself might refuse to join the organization, particularly if it were facilitated in any way by NATO or some other Western security organization. This represents an actual stumbling block owing to a consistent feature in Iran's otherwise zigzagging foreign and security policy—its demand that foreign military forces leave the Gulf. In due course, however, Iran might still accede to joining a Gulf security forum. Between the late 1960s and the 1979 Islamic Revolution, Iran suggested the development of a regional security forum, proposing an inclusive venue that would include even Iraq.[19] Since the end of the Iran-Iraq War, Iranians have continued to call for some form of regional security arrangement.[20] Because this has not happened, and because Iran cannot participate in GCC or Arab League meetings, the Islamic Republic has sought to pursue bilateral deals and discuss security-related subjects at non-security forums, including the Organization of the Islamic Conference. Even if Iran did not accept an invitation to join a forum at first, valuable work could begin on Arabian Peninsula security issues, and Iran could be drawn in at a later date, mirroring the progressive increase in size of membership in the NATO Mediterranean Dialogue.

Scope of Work

For a Gulf security forum, the scope of work can be lifted directly from proposals floated in the mid-1970s, which emphasized minimum common threat
perceptions and shared concerns. Saudi Arabian, Iranian, and Omani proposals
from that time identify the key tasks of the Gulf security forum as:

1. nonaggression pacts that stress the existential rights of regional governments and the inviolability of their borders;

2. mechanisms for resolving regional disputes peacefully;

3. cooperative security initiatives to maintain freedom of navigation and
   shipping safety in the Gulf and Straits of Hormuz; and

4. cooperative treatment of shared threats, such as subversion and
   terrorism.[21]

In designing a program of work, a Gulf security forum should build from the
impressive body of work completed in this field by the ACRS process before its
collapse in 1995. During its period of plenary activity, ACRS attracted the enthusiastic support of the six GCC states and Yemen (Iran and Iraq were not offered
membership), at which time a very active program of confidence-building measures was pursued. As noted in an earlier chapter, it may even be fair to say that
the demise of ACRS resulted from the rapid progression through confidence-
building measures and into the arms-control phase of its program.[22] Looking to
the future, a Gulf security forum—versus a collective security body—clearly fits
the local preference for increased dialogue as opposed to the transfer of national
military resources and decisionmaking to a regional collective.[23]

The development of existing security forums (see footnote) gives some idea
of what can be achieved in regional security forums within set time frames.[24]
In the first two years, a Gulf security forum could establish its processes, issue
a statement of principles and intent, plus develop a number of uncontroversial
but important ACRS agreements on SAR, INCSEA, and the establishment of
a communications network (e.g., the exchange of contact information between
key security officials). Within the first five years, regional states may conceivably have initiated exchange visits by military and security officers, educational
exchanges, and port visits by military vessels in transit. Gulf nations may also
be exchanging military information, including prenotification of certain military activities. In the five-year period, a conflict prevention center could be

developed to maintain an arms register for the region and a maritime security database. It might issue security-related white papers. Arms control could take place farther down the line, with the divisive issue of nuclear weapons best left untouched. To avoid dragging the paralyzing issues of Israeli nuclear weapons and a regional WMD-free zone into the equation, a Gulf security forum should instead tackle the issue of WMD indirectly, undermining the tense strategic situation that has, in part, led to the initial development of nuclear weapons in the region.

In developing regional responses to the transnational threats facing the Gulf, confidence- and security-building measures (CSBMs) will be invaluable. In addition, more regular communications between Gulf security officials will increase the potential for collaboration and intelligence sharing. The development of a regional conflict prevention center, meanwhile, could track transnational threats and produce white papers underlining the shared interests of Gulf countries in meeting these threats. In these areas, a strong model for the activities of a Gulf security forum would be the Association of South-East Asian Nations Regional Forum (ARF). As well as providing useful examples of confidence-building measures and preventive diplomacy initiatives focused on reducing interstate tensions, the ARF is also highly active in promoting greater harmony in regional approaches to transnational threats. For instance, Track 1 activities of the ARF support substantive working-group activity on regional approaches to shipping safety, oil spill cleanup, earthquake-hazard mitigation, sea accidents, terrorism, border security, uncontrolled migration, document security, and the prevention of drug trafficking and other smuggling. Track 1½ and 2 activities involve informal nonbinding closed-door dialogues between regional states on recurring and ad hoc issues of concern.[25]

In counterterrorism, the fight against organized crime and drug trafficking, and conservation and ecological issues, a Gulf security forum could undertake very useful work. As well as encouraging greater collaboration, it could create guidelines or understandings concerning sensitive issues such as the policing of joint land and maritime borders, and the pressing issue of "hot pursuit" over regional borders. A Gulf security forum could also push forward the case for getting the Gulf registered as an area of special ecological concern, thus allowing states to pursue and fine polluters operating in international waters. The forum could be particularly effective in increasing maritime security, perhaps developing an annual or biennial naval symposium like the West Pacific Naval Symposium or the working group on maritime cooperation of the Council for Security Cooperation in Asia Pacific.[26] Initially, maritime cooperation in the

Gulf could focus on the establishment of more routine patterns of navigation in the Gulf, to aid surveillance, policing, and safety. Thereafter, the Gulf countries could agree to standardized education and training for maritime control officers, and even appoint an overall maritime control officer for the Gulf, or just the Straits of Hormuz, the nationality of which would rotate among the regional states. Similar activities have been undertaken by Chile, Argentina, and Brazil in littoral choke points administered by the three nations.[27] Greater naval cooperation could facilitate sea-lane protection exercises and coordinated law enforcement, including maritime information-exchange directories, tactical-signals books to aid communications, and replenishment-at-sea manuals to aid interoperability between navies.[28] Existing regional maritime security NGOs such as the Marine Emergency Mutual Aid Center could assist with these missions.[29]

As the above analysis suggests, a new Gulf security forum would have limited goals and a modest, deliberate pace. In this approach, it would be a practical and low-profile step toward meeting U.S. objectives in the CENTCOM theater. The forum would need to address the security issues that Gulf countries care about most and would have to move at a comfortable pace. Yet indicators suggest that such a forum will do more in less time than observers suspect. Above all, a Gulf security forum can be effective because it is not simply an attempt to reinvent the wheel of the Tier II GCC collective-security effort by adding Iraq or Yemen. Whether Iran joins or stays out of such a forum, it will have been invited by its regional neighbors. If it participates in one working group or all of them, Gulf security will be stronger, not weaker. As Issam Salim Shanti has noted:

> It is the responsibility of the Gulf countries and the United States, as an essential player in the region, to organize a web of multilateral arrangements that could diminish tension and prevent conflict in the future. Multilateralism has become an urgent necessity if security is sought.[30]

Notes

1. Department of Defense, "Quadrennial Defense Review Report" (Washington, D.C.: Department of Defense, 2001), p. 11.

2. See Thomas Schelling, *Arms and Influence* (New Haven: Yale University Press, 1966); Schelling, *Strategy of Conflict* (London: Oxford University Press, 1960).

3. James Russell, "Nuclear Strategy and the Modern Middle East," *Middle East Policy* 11, no. 3 (2004), p. 107.

4. Michael Kraig, "Assessing Alternative Security Frameworks in the Persian Gulf," *Middle East Policy* 11, no. 3 (2004), pp. 4–5.

5. CENTCOM, "Southwest Asia: Approaching the Millennium—Enduring Problems, Emerging Solutions" (paper presented at the Southwest Asia Symposium 96, Tampa, FL, May 14–15, 1996), p. 59.

6. Naval War College, "Global 94: Volume III—Southwest Asia/Middle East Regional Estimate and Regional Action Plan" (Newport, RI: Naval War College, 1994), p. 65.

7. For a discussion of the Saudi-Iranian agreement, see Loftian, "A Regional Security System in the Persian Gulf," in Lawrence Potter and Gary Sick, eds., *Security in the Persian Gulf: Origins, Obstacles, and the Search for Consensus* (New York: Palgrave, 2002), pp. 126–127.

8. Craig Dunkerley, "Considering Security Amidst Strategic Change: The OSCE Experience," *Middle East Policy* 11, no. 3 (2004), p. 131.

9. Michael Yaffe, "The Gulf and a New Middle East Security System," *Middle East Policy* 11, no. 3 (2004), p. 129.

10. Rear Admiral John Sigler, interview by author, Washington, D.C., 2003.

11. Peter Jones, "Iranian Security Policies at the Crossroads?" in Jamal al-Suwaidi, ed., Emirates Occasional Papers (Abu Dhabi: Emirates Center for Strategic Studies), p. 15.

12. Jon Marks, "Buoyant GCC Grapples with Dollar Black Spot," *Gulf States Newsletter* 28, no. 726 (2004), p. 11.

13. Quoted in Lieutenant Commander Duk-Ki Kim, "Cooperative Maritime Security in Northeast Asia," Naval War College Review (Newport, RI: Naval War College, March 16, 2004). Available online (www.nwc.navy.mil/press/Review/1999/winter/art3-w99.htm).

14. Issam Salim Shanti, "Defense and Security Issues in the Gulf Region," in Abdulaziz Sager, ed., *Gulf in a Year, 2003* (Dubai: Gulf Research Center, 2004), p. 174.

15. Paul Melly, "Kuwaiti Planners Look to Reinvigorated Post-Saddam Northern Gulf," *Gulf States Newsletter* 27, no 705 (2003), p. 11.

16. Jon Marks, "Dubai, Qatar Confront the Realities of Life as a Global Hub," *Gulf States Newsletter,* February 20, 2004, p. 3.

17. Yaffe, "The Gulf," p. 12.

18. Loftian, "A Regional Security System," p. 127.

19. Taheri, "Policies of Iran in the Persian Gulf Region," in Abbas Amirie, ed., *The Persian Gulf and Indian Ocean in International Politics* (Tehran: Institute for International Political and Economic Studies, 1975), p. 275.

20. For instance, IRGC commander Major General Mohsen Rezai called for the development of a regional security group. See Bazargan, "Iran, Politics, the Military, and Gulf Security," *Middle East Review of International Affairs (MERIA)* (March 19, 2004). Available online (http://meria.idc.ac.il/journal/1997/issue3/jv1n3a4.html). Since 1998, Iranian minister of defense Rear Admiral Ali Shamknani has proposed a collective security arrangement to a number of Gulf states; see Loftian, "A Regional Security System," pp. 126–127.

21. M. H. Ansari, "Security in the Persian Gulf," *Strategic Analysis* 23, no. 6 (1999).

22. This case was made convincingly in Bruce Jentleson and Dalia Dassa Kaye, "Regional Security Cooperation and Its Limits in the Middle East," *Security Studies* 8, no. 1 (1998), pp. 223–225.

23. Kraig, "Assessing Alternative Security Frameworks in the Persian Gulf," *Middle East Policy* 11, no. 3 (2004), p. 149.

24. Case studies included ACRS; the NATO Mediterranean Dialogue; the NATO Partnership for Peace program; the Organization for Security and Cooperation in Europe; the Collective Security Treaty Organzation; the European Union Mediterranean Partnership; the eleven-member Mediterranean Forum; the Western European Union; the Nordic Council; the NATO-Russia Council; the Inter-American Defense Board; the Peace and Security Council of the African Union; the French-backed Reinforcement des Capacities Africain de Maintien de la Paix; and the Association of South-East Asian Nations Regional Forum (ARF).

25. An explanation of ARF activities is available online (www.aseansec.org/3530.htm). See also Yaffe, "The Gulf," p. 129.

26. Kim, "Cooperative Maritime Security in Northeast Asia."

27. Commander Pedro Luis de la Fuente, *Confidence-Building Measures in the Southern Cone: A Model for Regional Stability* (Newport, RI: Naval War College, February 16, 2004).

28. Kim, "Cooperative Maritime Security in Northeast Asia."

29. No Author, "The Role of the Armed Forces in Environmental Security" (Muscat: Sultan's Armed Forces, 2000), p. 1.

30. Shanti, "Defense and Security Issues in the Gulf Region," p. 174.

Conclusion

IN THE COMING decade, a worthy goal for the United States is to pursue the emergence of a more stable Gulf region, in which more responsible regional states cooperate against shared transnational threats. The key to achieving this goal is increased self-reliance in the GCC states, which have a reputation as net importers of security. Current U.S. Central Command (CENTCOM) strategy, developing out of the failure of Tier I and Tier II capability building, has left the Gulf states reliant on Tier III security assistance that has required the United States to station forces in the Gulf for more than a decade. In time, both the United States and the GCC became addicted to this form of security policy, which granted the United States firm control over the military situation in the Gulf and allowed the GCC states to outsource their security to a powerful external guarantor. Both sides quickly forgot that this dynamic represented the sole remaining option following a failure of policy, rather than a policy choice in its own right. Though it may seem that the Gulf is right where Washington wants it—with Iran frozen out and Saudi dominance on the wane—this short-term view could lock the United States into open-ended strategic parenting of the GCC. Instead, what is needed is a reappraisal of the operational, sustainability, and force-management risks involved in U.S. security strategy in the Gulf. Slowly, the balance of Tier III versus Tier I/II must be reversed, while stability in the region is maintained simultaneously. A Tier IV option (reduction of military tension in the region) must also be added.

In building the capability of regional states through security assistance and cooperation, the United States can reduce the sustainability and force-management risks associated with forward presence, while also reducing the operational risks inherent in a GCC-led first line of defense in the region. Already, GCC states play the leading role in ensuring their own internal security. In scenarios short of a major conflict involving Iran, it is no longer a pipe dream to imagine that they will play a greater role in their external defense with the recent shift from the overland invasion threat presented by Iraq to the littoral and aerial threat posed by Iran and other transnational adversaries. Furthermore, security assistance is the United States' most cost-effective means of bolstering Gulf security. As ambassador Chas Freeman once noted, U.S. taxpayers would prefer lower prices at the gas pumps even if they had to pay hundreds of billions of dollars to support a U.S. military presence in the Gulf, which he calculated to represent about an invisible ten-cent premium on each gallon of gas used in the United States. This premium probably represents a considerable underestimation of the cost of a U.S.-led approach to Gulf security. To date, all security assistance provided by the U.S. taxpayer to the GCC states represents a tiny fraction of the cost of one major deployment of U.S. forces to the region. As Dov Zakheim noted:

> In the eighteenth century, Prime Minister William Pitt the Elder argued that, "[O]ur troops cost more to maintain than those of any other country. Our money, therefore, will be of most service to our allies, because it will enable them to raise and support a greater number of troops than those we can supply with the same sum." His dictum holds true for America today. Helping our allies develop small but capable forces of their own—including but not limited to special forces—will ultimately result in both human and material benefits to the United States.[1]

Where local states can provide deterrent or defensive value approaching that of the U.S. military, it is incumbent on the United States to hand off primary responsibility for regional security and accept a loosening of control that will be more than offset by a reduction of sustainability and force-management risks.

The second key to transforming U.S. security strategy is greater focus on threat reduction in the Gulf, both through carefully guiding the GCC states to adopt nonoffensive defenses where possible and practical, and through supporting the development of a cooperative, comprehensive, and compartmentalized Gulf security forum. In the Gulf, Iran's intentions and military capabilities will continue to be shaped strongly by the overarching security guarantee represented by CENTCOM; but a balanced policy of military deterrence backed by the development of confidence-building measures will ensure that U.S. military presence has a positive rather than a negative effect on the development of Iranian military power. In this context, containment is necessary but not sufficient; meaningful threat reduction requires taking the offensive, including an unprecedented move from purely military-to-military activities to the more balanced political-military strategy described above. Cooperative security among all Gulf countries, not collective security for a select few, represents the way forward.

If the principles outlined in this book can be applied to future U.S. security assistance in the Gulf, we can imagine an attractive picture. Assuming that no major conflict has broken out involving Iran, the United States retains a minimal presence in the Gulf, yet maintains strong interpersonal relationships with Gulf security leaders, based on extensive exchange, training, and exercise programs. The United States also retains trusted and capable allies in the Gulf, each of which routinely exchanges intelligence with the United States through the standing expeditionary sensor grid (ESG) maintained by the GCC states, CENTCOM, and perhaps NATO allies. Though one or more states, perhaps the United Arab Emirates (UAE), provide a locus of inspiration to regional allies, the United States has once and for all abandoned the search for a regional "anchor state," or a new pillar, and instead relies on a raft of regional alliances that provides reliable access to the region. Finally, U.S. allies in the region are now more capable of handling the full spectrum of internal, transnational, and interstate threats to Gulf security. As a result, the United States is increasingly a niche provider of military support in the Gulf, reversing the decades-long situation in which the Gulf states played this role in their own security—a situation that may seem bizarre for those looking back from 2015.

Notes

1. Dov Zakheim, "The Quadrennial Defense Review: Some Guiding Principles" (lecture given at the Heritage Foundation, February 1, 2005). Available online (http://new.heritage.org/Research/NationalSecurity/hl864.cfm).

APPENDICES

Appendix A

Foreign Military Financing (FMF) Provided to the GCC, 1990–2006*

	1990	1991	1992	1993	1994	1995	1996	1997
Bahrain	0	1,000	500	0	0	0	0	0
Kuwait	0	0	0	0	0	0	0	0
Oman	0	3,000	500	1,000	0	0	0	0
Qatar	0	0	0	0	0	0	0	0
Saudi Arabia	0	0	0	0	0	0	0	0
UAE	0	0	0	0	0	0	0	0
GCC TOTAL	0	4,000	1,000	1,000	0	0	0	0
Iraq	0	0	0	0	0	0	0	0
Yemen	0	0	0	0	0	0	0	0

Source: Defense Security Cooperation Agency. Figures for 2005 are estimates; figures for 2006 are requests.

*All figures are in thousands of dollars.

1998	1999	2000	2001	2002	2003	2004	2005	2006
0	0	0	0	28,500	785	24,682	18,848	19,000
0	0	0	0	0	0	0	0	0
0	0	0	0	25,000	20,000	24,850	19,840	20,000
0	0	0	0	0	0	0	0	0
0	0	0	0	0	0	0	0	0
0	0	0	0	0	0	0	0	0
0	0	0	0	54,000	27,850	49,532	38,688	39,000
0	0	0	0	0	0	0	0	0
0	0	0	0	0	1,900	14,910	9,920	10,000

Appendix B

International Military and Education Training (IMET) Provided to the GCC, 1990–2006*

	1990	1991	1992	1993	1994	1995	1996	1997
Bahrain	0	0	74	103	56	75	108	149
Kuwait	0	0	0	0	0	0	0	0
Oman	164	214	97	92	54	131	119	117
Qatar	0	0	0	0	0	0	0	0
Saudi Arabia	0	0	0	0	0	0	0	0
UAE	0	0	0	0	0	0	0	0
GCC TOTAL	164	214	171	195	110	206	227	266
Iraq	0	0	0	0	0	0	0	0
Yemen	595	2,500	0	0	0	0	50	52

Source: Defense Security Cooperation Agency. Figures for 2005 are estimates, figures for 2006 are requests.

*All figures are in thousands of dollars.

1998	1999	2000	2001	2002	2003	2004	2005	2006
251	228	216	249	395	450	568	650	650
0	0	0	0	0	0	0	0	0
217	233	230	250	481	750	825	1,100	1,100
0	0	0	0	0	0	0	0	0
0	0	0	0	0	0	24	25	25
0	0	0	0	0	0	0	0	0
468	461	446	499	876	1,200	1,417	1,750	1,750
0	0	0	0	0	0	0	0	700
142	122	125	198	488	638	886	1,100	1,100

Appendix C

Nonproliferation, Antiterrorism, Demining, and Related Programs (NADR) Provided to the GCC, 2000–2006*

	2000	2001	2002
Bahrain	0	0	53 (ATA)
Kuwait	545 (ATA)	958 (ATA)	457 (ATA)
Oman	2,141 (ATA) 1,017 (HD)	514 (ATA) 273 (HD)	1,796 (ATA) 495 (HD) 20 (EXBS)
Qatar	0	472 (ATA)	50 (ATA)
Saudi Arabia	0	<50 (ATA) 10 (EXBS)	539 (ATA) 30 (EXBS)
UAE	1,043 (ATA)	535 (ATA) 340 (EXBS)	350 (EXBS) 50 (ATA)
GCC TOTAL	4,746	3,152	3,840
Iraq	0	0	0
Yemen	1,236 (HD) 947 (ATA)	1,023 (HD) 822 (ATA) 140 (EXBS)	750 (HD) 50 (EXBS)

Key: ATA—antiterrorism assistance; HD—humanitarian demining; EXBS—export and border security assistance SALW—small arms and light weapon disarmament assistance; TIP—terrorism interdiction program assistance
Source: Defense Security Cooperation Agency. Figures for 2005 are estimates; figures for 2006 are requests.

*All figures are in thousands of dollars.

2003	2004	2005	2006
543 (ATA)	393 (ATA)	0	0
65 (ATA)	180 (ATA)	0	0
641 (ATA) 85 (EXBS)	1,035 (ATA) 400 (EXBS)	400 (EXBS)	500 (EXBS)
0	662 (ATA)	0	0
80 (EXBS)	456 (ATA)	0	0
527 (ATA) 200 (EXBS)	274 (ATA) 250 (EXBS)	250 (EXBS)	350 (EXBS)
2,141	3,650	1,750 (ATA not yet known)	2,850 (ATA not yet known)
0	500 (TIP)	0	16,000 (HD) 10,000 (ATA) 1,000 (EXBS)
750 (HD)	827 (ATA) 773 (HD) 470 (EXBS)	700 (HD) 525 (EXBS) 148 (ATA)	800 (SALW) 754 (ATA)

Appendix D

Antiterrorism Assistance (ATA) Provided to the GCC, 1991–2004*

	1991	1992	1993	1994	1995	1996
Bahrain	0	0	0	0	0	0
Kuwait	0	<50	<50	0	0	<50
Oman	0	0	0	0	0	0
Qatar	0	0	0	0	0	0
Saudi Arabia	<50	0	0	0	0	139
UAE	<50	0	0	<50	0	0
GCC TOTAL (% of global total)	<100 (<1%)	<50 (<1%)	<50 (<1%)	<50 (<1%)	0 (0%)	189 (4%)
GLOBAL TOTAL	11,561	38,352	12,150	12,600	12,585	4,435
Yemen	0	0	0	0	0	0

Source: Defense Security Cooperation Agency.

*All figures are in thousands of dollars.

1997	1998	1999	2000	2001	2002	2003	2004
<50	251	228	0	0	53	543	393
<50	232	1,439	54	958	457	65	180
<50	396	398	2,141	514	1,796	641	1,035
<50	891	253	0	472	50	0	662
211	725	262	0	<50	539	0	456
<50	0	1,458	1,043	535	50	527	274
<561 (3%)	2,495 (24%)	4,038 (19%)	3,238 (8%)	<2,529 (34%)	2,945 (7%)	1,776 (1%)	3,000 (3%)
17,473	10,263	20,815	38,125	41,389	38,043	142,781	88,834
<50	145	296	937	822	0	0	827

Appendix E

Gulf Defense Expenditures, 1989-2003*

	1989	1990	1991	1992	1993	1994	1995
Bahrain	93	205	222	223	251	261	273
Kuwait	1,326	1,357	7,959	12,815	3,110	3,133	3,489
Oman	1,335	1,641	1,182	1,328	1,928	2,063	2,018
Qatar	n/a	n/a	781	781	330	308	700
Saudi Arabia	13,495	24,143	35,438	35,438	16,473	14,554	17,196
UAE	1,301	2,291	4,249	2,291	2,110	2,149	1,950
GCC TOTAL	19,084	31,173	49,831	52,876	24,149	22,468	25,626
Iran	4,215	3,810	4,270	4,270	1,977	2,340	3,000
Iraq	n/a	7,490	n/a	7,4902	2,600	2,748	1,250
Yemen	n/a	1,016	910	910	356	324	345

Source: Data compiled from various annual editions of the International Institute for Strategic Studies compendium *The Military Balance*, 1990–2004.

*All figures are in millions of dollars.

1996	1997	1998	1999	2000	2001	2002	2003
279	304	410	441	322	364	332	61
3,505	3,618	3,674	3,275	3,695	5,029	3,384	3,794
1,876	1,976	1,792	1,631	2,099	2,831	2,518	2,468
740	1,346	1,373	1,468	1,468	1,423	1,855	1,923
16,999	18,151	21,303	21,876	22,050	24,266	18,502	18,747
2,028	2,424	3,036	3,187	2,997	3,070	1,642	1,642
25,427	27,819	31,608	31,493	28,427	36,983	28,233	28,635
3,301	4695	5,879	5,711	3,957	4,968	3,077	3,051
1,224	1,250	1,428	1,500	1,400	1,372	n/a	n/a
354	411	404	429	499	531	731	798

Appendix F
GCC Succession Issues

Bahrain

Bahrain's King Hamad is the driving force behind modernization in the kingdom. He was born in 1950, which will make him sixty-five years old in 2015. Crown Prince Salman was born in 1969 and will therefore be forty-six in 2015.[1] Though the king's relative youth reduces the likelihood of frequent successions, it raises the risk that older relatives may seek to complicate the transfer of power to younger and possibly less experienced successors. King Hamad's reform efforts threaten to disrupt the ruling family's longstanding political and economic prerogatives, and the reform-minded Crown Prince Salman could be forced into compromises by Prime Minister Sheikh Khalifa or a number of other senior family members.

Kuwait

Until January 2006, Kuwait looked set to face a series of short reigns and quick successions due to the age and ill health of its key political figures. Yet after Emir Sheikh Jaber al-Ahmad al-Jaber al-Sabah died on January 15, 2006, the ruling family quickly moved to ensure that the elderly and infirm Crown Prince Sheikh Saad al-Abdullah al-Salem al-Sabah did not remain on the throne. Instead, the cabinet and parliament deposed the new emir in a consensual step and replaced him with Emir Sheikh Sabah al-Ahmad al-Jaber al-Sabah. The step was particularly unexpected because it breached the system of leadership alternation between the Ahmed or Salem wings of the royal family, allowing two al-Jaber rulers to ascend to the throne in a row.

The decision was a victory for common sense, vesting the highly capable Emir Sheikh Sabah with full authority. A modernizer and the de facto day-to-day ruler of Kuwait for a number of years, Emir Sheikh Sabah will be able to act with complete authority and this may improve the chances for much-needed reforms in the economic and political spheres. Emir Sheikh Sabah is neither young nor in perfect health, however, and he moved quickly to clarify the line of succession after him. Once again deviating from the alternation rule, the emir's younger brother Sheikh Nawaf al-Ahmad al-Jaber al-Sabah was named as crown prince. Crown Prince Sheikh Nawaf has long experience of government, having held the interior and social affairs and labor portfolios; he has also been deputy chief of the National Guard. He will be 78 in 2015. As long as the interests of the two wings of the royal family can be balanced through savvy dispensation of ministerial roles, governance in Kuwait has made a major leap forward towards meritocratic succession and more capable decision-making.

Oman

Sultan Qaboos, who will be seventy-four in 2015, has no children and is unlikely to sire any. Under existing plans, a successor will be chosen by a council of notables, creating uncertainty over who the successful candidate may be. If no clear result emerges, the Omani military has been authorized by Sultan Qaboos to enact the succession according to his intent, as communicated in a sealed letter, two copies of which are held by the trustees of the sultan within the army and the government. This situation could change if, as seems possible, Sultan Qaboos makes succession-specific alterations to the country's Basic Law in an attempt to move the sultanate toward the status of a constitutional monarchy.[2] In the meantime, a range of possible successors has been outlined, including favored uncles and cousins (notably Fahd bin Taimur and Fahd bin Mahmoud, or any of the three eldest sons of Sayyid Tariq bin Taimur).[3] What can be said with more certainty is that any of these successors would be hamstrung considerably by rivalries within the Omani elite and would have less ability than Sultan Qaboos to push through economic and political reforms that, while necessary, could threaten the interests of the governing elite's key families. A successor could also struggle to maintain the loyalty of the Dhofari tribes, who have accepted central rule from Muscat largely because of Sultan Qaboos's long-standing hard but fair treatment of them and because of his mother's Dhofari heritage.[4]

Qatar

Qatar's Emir Sheikh Hamad is the driving force behind modernization in his country. Born in 1950, he will be sixty-five if he lives until 2015, though he is known to have had two kidney operations that could reduce his ability to reign. Qatar's Crown Prince Tamim was born in 1979 and will be merely thirty-six in 2015.[5] As in Bahrain, the young emir is likely to face uncontested succession but may thereafter face internal challenges. Within the last decade, fractious family politics have caused one bloodless coup and one countercoup or more. The well-regarded reformist and former special-forces officer Crown Prince Tamim may find his relative youth offset by his elder brothers' apparent disinterest in politics, but he could face a greater challenge in senior Wahhabi members of the ruling clique, including Interior Minister Sheikh Abdullah bin Khalid al-Thani.[6]

Saudi Arabia

In Saudi Arabia, successions are also likely to be frequent, contested, and potentially inconclusive. Though nominally the passing of King Fahd has given full formal authority to King Abdullah, the new monarch will no doubt continue to be challenged on an issue-by-issue basis by his half brothers, the remaining members of the so-called Sudeiri Seven—the senior sons of Ibn Saud. Moreover, King Abdullah will himself be ninety-two by 2015; Crown Prince Sultan will be ninety-one. The next likely successor, Interior Minister Prince Nayef, will be eighty-two, and the remaining brothers of the Sudeiri Seven are not much younger. As Washington Institute scholar Simon Henderson has noted, "A period of several short successions is likely, with old age apt to impair the ability of kings to govern effectively."[7] Each succession creates a significant risk of disagreement among the wings of the royal family.

The Saudi royal family might choose to skip over one or more of the Sudeiri Seven, which would introduce a range of potential successors drawn from the grandsons of Ibn Saud, most of whom would be in their sixties by 2015. King Abdullah, Crown Prince Sultan, and Prince Nayef have been grooming their sons for this possibility since 2001, and by the end of the decade one of them could feasibly be close to accession. Whoever takes the throne, it is clear that power will remain diffused among the various princes. As an Oxford Analytica report noted, "It will be far more difficult for a single individual to dominate decisionmaking the way that King Fahd or King Faisal did in the past."[8] As in Kuwait, the effect will be to slow decisionmaking at precisely the moment when Saudi Arabia needs to take bold and decisive actions to reverse its course toward state failure.

The United Arab Emirates (UAE)

In the emirate of Abu Dhabi, the passing of the Gulf's elder statesman, former UAE federal president and local emir Sheikh Zayed, may end the periodic waxing and waning of policy that mirrored his activity levels in the latter years of his life. Before his death Sheikh Zayed prepared the next two generations of Abu Dhabi leadership, and in 2000 established an al-Nahyan Ruling Family Council to smooth the process of succession.

Ruling UAE federal president Emir Sheikh Khalifa will be sixty-six by 2015, and next-in-line Crown Prince Muhammad will be fifty-four.[9] Either man might rule for a considerable length of time and either would have sufficient seniority to dissuade potential challengers. Emir Sheikh Khalifa has a solid power base, built on a range of tribal alliances and backed by the patronage accrued during his day-to-day control of the Abu Dhabi Executive Council budget as crown prince. In the longer term, the reform-minded, energetic, and ambitious Crown Prince Muhammad is well placed to consolidate power, with four full brothers already holding key portfolios in the foreign, intelligence, information, and oil ministries.[10] Named the deputy commander-in-chief of the UAE armed forces, Crown Prince Muhammad now controls the Abu Dhabi Executive Council budget purse strings.

Like Abu Dhabi, the UAE's other principal emirate, Dubai, has not yet opted for a fixed, primogeniture-based system of succession, and the throne has instead passed from brother to brother. Dubai ruler Sheikh Maktoum bin Rashid al-Maktoum's sudden death in January 2006 triggered a smooth transition to his successor and younger brother, Sheikh Muhammad bin Rashid al-Maktoum, who will be sixty-seven in 2015. Following Sheikh Muhammad, it is possible that the throne may shift to one of the sons of either Sheikh Maktoum or Sheikh Muhammad.

Notes

1. "New Qatar Crown Prince Named," BBC News, August 5, 2003. Available online (http://news.bbc.co.uk/1/hi/world/middle_east/3124575.stm).

2. Paul Melly, Nick Carn, and Mark Ford, *Succession in the Gulf: The Commercial Implications* (Hastings: Middle East Newsletters, 2002), pp. 15–19; Simon Henderson, *The New Pillar: Conservative Arab Gulf States and U.S. Strategy* (Washington, D.C.: Washington Institute, 2004), p. 45.

3. "Oman: Qaboos Succession," Oxford Analytica, May 28, 2004 (available online at www.oxweb.com); "Oman: Majlis Elections," May 28, 2004 (available online at www.oxweb.com).

4. "Oman: Majlis Elections."

5. "New Qatar Crown Prince Named."

6. Paul Melly, "Qataris Line Up for New Political Dispensation," *Gulf States Newsletter,* April 16, 2004, p. 4.

7. Henderson, *The New Pillar,* p. 35.

8. "Saudi Arabia: Succession Stakes Rise as Leaders Age," Oxford Analytica, May 28, 2004.

9. Nick Carns, "Risk Management Report—UAE," *Gulf States Newsletter* 28, no. 728 (2004), p. 11. See also "Abu Dhabi Deputy Crown Prince Appointed," AlJazeera. net, December 1, 2003; available online (http://english.aljazeera.net/NR/exeres/ 7A28E8CF-7E0D-4395-9317-0B149D37C753.htm).

10. Paul Melly, "Qatar's Consensual Politics Complement and Clash with 'War on Terror' Thinking," April 28, 2004, p. 5.

Appendix G
Political Reform in the Gulf

United Arab Emirates (UAE)

It is worth noting that the royal families from one of the more stable and economically successful Gulf states—the UAE—have hardly begun to initiate meaningful reform programs. The Federal National Council, which has operated in an unexpanded consultative role since 1972, represents the high-tide mark of participatory politics in the UAE. The federal government and its constituent emirates appear disinclined to broaden the political franchise.[1] For the moment, the UAE's leadership feels that the country's booming economy makes real power sharing with the local population unnecessary. Instead, the UAE is addressing the primary internal threat to its stability—intracommunal violence and crime involving expatriate workers—through slow-developing initiatives to improve worker living standards plus longstanding measures such as surveillance, policing, and the threat of deportation. As Gregory Gause noted, foreign workers are not difficult to deactivate as a serious threat to security.

The dependence on foreign labor is not a problem politically. Highly transient and internally divided by nationality, employment conditions, residential patterns, and social networks, expatriate labor lacks the incentive and ability to act cohesively. Although labor has grievances, it has strong incentives to cooperate. Its interests are economic; its politics are at home.[2]

The emirates of the UAE have thus hardly begun to explore broader power-sharing arrangements with internal political groupings, and it is not clear what circumstances could convince the emirs to engage in political reform willingly. If reform begins, it will most likely originate in Dubai, where elected regional councils could be established within a short number of years, or in one of the smaller northern emirates (such as Ras al-Khaimah), which are ruled increasingly by younger and more reform-minded leaders.[3] The miniature rentier state of Abu Dhabi could remain in its present configuration for some time, particularly if Deputy Crown Prince Muhammad does not become emir for a considerable number of years.

Qatar

Boasting the most successful economy in the Gulf, Qatar might have concluded that it too could continue to rely on the established mechanisms of the rentier state to co-opt internal opposition, and need not engage in meaningful power sharing in the coming decade. Instead it has moved to the forefront of political reform in the Gulf. Emir Hamad initiated a "top-down" campaign of democratization that was slow to interest Qatar's 135,000 citizens, yet in the five years since Doha announced municipal elections, a slow blooming of interest has occurred in increased pluralism and representative government. In a landmark speech on April 5, 2004, Emir Hamad addressed the issue of modernization with a candor that is unprecedented in the Gulf:

> We must discard narrow allegiances and seriously work to build a democratic future.... [H]onesty obliges us to stress that the roots of wrath in our region do not spring from the Palestinian question alone.... [O]ther countries have suffered as we did from colonization, subordination, and protectorate status, yet they reformed themselves and set out steadily toward modernity.[4]

Qatar's route to parliamentary democracy will build on the solid base of incremental reforms undertaken since the establishment of the Majlis Ash-Shura in the 1960s, a consultative council that now wields some legislative influence, including some protection from emiri dissolution and the ability to issue votes of no confidence in ministers.[5] The Majlis Baladiy, a municipal council first elected in 1999, has acted as a nursery for the evolving political class, a number of whom may run in Qatar's first parliamentary elections. Scheduled for 2007, these votes will result in the election of thirty of forty-five members of Qatar's Shura Council. The Majlis Baladiy has also emerged as a forum at which Qatar's large foreign labor population (78 percent of Qatar's population of 575,000), can raise its grievances, providing the state with a way to address potential problems and provide strong economic incentives for nonnationals to cooperate with the government.[6]

Oman

In Oman, economic and political factors have driven Sultan Qaboos to share power with local interest and identity groups through relatively informal mechanisms, building on longstanding efforts to develop a tolerant and pluralistic form of government. These efforts culminated in 1996 in a form of constitution—the Basic Law—that may be expanded in the coming decade, formalizing the Sultan's incremental development of the concepts of Omani citizenship, rights, and the separation of powers, including an independent judiciary. The Civil Status Law has created mechanisms to register and issue identification to all citizens and expatriates, and—for the first time—record all births, deaths, marriages, and divorces.

Oman held its first elections on October 4, 2003, electing eighty-three representatives to the Majlis al-Shura, a consultative council that is mirrored by the appointed ninety-member Majlis al-Dawla, the legislative Council of State. Though the election granted universal suffrage to Omani men and women ages twenty-one or above, the turnout represented less than one quarter of the electorate.[7] It will take some time for Omani citizens—used to more direct forms of pluralism, including direct petitioning of the Sultan[8]—to become enthusiastic about the process, but the process is now under way. As academic Muhammad Salem al-Mazroui noted, reform will be necessary during the tough economic times ahead.

> Even though demands for reform have seemingly been preempted by the Omani government, the future predictably holds greater popular participation in store, especially as the country will have to face greater economic difficulties, more rampant unemployment, and a wider deterioration of individual income.[9]

It is unclear at what stage the Shura will gain greater oversight and legislative powers, allowing it to address popular displeasure with the systematic advantages established families enjoy in business dealings.

Bahrain

Bahrain's move toward pluralism has been more institutional than Oman's, and has resulted in some of the discomfort that can be expected when parliamentary democracy coexists with an autocratic monarchy. Following King Hamad's December 2000 declaration of intent to begin a reform program and a February 2001 referendum on the issue, Bahrain became a kingdom in February 2002, and has since taken steps to move toward a form of constitutional monarchy based loosely on the Jordanian model. Though progress has been made, the road has not been easy. King Hamad has had difficulty gathering support from a ruling family and Sunni elite that claim reform is proceeding too quickly, or from the Islamist opposition parties who believe it is proceeding too slowly.[10] Establishment hard-liners and Sunni "securocrats" such as the king's uncle, Prime Minister Sheikh Khalifa, have done much to undercut the popularly perceived value of political reforms. The Citizenship Law allowed Sunni Arabs from Syria, Yemen, and Saudi Arabia to receive citizenship to vote in the election, and in some cases these groups were bused into Bahrain during the elections of October 21–31, 2002.[11] Since these elections, which combined a low turnout with boycotts by many Bahraini political groups, the Bahraini establishment has also reneged on specific commitments to grant parliamentary oversight of budgeting, and has manipulated criminal law to prevent political associations from protesting against these developments or against the essentially limited powers of the forty-member elected lower house of the parliament, which is mirrored by a more powerful government-appointed upper house.[12] Assuming that King Hamad can prevent securocrats from undermining the reform process, he is likely to push forward a more inclusive model of Bahraini identity, integrating Sunni and Shiite elites and even some naturalized foreigners into the machinery of government.[13] Bahrain's civil rights movements provide excellent bases from which to develop political parties—a relative rarity in the Gulf.

Kuwait

For other Gulf states, Kuwait's experience of representative government sounds a cautionary note. Though parliamentary democracy is typically equated with political liberalization, in Kuwait the opposite has been true, with parliament acting as a brake on economic and political modernization. The overarching trend in Kuwaiti politics is that of an increasingly powerful Islamist and tribal (or traditionalist) bloc in the parliament, as evidenced in the July 2003 elections. Of the fifty members elected, only eight to fourteen could be described as secular, liberal, or progressive. Between seventeen and twenty-one came from parties that describe themselves as Islamist, including nine from radical groups such as the Salafi Movement, the Scientific Salafi Group, and the Islamic Constitution Movement (the renamed Muslim Brotherhood). The remaining winning candidates were independent tribal leaders, most of whom have strong traditional and Islamist tendencies.[14]

Further reforms to Kuwait's political system may not necessarily offset these factors. In time, Kuwait's voting rights may be broadened to include women, military personnel, and naturalized citizens, reducing the "elitist democratic" nature of the current system. The separation of crown prince from the post of prime minister opens the way to improved technocratic leadership, oversight of the prime minister, and even the eventual election of the premier. More non-royal members may be appointed to the cabinet, and constituency modifications may reduce the predominance of local tribal interests in the parliament.[15] Yet it is likely that the Kuwaiti government will share power increasingly with social forces that oppose economic, political, and social liberalization at precisely the time when these processes are becoming necessary to reduce tension and increase opportunity in the country. The Kuwaiti royal family, which tends to lag behind parliament on most political reform issues, may or may not have the ability or the focus to promote liberalization; and the parliament will be unlikely to promote such ends.[16] Thus, while increased democratization has helped to address broadly held concerns such as the difference between economic expectations and realities, and will assuage educated internal petitioners and external opposition groups, it has also given a voice (and a vote) to traditional and Islamist elements that support the imposition of Islamic law, oppose sectarian and gender equality, and reject other forms of modernization or interaction with the Western world, particularly the United States.[17]

Saudi Arabia

In Saudi Arabia, the ruling monarchy continues to undertake two very different approaches to power-sharing simultaneously. The first and more familiar is that of power sharing within the royal family and the Wahhabi religious establishment. As government decisionmaking ability is degraded by frequent and contested successions, there may be increased power-sharing among future kings, other members of the royal family, and the Ulama, which plays a strong role in legitimizing the ruling status of the al-Saud and blesses it during each royal succession. Without the Ulama's support, Saudi leaders may lack the authority to make difficult but necessary reforms, leaving national policy deadlocked on some issues and reducing the government's ability to head off destabilizing developments. The clerical establishment has already made itself appear indispensable in Saudi Arabia's counterterrorism effort, suggesting that the royal family will be forced to compromise with the Ulama on political and social reforms to retain clerics' support in the struggle against militant Wahhabism.

A second and more novel track involves an emerging policy of power sharing through political pluralism, through which the government could negotiate a new and radically different social contract with the Saudi Arabian people. This possible avenue of reform emerged from a series of announcements made by then–Crown Prince Abdullah between June and September 2003, which prompted public and media debate about the issue of representative government, and led to a series of petitions. Then–Crown Prince Abdullah appointed a royal commission to develop a gradualist reform plan that began with municipal elections in March and April 2005, resulting in municipal councils with an equal number of elected and government-appointed candidates. This vote will be followed by legislative debates on the potential role of an elected national assembly in budgetary oversight, and a national dialogue on broader political issues. When the government-appointed Majlis al-Shura (consultative council) was appointed in April 2005, it was expanded to 150 members and reshuffled to include more liberal voices. In upcoming years, plans indicate that the council will continue to be increased until it reaches a maximum of 360 members. Upon its next appointment in 2010, half of its members could be elected.[18] Alongside the development of popular representation, the government's executive branch is likely to continue down its current path toward meritocracy, employing a greater number of commoners and technocrats in cabinet positions.

Notes

1. Paul Melly, Nick Carn, and Mark Ford, *Succession in the Gulf: The Commercial Implications* (Hastings: Middle East Newsletters, 2002), pp. 32–36; Jon Marks, "Buoyant GCC Grapples with Dollar Black Spot," *Gulf States Newsletter* 28, no. 726 (p. 14).

2. Gregory Gause and Jill Crystal, "The Arab Gulf: Will Autocracy Define the Social Contract in 2015?" in Judith Yaphe, ed., *The Middle East in 2015: The Impacts of Regional Trends on U.S. Strategic Planning* (Washington, D.C.: National Defense University, 2002), p. 178.

3. Mohammed Salem al-Mazroui, "Elections and Referendums in the GCC States," in Abdulaziz Sager, ed., *Gulf in a Year, 2003* (Dubai: Gulf Research Center, 2004), pp. 50–51.

4. Paul Melly, "Qataris Line Up for New Political Dispensation," *Gulf States Newsletter*, April 16, 2004, p. 8.

5. Paul Melly, "Qatar's Consensual Politics Complement and Clash with 'War on Terror' Thinking," April 28, 2004, p. 2.

6. Gause and Crystal, "The Arab Gulf," p. 178; Melly, Carn, and Ford, *Succession in the Gulf*, pp. 21–23; Marks, "Buoyant GCC," p. 13.

7. Paul Melly, "Civic Modernization Not Radical Change for Oman," *Gulf States Newsletter*, March 5, 2004, p. 3.

8. Melly, Carn, and Ford, *Succession in the Gulf*, pp. 15–19; Marks, "Buoyant GCC," p. 12.

9. Al-Mazroui, "Elections and Referendums in the GCC," p. 47.

10. Marks, "Buoyant GCC," p. 11.

11. Paul Melly, "Opposition Charges Stir Bahraini Identity Crisis over Citizenship Voting Rights," *Gulf States Newsletter,* September 5, 2003, p. 4.

12. "Bahrain: Timid Reforms Fail to Tame Opposition," Oxford Analytica, May 28, 2004. Available online (www.oxweb.com).

13. Melly, Carn, and Ford, *Succession in the Gulf,* pp. 1, 5–9; Simon Henderson, *The New Pillar: Conservative Arab Gulf States and U.S. Strategy* (Washington, D.C.: Washington Institute, 2004), p. 41.

14. "Kuwait: Poll 'Win' May Not Help Government," Oxford Analytica, May 28, 2004. Available online (www.oxweb.com).

15. Al-Mazroui, "Elections and Referendums in the GCC," pp. 39–40. See also Ahmed Abdel Kareem Saif, "Political Developments: General Overview," in Abdulaziz Sager, ed., *Gulf in a Year, 2003* (Dubai: Gulf Research Center, 2004), pp. 29–30.

16. No Author, "Kuwaiti Reformists Seek Governance Breakthroughs," *Gulf States Newsletter,* April 30, 2004, p. 6.

17. Daniel Byman and Jerrold Green, *Political Violence and Stability in the States of the Northern Persian Gulf* (Santa Monica, CA: RAND, 1999), p. 8; Paul Pillar, "20/20 Vision? The Middle East to 2020," *Middle East Quarterly* 11, no. 1 (Santa Monica, CA: RAND, 2004), p. 63.

18. "Winning the Initiative: A Saudi Timetable for Elections and Reform," *Gulf States Newsletter* (March 19, 2004), p. 3. See also "Saudi Arabia: Modest Reforms Strengthen Shura," Oxford Analytica, May 28, 2004, Available online (www.oxweb.com).

Index

Page numbers followed by an *f* indicate a figure. Page numbers followed by an "n" and another number indicate a note.

patrolling and interdiction, 112–113; in state failure prevention, 111–112
Foreign Military Financing (FMF) program, xvii; by country, 208*f*–209*f*; GCC annual percentage of, 173*f*; procurement guidance in, 168–169
Foreign workers. *See* Guest workers
Forward operating sites (FOSs), 94
Forward presence, 102
Freeman, Chas, 9, 127, 193, 204
"Full-spectrum operations": in Iranian deterrence model, 56–59; U.S. training in, 96

G

Gause, Gregory, 23, 28, 103
GCC. *See* Gulf Cooperation Council (GCC) states
Global Concept of Operations, U.S. maritime, 94, 109
Global Hawk, 141–142
Global Strike Task Force concept, 97
Globalization, 20–21
Green, Jerrold, 128
Gross domestic product (GDP): annual percentage change in, by country, 30*f*; defense expenditure as percentage of, 174–176. *See also* Economic indicators
Ground forces, U.S., 108*f*, 107
Grove, Eric, 196
Guantánamo Bay, 35, 38
Guest workers: by country, 20*f*; terrorist targeting of, 37
Gulf Cooperation Council (GCC) states: border disputes in, 49; core competencies needed by, xii, xvi–xvii, 181*f*; counterterrorism support to, 110–112, 165–166; in funding of Desert Storm, 103; gross domestic product change in, 30*f*; internal security issues in: stabilization and key-point defense, 123–124, 146–147; terrorist network disruption, 122–123, 143–146; U.S. assistance with, 124, 163–165; interstate threats to, 50;

member states of, xi; military capabilities of: air forces of, *vs.* Iran, 131*f*; analyses of, 129–132; as collective defense organization, 128–129; defense expenditures, 126*f*, 174–177; force planning, 190n29; in Iranian conflict scenario, 114*f*, 130–131, 148–155; long-range strike capabilities, 149–150, 149*f*; maritime patrolling and interdiction, 146–148, 151*f*; missile defense assets, 152*f*–153*f*, 154–155; naval assets, 150–153; negative perception of, 125–129, 178–179; and network-centric warfare, 140–142; procurement trends in, 128–129, 131–132, 132–136; sustainment, 136–140; tiered objectives for, 9, 127–128; training exercises for, 170–171; WMD absence in, 150; per-capita income in, 175*f*; power sharing strategies of, 23–25; security cooperation program for, xvii–xviii; state failure indicators in, 27*f*; succession risks in, 22*f*; terrorist threat assessment for, 40–42; welfare reforms in, 18–20. *See also specific states*
Gulf security forum, 11–12; inclusive membership of, 196–197; Iran in, 196–197; models for, 199; NATO role in, 195; precursors for, 194–195; principles of, 195; Saudi Arabia in need for, 193–194; scope of work of, 198–200
Gulf War: GCC funding of, 103; Kuwaiti response to, 125–126; in shift to direct U.S. intervention, 9

H

Helicopters, in maritime patrolling, 151
Henderson, Simon, 129, 187
Hussein, Saddam, 104
Hydrocarbon supply: economic impact of interruption of, 4–5; Iranian interdiction of, 70; natural gas, 3–4, 3*f*; reserves, by country, 2, 3*f*; terrorist attack on, 38; U.S. consumption of, projected, 4